TILL I
Found You

MICHELLE FERNANDEZ

Till I Found You (V.2)

Copyright © 2020 by Michelle Fernandez

All rights reserved.

ISBN: 9781080595839

ASIN: B07V54LS2P

Editor—Michelle Morgan, Fiction Edit; https://www.FictionEdit.com

Cover Design—T.E. Black Designs; https://www.teblackdesigns.com

Interior Design & Formatting—T.E. Black Designs; https://www.teblackdesigns.com

Dedication

To Oliver Drew:

I know you're singing, laughing, and playing
with all the Angels in Heaven!

Playlist

Till I Found You—**Phil Wickman**

Collide—**Howie Day**

Love Someone—**Lukas Graham**

I Was Made For Loving You—**Tori Kelly**

Can't See Straight—**Jamie Lawson**

Heaven—**Kane Brown**

Your Body Is a Wonderland—**John Mayer**

Demons—**Imagine Dragons**

Broken—**Seether**

On My Own—**Ashes Remain**

The Mess I Made—**Parachute**

She Is Love—**Parachute**

Kiss Me Slowly—**Parachute**

I Won't Give Up—**Jason Mraz**

Circle Game—**P!nk**

Come On Get Higher—**Matt Nathanson**

A Drop In the Ocean—**Ron Hope**

CHAPTER
One

JULIAN

I GLARE AT THE PAPERS scattered all over my desk. I've gone over every last detail of the case file for the last several hours, a case that wasn't mine, to begin with. My office door is usually open, since that's how the security firm operates.

Full disclosure.

But now, my office door is shut because I stole this case from my teammate. And I'm a Grade-A asshole for doing it.

But this woman in the file blares inaudible sirens, calling to me. At the same time, something from my past pulls at me, haunting me, to look the other way. There's something about this woman that wrestles and confuses my thoughts.

I need to get my head straight, keep all emotions out and stay in control.

It's the only way I can do this job.

I rub my eyes with my fingers, look up to give them respite from the paperwork.

The client is Judge Frank Channing, the woman's father, a highly respected man of the courts. He has close ties with Charles 'Knox' Fremont, Head of Security and Founder of Knox's Security Intelligence Group. So, when Judge Channing called in a favor for protective detail to watch his daughter, Knox accepted him with open arms.

The Channing case is a complicated one and much different from the ones we've had in the past. Knox wants this mission handled with kid gloves. Miss Channing's past requires such sensitivity. Knox originally assigned Rochelle, our female operative agent, to shadow her, only because she wouldn't easily scare Miss Channing off.

I stare at the 4x6 polaroid photo resting next to the case file with all her information.

Name: Chloe Harper Channing
Occupation: Pediatrician - San Francisco General
Age: Twenty-nine
Height: 5'8"
Hair: Brunette
Eyes: Blue-Green (Aqua)

Damn… those eyes. They grab me… hook, line, and sinker.

My thoughts return back to the night I met Chloe Channing two years ago. Her angelic face is a flare in the sea of guests at the gala fundraiser event. When our eyes locked and I touched her hand, it was like a sucker punch in the stomach from Cupid. But it wasn't the right time to be involved with a woman.

I had no time for romance, nor wanted it.

The darkness deep in my heart and the lingering shadow that took residence there still haunts me. My life is complicated as it is. To add a woman to the mix would only screw me up even more.

I groan at the irony of second chances. What is it about this assignment that calls to me, compels me to protect Chloe?

My eyes veer to another photo, another woman, in an 8x10 frame on the corner of my desk. My heart aches every time I look at that photo. I kiss the pads of my two fingers, sending up a silent prayer, and touch them to her face. It's my sacred ritual before I go on any assignment and a constant reminder of why I do this job.

There's a rumble outside my office and the roar of a particular woman's voice I've been avoiding for the last two days. Being at KSIG for four years, I'd recognize her voice anywhere, her slight New York accent can't be missed and a voice that packs a punch.

Fuck! I'm in deep shit now.

I quickly gather the remaining papers and photos as the door flies open, slamming against the opposing wall.

"What the hell, Booker?" Rocky barges into my office, arms up in anger using my callsign. "I just came from Knox's office. Why'd you take the Channing case? You know I've been working it for the last four months—"

"I don't have time for this right now, I've got a flight to catch." I stand, pick up the manila folder and shove it in my brown leather shoulder bag.

"I don't care if you're catching Air Force One! You're not going anywhere until you tell me what's going on. That was a dick move you pulled, and you know it." She jabs her finger into my chest. "You have no business taking my case."

Ouch! I rub my chest.

"I finally got her to trust me and I can honestly say we've become friends," Rocky says with narrowing eyes.

"You can still be her friend," I tell her nonchalantly.

"You. Prick! What the hell is wrong with you?" She sent me an I-will-cut-your-throat look.

I glance at the door Rocky left open. I laugh to myself when I see each teammate tiptoe past my office to dodge the argument—except for Lincoln—who could never pass an opportunity to hear gossip around the office.

I shake my head when I glance at Lincoln leaning on the door-jamb with his usual shit-eating grin. I don't expect any less from the fucker.

Rochelle Yamaguchi, a.k.a. Rocky, is not merely a teammate, she's like a little sister to the team, our Samurai Princess and the youngest recruit to KSIG. Her innocent and petite five-five persona is never to be underestimated. She can hold her own and the team highly respects her. She's unassuming and intuitive—perfect for gathering intel—and the team witnessed firsthand she could kick some ass. One would never want to be on the receiving end of her stinging hands and side-kicks.

If I had first approached Rocky regarding the Channing case, she would've flat out shut me down. So, like an asshole, I went behind her back.

"Okay, you're right… I'm a dick and I should've talked to you first. Look, it's only for the next several weeks. After Miss Channing comes back from her vacation, you can pick up where you left off."

"Seriously? You're kidding. Is this all a big ploy to get a trip to the Bahamas?"

A ploy? If she only knew. I had to bribe Knox with an eighteen-year-old bottle of Macallan, his favorite scotch, in exchange for Rocky's case. Knox appreciated my persistence and once I got my approval, I immediately packed my bags and planned my flight out to the Channing Estate in the Bahamas.

"Lucky bastard… you're going to the Bahamas," Lincoln cuts in with wide eyes. "It's about time you took a vacation."

I shake my head. "It's not for pleasure, it's all work, donkey-boy."

Dylan Marshall, a.k.a Lincoln, has been my longtime friend and the closest I have to a brother. We were on the same SEAL team. Lincoln joined the KSIG team a year after I was recruited. Our brotherhood goes back to bootcamp where we met and trained for BUDs—Basic Underwater Demolition/SEAL. As active SEALs, we've saved each other's lives so many times I lost count. Our loyalty has been tested, proven, and remains stronger than with the other teammates.

Lincoln knows me better than anyone else on the team, but even he doesn't know why it's important for me to be on this case.

"Do you mind?" Rocky levels her eyes at Lincoln.

"No, I don't mind at all." Lincoln gives a cocky smile and does a hand wave. "Carry on, please," he snickers. Watching Lincoln and Rocky banter is like watching Ethel and Fred argue.

"This is an A and B conversation and doesn't have anything to do with *you*."

"Dear little one, need I remind you? This is my office too and what happens in this office—"

Rocky raises her hand in front of Lincoln's face. "Shut it, Linc." She turns to face me. "So, are you going to tell me why you stole my case, or do I have to guess?"

"You wouldn't understand if I told you," I tell her.

"Try me," Rocky says calmly as she moves to sit at the edge of my desk and crosses her arms.

I check my watch. Even though it's the company's plane, I have to get to the airport and San Francisco traffic during rush hour is going to be a bitch.

"I met her once… in passing. I was on an assignment a while back. And this job is something I need to do—"

"So, are you saying I can't do *my* job?" Rocky pats her chest.

"I didn't say that, nor did I tell Knox that, either."

"This assignment is undercover." She raises a brow. "How are you going to… wait, was she one of your conquests, a past hook-up?"

"No, Roc. You know I don't play that shit. I don't think she'll even remember me." Once again, I glance at the same framed picture of a smiling woman on my desk, then think of the woman in the case file. Why does this assignment call to me? Why her and why now?

"What if she does remember you? Then what?" she asks suspiciously.

"I have a backup plan."

Rocky angles her head. "I don't buy it. What's the *real* reason?"

I rub my face. "This is something I have to do. Please, Roc… understand me when I tell you this is important to me."

"I don't know if I'm pissed at you for going behind my back"— Rocky points her thumb at Lincoln—"or being partnered with this idiot as his bitch for my new assignment."

"Hey, I resent that!" Lincoln bellows. "You know I will take *really* good care of you." He wiggles his eyebrows, scanning Rocky from head to toe. "Finally got my date with a princess."

"It's not a date, dipshit… and for the last time, the answer is *no*." Rocky narrows her eyes at him while I stifle a laugh. She hates being called 'princess' by any of the team, and Lincoln loves taunting Rocky just to get a rise out of her.

I mumble to Lincoln, "Bro, I wouldn't start with Roc if you know what's good for you." I turn my focus back to Rocky. "I truly am sorry you got stuck with this donkey-boy," I say jutting my chin toward Lincoln. "If he gets too frisky, kick him where it hurts."

She glares at Lincoln. "I'll break both his hands and slice his dick off if he even *thinks* of getting frisky with me." She walks towards me, gets up on her tiptoes to kiss me on the cheek, then punches me in the stomach. I grunt from the light hit—well it wasn't that light. "Don't pull this shit again."

I pull Rocky into a hug. "I won't, I promise." I kiss the top of her head. "Thanks for understanding."

"No thanks needed, and I still don't understand. All I ask is please be safe. I have a hunch the unsub is getting closer than we think. That's why I had to befriend her to stay close and see what I could find out."

I nod and give her a smile. "I'll call you the moment I land to get more intel on Miss Channing. I gotta go. Wheels up in an hour."

Working at KSIG for the last four years was like working with family that I have grown to love more than life itself. Julian Cruz may be my name, but I'm Booker to the team, a callsign I'd earned when I was a SEAL.

During my deployments, the team teased me for bringing a book to read during our downtime, instead of playing darts or basketball on our makeshift dirt-dusted court. And when it came time to go over the mission plans, I reviewed and studied them as if I were back in school preparing for an exam.

My priority is the KSIG team now, much like when I was a SEAL, which was only four years ago but feels like a lifetime ago. I miss being a SEAL, loved protecting and serving my country, but eliminating the enemy on my homeland is more important to me.

Knox recruited me and made me an offer I couldn't refuse. It wasn't the over-compensated salary, but the fact there are very few deployments overseas since most of the contracts are domestic.

During the six-hour flight, I study the file again. Chloe Channing is not just a name in a file. She's flesh and blood. And I am going to do everything in my power to keep her safe. Not only did I want the unknown subject locked up or killed, whichever came first, I want to get to know *her*.

Why I feel this way about a woman I barely know is beyond me.

I stare at the photo. I'm drawn to her mesmerizing smile, aqua eyes that hypnotize me. Although these circumstances are not how I want to see her again, I truly believe there's a reason for everything. Perhaps fate is bringing us together.

It was two Christmases ago and the images are still so clear.

The Ritz Carlton venue had been decorated with sparkling gold and red ornaments and silk mesh streamers that hung from the ceiling. An impressive tree stood at the front of the ballroom by the stage with gifts underneath for the battered women and children. The band played holiday music and the singer seemed to enjoy the sight of the guests dancing below. The event hosted auctions, fashion shows, and accepted other donations to raise money for the organization.

My role was security detail. Among the attendees were state and city representatives, the Chief of Police and his staff, wealthy influencers, and hospital personnel from where Doctor Sarah Channing practiced medicine, the hostess of the event and Chloe's mother.

Although it was a simple assignment, I never let my guard down, especially with the exclusive guests in attendance.

A woman fidgeted next to the check-in desk and caught my eye.

She leaned on the desk with her right hand and adjusted the strap of her high heel with the other. Her dark chestnut hair was pulled up in a twist with soft wispy strands that softly fanned her face. My eyes followed the seductive lines of her body and the low dip of the dress that exposed her smooth back.

"Damn stilettos, what was I thinking? Remember why you're here… it's for a good cause," she mumbled. The attractive woman turned her head, looked up at me, and smiled. "These god-awful shoes are killing me. That's what I get for not breaking them in first."

I'm immediately captivated by her sexy kitten voice followed by her cute-as-hell rambling. The thought of having a one-night stand with her, the things I'd do to and with her, was making me hard.

But this woman had class and was indeed a lady to be respected.

I needed to think with the head above my belt and keep the other in my pants under control. I'd never jeopardize my job to satisfy my needs.

But this woman… there was something about her that tempted my will, my control.

I lifted a brow. "Sounds like you may need someone to give you a foot massage." The scent of peaches like spring morning over-whelmed my senses and I wondered what the stunning woman's name was.

She slipped her shoe back on and scrambled up from her slouched position, looking flustered by the rosiness in her cheeks. "I'm Chloe." She stuck her hand out toward me.

"Booker," I replied, and felt an instant spark when I looked right into her blue-green eyes.

Damn, she is so beautiful.

She bit her bottom lip and I wondered if she felt it too. There's no way I could ignore the chemistry. Her eyes twinkled and the look she gave me could make any man go crazy. Adrenaline rushed throughout my body, something I hadn't felt in a long time.

"Just Booker? Does it come with another name, like Bond— James Bond?" she joked with a slight snort, putting a hand over her mouth.

Fucking cute as hell.

I realized I'd been holding onto her other hand longer than I should've. "My apologies." I cleared my throat, letting go. "And yes, it's just Booker."

"I didn't mean to—"

I stifled a laugh. "It's a nickname my friends gave me."

"Is it for 'book 'em Danno'?"

"*Hawaii Five-0*... cute, real cute. What do you know about *Hawaii Five-0*?"

"My dad. He's a big fan and still watches reruns." Chloe looked over my shoulder, then smiled back at me. "So, are you going to tell me how you got your nickname? Or is that some secret bro-code?" She raised a brow then held up a finger. "Wait, let me guess... you have a little black book tucked in the inside pocket of your tux with a hundred numbers of all the women you've hooked up with."

I chuckled. "Is that what I look like to you, a player?"

"Well, if the shoe fits." She shrugged with a twist of her lips.

"Has anyone ever told you not to judge a book by its cover?" I said with humor in my voice. "Or in this case, don't judge *Booker* by its cover?"

"That was cheesy." Chloe giggled at my bad attempt at a joke. "Well, if I am so wrong, why do your friends call you *Booker*?"

"Despite popular belief, present company included, I like to read. One of my jerk friends gave me a hard time when he saw me reading a book and it stuck." I almost told her my *real* name but decided not to. My callsign is part of who I am, too.

"Interesting." Chloe tapped her chin with her manicured finger.

"Why so?" I asked.

"Something we have in common."

"Oh yeah? What do you like to read?"

"It's silly—romantic suspense. My girlfriends, Phoebe and Ryland, tell me to get my head out of the clouds and come back to earth because there's no such thing as a hunky, secret-undercover agent who will come to my rescue." She fiddled with her earring. *Hmm. Is she nervous?*

"Do you *need* to be rescued?" I insinuated as I gazed into her eyes.

"Maybe." Chloe let out a slight cough, looked down at her dress, a failed attempt to hide her flushed cheeks. "How can a gorgeous dress be so uncomfortable?"

"Well, I hope I'm not overstepping when I say this, but I think you look absolutely beautiful."

"Thank you," Chloe said softly.

"So, tell me, Chloe, what are you doing out here? Ditching your date?"

"Now who's judging a book by its cover?" She placed her hand on her hip.

"Touché." The corners of my mouth turned up in a grin. "What would you be doing if you weren't here?"

"Definitely not wearing this dress or these shoes. I'm more a hoodie-and-fat-pants kind of girl."

"Fat-pants, huh?"

"Oh yeah, everyone should have a pair. I love wearing them."

I'd like to wear you.

As discreetly as I could, my eyes quickly roamed her hourglass figure. Thunder in my veins, my heart bruised my chest and my balls tightened.

"I'd like to see what these fat-pants look like on you."

"Well isn't that an odd way to ask a girl out on a date, Booker?"

"Only if you're ditching your date."

"I don't have a date. I…"

"Chloe, I'm giving you a hard time. Besides, I have a rule. I don't mix business with pleasure."

She tucked a loose strand behind her ear and angled her head. "Well, that's too bad. I would've said yes."

Our eyes locked. Her gaze made my body jolt as electric energy permeated in the air. I couldn't shake these unfamiliar feelings soaring through my body.

What the fuck is wrong with me? How is she making me feel like this?

I cleared my throat. "If you're not ditching a date, why are you out here and not enjoying the festivities inside?"

Chloe squared her shoulders. "Actually, I am ditching someone… my mother. She's making me meet so many people." Chloe fiddled with the diamond charm on her necklace. "I'm sorry. Here you have a job to do and I'm a babbling four-year-old girl talking your ear off." She peered over my shoulder again, watching a few guests pass by.

"I like your babbling mouth." I would take her as a diversion any day. "It gets boring out here and frankly, I like the distraction."

"So, how long do you have to work out here? I saw your partners roaming in the ballroom. I think all the guests are probably checked in by now. Maybe we can get a drink aft—"

"Sweetheart, there you are! I've been looking everywhere for you," a woman's voice cut in. We both turned to the graceful woman coming from the ballroom. Her elegant, long-sleeve black ball gown, fit for the Oscars, swept the floor as she walked toward us. As the woman got closer, I recognized her as Doctor Sarah Channing.

"Hi, Mom." Chloe rolled her eyes and shrugged in defeat. "I was taking a break from all the pleasantries and talking to, err—Mr. Booker." She turned to me and slid me a look. "This is Sarah Channing, my mother."

"It's very nice to meet you, Mr. Booker." We shook hands.

"The pleasure is all mine, Doctor Channing." I politely nodded and felt like a fucking idiot. I've been flirting with our client's daughter. *What the fuck was I thinking? And how did I not put two and two together?*

"Please call me Sarah," she said with a sincere smile. "I hope everything is going well out here?"

"Yes, ma'am." My eyes dart to Chloe. "I believe all the guests have arrived."

"Wonderful. Also, please make sure you and your associates get some food, God knows there's plenty." Sarah turned back to Chloe. "Sweetheart, the announcements are about to start, and I need you to meet Mr. Kollsson. He's going to secure the finances to ensure the money raised from this event is accessible for the chapters in Oakland and Los Angeles. I want to make sure he adds your information to the accounts, aside from me…" Sarah's voice dissipated as she looped an arm through Chloe's and whisked her away. Chloe looked over her shoulder and gestured to me with her finger that she would return.

Later that evening, I kept a watchful eye from the entry doors. I observed Chloe mingling, laughing, and shaking hands with familiar faces. I didn't understand why I had a hint of jealousy prick at my gut when I watched her dance with random men. I couldn't keep my eyes off her, like she was the only one in the room. Every so often, I caught Chloe smiling at me as I stood stock-still against the wall. Everything about her was intoxicating. Her plump red lips, ever-changing blue-green eyes, and that sexy-as-hell body.

Why am I so drawn to this woman?

This is the most fucked-up joke Cupid could play on me… to meet this woman at the wrong time.

Remember, you're on assignment. Don't break your number one rule.

Two years later, and I still think of Chloe. I didn't realize how deeply I was entwined with her until I walked away from her that night. Now, I remember the intense attraction like it was yesterday.

I need to be on this case, but why now?

Maybe it's a self-inflicted obligation.

Maybe it's the guilt from my past haunting me to make things right.

Maybe it's the instant attraction I feel for her.

Maybe it's everything.

CHAPTER

Two

CHLOE

"CHLO, HURRY YOUR ASS UP! The Uber driver is here, and we're gonna be late," Phoebe calls from the living room.

"Okay, okay—hold your horses." I wave the tablet in my hand. "I almost forgot this. I want to catch up on some reading." I smile at my roommate, Phoebe, and shove the device in my carry-on.

"Heaven forbid you forget to bring your knight in shining armor with you," Phoebe teases sarcastically walking towards the front door.

We scurry out of our apartment, which nestles in a trendy upscale neighborhood in San Francisco. We fell in love with this apartment the moment we saw it. It's a typical bachelorette loft, girly yet modern: two bedrooms, each with their own bathroom, a guest room, and a dining area that leads to a large living room space and opens up to a quaint balcony overlooking the bay.

We don't cook much, but our kitchen boasts top-of-the-line appliances. Our Viking fridge houses white wine, various ice cream tubs, two flavors of coffee creamer, leftover pizza from our favorite joint, and take-out from China Town.

"I hope you have everything this time," Phoebe mutters as she locks the exterior deadbolt. "Passport? Ticket? Your brain, perhaps?"

"Check, check, and check." I giggle, examining the contents in my bag.

"Did you go over the instructions with Celina to get our mail for us? I know she's only ten years old, but I just want to make sure it doesn't pile up in the mailbox."

"Yup," I confirm. "And to feed the fish."

"Um… hun, we don't have fish." Phoebe scrunches her brows.

"Kidding. Jeez. I know I'm a scatterbrain, but I *do* remember some things!" I roll my eyes.

Just six months ago, a chilly forty-four-degree morning, on my routine jog around the neighborhood, when I had been stabbed by a mugger, I suffered a concussion which oftentimes made me forgetful.

My doctor said it was nothing to worry about. My failed attempt to recall the simple things like where I left my keys is not a concern. It's the loss of important events and memories that bother me the most.

I had forgotten to call Ryland—our other best friend—for her birthday. It was a legitimate excuse and an acceptable oversight since Ryland hadn't been around for the last two years. *But still.*

Then there were times when I forgot to meet Phoebe for dinner and drinks at the Tipsy Turtle Bar & Grill, our usual hangout. The most frustrating was when Phoebe would reminisce and I would blankly stare at her, dumbfounded by the memory I couldn't recall.

The drive to the airport took about twenty minutes. Phoebe planned our vacation down to every last detail, with a spa day and various excursions. It's the perfect getaway to unwind at my grandfather's beach house in the Bahamas.

"I have a feeling this trip will change your life," Phoebe says. "You'll come back a new woman."

Hanging onto Phoebe's words, I hope this trip will bring peace and healing. I look out the car window as the city passes by and comfort settles within me to be getting away for a while. I need this change especially with everything that's happened in the last year.

It's been an emotional nightmare and I want it all to disappear into a dark abyss. The void I harbor from my mother's death, then my breakup with Luke six months ago, and the physical healing and aftershock nightmares I've dealt with since my assault—it all adds up.

The checkpoint security line moves like snails since the July summer travel has commenced. I gaze at a man and woman in the other line, assuming them to be on their honeymoon. Their luggage appears to be new, they couldn't keep their hands off each other, and the big shiny rock on the woman's finger gives it away, as the woman keeps observing it. I imagine myself in the bride's shoes and sigh.

Someday.

In front of me, I make goo-goo faces at the squirming baby sucking on a pacifier as he stares back at me over his mother's shoulders. The baby spits out the pacifier that clips to his bib by a small lanyard. The woman turns to see what the baby's giggling about.

"He's adorable," I say. "How old is he?"

"Thank you. Noah's two." The woman bounces her baby in her arms. "Do you have children?"

"Oh, no," I reply and shake my head. "I'm still waiting for Prince Charming to come along." I quickly glance at the newlyweds. "I just love children… I work at San Francisco General."

"Really? Do you know Doctor Gene Peralta? He's Noah's pediatrician."

"Yes, of course. You're in good hands."

"Are you a pediatrician, too?" The woman switches her baby from one hip to the other.

"Yes." I rummage through my small canvas backpack, pull out a business card, and hand it to the woman.

Noah grabs the business card from his mother and attempts to put it in his salivating mouth. "No, no… that's for Mommy." The woman takes the card from Noah.

I giggle as it warms my heart. This is why I love my job. "Babies are so curious, aren't they?"

"Ain't that the truth. One time, Noah got ahold of my lipstick and mastered a Picasso all over the carpet. It took me five tries to clean it up before I decided to call in the professionals." We both laugh.

I take Noah's small hand in mine. "You're going to tire out your mommy, aren't you, Noah?"

"He's definitely a handful." The woman gazes at her baby and kisses the side of his head.

"Well, have a safe flight, Ms...." I elongate, trying to get the woman's name.

"Kayla Stevenson. Same to you, Ms...." —she looks at the business card— "I mean, Doctor Chloe Channing."

I remove my shoes and tablet from my carry-on bag and place them in the bin. I look over at Phoebe ahead of me and shake my head.

"This is insane! Do you have to keep waving that thing over my boobs? I know they look explosive... I assure you everything in my blouse is real and natural," Phoebe grunts out at the female officer.

Why does she have to be so complicated?

"Feebs, seriously? Stop being a jackass. And don't say *explosive* at the airport. Everyone is staring," I whisper-yell. "I swear, you're going to be the death of me someday."

Phoebe giggles, gets her belongings from the gray bin, and we both turn to look for our gate.

My overexuberant, loquacious and inquisitive best friend, Phoebe Kyndal Powell. We are polar opposites and I often wonder how we remained best friends throughout the years. But I still love her, nonetheless.

We arrive at our gate with at least another hour to board. Sam, my cousin, waves at us, saving three empty seats beside him.

"Chloe, PK, over here," Sam calls us, hands in the air.

"Remind me why he's here again?" Phoebe huffs.

"Would you turn down an all-expenses-paid trip to the Bahamas, thanks to my dad?" I remind her, looking at her dark hair and emerald-green eyes. "I honestly think he's here to babysit me even though he brought Sage with him. I'm pretty sure once we get there, they'll be off together doing their thing."

"You think he'll marry her?" she asks.

"Who knows?"

"I don't know what he sees in her."

I twist my lips. "Do I detect a bit of jealousy, Feebs?" I accuse.

"Hardly," she retorts.

There's a love-hate thing that exists between Sam and Phoebe. It stems from Phoebe crushing on him since high school which led to a summer fling before we started college at Berkeley.

"Remember, you agreed to be nice," I tell her raising a brow.

"Yeah, yeah… as long as they stay out of our way, I'll be fine."

I can't blame Phoebe for feeling annoyed. The *girls-only* trip had been botched, thanks to my father. This trip is a detox, a withdraw from *all* of San Francisco, including Samuel Channing. Dad did not budge at our plea, and I knew it was a case we were not going to win.

Sam's older by two years and the closest I have to a brother. His ash-brown hair needs a cut since it's getting long at the top, but he's still very handsome and charming.

"Hi, Sammy. Where's Sage?" I drop my bag to the floor and sit down in the vacant seat next to him. I look out the large panel window where an airplane approaches the jetway.

"She went to get coffee," Sam answers. "Something's bugging her… she's been off, not herself lately."

"You must not be doing your *job* right, Sammy-Boy," Phoebe smirks.

"Cute, PK. I'll have you know I can do the *job* every day and twice on Sunday." Sam winks at Phoebe.

"Only twice on Sunday? You're losing your touch. Now I see why Sage is so uptight."

"Jealous much?" Sam raises a brow. "Since when has my sex life been on your radar?"

"It's a very small blip on my radar."

"So, I'm still on your radar?" He wiggles his brows.

"Small… tiny blip." Phoebe levels her eyes at Sam's groin, holding up her finger and thumb an inch apart.

Sam steals a quick glance at her low-cut shirt that shows Phoebe's cleavage.

With two fingers Phoebe points to her eyes. "Hey, eyes up here, Sam!"

Sam chuckles, moving his eyes from Phoebe's breasts back up to her face. "Nothing I haven't seen before."

"Perv," Phoebe quips. "Did you forget you have a girlfriend?"

I clear my throat as I raise my hands up between them. "Okay, can we put an end to the Battle of the Sexes?" I let out a breath. "Sam, the thing is… this trip was only supposed to be me and Feebs. You and Sage, well… it puts a damper on our plans," I confess.

"Look, I've told Sage that Phoebe and I are old news—"

Sage finally appears holding two cups and a brown pastry bag in her hands. Her hazel eyes and shiny blonde hair cascade down her shoulders.

Sam looks up at his girlfriend. "Hey, babe. I was just telling my cousin the plans I have for us when we get to the Bahamas," Sam says. He kisses Sage on her cheek, taking one of the cups from her hand.

"Hi, Chloe… Phoebe," Sage greets softly, almost timidly. "I just want to say thanks for letting me tag along."

"Sure thing." I smile, then elbow Phoebe.

"Uh, sure. Not a problem." Phoebe didn't sound so convincing, but I'll accept it.

"Phoebe, are we good?" Sage asks.

"Yes. Why wouldn't we be?"

"I just want to be sure, considering—"

"I assure you… Sam and I are history. And I don't want this trip to be any more awkward than it has to be. I want to make this memorable for my best friend and to just unwind." Phoebe wraps her arm around me.

"Fair enough." Sage warmly smiles and takes a sip of her coffee. "I just want us to be good."

"We are good. I want you to have a good time with Sam." Phoebe returns a smile and slightly nods.

Sam let out a slight cough. "Well, now that that's all squared away… how are things at the news station?"

"It's good," Phoebe replies, her eyes back on Sam.

"Phoebe's going to cover the foundation's story. She'll interview a few of the volunteers and the women and children we've helped." I straighten my back with a gleaming smile. "I can't wait to start on that when we get back."

"Aunt Sarah would be so proud of you, Chlo. I know I am. Let me know when it airs." Sam takes a sip of his coffee. "By the way, how's the training coming along for the marathon?"

I shake my head. "Not this year. I'm not ready." There was a time when I felt safe and enjoyed running through my neighborhood. But the attack set me back and I hadn't really trained like I wanted.

I want to start training again but need to get my courage back. Running was my escape, to feel free. Now, I feel like I am running from something or someone rather than for myself.

I close my eyes for a moment, returning to that fateful morning. Flashes of my attack splinter my thoughts.

A dark silhouette appeared from the shadows. Olive eyes I could still see in the murky darkness, and a grin that sends shivers up my spine. The nightmares and the wound my attacker left behind reminds me he was there.

The announcement blares through the loudspeakers startling me out of my trance.

"Flight 2405 at one-fifteen to Fort Lauderdale will begin boarding," the lady at the desk says into the mouthpiece. "We will start with First Class and Premier seating."

CHAPTER

Three

JULIAN

THE AIR IS EXTREMELY HOT and muggy. The damp warm breeze rustles the palm trees. Caribbean weather has a mind of its own. There would be a torrential downpour for ten minutes and the next moment, the clouds disappear, and the sun shines as if the storm never happened. In the distance, the sky displays shades of pinks and blues as the sun begins to settle over a shimmering dark blue ocean.

I sit under an umbrella on the patio of the safe house that's nestled away in the hills. Once again, I'm going over the case file while I still have a couple of hours to spare. It's peaceful and tranquil here—until my phone vibrates.

"Knox, what's up?" I answer on the first ring.

"Frank received another letter a few days ago. The letter targets Chloe." Knox doesn't beat around the bush. "The unsub may take this opportunity to get his hands on her. My gut tells me this bastard will be out there instead of waiting for her to return home."

"As I told you before, the estate was like Swiss cheese. The unsub could easily get in and out of the property undetected. I installed the covert cameras and the security system. Tyco has eyes on the property now. I tried to show the old man, Ezra, how to use the alarm system, but he's clueless. So, I'll go ahead and remotely set the silent alarm every night after my rounds," I report.

With utmost discretion, I first installed the covert cameras. The estate is used as an Air BNB and I needed to be careful in respecting the renter's privacy. The cameras captured the pool man and gardeners with their normal routines, and the ins and outs of the resident staff—both Ezra and his wife, Olinda.

I have firsthand knowledge of enemy tactics. I don't expect the perpetrator to show his face on the property; that would be stupid on his part since the jackass has been careful enough to go undetected for the last year.

This perp is good, really good, and it pisses me off more than any other mission I've been on.

"I'm glad you took the liberty of tightening things up. I informed Frank that you've been securing things over there this past week. Once Chloe gets back to the States, Rocky will resume her role."

"I understand." I hope this maniac shows his face in the next few weeks so I can rid her of this asshole and know that Chloe is safe. "And what if this all blows over before she returns?"

"We'll cross that bridge when it comes… stick to the plan," Knox snaps. "The contract specifically states that your undercover assignment must *not* be compromised. You're the handyman and driver… and she knows nothing about the psychopath after her. Frank never told Chloe about the letters, her mother's murder, or that she's now marked."

I stare at her picture as a knot in my gut hardens. "I don't get it. Why doesn't he want to tell her? I think she has a right—"

"Frank doesn't want his daughter living in fear."

"I still don't agree." I rub my face.

This has got to be one of the hardest fuckin' cases I've worked.

"Agree or not, your job is the contract. Shadow her… and keep me posted."

"Yes, sir." I hang up without a goodbye. I grit my teeth, hating the sound of Chloe Channing labeled as a *contract*. But the fact of the matter is, her father is KSIG's client and I have no choice but to follow orders.

When I first joined the security firm, I met Tyson Cooper, or as the team called him, Tyco. He has the technical skills that could break into any database and dive deep into someone's background for finding things that couldn't be gleaned through normal channels. He gave me all the factual intel he could on Chloe Channing. But there isn't much about the unsub because the psychopath was good at covering his tracks and this angers me to high heaven.

Who is this asshole? And why is he targeting the Channings— especially, *why Chloe?*

For the thousandth time, I flip through the pages of the case file. Enclosed are copies of the letters addressed to Judge Channing and names of people associated with the family. There's photos of Chloe and her father at the coffee shop, a few at the hospital, hanging out with friends at the local bar, and some of Chloe jogging around her neighborhood. The file also contains police reports from Sarah's accident which took her life the summer prior to Chloe's attack and after I met Sarah.

Doctor Sarah Channing had been in a car accident that was anything but. At first glance, it merely resembles a hit-and-run. According to witnesses, a black GMC pickup ran a red light, crashed into Sarah's Mercedes Benz, and fled the scene. Tyco retrieved the police report along with video footage from the street cameras over that intersection. He confirmed a hit-and-run with a black truck— and it *did* look deliberate.

Shortly after the harrowing incident, a letter arrived at Judge Channing's chambers. The envelope did not have a return address.

Your wife is dead and she's next

I examine Chloe's police report again and again trying to piece together why she's a target even after her mother's death. No blaring sirens grab my attention, but I know there's a clue in here... I just have to keep searching.

Chloe kept a regular routine and it's probably how the attacker was able to get her alone. My stomach tightens as I read over the details.

It happened on a cold January morning. Chloe had gone out for a jog through her neighborhood when the unsub wearing a dark hoodie had attacked, stabbed, and rendered her unconscious. The suspect could've done worse, but another runner had come up and scared off the attacker who was smart enough to take the weapon with him as he fled the scene.

When Chloe awoke at the hospital the next day, she couldn't remember much. She didn't even remember waking up the previous morning for her run. The doctor diagnosed Chloe with temporary memory loss due to her concussion and said it was nothing to be alarmed about. Eventually, the doctor explained, she would regain more memories that might feel like déjà vu, or she may not.

Now, I wonder if it's coincidence or destiny to be on this case. Regardless, I have a job to do. Protect her and keep her safe.

Maybe, just maybe, once the job's done, I could resume that conversation from two years ago. I realize I'm taking a gamble that she may remember me, and if there's any chance she does, it's a chance I'm willing to take.

CHAPTER

Four

CHLOE

THUMP, THUMP, THUMP, THUMP...
      Oxygen in my nose, exhale through my mouth.
Repeat.

My breathing is fast and steady as my running shoes vibrate against the sidewalk. Music blaring in my ears. I'm in the zone, in my own world and away from reality.

The streetlights are still lit, and the sun has not made an appearance in the inky sky. Training for the marathon is best done early in the morning. There's an occasional passing car momentarily blinding me with its headlights.

My ears and nose feel cold in the January breeze.

I turn the corner to run alongside the park.

Trash can, tree, car, bright light; I say to myself as I run by each one.

Just ahead, around the corner I see another runner.

With no warning. We collide full force. Knocking the wind out of me, I lose my balance and fall backward hitting my head on the ground.

I touch the back of my head and feel wetness. Is that blood?

Headphones still in place, I can barely hear the song from the loud ringing in my ears. He straddles my body, imprisoning me.

I gasp for the air I desperately need but his heavy hands are on my throat impeding my efforts.

Tears stream down my temples.

A steely knife skims my face.

My heart races.

I'm terrified and feel helpless.

My vision blurs and I can barely see my attacker's face. But there is no doubt the narrow, beady eyes threatening me are filled with hatred and pure evil. I want to scream but the sound is stuck in my throat.

His breath reeks of cigarettes.

Then a fist crosses my face before the cold knife enters, stealing the last of my breath with excruciating pain. He grabs a lock of hair and slams my head against the concrete.

Then, only blackness.

THE JERK OF THE AIRPLANE LANDING ON THE TARMAC WAKES ME. MY heart races, I'm short of breath and a thin sheen of sweat coats my forehead.

My hand goes to my lower abdomen, where the phantom pain throbs. The asshole had left the scars to prove he was there. I'm unsure if the vivid images from my nightmares are real. In some way, I believe they really *did* happen, and this scares the shit out of me.

One thing remains, tattooed in my mind… the evil eyes give me shivers down to the pit of my belly and I tremble at the thought knowing my attacker is still out there. For now, there's comfort knowing I'm thousands of miles away.

When the police took my statement while I was recovering in the hospital, they deemed it random. But this never eased my mind knowing there's a maniac loose around the neighborhood. We live in a safe area with hardly any crimes reported. The weird thing I still can't shake is there were no similar assaults reported prior or after mine.

"Did you have another nightmare?" Phoebe asks, her hand on my shoulder, bringing me back to the here and now.

"Why? Did I say something?" I sit up letting out an exasperated breath, getting my bearings and unbuckle my seatbelt.

"Nothing in particular. You were mumbling again." Phoebe presses her lips together and gives a worried look.

"I'm fine." I make an imaginary X across my chest with my finger. "Cross my heart." I attempt a smile, but Phoebe knows me all too well as I try to push down my distress.

Phoebe is my rock. When I was released from the hospital, Dad tried to persuade me to stay at his home, in my old room, but I refused. I wanted to be in my own apartment in my own bed. Most nights, Phoebe slept with me so I would feel safe again, and she's the one who was awakened by my screams from the damn nightmares.

And although our neighborhood is considered among the safest places to live in San Francisco and our building has a doorman that announces all guests to the tenants, Dad still took every precaution by installing a security system at our home to ensure my safety.

I watch Sam fetch the carry-on bags from the overhead compartment and hand one to Phoebe. I look over at Sage across the aisle tapping on her cell phone which reminds me of Dad since I promised I'd call the moment I landed.

I pull out my cell phone and turn it on. I read a few texts from my colleagues and friends.

One from Celina promising she would take care of the apartment and mail.

A funny text from Ryland wishing she could be with me and Phoebe on this trip, asking not to *forget* about her.

A short message from Rochelle to call when I return and hook up for drinks.

Brennan, a friend and owner of the Tipsy Turtle, also sent a cute text saying he misses his two favorite drinking buddies.

And one from Dad reminding me to call as soon as I land.

I press Dad's name on my phone. "Pumpkin," Dad answers on the second ring.

"Dad. Hi. We just landed in Fort Lauderdale and are heading to our connecting flight to Papa's." I grab my carry-on from Sam.

"How was the flight?" Dad asks.

"Okay, I guess… I read a bit then dozed off." I yawn. "And what are you doing?"

"Oh, the usual." I hear him take a sip. I picture him with his usual short glass of brandy sitting behind his mahogany desk in his leather chair, maybe with a Victor Sinclair cigar and watching a rerun of Hawaii Five-O. "Listen, I know I've been a pain in your ass these last couple of months, but please be careful out there. Remember the buddy system, safety in numbers? And make sure Sam is with you."

Dad's tone is tense and full of uneasiness. I can't shake the distinct feeling there's more to his concern than he's letting on. The last several months, I've had this eerie feeling of being watched. Since my attack, my senses have heightened, and I am more aware of my surroundings.

Is it paranoia? Or have I just learned my lesson? Whenever I scan my surroundings, there's nothing out of the ordinary. Nevertheless, the ominous feeling sometimes overwhelms me.

Then there are the unexplained one-word postcards that arrived in the mail, addressed to me.

'Next'

Where did they come from? They never have a return address. And what did 'NEXT' mean? At first, I assumed they were advertisements but then another showed up. Now my gut warns me otherwise. Especially when the words progressed.

'You Are Next'

"I'm turning thirty in a couple of weeks, I—"

"I don't care if you're turning fifty. You are *my* little girl. *Always.*" He sounds off, obvious that he did not like my remark.

"Dad, since my attack you've been so protective, and I appreciate it, I really do. Don't be such a worry-wart. I was in the wrong place at the wrong time," I tell him, not sure if I'm trying to convince him or myself.

"I will always worry about you." Dad takes another sip. "Remember your first day going into third grade and you wanted me to drop you off about a block away?"

I nod as if Dad could see me. "Uh... kinda."

"Well, I did as you wished. But I was still there watching you to make sure you were okay."

"That was the day I met Feebs," I say, happy that I remember a moment in time.

"Yes... you two have been inseparable since. My point is, don't take my *worry-wart* away from me. I'm your dad and it's my duty."

Dad is amazing and all I have left. I certainly can't fault him for being a protective father.

"Okay, my worry-wart dad... I've gotta go. We're heading to our gate and will board soon."

"Love you, Pumpkin. Call me when you get there."

"Love you more. And I will."

It's a short trip on the charter plane to our final destination. As we approach the baggage-claim area, I notice a dark-haired man holding a sign with **CHANNING** written on it. We approach the tall, very tanned and handsome man. There's something familiar about him, but I can't put my finger on it.

"We are the Channings." Sam stretches his arm to him and shakes the man's hand. "My name is Sam."

"Hi, I'm Chloe Channing." The handsome man's hand wraps around mine and I can't shake the niggling feeling in the back of my mind. Goosebumps warm my skin as a familiarity blankets me. *Have we met before?*

"My name is Julian—Julian Cruz, and I'm here to drive you to the Channing Estate." His voice is low and raspy, and he's only looking at me.

Julian? Nope, doesn't ring a bell.

I open my mouth then quickly close it. I'm tempted to ask if we've met before, but I don't want to feel stupid if we hadn't. And how could I forget a face like his? He's got the most alluring dark intense eyes. His five o'clock shadow and dark chocolate hair are a bit longer than I care for. Nevertheless, I like what I see.

He's wearing tan cargo shorts, and his broad shoulders fit perfectly in the black short-sleeve shirt that exposes the ripples of his muscles on his forearms. And there's a hint of a tattoo on his bicep that I find sexy.

There's no doubt he's strong, and I'm so turned on the more I watch him. Julian's biceps bulge as he lifts our luggage effortlessly from the carousel and places them on the buggy.

My heart beats faster just thinking about what he looks like under his clothes. I want to lick the perspiration off his neck caused from the humid air like my favorite ice-cream flavor dripping from its cone. My thoughts wander, imagining Julian satisfying all the things I only fantasize about and read in my romance books.

Then my uncontrollable gaze goes south, curious of how well-endowed he is. I quickly shut my eyes and cover my face with my hand from embarrassment.

Holy shit! Why did I look there?

I shake my head and snap myself out of these thoughts. *What the hell is wrong with me?* This isn't like me and I need to get control of myself.

"Girlfriend, I see you staring at the eye-candy," Phoebe whispers, nudging my shoulder. I roll my eyes, not surprised at Phoebe's comment. "And babe, you might want to wipe the slobber." Phoebe giggles pointing to my mouth.

"Wha—I'm not..." I gasp and glide my fingers across my mouth.

"Sure you're not," she teases for good measure.

Julian and Sam load the luggage into the back of the Range Rover. Phoebe, Sage and I scoot into the back row and Sam takes the passenger seat. The drive over to the beach house is mostly quiet except for the radio playing steel drums of a familiar melody from Rihanna. It's dark out and there's no use looking out the window to take in the sights.

"So, Julian." Phoebe breaks the awkward silence. "Are you staying at the beach house, too?"

"No, ma'am. I have a small place a couple of miles away," he says gruffly.

"Please don't call me *ma'am*. I'm not my mother," Phoebe chides.

Julian's mouth perks. "Noted."

"So, what's your deal?" Phoebe continues.

"I'm helping out Ezra until he gets some permanent help."

"Hmm... I see." Phoebe pauses then glances at me with an I-have-a-plan look. "Do you have a girlfriend?" she sing-songs.

I elbow Phoebe's rib. "Stop asking so many questions. You're not working on an exclusive story," I say through gritted teeth. "Besides, I'm sure he's *got* a girlfriend... isn't that right, Julian?" I peer at the rear-view mirror where Julian's eyes meet mine.

"No, I don't have a girlfriend." The smile in his eyes contains sensuous flames.

My cheeks warm and I jerk my eyes to the side window. God, I hope he didn't see the flush all over my face. My heart skips a beat and blood rushes through my veins, and I wonder why I feel this way over a man I just met.

WE FINALLY ARRIVE AT OUR home for the next three weeks. A dowdy old man wearing glasses and a tropical shirt with black pants opens the front door. With a great smile, he waves at us as the car drives around the half-circle driveway. As soon as the SUV parks in front of the house, I hurry out of the back seat and give the man a hug like my life depends on it.

"Ezra! I've missed you so much." I circle my arms around the man. Ezra has aged a bit. His dark skin shows off more grays sprinkling in his black curly receding hair. Still holding his cane in one hand, he wraps his free arm around me.

"Oh, Chloe. It's been so long, I was afraid dat you forgit about me and Ms. Olinda," Ezra replies in his melodious island accent.

"I could never forget you," I assure him. "You remember my friend, Phoebe?"

"Yes, of course child, I remember Miss Phoebe. You da one chanting wid dem pom-poms throughout da house when you were dis tall." Ezra puts his hand mid-chest. "Look at ya now. Both ladies are beautiful and taller dan dis old man." Phoebe and I laugh.

"This is Sam's girlfriend, Sage Carmack." I point to Sage who gives a slight grin.

I glance at Julian as he carries the luggage into the house. I ask softly, "Why did you hire extra help? Are you okay, Ezra?" I eye Ezra's cane then his slouching back.

Ezra chuckles. "I'm not da stout man I used to be. Now, dis young man done some good tings around da house da last couple of weeks." Ezra rambles, rubbing his side. "He'd done fixed da lighting and da electric work." Ezra waves his hands pointing at the new lights that lit the porch. "Isn't dat right, Mr. Julian?"

"Glad I could help out, Ezra." Julian smiles and carries the last bag into the foyer.

"Ahhh. Now come on inside. Ms. Olinda is very excited to see ya and she's made a feast." Ezra enters the house and waves his hands prompting us to follow him.

I didn't follow the others. Instead, I stand in the middle of the foyer as they disappear down the hall toward the kitchen.

Feeling nostalgic, I close my eyes and take in a deep breath. The scent of the house, old wood and sweet plumeria, comforts me. It's a feeling of refuge and wonderful memories. I open my eyes and gaze at the rustic wooden floors and staircase that twirls to the upstairs bedrooms.

I smile to myself, remembering when I tried to slide down the banister a couple of times when I was a little girl.

To my right is the oversized living room with a fireplace, I angle my head and wonder if it was ever used.

To my left is the dining room with an elegant dining table and a chandelier hanging over. Just ahead is the hallway that leads to the kitchen and an enormous sunroom.

I tilt my head up to prevent the tears welling in my eyes from falling down my face. I'm a roller coaster of emotions. Although happiness flows through me, I'm sad and yet I feel relaxed and at peace, something I haven't felt in a while.

I savor every past event that plays in my mind. Mom's here, her scent of plumeria and the splashes of her feminine touches fill this house.

It feels good to remember.

Not knowing how long I've been standing there in silence, I suddenly feel a presence that tingles my skin, giving me goosebumps as I inhale a familiar scent of a man's cologne and yet it's not familiar. My heart races and my belly flutters for no reason.

"Jiminy Christmas! You scared the bejeezus out of me," I gasp as I turn to where Julian stands with his hands in his pockets behind me.

CHAPTER
Five

JULIAN

I QUIETLY GAZE AT CHLOE as she stands in the foyer. The second I saw her at the airport, it was like seeing her for the first time. As if I was a kid again, with the anticipation of opening a gift I begged Mom for and got on Christmas morning.

In this millisecond, I realize why I'm here. I take it all in and there she is, in all her beauty. She's so beautiful.

"I'm sorry, I didn't mean to frighten you," I keep my voice low and calm. "Uh... and *Jiminy Christmas?*" My mouth turns up in bemusement.

"It's my uncontrollable babbling mouth. It blurts whatever it wants." Chloe fidgets with her ear and softly giggles. *There's that nervous signature I remember and it's cute as hell.*

"I like your babbling mouth," I reply, returning a smile.

Chloe straightens her shoulders, angles her head, then scrunches her forehead. She looks at me as if I have two heads. With narrowing eyes, she asks, "What did you say?"

"I said, I like your babbling mouth," I repeat. Chloe's mouth opens and immediately closes as if she were going to say something. *Did I say something to offend her?*

"Is everything alright? Did I say something wrong?" I try reading Chloe's frozen look on her face but can't decipher it.

She shakes her head. "No... it's just, you said something..." Chloe whispers, almost inaudibly, but I catch it.

I have an intuitive feeling I must've triggered a memory, but I can't be sure. Sometimes, when a memory is triggered, it may come back as clear as she's looking at me, a flash of lightning that comes as quickly, or like walking slowly through a hazy fog. It can be jarring for someone who suffers from amnesia, so I need to be careful.

She stares at me for a moment. It was obvious Chloe didn't immediately recognize me when I picked them up at the airport. A part of me wishes she did remember me. I want to ask her if she's read any good books lately? Did she still wear her *fat-pants*? Perhaps catch up like old acquaintances.

I told her my nickname, the name I go by and what my teammates call me. But now, she knows me only as Julian Cruz, the *hired help*. Although I'm relieved, I'm also sad her amnesia took parts of her life away and Chloe's memory of the first night we met is forgotten.

Now, it's like starting over with her.

Clearing my throat, I ask, "Would you like me to bring your bags to your room?"

"It's okay, I can do it."

We both reach for the bags and our hands touch. The hitch of her breath alarms me. I grip the handle of one of her suitcases, waiting for Chloe's eyes to meet mine. And when they do, an electric spark zips through me down to my groin, but it's my heart that comes alive.

Does she feel it too?

There are unspoken words as if we know what the other is thinking and I'm tempted to test that theory. But I have rules and I need to make sure I don't break them. All the consequences ghost through my mind if that happens. I've seen it firsthand, losing a loved one after my instincts failed me because I was distracted.

I take in a deep breath and will myself to relax. I'm a professional and take my missions seriously. It's my job to control my actions in any situation I find myself in. And the way I can't control my emotions now, unnerves me.

One minute I'm in front of Chloe and the next, a ghost from my past haunts me. How is this dark memory buried so deep resurrecting from the abyss of my mind?

It's a warning. *Focus. Remember why you're here.*

"Please, let me take these for you. I wouldn't be a gentleman if I didn't do this." I give her a wink.

Chloe smiles as her hands rise up in surrender. "I guess chivalry still exists."

I lift the larger suitcase and she immediately takes the smaller one. "Holy hell, woman—what did you pack in here, everything *and* the kitchen sink? And you wanted to carry this to your room?"

"Stop your complaining, old man. You offered. Besides, I think you can handle it," Chloe says with a smile as I laugh loudly.

"No old man here. Give me a chance, I'll show you what else I can handle." I give her a coy smile. Chloe quickly turns around after I notice a flush of pink over her bisque cheeks. I watch her long legs and cute ass sway up the stairs and can't help but imagine them wrapped around me.

Undercover security detail is never an easy task, especially for this assignment. The irony of it all, I asked to be put on this case.

When we met back in San Francisco two years ago, I instantly liked Chloe and couldn't deny the attraction. And knowing her life is in danger wills me to be her protector.

My teammates tell me I have a *hero complex,* always wanting to be on every assignment possible. And maybe I do.

My assignment is to shadow Chloe, her undercover security guard, and nothing else. But I also want to solve this case and find out who the bastard is and put an end to him.

Earlier, I reached out to Rocky to gather personal intel on Chloe. Just as Rocky had done back at home, I need to befriend Chloe and earn her trust.

Chloe has a small and tight circle. Phoebe and Ryland are her best friends. There's Sam, her cousin, and Brennan, the owner of a local bar they hang out at.

Rocky got lucky in being part of Chloe's circle and getting to know all of them better. Rocky didn't suspect any of the friends as the perpetrator. However, Rocky suspects the unsub may have contacted Chloe in the last several months. It was unclear how many times Chloe was contacted, but Rocky had a feeling it was enough to rattle Chloe's nerves.

If that's the case, why didn't Chloe mention it to her father? Or the police?

My jaw tightens at the thought of this psycho getting anywhere near Chloe. Knowing all this about her, I want to slay all her demons, especially the one that's after her.

"This is my room." She opens the door, turns on the lamp as she sets her bag on the floor. "You can put the kitchen sink over there." She points to her bed as I catch her sarcasm.

After plopping the suitcase on the bed, I walk over to the window and sweep the curtains to the side with my hand. Seeing the SUV in the circular driveway, I make a mental note of where her room is.

I clear my throat as I look around her room and then peer inside the adjoining bathroom.

"Nice," I say as if I've never been in here.

I smooth my hand over the bed. It's a girly room with soft blue and yellow pastels and frilly pillows. The walls display beach artwork and seashells on the nightstand and vanity.

For a woman who wasn't trying in the least bit, she's sexy as hell as my gaze wanders to her silky chestnut curls that fall softly over her collarbone, then to her cleavage that peeks from her V-neck blouse.

Down, boy. I tell myself referring to my tingling dick in my shorts.

"So," I say, attempting to break the awkwardness. "What are your plans while on the island?"

"Not sure. Phoebe has a few things in the works, I'm sure."

"Well, I'm here to drive you around wherever you want to go." I shrug and my smile is automatic just thinking of how much time I will be spending with her.

Chloe softly smiles back. We stare at each other for a moment and I wonder what's going on in that pretty head of hers.

I should walk away and let her settle into her room, but her pull is strong and leaving her in the room is the last thing I want to do. And I have the feeling she's thinking the same thing too.

Chloe has those eyes that can lure any man in and swallow him whole. What is it about her? I want to reach over and touch her, act on my urge and taste her lips. But I need to lock my shit down. *Focus, dammit!* I run my fingers through my hair.

"No girlfriend, huh? I'm surprised." Chloe shifts from side to side in her Converse shoes, tugging me from my thoughts of her in my arms.

"Why?" I scrunch my brows, letting out a chuckle.

"I mean, look at you… you could be a model or a stuntman for the movies." Chloe's hands wave, pointing at my body. "I'm sure you've had your fair share of *wooing* women with a tight body, perky boobs, and hot ass out of their clothes and into your bed with that smile of yours."

I choke on my laugh, surprised by her being so forward. But she couldn't have been more wrong.

"You've known me for less than a couple of hours and you assume I sleep around with bimbos?"

"I'm sorry… I didn't… it came out wrong… again, my babbling mouth." She covers her lips with her hand when our eyes meet. "Is it getting hot in here?" Letting out a whoosh, she fans her face with her hand.

With Chloe's blushing, I'm going to enjoy getting a rise out of her.

"So, what about you?" I point my chin toward her.

"What about me?" Chloe jerks her head back.

"Do you have a boyfriend?"

"Is this your first tactic of wooing a woman… asking if she has a man before you proceed since you're a gentleman and all?"

"Let's just say flirtatious curiosity." I lean my shoulder against the opposing wall, arms across my chest. "Are you wooable?"

"Eh…" She shakes her head and gives me a look as if she just tasted something bad.

"What's that supposed to mean?"

"I have issues and let's just say I'm not the type guys would want."

"I disagree," I counter hating that she's bad-mouthing herself.

Chloe quirks a brow. "Disagree?"

"I'd want you," I say softly and stare deep into her blue-green eyes.

"Either you've been on this island too long or you must have smoked the ganja." Chloe put her thumb and forefinger together as if smoking a joint.

I chuckle not expecting that to come out of her mouth. "You're batting zero, sweetheart."

"Are you laughing at me?" Her hand presses against her chest.

"I would never laugh at you—*with you*, yes. Never at you," I say. "First of all, I'm not into bimbos. Secondly, I've been on the island for a short time and third, I don't smoke, at all. Finally, you are very beautiful and any man who doesn't see that is a fool."

I can't deny it. Something's definitely happening between us and there is no way I can ignore the chemistry stirring. With the gaze in her eyes and the pounding in my heart, I only wish there was no other agenda and my only plan was to get to know her better.

Can I do this job and protect her? Of course—protecting Chloe is the easy part.

Can I keep my feelings pushed aside so it doesn't affect my job? Possibly—it will be a challenge especially with the unexplained emotions, past and present.

I can't help my wandering mind. A quick flash of her in my bed. Kissing every inch of her soft skin, my fingers in her silky strands, tasting her plump lips, caressing her perky breasts and moving slowly over her.

Get your mind out of the gutter, Book!

I rub my face with my hand, ending the thoughts of having my way with her. By the time the night's over, a cold shower will be much needed. But, the *boys* in the shorts have a mind of their own. I have to think of something quick.

"So, tell me, Chloe… what do you do for fun?" I ask, shifting in my shorts. "Shopping perhaps."

"Excuse me?" Chloe tilts her head, most likely from the abrupt change of subject. "Is that how you see me? A clueless shallow woman that likes to shop?"

"Sorry. I didn't mean to offend you." I wrap my hand behind my neck and mentally slap myself.

"Although shopping is always fun, it's not on my list of priorities," she chides, putting me in my place for my opinion about women and spending money.

"Do you like to go running?" I ask hoping I can redeem myself.

"Uh, sure… why?"

"I usually jog in the morning before the sun comes up."

"That's the best time to go running."

"So, what do you say?" I raise a brow. "Would you like to go running with me?"

"Oh, I don't know. It's been a while for me. I wouldn't want to slow you down." Chloe chews on her fingernail.

"Nonsense. I'd enjoy the company."

"I'm here to relax." Chloe presses her lips together and hesitantly nods. "I guess it wouldn't hurt to get a little exercise in. It's a good thing I brought my running shoes with me."

"Great, it's a date. Let's start the day after tomorrow. This will give you a day to rest from your travels."

"A date?" Chloe crosses her arms over her chest and eyes me. "Julian, an early morning run is not considered a date in my book."

"So, you have a book on dating?" I chuckle hoping I can win her over with my teasing.

"That's not what I meant. But considering the topic, there should be a dating book on how a man should treat a woman."

My lips turn up in a smile as I take a step closer. "My mom raised a gentleman and I don't need a book." *Shit—don't do it… don't go there.* "How about I take you out to dinner, show you what a date with me is like." The words are out before I can take them back, before I can even try.

What did I do? I broke rule number one.

"Ha! And why should I go to dinner with you?" She sucks in her bottom lip and twirls the ends of her chestnut hair.

"Cuz you like me." I shrug.

She half-smirks. "You're so sure of yourself, aren't you?"

"I am." My cocky-ass grin widens on my face.

"I'll have to get back to you, since my vacation planner has me all booked. Shopping and all!"

"You do that… have your peeps get back with my peeps?" I joke as she smiles. "You have a beautiful smile."

Chloe's face softens as she giggles. "Are you trying to woo me?" Her fingers fidget in front of her.

"Is it working?"

"I…uh…"

"Do I make you nervous?" I put my hands in my pockets the only way I can control my hands reaching out to her.

In the little time I've been around Chloe, I've picked up on her little quirks. Her babbling mouth and random words. The way she blushes then soon after twirls her hair or bites her bottom lip, a tell-tale sign of her nervousness, I'm sure of it.

This woman before me, intrigues me.

She's witty, yet shy.

She's beautiful and modest.

Her innocent giggle is intoxicating.

Her smile melts me.

Chloe has some kind of hold on me. No matter how hard I try to downplay my feelings, she has this pull on me. I step closer to her and now I'm about a foot from her warm body.

The last time anyone made me feel like this was…

"I hate to break it to you, but I'm not nervous at all," she replies, as I look deep into her aqua eyes. "I've been burned, learned my lesson."

"Whoever burned you is a piece of—"

"A piece of shit. And because of *him*, dating is not on my radar," she says softly, mint on her breath.

"I would never burn you," I tell her.

"Why would you say that? You don't even know me."

"I'm going to rectify that." I breathe her in, the familiar scent of peaches and shampoo. "Have dinner with me. Let me show you how *you* should be treated."

"You're really good at wooing."

"So I've been told." I give my best, sexy, drop-your-panties smile.

Our eyes lock and with every passing second our connection grows stronger. Intense chemistry permeates the space between us.

"Chloeeeee!" Phoebe's voice echoes from downstairs. "Get your butt down here."

Saved by the fucking bell.

I clear my throat. "I think you're being summoned."

"Yes, I guess I am," she whispers. And fucking hell I want to kiss her so badly.

Damn—I need a cold shower!

CHAPTER

Six

CHLOE

"SAM, YOU'RE SO FULL OF it. That's not how it happened at all."
With narrowing eyes, I point my finger at Sam.

Sam crosses his arms. "Okay, *Miss I-Remember-Everything.*
Enlighten us."

Phoebe and Sage stifle a laugh at his jabbing joke.

"Hey!" I snap, not liking the dig. "I'll let you slide on that one,
jerk."

"Well, we're waiting." The corner of Sam's mouth perks up into
a grin.

I scan the faces around the table. Three sets of wide eyes with so
much anticipation for my side of the story.

Not Julian's, though.

The man's thick lashes and intense dark eyes seem to be
undressing me instead. And I can't help the heatwave that rises from
my spine to the base of my neck. I can't control the sudden burn and
know I need to get a hold of myself before I embarrass myself. *Look
away, Chlo.*

I cough and need to clear the vision I have of Julian when his body was just inches from mine a moment ago in my room. I mentally shake my head and focus back to the conversation.

"Here's what really happened. Everything was going smoothly. I handled the waves until Sam turned the corner around the buoy. Then this idiot"—I point at Sam—"made a sharp turn, zig-zagged, which made me lose my grip and he kept going without looking back."

"Bullshit!" Sam raises his arms. "You make it sound like I didn't come back for you."

My hand flashes up. "Sam, let me finish. So, after floating in the middle of the damn ocean for what seemed like forever, Sam *finally* circled back around. My point is, if you plan on going water skiing"—I arch a brow to Phoebe and Sage—"don't trust Sam as the driver."

"At least I came back for my *poor wittle cousin*," Sam mocks, making an impression of a crying baby. "Chloe needed to be *rescued*."

A sudden dull awareness flashes in the back of my mind. A fuzzy image of a man's face standing tall with broad shoulders, a clear bud in his ear connected to a coiled wire snugged under the lapel of his blazer, asking, *"Do you need to be rescued?"*

I shake my head as anxiety swirls in the pit of my belly.

Is it my imagination—I'm on my fourth glass of wine—or a forgotten memory? I can't decrypt the images and if the vision really happened, or not.

What the hell was that? A déjà vu?

"You okay?" Phoebe whispers, placing a hand on my shoulder.

"Yeah, I'm fine. I think the wine got to me, that's all." I brush off the concern, then slide a look at Julian.

It's meant to be a quick glance, but now I can't tear my eyes away. An acute awareness, a niggling feeling, sends chills to the back of my neck. His ruggedly handsome face seems vaguely familiar. Or is it the attraction stirring between us?

His eyes. Where have I seen them before?

I scan my mental rolodex but still can't place him there. It's like I'm lost in a maze in my own head. This is definitely one of those moments when being oblivious of my past frustrates me and I want to bang my head on the table in hopes of jogging my memory.

"Well, since Olinda didn't leave us anything to clean up, I'm heading to bed." Sam yawns. He turns to Sage and caresses her face. "Babe, you ready to hit the sack?"

"Definitely," Sage replies with tired eyes, then nods at Phoebe and me. "Goodnight, ladies. See you tomorrow."

Sam speaks up, "Maybe not, we have an early morning. Driving around the island." He takes Sage's hand. "Goodnight, ladies," he says, and they disappear down the hall.

"Chlo, I'm headed to bed too." Phoebe stretches her arms up and tips her head side to side. "You comin'?"

"I'll be up in a minute. I'm going to walk Julian out."

Phoebe stands and turns to Julian. "Goodnight, Julian. I guess we'll be seeing you around."

Julian nods with a grin as Phoebe retreats down the hall.

"There's no need to walk me out." Julian's voice is gruff. "I can lock up behind me."

"Are you giving the lady of the house a hard time about walking you out? Besides, I just want to make sure the doors are locked. I've made it a sacred routine."

"Well, it's a good routine to have and I don't want to turn down a beautiful woman's offer to walk me to the front door either."

I fidget with the hem of my shirt as we walk through the hall to the foyer.

Butterflies tickle the insides of my belly when I quickly glance up at him. His warm grin shows off his sexy-as-hell dimples. It should be a sin to be that good looking.

I've always had a perception; men like him are conceited and egotistical. But Julian surprised me and is quite the opposite. Sure, he flirted with me upstairs, but there's a difference between arrogance and the confidence this man exudes.

And something else about him, something sweet and dignified.

Still, there poses a question of the unknown familiarity, lingering at the tip of my mind.

My chest tightens and stomach hardens. I'm obsessing over the image of the faceless man in a suit and tie who'd asked if I needed to be rescued.

Rescued from what, or whom?

Desperate, itching for an answer, I inhale then exhale.

"Julian, I have to ask… have we met before?"

"What makes you think we've met before?" He raises a brow.

"Never mind." I shake my head suddenly feeling like an idiot for asking. "Of course, we haven't… it was a silly question."

I'm emotionally drained and don't want to elaborate. I don't want Julian to know about the crazy amnesia I endured from my attack.

My body and mind have been on overdrive for the past year. From my mother's death, the physical and emotional healing of my stab wounds, to the nightmares, and now these strange flashes.

I'm a patient of patience and in time, at least I hope, the images will eventually reveal some truths so I can be whole again.

Julian opens the front door, steps onto the porch and turns to me. His dark eyes flickering from the porch light above. "I'll see you tomorrow," comes his voice, velvety smooth.

"Yes, see you tomorrow," I answer, biting my bottom lip.

"Well, goodnight." Julian wet his lips with his tongue, right where I want to lick and taste and… *What the hell is wrong with me? Snap out of it.*

Julian takes my hand and brings it to his mouth. My skin is hypersensitive to his touch and I swear I feel a swipe of his tongue as his lips brush my knuckles.

An electric current ignites my lady-bits and my throbbing thighs. The hairs on the back of my neck begin to tingle, and my heart pounds so loudly in my ears I think I might go deaf.

Sexual tension lights the air on fire.

I struggle with the desire and my breath catches in my throat. Needing to break the connection, I stumble a few steps back until I'm on the other side of the doorway.

"Goodnight, Julian." I slowly close the door, lock it, leaving Julian in the dark warm night.

I ENTER MY BEDROOM TRYING TO subdue the silly-ass grin on my face. Phoebe sits on the queen-sized bed, brushing her hair.

"Well... how'd it go with your Latin lover?" Phoebe jumps to her knees on the mattress.

"Feebs, I thought you went to sleep." I toe off my shoes and chuck them in the corner of the room, not caring the least bit where they land. "And he's not mine."

"Don't hold out on me, you little hussy. He's freakin' hot! I think he's into you," Phoebe prompts. "Did he ask you out?"

I roll my eyes. We've been best friends since we were kids. Even though we're roommates now, seeing Phoebe on my bed reminds me of the many sleepovers as kids, long phone calls and sharing each other's clothes as teenagers.

After high school, Phoebe and I remained glued to the hip as Ryland, our third best friend, left for UCLA. She landed an internship in Switzerland then it led her to a career opportunity. I miss Ryland who's been the buffer between myself and Feebs. I have a feeling this is one of those times I need her in this room with me, to help me with Phoebe's meddling.

"No... yes..." I stutter. "God, I need Ryland right now."

"Well, too bad, Ry can't save you. Which is it, yes or no?" Phoebe strokes her long dark brown hair with my brush. "He's definitely fuckable."

"Shh... keep it down." I put a finger to my lips. "And who said anything about fucking him?"

"I saw how he looked at you. He has those *fuck-me* eyes." Phoebe calms herself and crosses her legs on the bed. "So...?"

"Yes, he asked me out to dinner, and no—I'm not sure I want to go."

"Why the hell not?" Her hand stops midway down her hair.

I let out an exasperating sigh. "I don't want to start something that isn't going anywhere." I open my suitcase and begin to hang my clothes in the closet and put some away in the dresser. "Remember what happened with Luke Jensen?"

"How dare you even mention his name. He didn't deserve your time then, and he sure as hell doesn't deserve it now."

"I know, but Feebs, I thought he was the *one*." Thoughts spin in my head when my mind returns to that night. The night I caught Luke with another woman. "Not only did he screw me over, he screwed that damn *nurse*. Funny thing, after I caught them together, I haven't seen her come back."

The relationship with Luke lasted four months. Luke's good looking with perfect golden-brown hair, hazel eyes, a clean-shaven, squared jawline, and sexy, gleaming smile. The most eligible bachelor in town and a successful surgeon at San Francisco General. He's secure and stable. The kind of man I would've settled down with.

After Mom died, Luke was at the funeral. As a matter of fact, all of the San Francisco General Hospital staff were there. Several weeks afterward, Luke checked on me to make sure I was doing alright. Eventually, our friendship grew into something more.

His mere presence has almost all the nurses at SFGH practically dropping their panties for him. But for some reason the delicious male specimen showered me with all his attention, spoiling me with flowers, extravagant dinners.

Then one evening, Luke told me he was running late... something about last-minute rounds and he needed to check on a patient before he left.

I took advantage and arrived at his townhome early to surprise him with fresh groceries to make him dinner. A couple bottles of pinot noir, two filets mignons, asparagus, and fingerling potatoes were on the menu. This was a stretch for me since I practically burn everything.

As I entered the front door of his townhouse, nothing could've prepared me for what I saw. Luke's scrub pants pooled around his ankles, hips thrusting against a woman bent over his desk.

Reyna Donovan, *that slut!*

I froze at the sight of the man who'd just shattered my heart into a million pieces. The air reeked of sex. The ecstasy on Luke's face, the moans uncurling from Reyna's throat and the slapping of their skin were like a dull scalpel cutting my veins so I could slowly bleed out.

Hot tears rolled down my cheeks and rage boiled in the pit of my stomach. The bag of groceries fell from my hands with a loud reverberating thump when it hit the wood floor.

Luke's head snapped at the sound. His eyes locked on mine. Reyna tugged down her skirt that was gathered around her waist while Luke quickly pulled up his boxers and pants.

"Fuck—Chloe!" he yelled, following me as I darted down the hall to the front door. "It's not what you think."

I squeezed my eyes shut, clutching the door for support.

"It's not what I think?" Adrenaline rushed throughout my body. "Maybe a wild guess, but I'm thinking *Nurse Donovan* was part of your last-minute rounds."

"Chlo, let me explain," Luke stuttered, trying to put words together, but failed.

I willed my eyes open, using all my strength to hold back the tears stinging the back of my throat. I looked at him, standing so close I could smell Reyna's perfume emanating from his naked torso. "How long... how long have you been fucking her?"

"I can't."

"Can't?" Bitterness sharpened my voice, wanting to claw out his eyes. "That's what you should have told Reyna before you shoved your dick in her."

He scrubbed his mussed hair back off his forehead. "I don't want to tell you..."

"Answer me, dammit!" I yelled, tears forming in my eyes.

"Shit, Chloe... does it matter?"

"Are you kidding me? It matters to me."

"Two months," he muttered.

"You bastard." I hissed, choking back the bile rising in my throat. "How could you? I thought—"

"What? That I loved you? Damnit, Chloe... we've been together for what, four months. How can I love someone I haven't had sex with?"

Rage in my eyes met his unemotional face. My heart exploded from the raging inferno building in my chest.

Luke never loved me. God, I feel so stupid.

Heated blood rushed from my face down to my hands, balled up in fists, nails digging into my palms. "Are you saying you love Reyna?"

"No. I don't love her. It just happened. A man has needs, baby."

My fist flew connecting to his jaw. "Go to hell." The pain in my hand hurt like hell, but it was well worth it. "And I'm not your baby, asshole!" I bolted out the front door slamming it behind me. If my mom were still alive, she would have been outraged and regretted introducing him to me at the fundraiser gala.

After Phoebe found out what Luke did to me, my livid best friend anonymously called one of the nurses' stations to start a rumor. These nurses were relentless with gossip. In no time Doctor Drop-Your-Panties became known as Doctor-Limpy-Jensen who took male-enhancement pills. The rumor lasted several glorious weeks.

Though I couldn't condone the move, I did appreciate Phoebe's efforts toward sweet revenge and solidarity.

"Chlo, you're my person," Phoebe says, snapping me back to the here and now. "Doctor Limpy is ancient history." She pauses as if an epiphany struck her. "You have to jump his boner."

"Who? Luke?" I jerk my head back. "You're joking, right?"

"No, you twit. I'm referring to Mr. Irresistible, lick-his-Latin-lollipop Julian." Phoebe giggles. "And if it doesn't work out, we're gone in a few weeks. No harm, no foul."

"Do you always have sex on the brain?" I didn't want to admit it, but the image of Julian makes me weak in the knees.

"Damn straight." She wiggles her eyebrows.

"How are we even friends, you slut?"

"I can't help that I'm in touch with my sexuality. Besides, ever since I got dumped by that douchebag Bryan, I've become a different person. Heartbreak can really screw with a woman's mind and heart… speaking of screwing."

I stare into Phoebe's emerald eyes. "Why are you so up in arms about me and Julian?"

"Hun, I want you to have a good time on our vacation. I said it once and I'll say it again. You will leave this beautiful island with a new perspective on life and lightning doesn't strike in the same place twice."

"I'm going to enjoy my vacation regardless. And Julian is not on the agenda."

"He is now," Phoebe counters.

"Give it up, Feebs."

"More like *you* need to give it up. God knows you've got some cobwebs up in there."

"I'm not going to have sex with Julian. Besides, I'm saving myself." I lean against the wall, suppressing a sigh.

Phoebe sticks her finger in her mouth to gesture a gag. "Oh, please. Don't get all righteous on me. I love you, Chloe Harper Channing, but you need to get your head out of the clouds and out of those romance books. We're in the twenty-first fuckin' century and chivalry is long gone. Prince Charming is the boy next door. That knight in shining armor is a divorce attorney in a three-piece suit. Besides, didn't Snow White step out of the gingerbread house to meet her hunky Fabio?"

"First of all, Snow White lived in a cottage with The Seven Dwarfs. Secondly, Hansel and Gretel were abandoned by their parents and they lived in the gingerbread house, and third, I don't read about Fabio."

"A woman living with seven men sounds like one big orgy to me. And parents abandoning their children proves fairytales are bullshit. Anyway," Phoebe argues, "you get my point."

"There's no point. Julian lives here and my life is in San Francisco. I'm pathetic, I know. I'm a twenty-nine-year-old virgin looking for someone I can share my life with and he's back at home... somewhere. I know it."

"Live it up for once and take off that damn chastity belt!" Phoebe exhales. "Look, I know you're saving yourself for the perfect guy. But what if Julian is that guy?"

"This conversation is over and I'm tired." I yawn. "Now, you can either go to your own bed or stay so I can tell you a bedtime story about Hansel and Gretel."

Phoebe scrunches her nose. "No, thanks, I'll pass. But I'm not done talking about this." She scoots off the bed. "Operation-Lick-His-Latin-Lollipop begins." Phoebe snickers as she dodges a pillow I throw at her.

I roll my eyes. *Ryland, I wish you were here!*

CHAPTER

Seven

JULIAN

"FOCUS DAMMIT... YOU'RE ON ASSIGNMENT," I berate myself as I pick up my pace. I need my morning run to release the sexual tension and overwhelming emotions invading my body.

The sun peeks over the hilltop and the temperature in the air rises to almost unbearable. Sweat beads down my forehead, my fists clench as my feet pound the gravel and vibrate my legs.

Linkin Park's "In the End" blares in my earbuds. It seems fitting somehow with the situation as I listen to the lyrics buzz in my ears. I run faster to calm my arousal. I'd hoped the thunderous bass could overpower my thoughts of guilt from my past and the attraction that compels me nearer to Chloe.

I need to lock it down, put my feelings aside and remember why I'm here.

My job—to protect her from an unknown asshole psychopath.

I just can't forget my first priority. Doing so would endanger us both, and I can't live through that kind of hell again. I barely survived the pain the last time I let my guard down and I'm still tormenting myself…. because it was all my fault.

Remember your orders. She's a client. As much as I hate the term… she's the contract.

I've overstepped with Chloe already, but I'll chalk it up as playful and innocent flirting. The visuals steal my thoughts. Her cheeks blushing, the way she twirls her hair, when she sucks her bottom lip between her teeth—that last one damn near makes my cock pulse.

Mom raised me better than that. I'm a gentleman and I'm immediately ashamed thinking of Chloe on my bed having my way with her. But I can't help it. Being in close proximity to Chloe validates there's something between us.

I'm sure she felt the same attraction, or did I misread her body language?

Her body—tall and graceful. Slender and curvy in all the right places. Those legs for days and perky tits. *Damn, what is she doing to me?*

I've had my share of protecting sexy, sensual women who threw themselves at me. They've tempted me with revealing clothing, occasionally inviting me to their bedroom and a few even groped me. A few of my teammates would have jumped on the opportunity to have no-strings-attached sex with those women.

I never crossed that line. Each of them was just a contract. It was business.

But Chloe… she's different, like a drug I can't get enough of and can't wait for my next fix. And I haven't taken a hit. But fuck if I don't want to. I want to kiss her lips and taste her tongue and feel her skin against mine.

I run for another mile, pushing myself until I have no more fight in me. The longer I run, the more my mind wanders again, back to my office.

Papers and photos from the Channing case had been strewn across my desk. I had just gotten the approval from Knox to work on the case.

I had stopped clicking the pen with my thumb and picked up the 8x10 picture frame sitting on the corner of my desk. Soft ash-brunette curls tumbled over her shoulders. Her golden hazel eyes sparkled, and she had the most endearing smile.

Amber. God, I miss you so much.

My thumb caressed the glass over the woman's face. This is my favorite photo of her. It was the day I proposed to her.

Across from me, I felt the weight of Lincoln's eyes glaring at me from his own desk. I could sense Lincoln wanted to say something, probably a stick-his-foot-in-his-mouth observation.

Lincoln's honesty is something I respect and often there are words of wisdom. In that moment, however, I was *not* in the mood.

Lincoln straightened a stack of papers and pushed them aside. "Don't you think it's time to let her rest in peace?"

"Linc," I snapped. "Not today." I know he means well. But asking me to tuck the last photo I have of Amber in a box with the others is like burying her all over again.

"Sorry, man, I hate seeing you like this."

I sighed, returning the frame to its rightful place on my desk. "She's been gone five years… I miss her."

"I know. I miss her too, bro." Lincoln's forehead creased. "You gotta move on," Lincoln said, closing his laptop.

I rubbed my face in frustration. The ache in my heart descended, finding residency deep in my soul. "I'm trying. My soul has been black since the day she died. *Five fucking years.* Do you have the answer, Linc? Tell me… how do I move on?"

"I don't know, man. Only you can figure that out."

"All *you're* figuring out is how to scratch your next itch," I bit back. As soon as the words left my mouth, I wished I could've taken them back. "What do you know, anyhow? Your wife didn't die in your arms."

"Uncalled for." Lincoln narrowed his eyes at me, scratching his jaw. "But, you're right. JoJo didn't die in my arms, but she still left me, and I dealt with it."

"I'm sorry, man. I didn't mean to—"

"I know my situation's different and I can't imagine what pain you've been through all these years. But I also know it's unhealthy. I'm honestly worried about you. You drown yourself with work by volunteering for any assignment you can get your hands on to keep busy. Give yourself a break. Take a vacation."

"I don't know if I can. I should've acted on my instincts when I saw that fucker walk through those doors. I should be six feet under, not her."

MY LEGS FINALLY GIVE OUT and I plop myself on the sand. I take a sip from the water bottle, my elbows on bent knees as I watch the waves break against the shoreline.

Grief is like the ocean's waves. Sometimes they're loud and fierce, drowning me where I sink deeper in pain.

Other times, the ocean is peaceful and calm, bringing me the solace I need. I can't forget Amber, but I need to learn how to live without her and move on.

The day Amber Cruz died was no ordinary day, it was her birthday.

A SEAL could be called away in a moment's notice and I took advantage of the time off.

I was stateside for the next two weeks and I surprised Amber with a road trip up the coast to Santa Barbara. We had reservations at a bed and breakfast, I planned a romantic dinner and looked forward to making love to my wife all weekend.

We lived in a cozy town outside of the Naval Base in Coronado, a good five-hour drive to the B&B. We set out early when the sun had not broken the skyline, hoping to get there before noon.

Although there was a hint of orange in the sky, it was still dark out when I parked the car at the gas station. Being a SEAL, it was natural for my instincts to stay on high alert.

I scanned the area and noticed a lonely Ford truck that had seen better days. I watched the man get out of his truck and enter the convenience store.

"I'm going to run inside to get a couple of drinks and snacks," Amber said after she opened her door.

"I'll get it for you, Ambs. Tell me what you want." I inserted the nozzle to pump gas.

"That's just it. I don't know what I'm craving." Amber shrugged.

"How about I buy all the snacks."

"Jules, don't be silly." She rounded the car, kissed me on the cheek and walked toward the convenience store.

"I'll be right in after I'm done pumping," I told her.

Although she was not quite showing, something about my pregnant wife made me hornier than I already was. Maybe it was her fuller perky breasts or the glow that illuminated her bisque skin tone, or maybe the fact that I'd been deployed overseas for three weeks.

I whistled at my wife as her cute ass sauntered into the store.

Amber smiled back at me. "Like what you see, Sailor?" She fluttered her lashes.

"Always." I wiggled my brows. "And babe, I get to see more later." It melted me every time Amber's dimples made an appearance and her eyes sparkled.

I placed the nozzle back on the mount when an eerie sound pierced the air. *Pow!* Then another—*Pow!*

I'd know that sound anywhere. *Gunshots.*

They came from the convenience store.

I wasn't armed, but my skills would be my best weapon. I silently prayed Amber was hiding and not harmed. I rushed to the storefront and peered through the glass doors before easing them open.

The clerk behind the register held a gun, pointed at the man on the floor whose blood was pooling from the side of his lifeless body.

My hands flew up in the air. "Hey man, don't shoot," I cautioned the young clerk. "I'm a SEAL... what's your name?"

"Nate," his voice shuddered.

"Okay, Nate, I'm going to check this man's pulse and while I do, you need to call 911." With two fingers on the man's neck, I checked his pulse. Nothing. "He's dead. Is there anyone else with him?"

Nate's face paled, hands still shaking. "No. Just him. He—he had a-a gun… I—I shot him."

"My wife. Where is she?" I looked around. "Amber!" I yelled for her in the small store.

My heart pounded, blood rushed through my veins, palms sweating. My legs moved frantically about the aisles.

"She's over there." Nate pointed to the aisle he last saw her. "He sh-shot her," Nate shakily told me as he put the phone to his ear. "He took out his gun and just fuckin' shot her… then I shot him when he was coming my way."

My body was on auto-pilot and the pit in my stomach grew with every step I took. Not only because my skills kicked in. But it was my wife, my life, that I was desperately searching for between the aisles in the small store that felt like an endless maze.

"Hello, 911? Yes, we need the paramedics… my, my name is Nathan… a man with a gun came into the store… yes, two people are shot… I don't know… just one person, I think he's dead… it's the gas station on the corner of…"

I tuned out Nate's voice and rushed to Amber's side when I finally saw her at the end of the aisle.

"Baby, I'm here." I placed both hands on her bloody shirt. "Hold on, baby." I tore open her blouse exposing where she had been shot in the chest. "Fuck!" I screamed. "No, no, no, no…"

I pulled my t-shirt over my head and pressed it against her harrowing wound, preventing more blood loss.

"Jules." Amber's voice was barely a whisper. "I-I'm s-sorry. I should've… I-I'm so co-cold." Amber's breaths turned to short pants, spitting blood from her mouth.

"Don't talk, baby. Keep your strength." I stared into her heavy hazel eyes, pushing the hair out of her face. "Help's on the way and they're going to fix you up." A tear fell from my eyes and landed on her bloodied chest.

"I don't th-think I'm going to make it"—Amber wheezed—"our baby," she stuttered breathlessly. She closed her eyes, placing weak hands over her belly. I placed my hands over hers.

"Don't fucking close your eyes. Come on, baby, open those pretty hazels... please, Ambs, stay with me." My bloodied hand caressed her soft cheek, wiping the tears streaming down the side of her face. "You're gonna be fine." I cradled her in my arms. "You're going to be a mommy and our baby needs you... I need you. Baby, please open your eyes, goddammit. Open your eyes."

Tears spilling down my face, I called out to Nathan, "Where the fuck are the paramedics?"

Amber opened her eyes to slits and proffered a tender smile. Her hand struggled to reach up and touch my face, wiping at my fallen tears.

"I love you, Jules."

I kissed her forehead. "I love you, Ambrosia... please baby... stay with me."

Swallowing the lump in my throat, her lifeless hand fell to the floor.

My world spun out of control.

Pain stabbed my chest, a twisting knife to my heart, then she was yanked from my soul.

My breath, my life, my happiness.

Fuck!

I broke twice that day, both for Amber and my unborn child.

No, no, no... God, why? Amber, please come back... don't leave me.

Then suddenly, my world, gone.

And with them, my reason for living.

Now there was no need to exist.

CHAPTER

Eight

CHLOE

"THIS FEELS SO AMAZING." THE radiant sun warms my face. I grab the sunscreen from the small round table between the lounge chairs and squirt a dollop on my palm.

This is exactly what I need.

Sun, relaxation and no worries for the next three weeks. The humid air is typical but at least there isn't a cloud in the sky to alert us of a sudden tropical storm.

Flipping through the pages of the latest *Cosmo*, Phoebe giggles at an article that grabs her attention. She holds the magazine up, showing the title to me. "This article is perfect for you… 'Flirting Moves No Guy Can Resist'."

"I know how to flirt." I retort.

"Yeah, right." Phoebe's wide eyes dart back to the words in the article. "This one you should try with Julian. It says, 'Walk by him with a super-sized tampon in your back pocket and there's a bonus if it falls out. If he picks it up, tell him you need them huge'." Phoebe busts a laugh so hard a snort sneaks out.

"There's something seriously wrong with you." I shake my head. I'm so annoyed at my best friend's baiting.

Although we are polar opposites, we are each other's person. *Heartaches and hangovers.* That's the mantra we adopted after Phoebe was stood up at the altar by Bryan Sullivan, her college boyfriend and ex-fiancé.

The endless nights of crying and red-rimmed eyes broke my heart to see my friend that way. Since then Phoebe's heart closed up and she's party-on Phoebe, with me being dragged along for the ride. Phoebe forced me to go to the god-awful clubs where men thought their pick-up lines really worked. We would drink all night only to wake up with cotton mouth and pounding heads. I know my best friend wants to be loved again; Phoebe's tough façade doesn't fool me.

Phoebe started having meaningless, no-strings-attached sex with men. She was a complete and utter mess and swore off any kind of relationship. After Bryan, Phoebe's philosophy is not to waste her life with just one man. I don't understand nor approve of my friend's lifestyle, but as long as she's happy, it's all I care about.

Phoebe was the first person to show up at the hospital and took time off from work to be by my bedside after the attack. She was the one who nursed my wounds. The one who cradled me when I woke from my night terrors in a cold sweat. Four months of therapy, and Phoebe was there every step.

Phoebe knows everything about me. But one thing Phoebe doesn't know is I want to pick her skinny ass up and throw her in the pool to cool her jets from the antagonizing rants about Julian.

"How about this one… steal his shirt and wear it… or tell him about a night terror you had." Phoebe smirks at the latter one. "Hmmm—skip the last one."

I shake my head. "Yes, let's skip the last one, shall we?"

I spread the sunscreen on my legs and arms. My fingers skim over my stomach and the pink welts from my stab wounds. I'm wearing my royal blue bikini and I'm not the least bit embarrassed by having my scars exposed. It's only me and Phoebe sunbathing with no one else around.

My fingers linger over the tender scar. It doesn't hurt anymore but it reminds me every day that *he* was there.

"I bet… actually, I double bet you will be panties-down, riding Julian's dick before the end of our trip," Phoebe blurts.

"Shit, Feebs, you're so vulgar."

"Don't act all prim and proper, Princess Chloe. You may still be a virgin, but I know you. You're dying to have that connection. And I saw how you two were looking at each other last night."

"I can't believe… I wasn't… okay, fine. You want to bet? Then let's do it." I tap my chin with my finger. Phoebe cocks her head, surprised at my response. "What's the wager?" I dare ask.

As much as I want to admit I'm attracted to Julian, I can't have him. And making this bet will keep me in check.

"You want to bet against me? I don't lose, Chlo, and you know that." Phoebe raises her sunglasses over her head, with a mischievous smile. "A pair of Christian Louboutin heels."

"That's an eight-hundred-dollar-plus bet, you bitch," I shout, straightening my back.

"Well, sounds like I already won."

Phoebe's right about one thing. She's never lost a bet.

Take Phoebe to Las Vegas or play the Powerball lottery, she's sure to have some winnings. One time, Phoebe put her name in a raffle at the mall for the hell of it and a week later, the sixty-inch flat-screen television was hers to claim, which is mounted nicely on our living room wall. Another time, she won Bruno Mars tickets just calling the radio station.

I need to win this bet.

Not for the sake of the very expensive wager, but because I don't think it's smart to hook up with Julian, a summer fling, I don't want that.

Not only was I over Luke, but my walls were back up and my heart guarded. To start something with Julian and for it to go nowhere is not in my plan during this vacation.

I raise a brow. "And when I win, you will be the bachelorette at our fundraiser auctions… as long as you're still single."

"That's not a fair bet, Chlo. You know I'll be single for a long while."

"Tables have turned. You don't sound so sure, now do you?" I volley with a shit-eating grin. "Besides, it's for a good cause." I raise my pinky finger. "Place your bet right here."

"I'm going to win"—Phoebe hooks her pinky finger with mine—"and I know just the outfit I am going to wear with my sexy heels on my date with Thomas… or maybe just wear them solo with nothing else."

It's quite entertaining for me to watch Phoebe with the countless dates that swagger through our front door. And I live vicariously through my friend, watching different men wine, dine, and spoil her.

We have man-codes. Very few men fell into Phoebe's keep-dating-code-green category. Most of Phoebe's dates were Code Yellow, something to try one more time, but they all eventually became Code Red, cease and desist.

"Is Thomas a Code Yellow? Won't this be your third date with him?" I ask, remembering the night he kissed her goodnight at our front door.

"Don't get excited. I'm not settling. It's just that he's an amazing kisser, and the things he does with his tongue…"

"Unbelievable." I roll my eyes.

"Yes, he most definitely is."

I vowed not to give up my virginity to just any guy, even though I almost gave it up to Luke. I made him wait for months before I was ready, until I caught him screwing Nurse Reyna.

Would I ever find that man?

The one who could tear down my castle?

Chisel away one stone at a time?

Or will I grow old and single with a dozen cats?

Phoebe drops her sunglasses over her eyes and returns to her magazine. "Now that's settled, I have a surprise for you later."

"Surprise?" My head jerks up. "What is it?"

"If I told you, then it wouldn't be a surprise, would it?"

I twist my lips. "I hate surprises."

"I know. But this one, you will *love*."

Loving surprises is a thing of the past for me. So much has happened in a year. So much change. Before, my life was simple, quiet. Being surprised has a whole different meaning for me.

Although this trip is to celebrate my birthday, this is my first birthday since Mom's death. Every birthday, Mom surprised me with an extravagant dinner party or a short getaway trip. Now with Mom gone, so were her surprises.

Then I get another surprise, yet again, ripping my heart out with Luke and Reyna. Shortly after that, my assault in the park and the aftermath nightmares that went along with it.

And what's with the sudden flashes?

I want peace, my head to be clear, and surprises are not something I look forward to on this trip.

My mind wanders to the postcards I tossed in the junk-mail basket at home, among the coupons, flyers and random items Phoebe and I held onto, just in case. At the end of each month, we would sift through it and throw out what wasn't needed.

The day before we left for our trip, an envelope arrived for me. No return address and enclosed was a photo of me and Mom at our favorite restaurant. I remember that day because it was Mom's birthday, the week before she died.

A red marker circled my face. Nothing else, no note and no indication who it was from. I probed for the meaning behind the photo. Just thinking about it sends icy shivers of panic down my back.

Were the postcards related to this picture?

I wanted to tell Dad. I know I should've but didn't want to alarm him. I decided I would tell him the moment we got back from our trip. Having this bit of information would've definitely pushed Dad over the edge.

To make matters worse, he most likely would have twenty-four-hour protective service on my getaway trip. That was the last thing I wanted. A bodyguard, watching my every move. *Creepy.* I know it's careless of me to think this way. Dad only wants to protect me, his only child.

But sitting poolside gave me some comfort knowing whoever mailed the postcards and the photo is thousands of miles away.

I need to get a grip.

Phoebe went above and beyond to make this vacation memorable and I refuse to be a Debbie Downer. Phoebe set up our itinerary with ziplining, parasailing, sightseeing, rum-tastings and even a spa day, which I'm looking forward to.

My eyes wander to the dock leading out to the bluest ocean, where a speedboat, two jet skis, and my grandfather's luxury yacht, *Serenity*, floats on the calm waves. I remember the day Papa bought the vessel and told me the story of why he named her *Serenity*.

I have a lot of my Nana's characteristics, at least that's what Papa told me. Nana was larger than life, beautiful and always thought of others before herself. They were married for fifty-nine years until Nana passed away from a heart attack at eighty-one. Then a year later, Papa passed away to be with his angel in heaven. Their love was epic, a true love story, in life and in death. Just like Allie and Noah in *The Notebook*, loving each other till the end.

My thoughts of my grandparents and their love chases the niggling fear away. How I long for some of Nana's wisdom now, and my Papa's strength. How had they done it? How did they know they were meant for each other?

I hope for their kind of love someday. I long for it, someone to surrender myself completely to. I not only want a loyal man, as Papa was to Nana, but also the passion, the desire. Things I read in my books.

Would I ever find a love like theirs?

I shake my head.

Maybe Phoebe's right, the true-love façade, the knight in shining armor is long gone. One thing is for sure, I need to get my head out of the clouds and come back down to earth.

Just then, Julian's head appears from below deck of Serenity.

Oh. Holy. Hell!

My pulse quickens at the sight of his naked torso. He's irresistible. I take in his tempting and magnificent physique.

Butterflies swarm in my belly when my eyes roam from the ripples in his abs to the ever-so-sexy 'V' that disappears in his tan cargo shorts. His bronzed skin glistens. His broad shoulders and muscles bulge, tugging the ropes, wires and the mainsail. Wearing aviator glasses, dark hair and a shadow of his profound jaw sends an electric current of lust straight to my apex.

I lick my lips and bite my fingernail, imagining myself in Julian's arms.

The warmth of his skin against my back. His arm wrapped around my waist as his hand slowly moves downward, slipping beneath my bikini, his fingers making their way down to my folds. With his free hand, he unties the string around my neck, letting my bikini top fall free. Julian's hand cups my breast as his fingers pinch my nipple sending a jolt to my sex.

I'm a prisoner to him with no plan for a jailbreak. I tilt my head, giving Julian better access to the oh-so-sensitive spot just behind my ear. With my eyes closed, my breath hitches as the delicate touches of his tongue licks my naked body.

He whispers in my ear, "It's time for your surprise…"

I moan with anticipation of what's to come.

"Wake up, it's time for your surprise." My eyes slowly flutter open as Phoebe shakes me awake, from my erotic dream.

Coming back to reality, I'm tired, and moody. "How long have I been sleeping?"

"About an hour." Phoebe hovers over me, blocking the sun.

I squint my eyes toward the boat where I last saw Julian. "That was the best nap ever," I mumble to myself.

"If I were to guess, you were dreaming of that sexy Latin lollipop over there." Phoebe hikes her thumb over her shoulder towards Julian. "He's all kinds of yummy, flaunting his abs in front of us."

"I would love to wake up to that sight every morning." I slap my mouth with my hand. "Did I say that out loud?"

"Ha! I knew you would see it my way." Phoebe takes a sip from a water bottle, turning to gawk at the shirtless man along with me.

A high-pitched voice interrupts our gaze. "What's up, my ladies." Ryland rushes through the double doors from the kitchen. She always did showcase her entry.

"Aaahh! Ryland!" I scream in surprise and jump from my chair. I run to the stunning sandy-blonde haired woman wearing a purple sundress and oversized sunglasses covering half her face. We hug like our lives depend on it. I lean back and look at Ryland, not believing it's really her. "Holy shit! You're here! You're really here!"

"Surprise-surprise," Ryland sings. "I couldn't pass up celebrating my bestie's thirtieth birthday."

"You sneaky little bitch!" I nudge Phoebe's shoulder. "I love this surprise."

"I knew you would." Phoebe affectionately wraps her arm around Ryland's shoulders.

Ryland slides her sunglasses down her nose, eyes on the boat. "Who is the deliciousness over there?"

"Keep your thong on," Phoebe tells Ryland. "That hottie belongs to Chloe."

"Damn, you've only been here for a day and you've already called dibs?" Ryland places her hand on her hip. "No fair."

"I do not have dibs on him," I cut in. "Phoebe is trying to set us up."

"And? What's the problem?" Ryland rests her sunglasses on top of her head revealing her blue eyes.

"Ry, you're not supposed to take her side." My lips pucker with annoyance. "I told her last night, I don't want to start something that isn't going anywhere."

"If you hook up with that hottie, you will most definitely be going somewhere! Check out the torso and that 'V'. Holy shit!" Ryland bites in her bottom lip and raises a brow.

"For Christ's sake, not you too. Aren't you supposed to be neutral, like Switzerland? And speaking of, how's your Swiss hottie?"

Ryland lets out a deep breath. "We're done… Switzerland and I are history," Ryland brushes off. "I think it's time I come back home."

"Seriously?" Phoebe's eyes brighten, releasing Ryland's shoulders. "Back home?"

I angle my head. "I thought you loved it there."

"I did, I do… the director informed me of two offices opening in Rhode Island and Oakland. I asked for a transfer, but since I was up for a promotion, he made me an offer and I accepted."

"That's awesome!" Phoebe claps her hands in celebration. "So, when do you move back home?"

"Before the holidays."

I have a feeling Ryland's hiding something. I know she's been dating a guy and every time we talked, she wouldn't shut up about him. "Why the rush? Don't get me wrong, I'm happy you'll be coming back but last I heard, you were so in love with the country and with—"

"Eli," Ryland says with sadness in her voice.

"And now you're going to leave him? Just like that?" I ask.

"I broke Eli's heart. He deserves better than me. I royally screwed it up." Ryland takes in a deep breath. "I ran into an old friend who was in town on business. We had an innocent dinner to catch up. Dinner and wine didn't turn out so innocent by the end of the night. One thing led to another… Eli saw him leaving my apartment the next morning, confronted me about it."

I stare at Ryland with disbelief. Like me, Ryland's just as prim and proper. At least I thought so. Maybe being in another country changed Ryland, or maybe it's the *old friend*.

"Well, holy hell," Phoebe chimes. "Welcome to the dark side, my friend."

"Who is this *old friend*?" I ask.

"His name's Jacob."

"You never mentioned him before," I say.

"College. I had feelings for him, but never told him. I even denied it myself. He dropped out junior year. Left without a goodbye. A month later, I got a letter from him. He had inherited his dad's ranch in Montana and needed to help his mother. He wanted me to come and see him. But I didn't." Ryland takes a seat on the lounge chair.

"There I was, grabbing some produce at the supermarket, and we ran into each other, literally. He looked amazing." Ryland sighs. "I thought I was over him, but all the old feelings rushed back. At dinner, he asked me if I received his letter since I never replied. He said he had feelings for me, and he wanted to tell me in person. He'd waited for me to come out."

"So, what now?" Phoebe asks. "Is Jacob back in your life?"

"No. It was a one-night stand... an *unbelievable* one-night stand."

"At least you have that. I'm still waiting for my unbelievable *one* night," I say, my head falling to Ryland's shoulder.

"I see a man over there who looks like he can give you just that," Ryland says softly.

I turn to see Julian standing on the dock. He's on the phone, facing the ocean. His cargo shorts hung low on his hips, hugging his perfect ass, sending electric pleasure to every fiber in my body.

Damn, even his backside is to die for.

"Anyway, I don't want to move back in with my parents," Ryland says, tearing me from my Julian-trance. "Feel like scouring the area for me to find a place to live?"

"We have the third bedroom." I look to Phoebe for a confirmation I knew she'd understand.

"Abso-fuckin-lutely," Phoebe declares.

"Say no more." I grin. "It's yours."

CHAPTER

Nine

JULIAN

"WHO ARE THE SCREAMING HYENAS?" Rocky asks on the other end of the line. "Sounds like you're at a beach party instead of working."

"One of Chloe's friends just arrived. Blonde, about five-seven. I heard Chloe scream her name—Ryland." I glance at the women by the pool.

"Oh, yes… Ryland O'Hare. What's not to know? She's the daughter of Gregory O'Hare, founder of O'Hare Financial Enterprises. She didn't want to be part of the family business. Instead, got her Ph.D. in biochemistry and landed a job as an investigator in clinical trials. She's been living in Switzerland for the last two years. Her parents are still married, living in a massive home in Pacific Heights. Let's see… she's the youngest and has three brothers, Jax, Kason, and Telis, who by the way are all single and fine as hell. Should I go on?"

"No need." I stifle a laugh. "Can we get back to Chloe? What else did you find out?"

Rocky checked the women's apartment for anything that could possibly help with the case. Since nothing in the file revealed who and why this maniac is after Chloe, maybe something there would indicate a possible lead.

"Those women really need a better deadbolt. It took me all of five seconds to pick the lock and be in before anyone noticed." I picture Rocky with a proud grin plastered on her face. "I did find something. Sending you pictures now."

A ping sounds on my phone and I swipe right to open to the image.

What the hell…

My eyes narrow at each new photo that came through. "That idiot mailed those postcards and a picture? Do you think she knows who the assclown is?"

"Not sure. They were thrown in a basket full of junk mail. My guess? She doesn't have a clue or she's hiding something," Rocky answers with serious calmness. "I also found some documents in Chloe's room from the charity events. The figures are fuckin' nuts. Millions donated to the Concrete Angels Foundation. Their projects receive a ton of support from politicians and people in high places, an impressive list of names. I didn't realize the Channings were well connected—"

"The charity event a couple of years ago," I mutter.

"Huh?"

Fuck. I couldn't have kept that tidbit to myself?

"That's where I first met Chloe," I say, knowing Rocky would find out anyway.

"Is that why you wanted this case?" she asks.

"I didn't say—"

"Jesus, Booker. Did she remember you?"

"I don't think so. When I picked her up at the airport, she didn't give me any indication she did. I'm guessing amnesia knocked that memory from her. I don't expect her to remember me. Not like we had some mind-blowing conversation." *That's a lie.* I won't mention I still remember every fantastic detail. "And if she did, the backup plan was to tell her the charity event was a onetime gig for me."

"Sucks that some of her memory was wiped. You think she may get it back? Something tucked in that brain of hers could potentially break this case wide open."

"Not sure she'll get anything back."

My eyes peer toward Chloe, sitting on the lounge chair talking to her friends. Her hair flying from the gentle wind as she pushes a strand behind her ear. I want nothing more than to take away any fear she harbors.

My brows furrow, questioning Chloe as if she could answer.

Do you know you're in danger? If so, why haven't you said anything? Should I tell you who I am? I shake my head. *No, that's absurd. She'll freak, and I will for sure lose her. Stick. To. The. Plan.*

"Earth to Booker... are you still there?"

"Sorry, Roc, I'm here... what'd you say?"

"Since Sarah Channing is dead, Chloe is the sole executor of the funds to be distributed to the various projects across the nation."

"What does this have to do with the case?"

"It's a hunch, hear me out... what if the unsub is after the money? First Sarah was the executor and now Chloe... it's the common denominator."

"Since you found the financials, have Tyco start working on the guests, then their colleagues from the hospital, volunteers and paid staff on this project."

The fact that the unsub is still incognito, and we are still at square one troubles me. Rocky stumbling over the financial documents is a good lead, the best lead we've gotten.

My operative assignment was security detail at the benefit the night I met Chloe. Aside from our brief encounter, the evening was fuzzy. It was futile trying to recollect the people she came in contact with.

"One more thing, I also found a letter from most likely an ex-boyfriend... a Luke Jensen. Coincidently, the letter was dated two days before her attack. Sounded like a gnarly breakup."

"She had a boyfriend?" I rub my outgrowing scruff on my jaw. "I wasn't aware. There's nothing noted in her file. Why would Tyco leave that out?"

"The two dated for several months and broke up after the new year. Apparently, Chloe dumped him after she caught him screwing one of the nurses. I looked into his background and I don't think he's the unsub. But Tyco'll keep an eye on him regardless. My guess is, it's someone connected to the foundation. Who else could it be?"

"I think you're onto something," I comment as I watch a seagull fly over me.

"Hey, Book... I gotta ask. We're operatives, agents... since when did we become detectives? Our role is only to shadow her."

"We're still doing our job. But there's something about this case. If we figure out who the unsub is, I can protect her better." I set the toolbox on the dock then stare out to the ocean. "By the way, how'd your assignment go with Linc?"

"Mission successful. We recovered at least thirty women in a container at the Long Beach ports. The women were held captive for a good month. I have never been so pissed and sad at the same time. When we opened the metal box, it reeked of urine, shit and God knows what else."

"Bastards," I say through gritted teeth.

"To top it off, Knox is being questioned by Agent Maggio from the FBI, wondering how the leader and his two pansy-ass sidekicks got bullets lodged in their brains."

"Sounds like a clean shot from a damn good sniper."

"I don't mean to brag, but those dickwads deserved it. I wish they'd suffered a slow death rather than my one-and-done clean shot between their eyes. The poor bastards didn't know what hit 'em."

"How was working with Lincoln for the first time?" Rocky is a solo kind of girl. So I'm curious if Lincoln was on his best behavior or if Rocky kicked his ass.

"Arrogant, egotistical, and he really does thinks he's God's gift to women. He needs to eat some humble pie. But he's a good operative. I'll give him that."

I laugh. "He's been through some shit. I really don't see him settling down with a woman anytime soon. He loves variety, as sick as that sounds."

"He told me about his cheating ex-wife. Sucks. But I guess that kind of hurt can change a person."

"A person's past can define someone's future," I add.

"Yes, but my mother once told me that your future is what you make of it. There is destiny and then there is *your* destiny. A Japanese proverb, I assume."

"Sounds like a fortune cookie to me." I envision Rocky rolling her eyes. She and her parents never saw eye to eye, especially with her becoming a sniper for the Marines then working for the CIA as a handler.

"We have choices, Booker. I don't judge. Linc chose to be who he is. Just as I made my choices and the same goes for you."

"You don't judge me for taking this case?" I ask apologetically.

"No, I get it. You met her a couple of years ago and I assume you like her. I've gotten to know her on a personal level. She's an amazing woman. Sacrificing her time to work on this charity foundation. It's admirable. She's got a wonderful heart and I can see why you're attracted to her and want to protect her."

"That's funny you say that."

"Why is that?"

"When I met her, it was, well… I don't know. It's hard to explain. Ever felt an inexplicable pull to a person, and they don't even know it's happening?"

"I can say I have… it was a long time ago."

I thread my hair back with my hand, look over my shoulder for a quick glance at Chloe. "I just hope once this case is done, she'll give me a chance."

"You're a good guy. If you let her see who you *really* are, it'll be hook, line, and sinker. I really believe that."

I chuckle. "I hope you're right. It's just that I have rules. She's a client and I have my orders. I don't cross that line."

"There's nothing wrong with blurring the lines," Rocky affirms. "There's a loophole, you know?"

"Loophole?"

"Chloe doesn't know why you're really there. Be yourself for a change. Let her know the real you. Don't be *Booker the operative*. Be Julian the great guy I know you are."

"Be that as it may, I still have a job to do." I reiterate.

"You can do your job and still be you."

Maybe she's right. "Listen, I gotta go. Thanks for getting the intel, Rocky."

"You got it. I'll call you as soon as I get a hit."

We hang up.

I pocket my phone, stealing another glance in her direction. The three women are laughing like cackling schoolgirls. And it warms my heart seeing her laugh. But I need Chloe to tell me about the post-cards, the photo, and that prick Jensen, but how?

I have to be delicate in my approach or it will be a shitstorm mission I will lose along with Chloe.

I stare at the horizon where the ocean meets an endless sky. Birds fly in formation toward the settling sun.

I thought of nothing and everything.

Then Chloe.

My chest pulses with irritation when I think of that bastard, Luke Jensen. Is it jealousy? It's something alright, uncontrollable and annoying. This Luke Jensen had her.

Assclown fucked it up! His loss and hopefully my gain.

I grab the toolbox and leap off the boat onto the deck. Chloe is finally alone lying on the chaise reading a magazine.

"Hey," I call out to her as I get closer.

"Hey back." She shoves the magazine behind her back then grabs her cover-up and pulls it over her waist and legs.

"You got a sec?"

Chloe gestures warmly to the lounge beside her. "Have a seat," she says, straightening in her seat.

I set the toolbox down next to my feet and take the chair across from her. "First, I want to apologize."

"Apologize? For what?" Chloe's brows furrow.

"For being forward last night. I hope I didn't make you uncomfortable," I say, my forearms on my knees. "I'm normally not like that. I just don't want you to get the wrong idea about me."

I examine her sun-kissed expression. Wind gently breezes through her hair, carrying her scent of coconut and peach. Chloe's body is calling to me. The way the sun glistens on her oily skin accentuating her smoothness. Staring at her perfect golden-tanned skin is giving me that funny feeling below my belt again.

My eyes lock on Chloe's ever-changing blue-green ones. There's a softness in her gaze that calls to me, a silent cry for help. Am I reading it all wrong? It's possible since I know more about her than she knows herself.

"I'm fine. You didn't make me feel uncomfortable at all." She twirls the ends of her hair as her eyes look up at a bird flying overhead.

"Well, that's good," I tell her.

"So, anything else on your mind?" Her eyes gently look back to mine.

"I know you probably have plans with your girlfriends… but I wasn't kidding when I said I want to take you out to dinner."

"I'd love to have dinner with you, Julian." I'm in shock with her answer considering she brushed over my invitation last night. The corners of her mouth turn up into a smile and she's so fucking adorable. "It's just dinner, right?"

There's a bit of a sting to her casualness of dinner *just being dinner*. "Right… just dinner."

"I didn't mean it like that. I really am looking forward to having dinner with you," she says shyly. Her eyes dart to the ocean behind me then back to mine. "Listen, my friend Ryland just arrived, and we plan on going to the new club downtown. The Atlas? I'm not telling you this so you can drive us there… I want to know if you would like to join us… join me?" Chloe tucks a strand of hair behind her ears.

It takes all my willpower to hold myself together. She hypnotizes me with her smile and profound beauty, and she doesn't even know it. Self-control is what I need especially when my heart begins to race as I gaze at her face, feeling like a fourteen-year-old with a crush.

"I'm not a dancing kind of guy."

"Well, maybe tonight you'll find that beat in your step."

I shrug, relenting to her irresistibly cute-as-hell smile. "Maybe I will."

CHAPTER

Ten

CHLOE

C *LASSY, NOT TRASHY.* I BARELY recognize the woman in the mirror.

Ryland and Phoebe had a field day with my makeup. It's heavier than I normally wear it, but I love it all the same.

Smoky gray eyeshadow accentuates my blue-green eyes, the blush highlights my cheeks and taupe gloss shimmers on my lips. Gold hoop earrings, bracelets, and a necklace finish the ensemble.

My stubborn waves were straightened to fall like a thick silky curtain. I cringe as I slip into the strappy high heels I bought just for this occasion, forgot to break in and pray I don't end up with blisters at the end of the night.

Is this really me?

I smooth out the too-short, emerald-green dress. A low-scoop neckline barely held by spaghetti straps suggests ample cleavage and an even-lower scoop exposes my back. Phoebe insisted on this dress, saying it would grab Julian's attention.

"Oooo, girlfriend!" Ryland walks into my room wearing a very tight black strapless dress. "Now if that doesn't call to Julian, then I don't know what will."

"Hot damn, Chlo," Phoebe bellows behind Ryland as she saunters in, wearing a gold sequin dress showing off her legs. "There is no way he could resist you."

I laugh at their responses, my self-esteem boosts.

"Thanks. And you ladies look amazing." I do a once over on each of my friends. They are both absolutely stunning. "I can't believe I invited him to come with us."

"Well, if you didn't, I was going to." Phoebe gives me a cunning smile. "I'm winning this bet. And, hun... Julian is going to have you on your back sooner than later."

"We'll see about that," I retort and roll my eyes. As much as I would love to give in and possibly lose this bet, I'm not sure how to separate my emotions with the physicality of sex. I don't know how Phoebe does it.

"Wait, there's a bet?" Ryland asks, her hand on her hip.

"Julian is going to pick the lock on that chastity belt so Chloe can finally get laid."

Ryland's eyes grow wide. "I want in on this bet too!"

"Not a fat chance," I say. "Dealing with Feebs is enough. I can't have you in on this one too!"

"Not a fat chance you will be winning this bet anyway." Phoebe laughs as she looks in the mirror. "C'mon, I'm ready to get this show on the road and have me some C.P.R. time with my girls." Phoebe leaves us in the room. Her clacking heels can be heard on the wooden staircase as she descends.

"Ry? Remember that...C.P.R.?" I gaze at my friend's reflection through the mirror.

"How can I forget? Chloe-Phoebe-Ryland time!"

I wrap my arms around Ryland. "I'm so glad you're here," I whisper and choke back a tear.

"I've missed you, Chlo-bug."

"I've missed you too, Ry-Ry. And I'm glad you're coming back home." I pull back and meet Ryland's eyes.

"Me too." Ryland tucks a hair back behind my ear, softly smiling.

"It's been a freakin' whirlwind since I got here. I never really got to ask you…how are you?"

I angle my head, confused. "I'm fine. Why?"

"I mean, *how are you doing*? Your mom, your attack, the breakup with Luke?" Ryland's concerning voice almost sounds motherly. "I know we've talked, and Phoebe's filled me in…but Luke and then the nightmares? I just want to hear it from you."

I take in a deep breath and look into my friend's blue eyes. Ryland Marie O'Hare, my friend since birth. Ryland isn't as outspoken as Phoebe, but she knows how to get her point across. Ryland's the mother hen out of us. A patient listener, giving advice, and the buffer between Phoebe and I when we disagree, which is quite often.

A memory tickles my mind, when Phoebe and I got into a quarrel and didn't talk for a couple of days. Ryland tricked us into a sleepover, not knowing the other would be there. It's a good balance between the three of us and I wouldn't have it any other way.

"I'm fine… really," I tell her. "It was rough at first. Things are getting better. My kids at the hospital and the upcoming charity benefit have been keeping me busy." I don't want to rehash all the details of the past year. It's not that I don't want to divulge them to Ryland, it's just when I do talk about it, I feel like I'm resurrecting things I don't want to face. And there's that niggling fear that sprouts goosebumps I can't explain.

"Busy is good. I-I'm sorry I wasn't with you after your attack. I'm a horrible friend," she says apologetically.

"Oh my God, you're not horrible." I place my hands on Ryland's shoulders. "Remember that time when I had the chickenpox?"

Ryland nods. "Mmm-hmm."

"And you came over and brought chicken noodle soup, thinking it would be the cure for it?" We both laugh for a beat. "And you put Calamine lotion all over my body and taped mittens to my wrists?"

"Oh God! I never told Mom and Dad I took the bus to come and see you." Ryland's mouth curves up into a smile. "Instead of my parents punishing me for not letting them know, I got the freakin' pox."

We laugh again, harder this time. "Ry, that's one of many countless times you've been there for me."

"But your attack… I should've hopped on a plane and got my ass over to see you."

"Well, you're here now. Let's not rehash anything. Maybe another time." I take in a deep breath and give her one last hug. "I'm ready to go dancing. How about you?"

"With Julian?"

The sound of his name makes my heart thunder and the butterflies take flight in my stomach. I'm nervous to see him, even though I just saw him a few hours ago. I can't help the smile that's spread over my cheeks. "I hope he'll be there."

"He'll show. Can I offer you a piece of advice?" Ryland's voice is soft and enduring. "Phoebe's right, ya know. You need to let your hair down. I know you're saving yourself or making an excuse because we're only here for a few weeks. But sweetie, if it feels right…don't let him go. Trust me, I made a big mistake letting Jacob go and I regret it now."

"I don't know what it is about him. I do like him, though. I feel like I've met him before."

"Why's that?"

"He looks so familiar."

"Maybe he has one of those faces," Ryland suggests as she checks her makeup in the mirror one more time.

"Julian's face is not *one of those faces*." My world has tilted on its axis picturing his dark brown eyes, deep-set dimples, and amazing body. He's reduced me to a puddle of stirring emotions. "I hate that I've lost some of these bits and pieces of my memory."

"Did you ask him?" Ryland prompts, tilting her head.

"Sorta…well, not really." I half-shrug.

"Ask him. It's that simple." Ryland looks at her watch and grabs my hand. "Let's go. Sam and Sage are waiting and Feebs will tell him to leave our asses here if we don't get downstairs."

It was time to let loose. It was time to take charge of my life again and be the confident woman I once was.

THE LOW THUMPS POUR THROUGH the subwoofers and vibrate my body. Criss-crossing rays of light shine in the dark trendy club. The featuring DJ, Fantasia, stands center stage. She's wearing a thin strap of fluorescent green material covering her breasts and hips, her skin radiates as the lights flicker on her glittery body. Fantasia bops her head to the beats, bracing the headphone earpad between her head and shoulders as her fingers play with dials and knobs. Up above, dancers in floating cages take part in the beating symphony.

Dancing bodies overcrowd the floor to almost max capacity; couples gyrate and wave their hands in the air. Men on the sidelines, beers in hand, gawk at the women flaunting themselves in their tight dresses that are barely covering their assets.

I'm holding my friend's hands as Ryland and Phoebe weave between the crowd of people toward the bar. The bartenders are busily serving drinks from the endless glass shelves housing exotic bottles from all corners of the world.

The last time we three ladies were out on the town was Ryland's farewell party for her promotion in Switzerland. Drinks had poured until last call, and I have a feeling tonight's would too.

First order of business, to have our first toast before the night begins. We order two shots each, filled with Jack Daniels, Johnny Walker, and Jim Beam. Our ritual cheer to the *Three Wisemen.*

"Here's to Jimmy who loved us, Johnny who lost us and the lucky Jack who got to meet us!" we chant in unison, clinking our glasses. I wince after tossing the liquid back, feeling the burn as it numbs the back of my throat.

"One more shot, ladies," Ryland yells over the music, holding her second glass in the air. "I've really missed you guys."

"Don't get sappy on me," Phoebe chides. "This is supposed to be a fun night. To heartaches and hangovers."

"Awww. Ry loves us." I raise my second shot glass, my arms around Ryland. "To heartaches and hangovers."

"Cheers, my bitches!" Phoebe raises her glass, winks and tosses the liquid back.

"God, this is so disgusting," Ryland shouts. "Why'd we start drinking this shit?"

"It was the night we went on that ski trip to Utah with your family. After I sprained my ankle, Jax carried me to the bar. We were cold as hell and the bartender made this shot for us to warm us up and maybe to ease the pain in my ankle. I think we all got too warm having about a dozen of those because I don't remember the rest of the night."

It was our third year in college and a much-needed trip during winter break after finals. Phoebe and I had flown to Ryland's massive family home in Utah where we spent an entire week with Ryland, her parents, and three brothers. I learned to ski and sprained my ankle in the process. Even back then, Phoebe and Ryland schemed for me and Jax, Ryland's youngest brother, with their failed match-making skills.

Phoebe's mouth drops open, wide eyes looking at Ryland, then they both laugh. "Holy shit! I can't believe you remembered that, Chlo," Phoebe blurts.

"I guess I do." I shrug, flashing a smile. "It was one of the best trips we've taken."

"Well, we're going to make memories on this trip." Ryland grabs both our hands. "Come on, let's dance."

The crowd thickens on the dancefloor. Bodies pulsate when Fantasia plays a beat from Jay-Z. Holding Ryland's hand for support, I force a smile as I struggle in my four-inch heels.

I glance to my right, Phoebe's body in motion, hip to hip with a tall, dark and broad-shouldered man. Phoebe knew how to pick 'em, and chances are she's having a nightcap with her dance partner.

I look to my left, where Sam and Sage barely move, lips connected, their hands stroking each other's backs. I can see Sam really loves Sage and his happiness is all that matters to me.

A copper-haired man politely taps Ryland's shoulder and

speaks in her ear. Ryland nods with a beaming smile. She gestures to me that she will be dancing with her mystery man, leaving me solo.

Buzzed from four shots of the Three Wisemen and several Embassy Cocktails, I don't mind dancing alone.

I feel sexy, confident. I'm in my own world, owning it.

The next song from Bruno Mars floods the atmosphere with a collective roar. Liquid courage pulses through my veins, compelling me to twirl my hands in the air, feeling free, liberated. I close my eyes, feel the tempo, as I sway my head and hips.

I open my eyes and glance over at my two best friends. Their bodies flirtatiously move against their male companions, as they smile and laugh with them.

Those women never cease to amaze me. They are stunningly gorgeous, and it never fails that they would have at least a handful of phone numbers by the end of the night.

Just like old times.

A tingle jolts up my spine. I freeze when I catch Julian leaning against the edge of the bar. Our eyes meet and he flashes a smile. With his intense gaze, heat radiates down my spine as if he's undressing me. Desire electrifies my insides and my heart pounds in my ears, drowning out Fantasia's beats.

I suck in my bottom lip between my teeth, drinking in his six-foot-plus form. He's alluring, mysterious, exuding a confidence I find sexy as hell. His dark eyes never depart from mine, watching my every move. Sculpted cheekbones and that squared stubbled jawline leave me wondering what his mouth would taste like.

Unlike me, he'd kept his attire simple. Herculean shoulders and a hard chest fit nicely against his gray shirt, with sleeves rolled up to his elbows. He brings the amber liquid to his mouth. I enjoy the view, but my brain taunts my memories.

Where have I seen his gorgeous face?

Then my heart nearly stops, and insides churn when a voluptuous sultry blonde in a skintight red dress grabs Julian's attention, literally pulling him to her. Soon there's another. One of the blondes strokes his forearm as the other plays with the buttons of his shirt.

Her red lips lean close to his ear. Julian's mouth turns up in a cocky smile.

My mouth suddenly feels like I swallowed cotton balls. I pull my eyes away, but the trio remains in my periphery.

Why am I jealous?

Julian shakes his head and appears to stifle a laugh. My insides jump for joy, seeing the blondes walk away with a look of rejection written all over their faces. It's euphoric.

Then comes Julian's stare again, animalistic as it captures me like I'm his next meal.

Did he just turn down those women? Was it for me?

Julian's expression is unnerving. Once again, my brain probes as I try to recall the faceless man who'd asked, *do you need to be rescued?* It echoes over and over in my ears, despite the loud music filling the club. I'm obsessed with this vision. It gives me a sense of peace and I want to go back to that moment in time to whoever asked it.

Is this memory a dream or reality?

Is there a connection with Julian and the vision? It only occurs when he's near.

The alcohol jars my senses, embattling my heart and mind in a tug-of-war. Our eyes lock as if no one else is in the room.

I exaggerate my sway. The short hem of my dress only inches from my ass, accentuating my long legs, my best assets. I flip my chestnut brown hair over my bare back, shamelessly flirting in hopes Julian would give in to the temptation and come join me on the dancefloor.

I know at this point I'm losing the bet, but I wouldn't dare tell Phoebe.

Then a set of clammy hands trace my arms and circle me from behind. I shudder at the sudden tight grip at my waist as a man begins to gyrate against me, his groin forceful against my backside.

My face burns as I remember my attacker's hold. Murderous eyes assault my thoughts, haunting me from that fateful morning. I squeeze my eyes shut, my muscles tense. I want to vomit. I need to gain control, something I learned in my sessions with Doctor Zhang.

Feeling the suffocation, I shift, take in a deep breath and spin to face the uninvited man. I steady my pulse, shaken by his repulsive breath that smells of alcohol and musty cologne.

"C'mon, sweet cheeks," the man drunkenly slurs inches from my face.

"Get your hands off me." I push my hands to his scrawny chest, shoving him hard to separate myself from him. He tightens his grip, almost hurting me. But Mr. Scrawny wouldn't budge.

Looking over the man's shoulders, I no longer see my friends or Julian at the bar. I'm alone facing my attacker.

Then—slam—he appears beside me ready to pulverize Mr. Scrawny.

Julian's dark eyes narrow, burning with rage. His strong hands slam against the man's lean body, disconnecting his dick-dancing hold on me.

"What the fuck!" the man shrieks, faltering back.

"Get your fucking hands off her," Julian growls through gritted teeth. Although it's dark, I can see the pulse in his throat and the redness in his eyes. His voice is commanding. "She's with me, asshole."

"If she's with you, why is she dancing with *me*?"

"I suggest you walk away." Julian's jaw tightens, his hands in tight fists with a warning glare.

Hot panic surges in my chest. The last thing I want is a fight to break out in the middle of the club. Stepping back, Mr. Scrawny realizes he has no chance. Julian can clearly kick his ass from here to Timbuktu without breaking a sweat. Despite my feelings against violence, I'm relieved Julian showed up when he did.

"Julian, please"—I wrap both my hands around his bicep—"it was innocent. He's obviously drunk and just being a guy. I was handling it and you don't need to protect—"

"Chloe, his dick was up your ass...unless you like that sort of thing."

"And what if I did like it?" I yell over the loudness of the club, irritated by his sly suggestion.

"You can't be serious." Julian's hand threads through his dark hair.

"What if I am serious? And what's it to you? It's not like you're my boyfriend."

"One thing you were serious about was eye-fucking me all night. You moved your hot ass to get my attention…and sweetheart, it did, as well as every other horny bastard here. And every woman that approached me, you stopped and watched what I would do."

Is this guy serious? "Conceited much?" I argue. "And here I thought you were different."

He shot me a cocky smile. "So, you do think about me." He places a finger under my chin, tilting my face up so I have no other choice but to meet his eyes.

"What? Think of you, ha!" I am so irritated by his coolness and aloof manner. "And what about you? You're not so innocent. You were *eye-fucking* me, too!" I say returning his words back to him. "So, don't stand there and act all high and mighty."

One minute I'm dancing, my body absorbing the atmosphere. The next, I can't control my babbling mouth arguing with the sexy, dominating man in front of me. Julian is so intoxicating, and he clouds my senses when he's near me. I need to walk away, I need distance.

I yank my hand from his hold and turn toward the bar. Julian stalks a few steps behind me, as I slide him a hostile glare over my shoulder. Now the overcompensating gentleman is beginning to piss me off.

"Will you stop following me? You're not my bodyguard!" I don't know whether to knee him or grab his face and devour his lips.

Strong arms swoop around my waist, turning my body to meet his. My foot staggers and I fall into his arms. His left hand braces my lower back and the other holds the nape of my neck. His sweet warm breath of alcohol just inches from my mouth.

I'm frozen in utter shock as he presses his lips to mine. Kissing me, adoring me, claiming me.

Taking my breath away, a soft gasp escapes me at his commanding takeover as tingles of desire race through me. I want this, there's no denying him, giving myself freely to the passion of his lips.

My hands snake to the back of his neck. I open my mouth slightly, an invitation. I want more. His tongue dips between my lips. Julian tastes of sweet rum and Coke, more delicious than my fantasies.

The crowd muzzles as if we are the only ones in the room, nothings moving. Stillness all around. My heart slams against the inside of my chest. All the pent-up frustration dissipates, and my desire intensifies.

His kiss is strong, yet gentle, igniting every fiber of my being.

I press my hand to his muscular chest, feeling those hard pecs through his shirt. The glorious display of his naked torso on the boat earlier makes the apex of my thighs throb and moisten. As if I can't get any closer, his assault continues, embracing my body tighter to his. Feeling his impressive erection against my stomach.

Julian's hands move up the sides of my body, his fingers skim my arms, sprouting goosebumps. My muscles relax and my body goes boneless. How the hell am I still standing?

As much as I want to be reckless and wrap my legs around Julian's waist, it isn't smart. I can't get involved and then have my heart broken all over again. But I think it's a bit too late for that. My heart has taken the driver's seat of my emotions and I've lost control.

My common sense reigns, as I manage to push him away. Licking my bottom lip, savoring the last remnants of his mouth, I narrow my eyes.

The alcohol finally losing its grip. It gives me some semblance of self-control. Searching for a plausible explanation, I know I can't continue.

"Stop…wh-what are we doing?" My face clouds with unease. I'm so aroused by Julian's close proximity, hair mussed, his seducing eyes send a rippling desire straight to my sex.

"It's called kissing, sweetheart. Letting every dick-dancing asshole know you're *mine*."

"*Yours?* Are you trying to prove that to Mr. Scrawny?"

"You named that asshole?" His brow raises giving a look of disgust.

"I've got a name for you, too." I try to sound irritated but I'm anything but. And it's because I really like him, and he rescued me from a drunken asshole who wouldn't take no for an answer.

"Names like, devilishly handsome, sexy—" Humor coming from his husky voice.

"Arrogant, egotistical, big-headed—" I snap back.

"I'll show you big-headed." He chuckles as his knuckles skim the line of my jaw. "Come on, you walked into that one."

I roll my eyes, disguising my reaction to his charming humor. I enjoy the banter as much as he does. Seeing the amusement in his eyes, I can't help but laugh as I whirl to the bar and know he'll follow.

I hop on an empty barstool, relieved to give my aching feet a break. I wave my hand at the bartender to get his attention.

"What'll it be, miss?" the bartender asks, wiping the wooden counter with a damp cloth.

"Two shots of the Three Wisemen."

The bartender nods, turns and retrieves the three bottles from the back shelf. He pours an even mix in a short glass and places the rust-colored liquid in front of me.

"No shots for me," Julian says behind me, assuming the other glass was for him.

"They're for me." It's a bad idea, but I need the buzz back to calm my emotions running amuck.

Sliding himself beside me, Julian leans in. "Hey, talk to me." His fingers trace my arm.

I press my fingers to my temple and mentally count to ten. I need to reassemble my thoughts after feeling like putty in Julian's embrace only moments ago.

"Look, I can't go down this road with you."

"I'm not going to apologize for kissing you. It's very arousing to know how you respond to my touch. But I want to respect your wishes and, being the gentleman I am, I won't cross that line if you don't want me to."

It frustrates me how I'm vulnerable to him. I feel like a presumptuous teenager letting him get every angle on me.

"Julian, I can't."

"Just tell me one thing—did you feel something?"

"I did," I tell him without hesitation. "It's just that some jerk at home hurt me and I'm not about to get involved with a stranger I've known for a couple of days. It's not fair to you and especially to me." I grab the glass and tip my head back then place it upside down. *Gross!*

Before I grab the other glass, Julian snakes it and downs the liquid concoction.

"Hey, that was mine!"

"Holy fuck! You like that shit?" He wipes his mouth with his wrist, choking back the last drops.

"They make me feel good… Jack, Jimmy and Johnny are my heartaches and hangovers."

"I'll show you what *good* feels like." He places the empty glass on the counter.

"Do you always have a comeback?"

"You're cute as hell when you're angry," he cuts me off.

"I'm beyond angry." And I am. I'm mad at *myself* for letting my body surrender to his touch and losing the drink that's supposed to escalate my buzz.

"You're also breathtaking." Julian's fingers move to my chin, as the pad of his thumb grazes my heated cheeks. The trace of his finger renders me speechless.

My anger abates somewhat under the warm glow of his smile.

Pleasure, once again, spirals in my belly down to the depths of that G-spot longing to be touched.

Even in the dark club, pink and purple spotlights dancing around, I'm almost sure he could see my cheeks turn crimson.

My attempt in preventing a smile is a fail and the corners of my mouth perk up.

Oh. Holy. Hell. Am I falling for him?

CHAPTER

Eleven

JULIAN

"ANOTHER THREE WISEMEN FOR YOU, miss?"

"She will not be having another," I tell the bartender, my eyes lock on Chloe's blue-green ones. The bartender nods politely and walks away. "No more drinking for you. We have a date tomorrow at six a.m."

"Date? I never agreed to a date and especially not at the crack of dawn."

"You did. And if I remember correctly, you said, and I quote, *it's the best time to go running*." I tuck an errant strand of hair behind Chloe's ear. She swivels on the round leather barstool.

"Running at six a.m. is not a date!" Chloe squares her shoulders. "And I have plans."

"Plans? I hope you're not one of those Spartan athletes and gonna make me do those god-awful burpees?"

"You're cute as hell when you're nervous, you know that?"

A female bartender approaches us. Her low-cut tank-top,

revealing her engorged jiggling tits is unavoidable. "Another rum and Coke for you, sexy?"

"No, just two bottles of water for me and my girl."

The woman bends down, opens the small refrigerator below the counter and places the two bottles on top. I take out several bills from my back pocket and toss them on the counter.

"For the record, I'm not nervous. But I'd like to do a brisk walk instead. My feet are killing me right now and I predict they will be the same tomorrow."

"No deal, sweetheart. You're running tomorrow. I will pick you up at six a.m. sharp. So, dust off your princess running shoes because it's about to go down." I tap her nose with my finger, enjoying getting her all riled up.

Her smile, the looks she gives me, her beauty makes all the chaos disappear into a foggy haze.

Chloe pouts, slightly jutting out her lower lip. The sight of her delicious mouth I tasted moments before and the vision of my hand knotting in her hair, skin on skin, and having my way with her sends blood rushing back to my dick.

She's everything I want, but someone I shouldn't have. But I can't help myself and I'm falling under her spell. The kiss on the dancefloor was fueled by the adrenaline of anger and desire, along with this mission that's been fucking with my head.

Chloe bends down at the waist, slips off her one shoe and rubs her heel. "I hate these shoes. That's what I get for not breaking them in first."

Hmmm, sounds familiar.

I muse about how gorgeous she looked in the red gown, her hair pulled back and her cream-colored skin tugs at my memory. I laugh inside, remembering the conversation about her feet hurting and not breaking in her shoes.

"Looks like you need a massage." I quirk a brow, remembering what I told her that night.

Chloe's eyes close momentarily, causing her to almost fall from the stool.

I catch her and pull her up. "Hey, you okay?"

"I'm fine. I-uh…" She shakes her head. "Have you ever had a déjà vu?"

"Hmm. Maybe once or twice. Why?"

"I feel like I've had this conversation with you. But that would be stupid because this is the first time I've met you…right?" She angles her head expecting an answer I can't give her.

I twist off the cap from the water bottle. "Here, drink this."

"Thanks." Chloe takes a sip. "It's probably the alcohol."

The night at the gala is crystal clear for me. I have a feeling I may have triggered yet another forgotten memory. My mouth curves into an unconscious smile.

How much does she remember?

She hasn't changed at all, she's still beautiful. Chloe is like a change in the weather. Even back then, she cleared the clouds that hovered over me.

This is the reason I need to be here, to protect her. Keeping her at a distance in order to do my job is damn near impossible. I can't remember a time I ever lost control. Whatever Chloe is doing to me is becoming undeniable.

I swore I would never go down this route again, having feelings for someone else. Even though the guilt and uncertainties are inevitable, they are slowly disappearing into a haze.

My heart has a gaping hole and somehow, being in proximity to Chloe, she's its healer, the cure for my dark soul, making me whole again.

Needing to touch her, I lean closer, to test her response. I told her I wouldn't cross that line, but her pull is magnetic. I tuck another strand of hair behind her ear, then my fingers graze her temple and down the delicate lines of her face.

Chloe's breath hitches and she grips my wrist as I palm her face. She rests her soft cheek in my hand. Chloe inclines her head and there's a gentleness in her voice. "What are you doing, Julian?"

My forehead touched hers, breathing her in. Peach scents from Chloe's hair fill my nose. "Just tell me to back off, Chloe."

She's still for a moment. And I'm afraid of what she'll say next. I want her and I know she wants me too.

"I don't want you to back off, Julian." I hear her murmur, even with the bass of the music echoing throughout the club.

Sexual tension and desire electrify between us. The pad of my thumb caresses her cheekbone. Chloe wraps her hands around my neck and pulls me closer. She presses her lips to mine.

I cup her face with my hands and gently graze her soft lips with my eager mouth. This time, the kiss is slow and sensual. Chloe's mouth opens slightly, giving me freedom to make my entry. Our breaths increase as our tongues tangle with one another.

I stroke, lick and taste Chloe.

My fingers itch with impatience, with the need to roam her body and explore every inch of her.

She pulls away, her blue-green eyes hypnotizing me, paralyzing me.

"Don't hurt me," she tells me, as if there's fear in her eyes.

The world around me stops with those three words.

Does she have any idea how sensuous her voice sounds? Does she have any idea that I'm falling for her?

I tune out the thunderous bass, the clatter behind the bar, the laughing women passing by and the bellowing dancers on the floor.

I'm fucking losing control.

Rocky's words ring in my head: *Don't be Booker the Operative, be Julian the great guy I know you are.*

"I would never hurt you, Chloe."

She's sexy, gorgeous, and I want to feel the naked curves of her body against mine. I crash my lips to hers, reclaiming her mouth once again.

Her perfect lips mold onto mine.

My kiss is urgent and exploratory.

Our tongues entwine in a frenzy.

A low moan vibrates in the back of my throat. I kiss her as if she is my last breath and I need her to survive.

I want her more than anything I've ever wanted. I want to hide her away from the rest of the world. From this moment, I'm no longer doing my job. I'm going to protect her because I know what it would cost me if I lost her.

It's all too perfect. She's perfect.

Chloe's warm hands move slowly to my waist. My dick pulses, enough to render me weak.

We need to stop. Need to get a grip, we're in a public place, for crying out loud. And she's been drinking.

Might she regret this tomorrow? I can't do this to Chloe, as if she hadn't been through enough already.

I slowly pull away, immediately missing her lips.

"What the hell are you doing to me?" I muster.

"What are you doing to *me*?" Chloe echoes, as she eyes me through her thick lashes.

"I want you… God knows I want you, Chloe Channing." Her name easily slips from my mouth.

Suddenly, there's an uneasy feeling, a cold shiver creeps up my spine. I scan the crowded club.

Was it Amber's presence or something else?

Memories of my wife fill my mind, that dark place Chloe's saving me from. Losing Amber was devasting and I wouldn't wish it even on my worst enemy. I lost Amber for not following my instincts and I am not about to fail again.

But I suddenly feel off. My mind and body are on high alert. A cold knot forms in my stomach. I can't shake the feeling of being watched. My skin prickles, the muscles of my forearms harden, my jaw tightens. These emotions are clouding my judgment and they need to dissipate. I need to lock that shit down. *Goddammit, Chloe's life is at stake. What the fuck am I thinking?*

Someone or something ignites these familiar instincts. I straighten, eyes roaming the dark room, ready to take Chloe out of here and back to the house. Nothing blares sirens or sets off alarms. So, why am I feeling on edge all of a sudden?

"I-I can't do this…to you. We can't." I shake my head slightly and the look on her face tells me I've upset her.

"God, Julian…you can't do this to me. Play with my feelings. You said you weren't going to hurt me," Chloe snaps.

I release a deep breath. "Chloe, you deserve better. But—"

"But what? You're so damn confusing. And I thought the female species was a mystery."

"I like you, a lot, and from the moment I picked you up at the airport, you're all I think about."

Chloe lifts her hands and cups my jaw. "I like you, Julian, and I'm not afraid to try."

I smile, easing the tension. "Not afraid to run with me tomorrow?"

"Oh, jeez! You're insufferable. I'll do the damn run tomorrow… on one condition."

"Yeah?"

"I get a foot massage."

I cock my head back. "Deal."

CHAPTER

Twelve

CHLOE

THE ALARM BUZZES, STARTLING ME from my sleep, annoyed by the ringtone set for the god-awful hour. *Party in the USA by Miley Cyrus.* I grab the cell from the nightstand. *Five-fifteen.* I tap the screen to silence it. I pull the quilt over my head, lying in the drowsy warmth of my own bed.

Why the hell did I agree to this?

I grunt at the slight throbbing in my head and curse the alcohol I drank last night. The Three Wisemen may have made me feel good, but the aftermath never did.

Heartaches and hangovers.

I reach for the water bottle and aspirin on the nightstand I forgot to take last night then lean back on the propped-up pillow against the headboard to down the two pills with the much-needed water.

The night before scrapes through my mind. I shudder at the thought of Mr. Scrawny's creepy hands and disgusting dick-dancing thrusts. When I told Julian I had it under control, it was a lie. Underneath all my bravado, I was scared.

Shrapnel images tear at my thoughts from the morning I was assaulted. Although the visions are foggy, I'm well aware they happened, and it knots my stomach just thinking about it. Not only did Julian seize the apparitions dancing in my mind and chase my fears away for the moment, but he also protected me from the unwanted hands of the drunken man.

Then that mind-blowing kiss and the emotional rollercoaster. I touch my mouth, remembering his lips on mine.

I'm completely and utterly lost in him.

The huskiness of his voice.

The gentleness of his fingers when he traced my curves.

I am putty in his hands and can't comprehend why I'm falling for Julian in such a short amount of time. I swore I wouldn't.

I reprimand myself, whether or not last night's alcohol consumption played on the ups and downs. The echo of Julian's voice has me questioning this new whirlwind of emotions. It's like the world has tilted on its axis.

How is it possible I have strong feelings for him so soon?

Was it the passionate kiss we shared? The flirtatious bantering?

Or is it the way he looks at me with those dark, possessing eyes?

Or could it be, deep down, it's something else, a familiarity?

Why can't I place him?

My brain is on overdrive, hurtling down memory lane. I'm determined to know where I've seen him before.

Déjà vu or not, I have to figure this out.

I need to fill the void that clouds my lost memory and tortures my thoughts, playing the game of hide-and-go-seek. The only way to figure it out is to ask him, as Ry suggested. Would it be that easy? I need to be strategic in my questioning without letting him know I'm some crazy person who suffered amnesia.

It's too early to think about it. I shake the thoughts out of my mind and manage to roll out of my comfortable bed. After I twist and stretch my tense back, I throw on my old UC Berkeley t-shirt, put on my shorts and slip on my running shoes. I trudge down the stairs dreading the chore of what's to come.

I smile when I spot Julian waiting for me in the foyer. My breath hitches at the sight of his magnificent form. The rich outlines of his broad shoulders strain against his sleeveless blue t-shirt revealing the muscular lines of his tanned arms. A simple pair of black running shorts sit low on his hips and weakens my knees.

He's leaning against the wall, legs and arms crossed, a half-cocked grin. I bite my bottom lip. *Holy shit. I'm in trouble.*

Julian pushes off the wall and steps closer. "Good morning, sweetheart. You ready?"

"Not really," I say as I pull my hair up in a ponytail, trying to hide the blush that warms my cheeks. "I hope your plans have to do with a brisk walk."

"Nice try." Julian raises a brow. His thumb and forefinger pull at my chin, forcing me to look up at him. Inches from my lips, the warmth of his minty breath tingles my mouth.

I wet my lips in anticipation.

Kiss me again. Please.

For a moment we stare into each other's eyes, his fingers chase the goosebumps over my bare arm, sparking desire deep within my belly. "I promise, I will go at *your* pace." His low raspy voice shocks my body awake.

What did he mean? *Go at my pace?*

I lean in, inviting him to kiss me, wanting to feel his lips on mine.

Julian shifts, and within seconds, he consumes me with his mouth as he takes possession of my tongue. His thumb circles at the nape of my neck igniting the bliss as he deepens the kiss. My fingers press into his biceps. I can never get enough of him and the hard press of his body against mine. I lightly moan, breaking the silence in the foyer.

The kiss ends and Julian lets out a slight cough, then chuckles as he hands me a water bottle and small towel. He takes a step back. "If we don't get going, I may have to change my plans and take you somewhere private."

"Yeah, yeah. Promises, promises." I tease playfully rolling my eyes as I hop off the bottom step. Maybe a morning jog is a good thing, to wear off the salacious tingles that prowl between my legs.

Every step, one in front of the other, I study Julian's every move.

I'm trying to figure out why he feels the need to shield me as if I'm made of glass. The way he's closest to the road, guarding me from oncoming traffic. Is he being a gentleman, showing some chivalry?

He scrutinizes every car and glares at every person we pass as if he's ready to pounce on them. Although his actions are a bit over the top, it also increases my attraction toward him. It's actually a turn-on to be so protected.

I survive the five-mile run. Although my legs throb, Julian and I agree to jog every morning to build up my stamina once again...and to overcome my fear, but he doesn't need to know that. I need this, to shake the anxiety and the poisonous images that claw at the walls of my mind.

We end our run on a secluded hillside where Julian's white Jeep is already parked. He takes out a picnic tote from the back seat and pulls out a blanket to spread it on the grass. One by one, he takes out plastic tubs from the basket. There's fresh fruit, yogurt, granola, water bottles and chocolate-chip cookies for dessert.

"Breakfast is served." Julian extends his arm, gesturing for me to have a seat on the blanket.

This man. Would he ever stop surprising me?

"When did you get all this food?"

"Got all this at the market yesterday." Julian brushes his hair back with his fingers. "I've been looking forward to this morning. I hope you like it."

"This is great. Thank you." I sit on the blanket, crossing my legs. My eyes focus on the ocean where the ships and sailboats look like toys in a tub. "This view is amazing."

"I found this spot last week after hiking up here." Julian points out over the hill. "Look...over there. Your beach house."

I squint. "Oh yeah, I see it." The distinctive dark blue rooftop isn't hard to spot even against the ocean's color. I take in a deep breath of the sea breeze. "It's peaceful up here."

"It's one of the reasons I brought you here." Julian peels off the tops of the plastic bins and hands me a plastic fork and spoon. "Figured we could get to know each other better."

"Putting your wooing skills to work, I see." I peel the aluminum cover off the yogurt cup and scoop a spoonful in my mouth.

"You haven't seen anything yet." Julian flashes his dimples with his megawatt smile. "I've got a few plans up my sleeve for you."

As we dig into the healthy breakfast, there's small talk about the run and other routes to take for the coming days. The more we talk, the more my curiosity awakens. Questions flutter through my mind. I ponder what he'd said earlier. Plans? As in a future? I don't want to think too much of it. But what if...did he mean plans beyond the next three weeks?

Every time I look into Julian's eyes, there's a tenderness in them. My mind reverts back to Luke who never did anything as simple and romantic as this hillside breakfast, let alone talk about a future with me. Luke's future was getting Chief of Staff and putting a notch on his bedpost with every nurse he slept with.

I don't want to jump ahead of myself being that we've only known each other for such a short time. But with Julian, I can see a future with him. Is it possible?

The sun above warms my cheeks as a soft breeze blows my hair across my face. I finger a loose strand behind my ear. My heart pounds when I turn to see Julian looking at me rather than the view. Slowly and seductively, his eyes sweep over my face, down my shoulders and stops at my breasts.

Julian coughs nervously. "You did good today. Not bad for a *bear*."

"A bear?" I ask with confusion.

"Yeah, Oski the Bear? UC Berkeley?" Julian eyes my shirt.

I look down at the mascot cartoon printed on my shirt. "Oh, yeah...right." A grin tugs at my lips. "Feels like ages ago."

"Tell me about college." He leans back on his bent elbows and his muscular legs straighten.

"Not much to tell. Phoebe and I were stuck at the hip, being roommates the entire time. The only thing that differed was our major. She studied communications. I studied biology and child development, which landed me in the medical field working as a pediatrician at San Francisco General. I love being a doctor, taking care of kids. Then there's Ry, she went to UCLA and got a job in Switzerland."

Julian forks watermelon from the plastic bowl and pops it in his mouth. I want his bruise-biting mouth on me again, to possess and consume me. To have his hands all over me, his hardness pressing on my softness.

"Hellooo. Earth to Chloe." Julian waves his hand over my face. "Where'd you go?"

"Huh? Oh. I'm sorry. What did you ask me?" I shake my head, coming out of my fantasy.

"Why'd you want to be a pediatrician?"

"My mom. She was a doctor and I love children."

"Tell me about her."

I hesitate. My heart crushes just thinking of Mom, remembering the day Dad called with the horrific news. It was the worst day of my life.

Then Dad had told me again, reliving it a second time after I had awakened from my attack and asked where Mom was. The painful images burn in my mind. The flowers on Mom's casket, the sun beating down through my dark dress as I squeezed Dad's hand watching it descend in the ground.

I look out to the ocean, concentrating on a sailboat dancing on the waves. I swallow the sting in my throat, before I continue. "She, um, died in a car accident last year."

"I'm sorry. I didn't mean to bring up bad memories."

"It's okay. I've learned talking about it can be healing," I reply. "She loved being Doctor Sarah Channing. It wasn't just a career. It was her life. It's who she was. And I wanted to be like her." I pull at the blades of grass on the side of the blanket. "She was amazing."

"I think you're amazing...dealing with kids." Julian slightly shakes his head. "I couldn't do it."

"You don't like kids?"

"I love kids. I look forward to being a dad someday. Having a mini-me being stupid, chasing girls. And if I had a little girl, a princess, she would have me wrapped around her little finger, protecting her from all the stupid boys." Julian stifles a smirk, unsuccessfully. He takes a deep breath before he continues. "What you do…day in and day out, children hurt. It would break me."

My breath catches and I just about melt at what he just told me. Julian tugs at my heartstrings. My attraction toward Julian grows knowing that children can render him helpless.

Alpha yet gentle. Could he be more perfect?

Where has this man been all my life?

"Yes, children do have their ways of consuming your heart. They pretty much yanked on my mom's heartstrings, so much she started a foundation."

"A foundation?" Julian straightens, showing interest.

"Yes. The Concrete Angels Foundation. My mom set it up to get women back on their feet, help them with job placements, get their kids back to school." I look up to the cloudless sky, thinking of how it all began.

"My mom started this campaign because of a mother and daughter—Stacey and Lily. She found the two sitting on a bench, just outside the trauma unit. It tore her heart in two seeing them there. They were dirty and the bruises were something my mom couldn't ignore. Lily was ten and she was holding her arm, crying." I sigh and shake my head, remembering how Mom came home devastated about the little girl's arm, wondering how anyone could be so cruel to hurt such an angel.

"While Stacey was getting treated for her broken ribs, my mom sat with Lily while she got her cast put on. To comfort the little girl, my mom told Lily she was an angel with a broken wing. That's kinda how the foundation got its name." I sip my water, meet Julian's eyes still on me. "I hope I'm not boring you."

"No, not at all. Please go on." He pops a bite of granola in his mouth.

"Very well. My mom tried to get Lily to tell her about the abuser. But it was no use. Lily said she broke her arm when she fell from the kitchen counter trying to get cereal from the cupboard. When my mom asked about the bruises, she said it was from play-ing. The only thing Lily slipped about was saying she and her mom were kicked out of their own home by Lily's asshole dad." Rage boils in the pit of my stomach, even all these years later. "Men like him are pond scum, cowards. But my mom couldn't get her to talk more about it."

"Did Stacey press charges?"

"No, she was also afraid. And because of it, the police couldn't do anything."

"Without their statement, the police's hands are tied," Julian confirms, his attentive eyes hold mine. "What happened to them?"

"Since they had no money, and nowhere to go, my mom placed them in a Holiday Inn, paid the entire month."

"Do you keep in touch?"

"Yes. They're doing great." My eyes widen, joy bubbling up. "Stacey now runs the foundation and as for Lily, straight As, in a few clubs at school and lots of friends. She's an awesome kid."

I open a bag of cookies, break off a small piece and pop it in my mouth. "I wish Mom were here to see how much the foundation flourished all because of her, Lily and Stacey."

"And what about you? Are you involved with this foundation?"

"I am. But I have no idea what I'm doing. With the help of Stacey, a few staff members and volunteer counselors that have been there since day one, it practically runs itself. That's the beauty of it. I just want to make my mom proud and don't want to let any of these women and children down."

"I'm sure you're doing a great job."

"Thank you." I shrug. "It's a lot of work. And I love all the women and children we help. In the end, that's all that matters."

"That's admirable...what you're doing." Julian places his hand on mine, grazing his thumb over my knuckles. I bask in this moment, unspoken emotions swelling my heart. Other than a few people, I haven't talked about Mom and the foundation to anyone. I feel comfortable enough to talk about it with Julian and somehow, he makes me forget the pain.

"I don't do it for merits, but to give these women and children a place to go. To get better, be better, away from those assholes. We give them some kind of hope and dignity. That's why I do it."

"You're amazing, you know that?" His voice is compassionate.

I half-shrug, softly smiling. "Enough about me. What about you? Dad, mom, siblings?"

"My turn, huh?" Julian laughs.

"Yup. You said you brought me up here to get to know each other better. So, fess up, Julian."

His hands raise in surrender, then he leans back on his arms. "Well, my father passed away when I was only five."

"Oh, Julian. I'm so sorry." I press my hand to my chest. What is it with people saying 'I'm sorry' when someone dies? I shake my head realizing I'm one of those people. Julian and I have this in common, a parent who died too soon.

"The memories of him I still can remember, I will always cherish. Little league games. Sunday dinners." Julian's chuckle fades. "My dad had this contagious laugh, you just had to laugh with him even if you didn't get the cheesy joke. He would tell me and my mom about his day, how he saved people and put the bad guys in jail. But the one memory that holds strongest is when he would leave for his shift, wearing his police uniform. For a kid like me, he was a giant. Invincible, like Superman. Until the night my mom got the news and our world crumbled. A kryptonite bullet killed my dad. From what we knew, it was after his shift, my dad saw a woman being harassed in an alley. He parked his car to help her and those punks shot him during their scuffle."

Pain squeezes my heart hearing the despair in his voice. "He was a hero."

"He was to me and so many others. I wanted to be like him."

"And did you? Follow in his footsteps?"

"I ended up in the Navy. A SEAL."

"You're still a hero." I give him a gentle smile to lighten the conversation. "Are you still in the Navy?"

"No. My contract was up. I didn't reenlist and decided to pursue other things."

"Like?" My interest and curiosity grow at the man before me.

"Being a handyman for the Channings." The corners of his mouth quirks.

"A cute handyman."

"Cute? Sweetheart, cute is for puppies in the pet store. I think hot, sexy or strong is better suited for me." Julian puffs out his chest and holds his head high.

"Unbelievable." I roll my eyes.

"That'll work too."

"Oh jeez! And how about your mom?"

"She's an interior designer and mostly works on celebrity homes or international accounts. It was she and I until she remarried three years later. Then came my kid sister Fabi. She lives in Paris. Landed some killer job with Louis Vuitton. She travels the world, has this whole lavish lifestyle."

"Wow, how exciting."

"Her name fits her—Fabiola-the-fabulous and full of life. You two would definitely hit it off. I would love for you to meet her someday, if she could pry herself from her work."

My hopes rise. Meet his sister? More plans for the future?

"Aside from Fabi being a pain in my ass when we were kids, she's much like you, positive outlook on life, strong-willed and focused." Julian unscrews the cap from his water bottle and tilts it back.

"And your stepdad? What's he like?" I take the last bite of my cookie, brushing crumbs from my hands.

"He's a good man. Took me in as his own and taught me how to be a man. He filled the gaps as my dad and made my mom smile again."

"Stories like that make me sappy." I give him a soft smile.

"Yeah? Why?"

"I'm a sucker for true love. Second chances. It's funny… I read a lot of romance books." I shrug. "Feebs gives me shit about it all the time."

"Nothing wrong with believing in true love," Julian counters, his eyes meeting mine.

"It can be when you're let down." I look away and pick at an imaginary lint on my shirt.

"Tell me about the jerk who broke your heart."

"Who? Luke?" I stall to answer his question. I shift, bending my knees so my feet are under my bottom.

"If he's the one who broke your heart."

"Why?" I twirl the ends of my hair. I don't want to talk about my ex to a guy I am very attracted to. And every time I think about Luke, I feel so stupid that I was played. "Why do you want to know?"

"I just want to know what I'm up against."

My breath hitches. The fortress I built around my heart after my heartbreak, Julian's slowly tearing it down with his proverbial sledge-hammer. The things he says to me, the way he looks in my eyes, into my soul… *Why do I feel like this? Is it too soon?*

I need to calm my racing heart. "Up against?" I whisper.

"I know it sounds crazy, but I enjoy being around you and I like you a lot. Like I said, I am going at your pace. Run, jog, a brisk walk…whatever it is…*your pace.*" Julian tucks a lock of my hair behind my ear. "I know you may have this perception about me that I'm some kind of player. My mom raised a gentleman and she would kick my ass, then kill me, if I ever treated a woman like she was unworthy. So, please tell me about him."

I can't believe my ears. Was Julian serious? It's unreal. I hate to compare the two men, since Luke doesn't hold a candle to Julian. Luke never said things like that to me. Sure, Luke wined and dined me at expensive restaurants, but it was to impress me with his wallet —and to impress Dad.

"Well, there's nothing to compete against." I turn my head and stare out to the ocean. Of all the memories I lost, the image of Luke and Reyna is crystal clear, an image I so wish I could erase. "I wanted the brisk walk, but I guess Luke wanted to run." I give a pathetic laugh. "I caught him screwing someone else."

"Ass-clown."

"Yeah, he definitely was. I thought he was the one that…" I taper my voice, not wanting Julian to know I haven't given myself completely to any man. "Let's not linger on the past. Change the subject?" I plead.

"I would never do that to you." His voice is sincere. His hand frames my face and I almost forget what we were talking about.

Julian leans in closer. I can see the gold flecks mixing with his dark brown eyes. His hand wraps around my neck. I can sense Julian being cautious as he pulls me nearer. I surrender to his tender touch. He gently brushes his lips over mine. My belly somersaults as I sink into the kiss.

"Mmm. Sweet, chocolate-chip Chloe kisses," he murmurs under his breath. His lips delicately press to mine once again.

My hands grip his broad shoulders as he gently lowers my back onto the blanket. He cups my face. His tongue continues to explore my mouth, teasing and tangling with mine. A groan sounds from the back of his throat. His fingers sensuously trace down my arm, leaving a trail of electric sparks.

"Fuck, Doc…what are you doing to me?" Julian says in one breath.

This man has taken my breath away as I melt into him. I want to fight the overwhelming need to be with him, but his gravitational pull is too hard to resist.

What's happening between us? Emotions swim in my mind.

Is it merely the ambiance of the tropical island?

Are Julian's charming words convincing me I'm falling under his spell?

Am I just a sucker for the romance?

There's a strange comfort being with Julian. Images come back, eating at the corners of my mind, once again. Blurry and yet vivid scenes of a handsome stranger in a tuxedo. The sound of his voice and the distant words echo.

I struggle to remember, feeling paralyzed. Then something clicks in my brain. Julian's voice, his eyes, his hands, his touch. Is *Julian* the man in the image? It can't be. Impossible.

Do you need to be rescued?

Sounds like you may need someone to give you a foot massage.

My mind spirals back to earth. I slow the kiss, gently pushing him away, and study his familiar face. I want to ask if we've met before, but the words are stuck in my throat. Our time is limited, and I don't want to ruin this perfect moment.

"What's happening between us, Julian? I need to know." My breath tethers between us.

"I adore you, Chloe." Julian's voice is calm and seductive. "All I know is this feels right." He presses a chaste kiss on my lips.

A certain sadness stings my heart, knowing our fling would end in a few weeks. My vow to not become involved is shot to hell.

There is no denying it, I'm falling for this man.

CHAPTER

Thirteen

JULIAN

S*HE'S SO FUCKING PERFECT.*
  I moan as our tongues intertwine, tasting and drinking her in. I'm addicted to her slow, quenching kisses. I can't get enough of her.

Sexy, beautiful and still a mystery. Chloe consumes me. It wasn't about the mission anymore. It was about a woman I deeply care about. How was it even possible for me to be falling hard and fast?

It seems Chloe has no idea the powerful, inescapable pull she has over me that renders me to lose all control. I tighten my embrace, the contours of her body molds perfectly against mine. Her nails trace my back, sending chills through the material of my shirt. There's no denying it. Chemistry sparks between us, and I can't help but act on my desires.

Emotions play in my head like a hockey game, fast-paced and everchanging. My heart and mind violently pass like a puck from one opponent to another. The mission, my past, my rule I resolve to follow—all become compromised when I am this close to her. Chloe annihilates my control and I need to distance myself.

I need to stop and take back control.

I gently pull away. "Fuck, I'm sorry, Chloe." My forehead rests on hers.

"What is it? Did I do something wrong?" Her voice becomes nervously unsteady. She looks up to meet my eyes.

I push myself off the blanket. I wipe my face with my hand, hoping to clear the frustration riddling my mind. This woman is driving me crazy and I can't see straight. Sometimes I wish Chloe would just deny me. It would have been a hell of a lot easier to be her bodyguard. But she's doing nothing of the sort. She's being herself and that's my weakness.

"No. You did nothing wrong. Actually, you're perfect. I shouldn't have—"

Chloe pushes back her hair that the wind blew in her face. "So, what is it?" She watches me pace, making tracks in the grass. "I'm trying to figure you out, Julian."

"I'm trying to figure me out, too. Hurting you is the last thing I want to do, Chloe. But I'm afraid that is exactly what will happen." I pinch the bridge of my nose. "Doc, there are things about me…"

That's all I could get out without blowing my cover. Not to mention the deep scars, a tortured past I have been trying like hell to keep buried.

If she found out I've been lying to her, I will hurt her and lose her.

Chloe's scaring the shit out of me. From the first encounter when I met her two years ago, and now, being with her on this island is stirring up emotions, too quickly.

This mission, my undercover assignment, it's fucking with my head.

Chloe makes my head spin, making me forget about my assignment and remember Amber all at the same time. How can I fall for Chloe when I can't let go of Amber? Chloe's healing my heart, yet when I loosen the grip on my past, Amber's last words echo. *I love you, Jules*, would somehow resurface.

I thought I could handle it. I'm dead wrong.

"I also recall telling you I was willing to try," Chloe reasons with me, shaking me from my internal debate. "Go at my pace as you eloquently put it. There's something about you and I can't explain it…like we've met before. Do you feel the same way or is it all in my head?"

Fuck! She's remembering.

I should've known Chloe would remember something. We've spent the last couple of days together and it's bound to trigger something. I want this charade of the handyman/driver to be over, desperate to tell her about the first night we met, and the fact I'm here to protect her.

She needs to know.

But I can't just come right out and tell her. She would probably go ballistic.

So why else would she ask the question?

Although I want to be truthful, I'm under strict orders. I'm between a rock and a hard place. I only have one choice, and not an easy one to make. *Lie to her.*

"Are you sure it wasn't the alcohol talking?" I ask referring to last night at the club.

Chloe stands, her arms rise in frustration. "Is that what you think? The feelings I have are from being drunk?" It's her turn to pace, arms waving at her side. "Julian, I'm not drunk now. I don't know what it is…last night, when you protected me, then you kissed me…I just…I'm going down a spiral of emotions…help me out here. Throw me a life preserver because I'm feeling really stupid right now. I just don't want to get caught up if this isn't—"

I close the distance between us, gently framing her delicate face, effectively cutting her off. "Look, I'm sorry."

Chloe stills beneath my touch. "I'm rambling again, aren't I? I've been through a lot this last year that could last me a lifetime. Baggage, you know? Now, you…me…us…I can't explain it."

"I know about baggage and I need you to understand this was—"

"A mistake! I get it…forget it happened." Chloe shakes her head, tearing her eyes away from me. "What was I thinking?

Getting involved with someone, and then what? Leave in a few weeks?"

"Hey, look at me," I say softly. "I don't think it was a mistake." My thumbs caress her cheeks. "This *pace*... let's see where this path will take us. No rush. No expectations." I wrap my arms around her, my fingers playing with the ends of her hair. "Okay?"

"Yeah, okay." Chloe sighs as she traces the letters on my t-shirt.

I lean back, my hands descending to her waist. "Let's say we pack up. I'm sure your friends are waiting for you."

"As much as I want to stay, I don't want to ruin Phoebe's plans."

I'm deep in thought as we wrap up the leftovers and toss them in the picnic tote. Chloe has cracked the armor around my heart, then deeper, tapping the shoulder of my very dark soul. I didn't realize how hungry I was for her after I kissed her. Now my mind fills with thoughts of taking Chloe back to my place, stripping her naked and feeling her skin on mine.

She is so damn sexy.

After Amber, I dated, and even slept with other women, only to erase the pain. But with Chloe, kissing her is pure and honest, and it's real. But I need to slow it down. A *brisk walk*, the perfect innuendo. I still have a job to do. A fucked-up job. To protect and covet her are the hardest things I have to do because there's a secret, one I can't compromise—both my orders and the damn psychopath that's after her.

"So, are we doing this again tomorrow?" Chloe asks, towing me back to earth. "The breakfast was a nice touch."

"Huh?" I focus on her face and bringing myself out of the deep thought I was in. "Oh, yeah. Being that it's been a while since you've run, your legs will be sore. So, we will take it a little bit easier tomorrow."

"We could just do breakfast."

I chuckle. "Do you like pancakes?" I open the passenger door for Chloe to climb in, then place the picnic tote in the back. I stroll across the front of the Jeep and settle in before starting it up.

"Pancakes are my favorite," she says as she reaches behind her to grab the seatbelt.

I turn to watch Chloe buckle herself in. "Listen, let's not over-think this thing that's happening between us. I've only got a few weeks with you and I want to enjoy every minute together. No more fighting and no more questioning it, okay?"

"Okay," she replies, captivating me with her smile.

We ride back in silence. My thoughts return to the mission. With the case file sitting at the safe house, knowing the facts of what happened to her the last year, my stomach twists and I grip the stir-ring wheel a bit tighter.

She's been through enough and I need to be selfless. Even though she's told me more information about the foundation, it still isn't enough.

Chloe isn't as involved as I originally thought. But why are the foundation's financial documents at her home? What is so important that she has to have them in the security of her bedroom rather than with the staff or with Stacey? Did she not trust them? It's a good thing Tyco ran the background checks on the staff members and their affiliates. So far nothing appears suspicious.

I have to peel back her layers and dive deeper into this founda-tion. I know there's more to her than she's letting on.

What clues are hiding in plain sight? Why murder Sarah Chan-ning? Why is Chloe a target?

Murky thoughts of the photo Rocky sent me earlier replay in my mind. It's evident the bastard is after Chloe by the red circle around her face. Is Chloe that naïve to not realize this? Did she mention it to her father and in turn to Knox? But Knox would've said something to me.

"Hey, you okay?" Chloe turns to face me, interrupting my thoughts.

I nod. "I'm fine." I place my hand on her knee. "Just thinking, that's all." I've been playing a role of secrets and lies. I'm afraid Chloe will see right through me.

Guilt and betrayal.

Pain and turmoil.

One thing remains true, I want to take care of Chloe, keep her safe, no matter the cost. Even if she discovers my true identity, it's a sacrifice I'm willing to make.

"What about?"

"You." I glance at Chloe, seeing the rosiness in her cheeks. Not sure if it stems from being in the sun all morning or my comment.

"Me?"

"Just how amazing you are. The wonderful things you're doing for the foundation. How do you find the time to do it all?"

"That's a good question. I guess, the volunteers and the staff have made it easy. Sometimes I take the workload home with me."

"Why would you need to take the workload home with you?"

"Since I'm at the hospital all day, I don't like staying at the shelter too late. It can get a bit creepy in that part of town. So, I take home some of the financials to make sure all things match. Checks and balances…stuff like that."

One thing I can count on is Chloe's openness. I pride myself that I've been able to make her comfortable enough to talk to me. "Financials?" I ask.

"The staff doesn't need to know the amount of donations in the accounts. It's my responsibility to touch base with the outside financial firm that oversees the funds to make sure the various shelters have what they need to run efficiently."

"Hmm." I look intently at the road ahead as I keep driving. My thoughts flash back to the night when Chloe was hiding from her mother in the grand hallway. Doctor Channing mentioned a man Chloe needed to meet, about adding her name to the accounts.

What was that fucker's name? Mr….Koll-something.

"Why the sudden interest in the foundation?" She sits back, her brows furrow.

Damn. Too many questions.

"Maybe I'd like to donate something to your foundation." I hate lying to her but need to think quickly while I'm ahead.

I loathe this part of my assignment. If Chloe finds out about me being her protective detail, she will be devastated. The last thing I want is to hurt her.

My mind's like a damn seesaw. But it's more important for me to have Chloe find out about the lies and possibly hate me, than for me to mourn another dead woman.

"A donation? Really?"

"What you do is amazing. Maybe I can talk to my mom and sister to help out."

Chloe beams. "You would do that?"

"Of course, sweetheart."

We talk more about how I will give Mom and Fabi a call to ask what they can do for the foundation. Chloe seems ecstatic and the conversation lightens, shifting to Chloe's plans at the spa with her friends. I offer to drive the women there and pick them up after. This gives me enough time to touch base with KSIG and inquire if there have been any more leads.

AFTER I DROP THE WOMEN off, I head to the safe house to review the financials Rocky emailed to me. I read a familiar name. O'Hare Financial Enterprises holds all the funds—the bank is also Ryland's family business. I search for a name of someone managing the account but can't make a match in the file.

A needle in a fucked-up haystack.

One thing is for sure, there's millions of dollars spread across several accounts in the OFE bank. Budget sheets for the various shelters and homes show the incoming donations and the allocations of its spending. It's impressive and very organized, to say the least. Except for one account and the unexplainable debits. Is Chloe aware of the withdrawals?

When I spoke with Tyco, he wasn't sure what this account entailed. Being one of the best hackers I've met, nothing's impossible for Tyco, who is still working to discover who is withdrawing from it.

Since there's nothing more I could do until I got new information from Tyco, I shove the file in the safe in my bedroom. I instruct Tyco to look into the O'Hare's and any of the bank's employees involved with the foundation. God forbid the O'Hare family is involved with Sarah's death and Chloe's attack—it would devastate Chloe. But no matter the cost, I must figure this out and find the missing pieces.

I head back to the spa to pick up the ladies. While I wait in my Jeep, my mind travels down memory lane.

When I was stateside, I would take Amber to and from work, a quaint day spa where she worked as a receptionist. It's been five years and Amber somehow pulls me back with so many things that remind me of her.

But now with this longing for Chloe, to have feelings once again, guilt stirs in my heart. My emotions are in a whirlwind and I need to hear the sweet sound of reason.

I reach for my cell phone sitting on the dashboard and tap the first name at the top of my speed dial.

"Julian?" a woman's slight Spanish accent answers on the other end of the line.

"Hi, Mom." The sound of her voice is like a warm blanket covering me.

"Is everything alright? You never call me when you're working."

"I'm fine." Indistinct chattering filters through the other end of the line.

"Charles will have your head for making personal calls while on the job. Isn't it a cardinal rule?" Mom never liked calling my stepdad *Knox*. She thought it was our code word between us, a nickname of some sort. And frankly, I don't know why we call him Knox. He never told us how he got that callsign.

"I called to hear your voice."

"I know that tone, Julian Diego Cruz. What's the matter?" Her motherly voice is firm.

How does she do that? Damn maternal instincts.

I envision Mom in the office sipping on a hot cup of tea, wearing her St. John attire and her hair in a neat bun at the top of her head, peering over various colors of fabric and material spread across a long table.

I hear a younger high-pitched echo, most likely Nikki, her assistant. "Mrs. Fremont, line one," Nikki's voice comes through the line. "It's Paul from PWF Textiles."

"Tell him I'll call him back," Mom tells Nikki. "I'm talking to Julian."

"Julian? Tell him hello and I'm still waiting for him to take me to lunch," Nikki teases. A click sounds, most likely Mom's office door closing shut.

"I swear...that Nikki has had a crush on you since I hired her straight out of college six months ago." Mom giggles.

"She needs to find a man her age." I rake my fingers through my hair. "Did I catch you at a bad time?"

"Mijo, I always have time for you. Please, tell me, are you okay?"

"I'm fine. Have you heard from Fabi?" I ask, easing my mother's concerns and to lighten the mood. Every time Mom speaks of Fabiola, it buoys her spirits, being such a proud mother.

"Yes. I spoke with your sister this morning. She has a new man, you know."

"Another one?" I roll my eyes. "When is she ever going to settle down? That must be, what...the fourth guy in the last year?"

"His name is Remi," Mom says, her voice gleaming. "And she told me she really likes him."

"That's what she said about the last one," I huff, resting my head on the seat.

"Well, Remi will accompany Fabiola when she comes home for the holidays. So, when you talk to her, be nice." Her voice is cool and stern.

"I'm always nice to my baby sister. But I have a big-brother duty to at least give this Remi guy the third degree. Maybe Dad and I can take him on one of our hunting trips?"

"Julian, I said to be nice."

"I am being nice. To my sister. I never agreed to be nice to *him*." I chuckle at my ribbing.

"Aye, Julian. Fabiola will hate you." Mom's screech laces with humor.

"Eh, she'll get over it," I chide, switching the phone to my other ear.

"Certainly, you didn't call me to ask about your sister?" A moment of silence as I hear my mother take a sip. "What's going on with you, Julian?"

"Nothing. Can't a son call his mom?"

"Hmm. Nice try. I may be an old lady, but I'm certainly not a dumb one to know something is up."

"How?" *Damn, she must be clairvoyant.*

"It's in the sound of your voice."

"I'm working on a case."

"And? That's all you called to tell me?" Mom asks skeptically. "You don't talk about your cases with me…ever. Rules, remember?"

"I was thinking of Amber, again."

"Oh, sweetheart. You need to stop blaming yourself and move forward."

"Move forward?" I take a deep breath. "I'm never going to forget her."

"And no one is saying you should. I'm saying you need to stop living in the past."

I pinch the bridge of my nose. "The thing is, it's more betrayal I'm feeling."

"Betrayal? I don't understand."

"This case…" I watch a few women exit the glass doors of the salon. "I feel like I am betraying her."

"I'm lost, sweetheart. Betraying who? What does this case have to do with Ambrosia?" Mom quiets, waiting patiently for an answer.

I hesitate, measuring my response. Mom never judges her children's love lives—case in point, Fabi with her new man, Remi. "This woman… I met her two years ago…and I don't want to screw it up."

"Mijo." Mom takes a concerning, sincere breath. "I was wondering when this day would come. Now listen to me. After your father died, I wasn't sure how I could live without him. Your father's death sucked all the energy I had. I laid in bed for days, weeks even. I couldn't look at you because you reminded me so much of him. Charles was your father's best friend and he promised your father he would watch over us. He checked on me every day, making sure I was getting better for myself and for you. Helped me cope and healed my heart, putting the pieces back together. If you're lucky enough to get a second chance, don't pass it up. As much as I still love your father, always will, Charles was my second chance. In the end, we all want to be with someone, to belong."

"But isn't it too soon to feel like this?"

"Oh, my sweet son. There is no timeline. The heart is a crazy thing. You will always love Ambrosia and that will never go away. You just need to let this woman into your heart, make a little bit of room for her so you can heal." My mother's voice comforts me. "Some people don't get second chances. If this is yours, take it, Mijo."

"It's funny…she says she's not afraid to try. But I'm afraid." I squeeze my eyes shut.

"Afraid of love?"

"Yes, but also…afraid of failing. Just as I failed Amber."

"You need to learn to let go of the things that are holding you back from true happiness. Only you are in charge of your future."

"*Your future is what you make of it. There is destiny and then there is your destiny,*" I whisper, Rocky's words ringing in my ears.

"What did you say, Julian?" The pitch of her voice rises through the line. "You broke up."

"Nothing. It was something Rocky told me earlier." In spite of my fear, a smile tugs on my lips. Were both of these women right? *Is their encouragement really enough?*

"Julian, I wish I could snap my fingers and make things better for you."

I let out a long breath. "I know, Mom. The thing is, my assignment is to protect her. Some jackass is after this woman. And she's so distracting, she doesn't even realize it, whether she's in front of me or not. I'm afraid I'll let my guard down and miss the threat, just like I did with Ambs."

"I know you can't tell me too much about your assignment. But I also know you are very good at your job and you will do everything in your power to protect this woman. I have raised you to be an amazing man and I am prouder of you than you will ever know. If I believe in you, you need to do the same."

"You're pretty amazing, you know?" I hope Mom can hear the smile in my voice.

"I've been told."

I chuckle. "I love you, Mom."

"I love you, Mijo. Now, go be the badass agent I know you are."

CHAPTER

Fourteen

CHLOE

"SHH, KEEP YOUR VOICES DOWN." I look around the spa at the other women, their eyes narrow at me and my friends.

Despite the relaxing day so far, there is no way I would be able to avoid the third degree. We finished getting our hot stone massages and milk baths. We sit in our oversized salon chairs, hair wrapped in white towels and cuddled in our white cotton robes while indulging in our mani/pedis.

Candles softly shimmer around the room and set the ambiance. Scents of lavender and eucalyptus fill the air and soft harp music plays in the background.

"You kissed him?" Ryland whisper-yells. "I can't believe we've been here for the last three hours and you didn't say shit."

"You didn't ask." I shrug, taking a sip of lemonade.

"I can't believe you missed it, Ry," Phoebe cut in, sitting on the other side of her. "Oh, yes...I remember now, you were dry-humping your red-headed hottie."

"My guy was hot, wasn't he?" Ryland adds, carefully fanning her face.

"Yes, Ry. Tell us about your night." My mouth turns up in a playful smile, grateful for the diversion.

"Who? Seth? Nothing happened. We danced. End of story." Ryland half-shrugs. "His friends made a last-minute trip from Miami and he's getting married next weekend. And I am not the kind of girl to be someone's last booty call before he's someone's ball and chain. And what about you, Fee? Your tall dark and handsome was—"

"Fuckin' amazing," Phoebe squeals. "May I emphasize *fucking*. I love no-strings-attached sex." Phoebe licks her lips seductively. "He was Seth's best man. And he really is the best with what he did last night." She wiggles her eyebrows.

"I swear, you must have a guy buried deep inside you to talk the way you do," Ryland pipes out.

"Oh, Matt was deep inside me alright." Phoebe's shit-eating grin brightens her face.

"Slut," Ryland chides.

"Tramp," Phoebe retorts. "Anyway, let's get back to the juicy stuff." Phoebe tilts her head, glaring at me. "Well? Spill it, hun."

"We kissed." I smile, heat warming my cheeks.

"Were they drop-your-panties kisses?" Ryland asks.

"God, yes… He's so perfect yet frustrating. I feel like I've known him forever and yet he's so mysterious. It's just that…"

"Uh oh, I know that look." Ryland narrows her eyes, waving her finger.

"What look?" I counter.

"You fell for him."

I lean back in the chair. "I don't know. I like him a lot."

"All I know is I'm getting my Louboutin heels." Phoebe declares, sipping her lemonade through a straw.

"I didn't have sex with him."

"*Yet*…and trust me, you will. He's too hot to pass up. So, tell us… did he kiss like this?" Phoebe swirls her tongue around the straw.

"Ew, gross!" I gasp at Phoebe's failed attempt at a ridiculous French kiss with her straw.

"No, she kissed Julian like this." Ryland joins in as she licks the side of her own straw, starting at the bottom and up to the tip. Ryland and Phoebe's laughter fills the room.

I shake my head. No boundaries, no filter. It never ceases to amaze me how crude my friends can be. "You two are pathetic, you know that?" I shift in my chair, facing the opposite direction and away from my friends. An older woman sits to the other side of me, mouth agape. "My apologies," I say, feeling my cheeks warm from embarrassment. "My girlfriends don't get out much."

"No need to apologize. How I miss those days." The woman giggles.

"They're a bit boy-crazy when we go on our girls' trips."

The woman places her soft hand on my arm. "I met my Henry on a trip similar to yours. And with the same kind of girlfriends." The woman juts her chin toward Ryland and Phoebe, both giggling like hackling schoolgirls. "My Henry and I had passionate sex the entire time," she whispers. "Oh girl, he still has moves that make my toes curl."

"Oh, yeah?" I'm taken aback by the older woman's candid confession.

"I have no shame in talking about my Henry like this among women. He's the reason we've been together ever since. He's made me the happiest woman. Now we are celebrating our forty-fifth anniversary."

"How beautiful." I smile. "Happy anniversary."

"Oh my, here I am, spilling my secrets." The woman extends her hand. "My name is Rose."

"Nice to meet you, Rose." We shake hands, fingers barely touching, careful not to ruin our wet nails. "I'm Chloe."

"What a pretty name."

"Thank you."

There's something heartening about Rose, as if I can ask her anything. I turn the question over again, looking down at Rose's hands, soft and delicate, just like Nana's. I lift my eyes to meet the woman's blue-grays, warm and enduring.

Then the question flies from my mouth. "Rose, how did you know? How did you know Henry was...*the one?*"

"Well, it was a no-brainer...you feel it in here." Rose places her hand over her chest. "There's an unexplainable chemistry, like fireworks exploded in my heart. When Henry kissed me for the first time, God I still remember it like it was yesterday." She pauses, smiling at the memory. "When you kiss him, did you feel the fireworks?"

I nod. "Mm-hm."

"And when you first saw him, how did you feel?"

I thought of the day I saw him at the airport when my thoughts tickled my brain. Was it the first time I met Julian? Why were my feelings deepening so quickly, and all the while it's comforting? "He drowns me, Rose...and I don't want to come up for air. Is that what you mean?"

"Yes, that is *exactly* when you know he's the one." Rose pauses again, giving me the sincerest smile. "I can see you like him very much. Your eyes say it."

"They do?" My brows furrow, searching for a plausible answer.

"Yes. Eyes are never quiet. As much as you may want to hide your feelings, or deny them, you forget our eyes will speak. They say you want to let your heart do what it does best, to love someone. And..." Rose's voice lowers conspiratorially. "You will most likely have that passionate sex your body is yearning for."

"Rose!"

The woman laughs as I gasp from her shocking comment. "I don't mean to be so forward. But, am I wrong?" she adds.

I bite my bottom lip, then shyly shake my head. Rose wasn't wrong. Not in the least.

"I know the heart and mind fight battles. But sometimes we need to shut off our mind and just go with our heart."

"I'm afraid he'll hurt me," I say.

"Who isn't afraid? I'm sure your girlfriends over there are afraid as well. Might explain why they're still single, hmm?" Rose looks over at my friends on the other side of me. "Of course, the heart is afraid, but it is also very brave. It knows when to take a chance. You just need to be brave enough to listen to your heart. Can you picture this man out of your life now that he's part of it?" Rose peers down at her toes. "I think my piglets are dry." She pushes herself off the salon chair. "If the answer is no, then I suggest you don't let him go."

My heart cracks at the thought of dismissing Julian out of my life now that he's part of it.

How does this man consume all of my thoughts?

He makes me feel whole again when I didn't know I was incomplete, to begin with. I ache for him and although I'm supposed to be spending this time with my friends, I want to be with him.

"Our time is limited." I sigh. "He lives here, and I don't."

"The best kind of love is unexpected—"

"Oh, Rose, I don't love him. We just met."

"That's exactly what I said about my Henry. If there is an instant connection, I call it fate. Fate is love. You were meant to meet him. And I truly believe it'll work out." Rose pauses, tender eyes pitching to mine. "Well, I best be going now. My Henry is picking me up soon."

"It was nice talking to you…and thank you for the advice."

"My pleasure, dear." Rose turns and disappears through the dressing-room door.

The wisdom I longed for and needed to hear comes from a complete stranger. I place my hand over my heart. Looking at Rose's unoccupied chair, an angelic vision of Nana sweeps my mind.

Thanks, Nana. I know you're watching me.

"I'm so glad Thomas and I have an understanding that it's purely physical," Phoebe tells Ryland.

How does Phoebe do that—sex without love?

I think back to Julian's heart-throbbing kiss at the club, then on top of the hill. Butterflies swarm in my belly and a warm glow flows through me.

Was Julian the one I've been waiting for? Did he feel the same connection? It certainly appears so. I can still feel his hands against my body sending goosebumps up my back. His eyes, wild with lust. His raspy voice telling me I belong to *him.*

Are my emotions getting the best of me?

It didn't matter. I'm going to see where this thing we have will go regardless of our limited time and toss my plan out the window. Phoebe, Ryland, and now Rose's words seem to chant in my ear.

Take a chance.

"Don't think I've forgotten about you and Julian." Ryland shifts toward me, squaring her shoulders. "Spill it. And don't leave anything out."

I take a steadying breath. "Okay, yes, he's an amazing kisser. Like toe-curling, panty-dropping, wrap-my-legs-around-him, tastes-so-good kisser. I don't know what it is, but I can't control myself around him."

"Are you saying you're finally going to let your hair down, take a chance on him?"

"Toss the Chloe Plan, sweetie," Phoebe adds. "Do you really want to look back twenty years from now and wonder why you didn't go for it with Julian?"

The infamous Chloe Plan—fall in love with Prince Charming, have 2.5 kids, a house with a white picket fence, and live happily ever after.

"I like my plan," I say, sipping my lemonade. "Feebs, how do you do it? Have no-strings-attached sex?"

"Seriously? Well, he inserts his hard di—"

"Don't be a dumbass," I yelp, stopping her before she finishes her sentence. "It was just a question."

"Well, you asked, *dumbass*." Phoebe twists her lips. "I know you two think I'm a nympho, but I swear I'm not."

Ryland and I laugh hysterically. Women from every corner of the salon scowl at us for interrupting their solace.

"Okay"—Phoebe displays her forefinger and thumb in the air, barely touching—"maybe a tiny bit nympho. There used to be a time having sex with the one you love was the way it was supposed to be. But after Bryan, I don't believe in love anymore. He messed it up for me."

"Feebs, I hope someday you fall in love again." I tilt my head. There's a sadness there even if Phoebe won't admit it. Phoebe once had a heart of gold and unfortunately, it turned to a heart of stone, rejecting any man who tried to give her attention.

"It will take a miracle for Feebs to fall in love again," Ryland says. "What about you, Chlo? Planning on having no-strings-attached sex with Julian?"

"He's pretty fuckin' hot," Phoebe confesses, and Ryland makes a sizzling noise that has all three of us grinning.

"Exactly. I can't wait to see him naked." I mumble. I cover my mouth with my hands. The words were out before I can take them back.

"Thatta' girl." Phoebe raises her hand to Ryland for a high-five. "Time to embrace your inner slut."

CHAPTER

Fifteen

JULIAN

SOFT WARM HANDS CARESS MY torso, fingernails tracing down my abs. Our bodies tangle in endless waves of bedsheets. She's in control, straddling me, moving rhythmically against my hips, fueling my desire.

I palm her breasts, teasing her nipples with my thumb and forefinger.

I need to taste her mouth.

With both hands, I scoop the sides of her face and bring her closer to me. Our tongues dance in a frenzied pace.

Fucking delicious.

She breaks the kiss, and I immediately miss the contact. Her perfect wet lips trail kisses from my mouth, languidly down to my jaw. Her warm breath and tongue against the crook of my neck as it ignites sparks to my awakened dick.

I let out a groan, and she returns a sexy sigh.

Tasting. Feeling. Claiming.

Her firm tits press to my perspiring pecs.

I've waited too long for this.

Skin on skin.

Sweating. Pulsing. Throbbing.

Holy fuck, sweetheart, you feel so damn good.

A faint vibration disconnects our kiss. "Your phone…is buzzing…someone's calling," she pants between kisses, nipping my jaw. "It might be important."

"Later…they'll call back…you're more important." My fingers thread through her mussed hair. "No more talking. C'mere, I want to taste you, baby." Something's different about her kiss, yet familiar. I pull my mouth from hers and gaze into her eyes.

"I love you, Jules." Her voice echoes, sending chills down my spine.

Amber?

Amber's fingernail traces my jawline. Her beautiful smile—she's biting her bottom lip. Wayward hair tumbles down her shoulders.

I squeeze my eyes shut.

I shake my head to steady the image.

This can't be…

I open my eyes again, rub them to clear the vision.

Chloe?

"I remember now," Chloe hisses. "It was *you* all along." Her blue eyes taunt me. Brown curls tickle my chest. The pad of her thumb grazes my lip. Chloe leans in and whispers, "You lied to me, Booker…*you lied to me.*"

The vibration grows louder. *Buzz-buzz-buzz.*

"I didn't lie!" I yell, springing myself out of bed. Anxiety pulses through my veins and sweat drips from my body.

Am I going crazy?

My bare feet touch the floor as I get my bearings. A gray half-moon shines through my bedroom window. A woman was here, yes?

No.

I exhale a shaky breath to calm the thunder roaring in my chest. I'm alone.

A fucking dream.

My cell illuminates the nightstand. *Tyco.*

I rub my eyes again, squinting at the time. *Three twenty-two.*

I sit at the edge of the bed, swipe to answer the call. "It's too early for—"

"Took you long enough." Tyco's voice sounds through the line. "I've been calling you for the last thirty minutes. I was about to send the hounds after you."

"This better be good," I grunt.

"Sorry, Book. I couldn't sleep...after my night with...what was her name again? Chelsea? Chastity? Fuck. Anyhow, I still had all this pent-up energy after I left her place, thought I'd put it to good use. You know me, once I get going, I can't stop—"

"Jesus, Ty. How many cups of coffee have you had?" I hear Tyco slurp, most likely his special black coffee with two extra shots of espresso.

"Only four."

"Easy on the liquid crack. Not good for you."

Tyco chuckles. "Yeah, yeah. So, as I was saying...I got to working on the Channing case when an alert came across my monitor. I didn't wanna wait till morning to call you after I saw it."

"Spit. It. Out."

"Luke Jensen—the guy you wanted me to keep an eye on? He took a redeye out of San Francisco last night."

"And? Do I need to guess where he went?"

"Miami." Tyco slurps his coffee again.

My jaw tightened. "Fuck."

"Too close for comfort, if you ask me. He's staying at the Intercontinental for the next several days. Knox sent Lincoln to keep an eye on him," Tyco adds. I can hear the clicking of a keyboard.

"I wasn't aware Lincoln got put on this case." And now I need to contact Lincoln. *Why is he on Jensen?*

What am I missing?

"Well, you know Knox...he's covering all bases. He's a good guy and always pays back any favors that are due especially for District Attorney Frank Channing."

"Yup, that's Knox...never forgets and would take the shirt off his back."

"Anyway, two nights ago Lincoln trailed Jensen and get this…he met up with Tellis O'Hare, Ryland's brother. They had dinner and drinks at the Press Club. At one point, Jensen slid an envelope to O'Hare."

"What else?"

"Nothing. That's it."

"What do you mean *nothing*? Is Jensen linked to the photo that was mailed to Chloe, the letters to Frank?"

"I checked on Jensen's whereabouts the morning Chloe was attacked. He was at a medical conference in Rhode Island. I even went further to check his whereabouts during Doctor Channing's hit-and-run. Jensen was in surgery. He's not the unsub."

"Let me get this shit straight…you woke me up at the ass-crack of dawn to tell me Chloe's ex-boyfriend had dinner with Ryland's brother and is on his way to Miami…and this asswipe is *not the unsub*? I need you to look into Tellis O'Hare…God, I hope Ryland's brother is not involved or it's going to be a shitstorm."

"I've got more, donkey-boy." Another pause from Tyco, slurping his coffee. "I looked into the accounts, that slush fund—"

"What'd you find out?" I ask quickly.

"Doctor Channing opened the CAF accounts with a Mr. Russell Kollsson."

"Sounds familiar." *Familiar indeed.* The name gnaws at the corner of my brain until it suddenly dawns on me. Doctor Channing needed Chloe to meet this man the night of the gala.

"Kollsson *was* her financial advisor," Tyco says.

"Was?"

"He's dead. Multiple stabs to the chest. Apparently, he'd left early from work. His secretary told the detectives he was feeling woozy."

"*Woozy?*"

"Yup. Her words. She offered to call him a cab, but he refused."

"Fuck." I scrub my face with my hand. "How long ago?"

"Two months. Toxicology report found benzodiazepine in his system. Explains the woozy part and the reason why Kollsson couldn't fight the assailant. Unfortunately, there were no cameras in the parking structure for detectives to review."

"Another dead end." My muscles tense and my teeth clench.

"Nah...just more breadcrumbs for me to follow." Tyco's confident voice radiates through the line knowing he loves the challenge. If there's a trail, leave it to Tyco to follow it and get the answers needed.

"Doctor Channing, Kollsson..."

"Wait there's more folks...behind door number three...half a mill was wired to a Swiss account the week prior to Doctor Channing's murder. Not to mention hundreds of thousands withdrawn since then. I'm working on the Swiss account as we speak."

"Let me guess: Kollsson."

"Actually, no." Tyco's fingers click-clack on the keyboard. "Doctor Channing made the wire transfer."

"Doctor Channing? This is becoming one big clusterfuck. Okay. Keep digging."

"Funny, that's what she said to me last night." Tyco chuckles.

"Asshole. I don't need to hear about your sex life."

"At least one of us is getting some."

"Fucker."

Tyco laughs again. "Yup, that's what she said, too."

"Ty, focus. Did you get any prints from the photograph or the postcards that Rocky retrieved from Chloe's apartment?"

"Working on it. They're backed up at the lab."

"Backed up? Are you shitting me?"

The KSIG firm added their own in-house lab six months ago, after growing tired of waiting on the city for results. Unfortunately, Sabrina Kent is running the lab solo, and with the surmounting cases, she's overworked and understaffed.

"Sabrina needs some help over there." I run my fingers through my hair. "I'll talk to Knox about hiring an assistant to help her out."

"I could always work my charm to get bumped up to the front of the line."

"Keep your dick in your pants, playboy. You know how Knox feels about office fuckery."

"Sabrina has a boyfriend. And Knox gave me an earful and my dick is in check. So, I don't need his *son* lecturing me, too."

"Asshole. Just send what you have to my tablet." That's the thing about being the boss's stepson, the guys will forever give me shit for it. But, it's all fun and games until someone fucks up at the office.

"Ten-four. Tyco out." He hangs up.

I toss my cell on the nightstand with a clap. I rub a hand down my face, yielding to my bed, where my mind wanders back to the dream. Too-clear images splinter my thoughts, flickering like a slideshow. Visions of Amber fuel my guilt, my betrayal toward her. Another vision follows, whispering my desire to Chloe.

I'm going straight to hell.

My growing feelings are strong for Chloe, fast and hard. The longer I'm on this case and around her, it's harder to resist her allure. Every bone in my body aches for her. I feel out of control and I can't keep my mind straight.

For two years I stayed away from Chloe, but every time I tried to push out the memory of that night, it was no use. Now that I've kissed her, game over. I refuse to have history repeat itself. If it did, I wouldn't be able to live with myself.

No way in hell am I losing Chloe. She is not Amber.

After hearing more intel from Tyco, I have to get my shit straight —now more than ever. I take a deep breath, need to snap out of it, to focus on my objective.

There's no use trying to sleep, too much information to deal with in the early hour. I go to the kitchen, pull out a mug from the cabinet and place it under the one-cup coffee maker. It took about thirty seconds for my mug to fill with hot coffee.

No sugar, no creamer, just how I like it.

Now that my brain juices are flowing, time to connect the dots.

Doctor Channing's dead.

Chloe's attack.

Kollsson's dead.

The CAF accounts and a million dollars withdrawn and then more in the last year. Luke Jensen with Tellis O'Hare—what was in that damn envelope? Why the sudden redeye flight, and who was Jensen meeting with?

I head back to my bedroom and open the hutch door to a hidden safe which houses the case file, iPad tablet, my HK VP9, an extra mag and a box of ammo. I take out the tablet, leaving the safe door open.

I review the financial documents yet again. I press the home button, type the code then open the blue file-folder icon. The documents appear one by one. Swiping the screen until I come upon the week before Sarah Channing's death.

There, in bold: $1,000,000 transfer processed by Sarah Channing.

How had I missed it?

None of this shit makes sense and it pisses me off to high heaven.

Frustration overwhelms me as I place the tablet back in the safe and lock it. There isn't much I can do now but wait for the results from Tyco.

Needing a hot shower to relax, the stream of water warms my back. Thoughts drift again to my dream. It's the first time I've dreamt of both Amber and Chloe in one night. Shrapnel images embed in my memory: Amber's lifeless body as I cradled her, not letting go even as the paramedics finally showed up.

It was no use for the medic to do anything; Amber was already gone.

I look down at my open palms, at a speck of phantom blood on my hands. The demons woven throughout my soul claw at my chest. A rock of shame, guilt, and betrayal, sink to my gut, weighing me down.

There in the shower, I fall to my knees.

How could I have dreamt of both Amber and Chloe?

I want the mission to end, and when it does, I know exactly how I will finally lay Amber to rest and give myself peace of mind.

I step out of the shower, towel-dry and wipe the steamed-up mirror with my hand. I stare at my own face, then down at my hands gripping the edge of the counter, my head hangs low between my shoulders.

"Pull your shit together, fucker," I mutter.

Self-control and rational thinking—that's who I am.

Yet I've completely lost it the moment Chloe entered the picture.

I can only blame myself for my actions these last couple of days, being in close proximity to her. But the new intel steadies me back into position.

No more indecision.

No more letting my guard down.

I need to refocus not just for my sake, but for hers.

White-hot rage courses through my veins at the thought of just how far this unsub would go. The man wants Chloe dead, there's no doubt about it. There's no way in hell this asshole is going to get his hands on her.

CHAPTER

Sixteen

CHLOE

"THIS FEELS SO AWKWARD." I concentrate on the formation of squaring my shoulders, bent elbows and clenching my fists in the air. The soft breeze is a relief, cooling my bare skin from the humidity and the sun's beating rays. "Am I even doing this right?"

We were back at the hilltop where we had our picnic the other day. Julian shifts his attention from my legs to my feet. The toe of his running shoe taps the insides of my feet, nudging them apart.

"More space here and stay on the balls of your feet. The weight should be even," he instructs, and I roll my eyes.

This is the third morning of punching, kicking and blocking. And quite frankly, I'm getting tired of Julian's mission of making me the next Rhonda Rousey.

Turn this way, pivot that way. Punch, kick, protect.

The moment I make up my mind to go at a faster *pace,* Julian makes a U-turn and keeps going the other way. All morning, just like the last two days, I've batted my lashes and licked my lips, but nothing seems to faze him. Had he lost his attraction for me? Just like that?

The abrupt shift makes me feel off balance.

The flirting gone.

No more kisses.

The touches are there, but only to position me to correct my stance.

Gone is the playful and seductive man I met a few days ago. I'm on Julian's damn rollercoaster stuck in the turning loop and I'm hanging upside down hoping somehow this emotional malfunction will get back on course.

The about-turn gives me whiplash and I don't know what to make of it. Should I go with the flow? Ask him why the sudden change of heart? Should I cut ties with him and treat him as the *hired help*? The latter question flickers and fades quickly, knowing I can't do it.

The chemistry that once brewed between us has dissipated. What happened to the old Julian? The one I was falling for…

Julian levels his eyes at my hips, shaking his head. There's dissatisfaction with my stance. He places his hands on my hips, angling me at a forty-five-degree pivot. His fingers send an electric current with an aching of need and wanting more of his touch.

I give him a coy smile, trying to hide my euphoric emotions, but the unavoidable burn heats my cheeks as I study him.

"Concentrate, Doc." His brows knit together. "Be serious."

"I'm trying. But you're tickling me," I huff, biting my bottom lip. "But I don't mind you touching me there."

Julian shakes his head, dismissing my flirty banter. "Don't be so stiff," he instructs, mirroring his hips with my movement. "Loosen up here…like this."

"I think *you* need to loosen up," I sneer, raising an eyebrow.

Julian smirks, then repositions his hands to my elbows, his thumbs graze my breasts. Sensations tingle my now taut nipples as the friction rubs over my sports bra.

Did he do that on purpose?

"Keep your elbows here." Julian's voice is low and serious as he places my elbows closer to my ribcage. "Need to protect your body."

"Is this better, Mr. Bossy?"

"Mm-hm," Julian said, eyes squinted with expressed irritation.

"I didn't sign up for this."

"Look, I know you don't like this. But you'll thank me later."

"I doubt it."

Keeping my focus on Julian, confusion blankets my thoughts. Confused and head over heels at the same time. I can't help being irked by him and all the while wanting to throw my arms around his neck and taste his lips again.

All morning, he touches my body but gives no sign of wanting more than just to readjust my fighting posture.

Regardless of his rejections, I can't help the goosebumps as his calloused hands smooth over my biceps, then stop at my shoulders. "Too tense. Relax here."

"I'm too tense? You should hear yourself." Sarcasm is my best friend this morning. I can't resist. In fact, he seems more irritated and I'm enjoying getting a rise out of him.

The nerve. I'm tense? I'll show him tense.

He smirks once again, ignoring my comment. His fingers move down my arms. His large hands cover my balled-up fists; his thumbs softly graze my knuckles. His brown eyes meet mine. Silence stretches between us.

"Need more tension in your fists. Remember when you punch your attacker, it needs to sting."

Sting? I want just one kiss to ease the sting piercing my heart.

"Relax my shoulders. Tension in my fists. Why are we doing this, Julian? We've been at this and you still haven't told me why the sudden change of...*pace.*" I lift a brow, underscoring the double entendre.

Julian opens his mouth then closes it, taking too many seconds to answer. "I'd rather you be safe than sorry."

I stare at him, letting the words sink in. "What makes you think I'm not going to be safe?"

Julian lets out a breath. "Before Fabi headed off to college, this was the first thing I taught her. The mace I gave her wasn't going to be enough. And with her late classes, knowing what to do if she were ever attacked, gave me peace of mind." Julian lifts both palms in front of him. "Okay, give me a left-right jab."

"Like this?" I punch straight to his open palm, making impact.

"Yes, good." Julian nods. "I'm glad I was able to show her because the following spring break, she was attacked by a jealous ex-boyfriend."

I gasp, eyes wide. "Was she hurt?"

"Some bruising and scratches. But at the end of it all, she kicked his ass good. Was she *sorry*? No, actually, she was *safe*. Even my mom knows how to kick some ass."

"Your mom? You showed her these moves too?"

Julian's mouth curls up. "Yes. I think every woman should know how to take care of herself. I just don't want anything to happen to you." His last words make my emotions go in all different directions but find purchase in my heart.

Julian wraps his fingers around my wrists. "After you punch, make sure you bring your hands back to your jaw. Always protect your face. If your attacker hits you here…" Julian demonstrates a slow right hook, his knuckles softly tap my cheek. "Game over."

With both hands, Julian palms my jaw. "I would hate to have this beautiful face battered and bruised…or worse."

An image triggers.

Evil eyes filled with hatred.

The weight of my attacker straddling my waist, pressing me into the concrete.

Hands around my neck.

The stinging blade and the bone-crushing hit to my face knocking me senseless.

I swallow the bile in the back of my throat and shut my eyes to push back the threatening tears. My fists begin to tremble as a cold shiver creeps up my spine despite the warm breeze enveloping me.

"Hey, you okay?" Julian's voice brings me back to our secluded hilltop where we stand. "Look at me. Where'd you go just now?"

I bend over, hands on my knees to steady my breathing. "I…it's nothing."

"Bullshit. You're ghost white." Julian pulls me up, forcing me to look at him. "Talk to me, Channing." There's a raw grit in his tone. His jaw clenches, then unclenches.

We look at each other for what seems like an eternity. In his brown eyes, I see concern and rage.

"I can't talk about it." I shake my head, hiding the fear in my own eyes.

"Can't or won't?"

"Both."

I don't want pity. I don't need him seeing me as a frail stray dog that needs to be brought back to health.

"You know you can talk to me about anything." He tucks a loose curl behind my ear.

"Then tell me what I did wrong."

"What are you talking about?" He cocks his head back.

"Why haven't you kissed me? I swear your mood swings are giving me whiplash." I cross my arms over my chest and glare.

"Chloe." My name is a sounding plea. "There are things I wish I could talk to you about and things I really shouldn't. You make me feel things I'm not supposed to." He scrubs his hair back with his hand as he turns away from me. "I need to figure this out."

"Figure what out?"

"You. Me. Us. Fuck! I have a job to do." He spins to face me. "And it's not good for me to be commingling with my employer."

"Is that what I am to you? Your employer?"

"I didn't mean it like that. I do care about you, more than you know."

"Fine," I sneer, then purse my lips together.

"Fine?" Julian echoes. "Having a sister and mom...*fine* is never a good answer."

"What else do you want me to say? You've been pushing me away and I thought we had an understanding. We weren't going to fight, enjoy our time...remember? You told me—"

"I know what I said, and I shouldn't have. I'm sorry."

My stomach lurches as his words knock the wind out of me. My overwhelmed emotions are raked over hot coals. He might as well have taken the proverbial knife, stabbed me in the heart and cut the strings attached to it. So, where does this leave us?

After a beat of awkward silence, our staring contest finally ends when I speak up.

"Well, that's the most I've gotten from you in the past couple days. So, let's call it what it is. From now on, I'm your employer."

"Chloe." His voice is low and apologetic.

"Don't *Chloe* me, Julian. You said it loud and clear. No need to explain anything else." I slip back into formation. Now there's a reason to hit him in the face. The humiliation, anger, and regret will be the fighting forces behind my punches.

Un-fucking-believable.

I plant my feet. Square my shoulders and bob my head side to side. Balled fists lifted and ready. "Although I didn't ask for these lessons, I guess we should finish. Let's just do this. I need to learn, right?"

"Okay," he answers hesitantly. "You ready?"

"Mm-hm." I nod.

Julian bounces from side to side, pats and lightly slaps unguarded parts of my body.

"Need to be quicker than that, Channing."

"Shit. I wasn't ready."

"You must always keep your guard up. Come on…fists up…tuck in your elbows. Feet apart and relax your shoulders…and pivot your hips. Gotta be light on your feet. Now take your shot."

"I'm a lover, not a fighter." I lick my lips and blow him a kiss.

"Are you trying to woo your attacker, Doc?"

"I don't know. Is my attacker wooable?" I flirt.

"Not today." He points to his chin.

"That's what I thought," I say.

"Give me a clean shot, right here." He delivers a hit-me-with-your-best-shot smile.

I take a deep breath and throw a right hook.

Missed.

Then a left hook.

Missed again.

A right uppercut.

Missed.

Dammit.

I blow out an exasperated breath. I have an idea. I quickly remove my tank-top, leaving only my sports bra to show off my flat and tight abs.

Julian's mouth opens slightly, as he stares at my naked torso.

I reposition myself as he continues his mouth-watering glare. A jab straight to Julian's chin makes impact with my fist.

"Holy shit." Wide-eyes, I shake out my throbbing hand. "Did I hurt you?"

Julian rubs his jaw. "It'll take more than that to hurt me."

God, that felt good.

"Good hit. Let's do it again. But this time, use your legs. Try to hit up here." He points to the side of his stomach.

Adrenaline invading my body, I take a step forward. Julian takes a step back. It's a mirroring of the mime game.

Julian steps forward; I step back.

Julian sends a right hook; I duck.

A grin appears on his face.

Proud of dodging Julian's swing, my insides are boiling like a tea kettle ready to whistle. Heat fuels my right leg, then smashes his guarded torso.

"Nice. Now a combo."

I'm getting the hang of it. The fight in me is exhilarating and I love every minute of it. Sweat beads down my temples. Narrowing eyes darting to an opening. Alternating from a kick to a one-two punch, I make impact.

Julian grunts. "Damn. I think my apprentice is a fast learner," he says, holding the side of his stomach.

"Tired already? You're not giving up on me, are you?" I ask him, stilling bobbing.

Julian's left leg sweeps under my feet, and I stagger backward. His arms wrap around my waist, as my hands catch his shoulders before hitting the grass.

"I will never give up on you, Chloe Channing."

CHAPTER

Seventeen

CHLOE

I WAKE UP DISORIENTED AND lost in the silence that surrounds me. I canceled the *Rhonda Rousey* morning session and avoid any reason to be near Julian. I pull the covers over my head, drowning out the sun's rays sneaking through my windows.

Avoidance is my best tactic to staying away from Julian. It's an emotional sting to my heart and a punch to my gut as if I'm put back in the black hole just like when I found Luke with Reyna.

How could the pain from Julian's denial feel just as bad as what Luke did to me many months ago? It's because Julian possesses my heart.

I grunt. *Love sucks.*

I shove the covers off and pick up my cell phone to check the time.

Nine-fifteen.

Scrolling through my text messages, I smile at the long text from Celina letting me know she got the mail and rambling on about her dog and cat fighting.

Three text messages from Julian.

4:12 am: We need to talk.

6:20 am: I need to clear the air.

8:25 am: There are things you don't know about me and I don't want to hurt you.

My finger hovers over the delete button. What could he possibly say to make me feel better?

Did our conversations and kisses mean anything to him? I'm not too sure how I'm going to handle Julian coming around the house after the day I've had with him on the hilltop.

Please don't be here. Please don't be here, I chant, eyes clenching.

I hear my friend's faint voices downstairs. I slowly scramble out of bed, head to the bathroom. I wash my face and brush my teeth. The reflection in the mirror is a pathetic woman, red-rimmed eyes from being up all night, tossing and turning. My mind wouldn't let me rest. Every time I close my eyes Julian is front and center.

Only a couple more weeks then I'm back home. Julian will soon be forgotten.

I mentally slap myself.

How can I be this stupid? I shouldn't have ever listened to Feebs.

I shake my head and roll my eyes. "Easier said than done," I say to my reflection. Flashbacks of Julian come to mind. I stifle a laugh, remembering the first night I arrived, laughing at his arrogant banter in my bedroom.

I touch my mouth, missing Julian's lips when he kissed me at the club. The hilltop picnic and the things he told me about possibly meeting his sister, his mom. Then the punch to his jaw that he deserved for leading me on.

I slip on my bikini. A lazy day under the sun and a book to read sounds pretty good.

AFTER A COUPLE OF HOURS in the sun, I stare out at the glassy ocean in front of me, drinking in the calm crystal-blue shimmers. Even with the wide view of nothing but sailboats, all I can think about is Julian.

His intense dark brown eyes always made it hard to look away. His touch ignites an electric charge and awakens all my senses. I would gladly surrender myself to him over and over again.

Every part of me screams Julian is the one. But I need to get over him. But how?

I fight the tears stinging behind my eyes. Although I'm hating every bit of my life right now, I need to get a grip. I refuse to let Julian ruin what is left of my vacation.

"Paging Doctor Channing... Hello, Chloe..." Ryland says, pulling me from my thoughts. "So, what do you think?"

"Think about what?" My legs dangle on the edge of the pool, my feet dipping in the water.

"The sangria?"

I raise the glass to my mouth. "It's delicious. Just what the doctor ordered."

"Everything alright?" Ryland asks.

"Yeah. Peachy. Why wouldn't it be?"

"Because you've been in la-la land. Would there happen to be a hunky Latin lover consuming your thoughts?" Phoebe sits in a large inflatable lounge chair in the pool, sangria in the cup holder, her fingers skimming the top of her glass.

"I don't know...he switched." I roll my shoulders and blow out a breath.

"What do you mean?" Ryland is bobbing in the middle of the pool, her hair floating above the water.

"He's backed off and I guess I will too. He's not the same person. As if the weight of the world is on his shoulders."

"How can you tell? You barely know the guy." Ryland asks.

My thoughts scatter like a jigsaw puzzle thrown across the table. Not only am I trying to piece together the mess of flashes, but I'm also trying to figure Julian out.

Why the sudden change?

Still, the niggling in the back of my mind keeps telling me we've met, and I need to find this missing piece. If we met before, why didn't he say anything?

"I know him well enough... For starters, I've tried several times to kiss him and he turned away."

"Maybe you had bad breath?" Phoebe teases.

"Bitch." I kick the water, splashing Phoebe in the face, then sip my sangria.

"Hey, watch it," Phoebe screeches, using her hand to shield from the splash.

"I'm serious. He hasn't touched me since the day after he picked us up from the spa. You'd think after the kiss we had; he wouldn't be this way." I wrinkle my forehead. "Instead of going on our jog, he teaches me self-defense?"

"Better late than never," Ryland says, before swimming to the other end of the pool.

Phoebe lowers her sunglasses down the tip of her nose. "Hun, you're overthinking this thing with Julian. Maybe it's *you* who's sending him the wrong signals. Have you thought about that?"

Ryland swims back toward us and steps out of the pool. She dries herself off with a towel. "Why don't you ask him what's bothering him? Ask him if he still wants to make it work with you?" Ryland ruffles her hair with the towel. "If you don't ask, you'll never get the answers. And I'm testimony to letting the million-dollar question pass by."

"I think I already know the answer, Ry. Besides, like I said before...this thing with Julian was a bad idea. Only a couple more weeks and we'll be back home."

"What if Jacob had told you he wanted to work it out?" Phoebe asks.

"I would go for it," Ryland answers, lifting a brow at me. "Ask him, babe. What have you got to lose?"

My dignity.

I push myself up from the side of the pool. Everything starts to spin, and it takes me a minute to focus.

A kaleidoscope of memories tumbles through once again. Before the fog could clear, I hold the images a little longer this time.

A red elegant gown.

A man standing next to me.

A drop-dead smile and sexy-as-hell dimples looking down at me.

"Whoa." I place both hands to my side to balance myself. "Head rush."

Ryland rushes to my side before I slip and fall into the pool. "Oh my God, sweetie. Are you okay? Here…sit down." Ryland escorts me to one of the lounge chairs. "Drink this." She gives me a bottle of water.

"I'm fine." I tip the water bottle and take a drink. "I just got up too fast."

That's a lie.

Phoebe scrambles out of the pool and is at my side. Her body blocks the sun from my face. "You've been having these spells lately. It's kind of scary. Maybe you should see a doctor."

"I am a doctor and I'm fine," I clip. "I didn't sleep well last night, that's all."

"Nightmares?" Phoebe asks, her eyes soft, concern lacing her voice.

"No. I just couldn't sleep." I didn't want to let my friends know that Julian consumed my thoughts and he's the cause of my sleepless night of tossing and turning. But I'm sure they know that already.

"Maybe you should rest," Ryland tells me. "You look tired."

I meet my friends worried gazes. "I'm fine. Stop looking at me like that. I just—"

"We should skip the skydiving." Phoebe looks at Ryland. "I could reschedule or get a refund—"

"No. Don't. You two go have fun." My cell jingles the *Hawaii Five-O* theme song. Without looking at the caller ID, I know who it is. "It's Dad. I gotta get this."

"Kay." Phoebe kisses the top of my head. "We'll see you later."

Both ladies disappear through the double doors, leaving me with the warm sun. The ringtone plays again. I grab my phone on the table beside me, I swipe my finger across the screen.

"Hi, Dad," I greet.

"Hi, Pumpkin. How's everything?" His deep overpowering tone fills the line.

"It's good…just hanging out by the pool."

"I haven't heard from you in a few days. I was beginning to worry."

I can hear an undertone, something distinct. Concerned desperation starts to alarm my thoughts. "Dad? Is everything okay?"

"What makes you think there's something wrong?"

"I know that tone." There's silence as if he's deciding on how to answer my question. "Dad?" I call for him.

"I wanted to hear your voice, that's all."

"I'm here with Feebs and Ry. Not to mention you had Sammy come along. What else could get you so worried?"

Almost every conversation with Dad is like a broken record. He's always worried over me ever since Mom died and especially since my attack. And I can't fault him.

I'm their rainbow child, their miracle baby. Mom and Dad tried for years, failed pregnancies one after another until I came along. So of course, Dad's wariness and needing the validation to know his only child is doing fine is the least I can do to bring him peace of mind.

"I'm just here at the office…and I was looking at the picture of you and your mother. The one at the charity event," he sighs, and his voice fades. "You both were so beautiful."

I sit straight up and square my shoulders. Could it be any more of a coincidence?

"Uh, Dad. What color dress was I wearing?"

"Color of your dress? Why?" he asks, suspiciously.

"Please, just answer the question," I implore. Images of the past charity events dance in my head. It's time to start putting the puzzle pieces together.

"You're starting to sound like you're in the courtroom. Maybe you should've been a lawyer instead of a doctor."

"Please, Dad... I just want to know."

"You're wearing a red dress. Now, are you going to tell me why that is so important?"

Well, there's one puzzle piece placed. Red dress, check.

"I-I just was curious, that's all." I feign innocence.

"I don't buy it. You never were into dressing up and all of sudden you want to know...what gives?"

"I've been..." I take a breath. "... having flashbacks."

"What kind of flashbacks?" he asks quickly.

"It doesn't matter."

"Of course, it matters. Tell me what you see."

I clear my throat. "Me in a red gown."

"That's it? Anything else?"

"A man in a suit. I can't see his face. Not completely." I twist my lips. "I'm sure it could've been any of the men you and Mom introduced to me that night."

"Hmm. I wonder what's triggering these flashbacks?"

"Mom's hosted about five of these things and last Christmas was the first time we skipped it. Maybe the stress of planning it without her."

"Are you saying you're not up to hosting this year's event? If not, you should have Stacey—"

"I can do it. I *want* to do it. These women and children need this event, need me...and we need the donations."

"Your mother would be so proud of you. I certainly am. Picking up where she left off."

"Yes." I know this, too. "I've swindled Feebs and Ry to participate in the dating auction."

Dad chuckles. "How'd you pull that off?"

"Let's just say there's a wager riding on this." My mouth turns up.

"Whatever works. With Phoebe being the new face for Channel 3 Primetime Media and Ryland's family history, you'll be sure to raise some money for the event."

"I already have about ten stunning women lined up for this. It will be a success, like it's always been."

"Yes. It always is." Dad clears his throat. "Pumpkin, I wanted to ask about…Julian Cruz?"

I jolt at the mention of his name. *Well, this conversation is unexpected. Does Dad know about us?*

Dad would go ballistic if he knew about Julian and I, and would most likely fire him.

"Um… He's okay. Why do you ask?"

"Heard he did some improvements around the house."

"Oh… I guess so. He installed a home security system. Was that your idea?"

"Yes. I thought it would be a good investment. He's not just the handyman. He's also paid to drive you around. That is a non-negotiable."

"Wha-why?"

"Because I'm paying him to do it. That's why."

Needing to know more about Julian and who he really is, are questions maybe Dad can answer. I only know of his family and the fact that he was in the Navy.

But what else makes him tick?

Why the emotional switch?

Whenever I look in his eyes, there's a deep-seated mystery.

Where is he from?

Is he temporary or a permanent hire?

"Dad, why don't *you* tell me about Julian. How much do you know about him?"

Silence stretches through the phone line, as if Dad's trying to summon the answer. "Enough to know he needed a job. He's ex-Navy, married I think…"

A woman's voice echoes in the background. "Mr. Channing. Charles Fremont is on line three. He said it's important that he speaks with you."

"Thank you, Martha. Give me a second," Dad tells his secretary. "Pumpkin, I've got another call I need to take."

Chauffeur? Hogwash. Dad hired Julian not knowing more about him? Unlike him.

I recall a conversation I had with Dad and why Sam had to accompany me on this trip. *Incognito babysitter.* But Sam had been so preoccupied with Sage, maybe this was Dad's creative sham to hire a backup babysitter. Or, in laymen's terms, a bodyguard.

But why? What is Dad not telling me?

"This conversation is not over, Dad."

"It is for now. Call me sometime, will you? I'd like to know you're doing okay over there. I love you, Pumpkin."

"Love you too." I hang up. With my cell still in my hand, I tap the edge of the phone softly on my chin, deep in thought.

Married? And maybe another babysitter...or bodyguard?

At least that's something. Is this why he's been acting distant?

A shift in the air sprouts goosebumps up my spine. "Jiminy Christmas," I gasp, my hand on my chest. "You really need to stop sneaking up on me like that."

"Sorry. I didn't mean to startle you." Julian walks around and stands in front of me. "I ran into Ryland and Phoebe out front. Are you okay?"

My God! He really is beautiful. His tan olive skin, dark brown eyes, and chiseled jaw with just enough shadow it makes the butterflies in my tummy take flight. Broad shoulders and muscular corded arms. Julian smiles, flaunting his sexy-as-hell dimples I adore so much.

Hmmm...my flashback... Dimples?

I pull the towel over my stomach, hiding my scars. "I'm fine. I just got lightheaded. I blame Ryland's famous sangria."

"You didn't want to go skydiving?"

"Honestly...not really. It's Phoebe's idea and a dare on her part. I like my feet planted right here." I pat my foot on the cushion.

"May I?" Julian asks, pointing to the opposing lounge chair.

"Sure. Have a seat."

Julian sits across from me. His elbows on his knees and fingers clasped together. He's wearing a pair of board shorts and his white t-shirt clings against flexed biceps and broad shoulders. Everything about Julian screams sex appeal and mystery.

I focus on Julian's hand. I don't see an untanned ring line around his finger as some sign of a wedding band. In the back of my mind, I wonder about Julian's wife and why they were no longer married.

Does he still love her? Do they have children? How long were they married? Why aren't they together anymore?

"Want to tell me about them?" Julian asks.

"Tell you about what?" I angle my head, wondering what in the world he's asking about.

"Your flashbacks." He raises a brow.

"Did anyone ever tell you it's not nice to eavesdrop?"

"Did anyone ever tell you not to bottle things up? That it's good to talk about things?"

"Pot, meet kettle." I chide.

"What's that supposed to mean?"

Give and take.

I'm not one for games, but if Julian shows me a piece of what he's hiding in that proverbial locked box of his, then maybe I will open up my box, just for him. The one question burns in my mind.

Why is it so important to know more about him? The answer is simple, but yet not so. Am I falling in love with Julian Cruz? No, too soon. Right?

I have to take a step back. No pretenses, no expectations.

I revel in the moment and enjoy the time I've had with him. Julian has somehow breached the walls that have been protecting my heart. But when the time comes for us to part ways, I have to be strong enough to say goodbye.

The heel of my hand presses against my chest, coddling the rising ache. I can't bear another *heartbreak*. And I know I will not be able to recover from this one.

CHAPTER

Eighteen

Julian

S AM AND THE WOMEN ARE BARRELING through the kitchen, then through the sliding-glass window that leads to the pool area. It looks as if they're going to be out all day with oversized beach bags in their hands.

I look over to Chloe, still in her bikini, laid out on the lounge. She's covered her scars with the towel, and I grit my molars, knowing exactly how she got them.

I sit across from her and take her all in. Sexy long legs and smooth tanned skin. I force a swallow down my throat as a strong desire rings straight to my balls at the sight of her taut nipples peeking through her white bikini top.

Damn, get a hold of yourself.

"You're here," Sam pipes out, ripping me from my gaze. "Take care of my cousin, yeah?"

I clear my throat. "Always," I say as I look up at Sam and give him a chin lift. I turn back to Chloe, crease my forehead. "Are you sure you don't want to go?"

"Personally, I think she wanted to get out of my dare to skydive," Phoebe says, hand on her hip.

Ryland speaks up, sliding her sunglasses over her face. "Maybe if you're feeling better, you two could meet us at the bar later tonight?"

Chloe looks up at her friends. "Maybe. I'll let you know."

"Thanks for your ticket, Chloe," Sage says. "I'm not one for skydiving either. But there's a first for everything."

Chloe smiles. "You're welcome. Glad it wasn't a complete waste."

Sam trusses the backpack over his shoulder. "Alright, ladies. Enough chatting... Let's go. We're going to be late for our slot. And this place is on the other side of the island."

Ryland kisses the top of Chloe's head. "I'll call later to check on you."

"Okay. Love you and have fun." Chloe waves at them as they leave us alone with the sun on my back and Chloe looking ever so gorgeous with her brown hair dancing in the breeze.

There's a stretch of awkward silence between us. I didn't want to drop the subject of her flashbacks. Something triggered them. What was it that she remembered? Was it her attacker?

"So why aren't you really going?" I ask again.

"I had one too many of Ryland's toxic sangrias and I got dizzy."

"Hmm... I don't buy it. Your flashbacks made you dizzy, didn't they?"

"How would you know about that?" Chloe raises a brow.

"I know all about flashbacks, Chloe," I admit. "I was a SEAL—I've done and seen unspeakable things." I stand and walk to the edge of the pavement, my hands on the railing, taking in the open skies and dark blue sea.

"After every deployment, it was mandatory we talk to a shrink," I continue.

I hated sitting in that God-awful plastic chair for several hours to recall and spit out the horrid images. Sounds and scents of gunfire, the bloodbath and the screams of all humanity.

Maybe my brain is fucked up. But deployments kept my mind occupied from thinking about Amber. I needed to be on the missions, the damn flashbacks of my dead wife would stay out of my head. My bloodstained hands holding her in my arms, the sound of her voice and the last of her breath stings my psyche.

I look out to the calm ocean, hiding the distraught look I'm sure is in my eyes. I rake my fingers through my hair and take a deep breath. My life means nothing without her. Amber was my reason to live.

So, yeah, I guess my head is fucked up. Even the doctor suggested to my Commanding Officer that I take a leave due to being unstable. *Damn shrinks.*

Although I didn't agree with the therapist, I had no choice in the matter. I was trained to be calm under the most intense pressure, but after Amber's death, I was a killing machine, ruthless and suicidal.

Even my teammates voiced their concerns. After a month on leave, I returned and made them all think I took control of those demons.

I slowly turn to face Chloe. Her blue-green eyes meet mine. There's compassion in her gaze, and it comforts me. I don't deserve Chloe, but I can't bear the thought of anyone else having her, either. She most certainly doesn't deserve to be tangled with my demons that somehow resurfaced. She's worthy of so much more.

"Don't feel sorry for me, Doc."

"On the contrary. I think you're a hero."

"A hero?" I stifle a laugh.

"You risked your life, fighting evil around the world, protecting and serving our country." Chloe pauses, shifting her feet on the concrete. "So, do you still get flashbacks?"

"Not as much. But when I do, I know how to deal with them better."

"How?"

"I talk about them." I walk toward Chloe and kneel on one knee in front of her, my forearm resting on my leg.

"I don't want you to feel sorry for me," she says fidgeting with her nail.

"I would never." I brush back a wayward lock of hair behind her ear. "You have no idea what I think of you."

"Then tell me because it's killing me to guess what's going on in that thick skull of yours."

"Thick skull? I'll show you thick." I chuckle, lightening the mood.

"Seriously? You're going to go there?" Chloe smirks. "Always a comeback."

I need to set things straight. But I'm such a chicken shit. I know I'll lose her.

A fog of guilt clouds my thoughts at how I've masqueraded since our first meeting. I wanted to tell her I've thought about her for the last couple of years. And from the moment she'd rested her cute feet at my table, I was mesmerized.

How would she react to the truth?

Chloe could punch me in the jaw again and I would gladly accept it for keeping the truth from her. Laughing to myself, remembering how she played dirty taking her shirt off and leaving only her sports bra on. I could still feel the phantom pang.

Beautiful, sexy, strong, and she has a killer right hook.

I clear my throat needing to abate this conversation. "Tell you what. You hungry? Let's eat and I will tell you what I think."

With a tender smile, Chloe nods. "Promise?"

"SEAL's honor. Go get dressed and we can grab a bite to eat in town."

I start up the Jeep and head toward town. With the top off and the music playing, I glance over at Chloe. She's so damn adorable wearing her white Converses, cut-off jeans and red tank top.

I love how the sun kisses her cheeks. Her smile is so carefree and beautiful. The sight of her chestnut hair whipping around her face has my heart pounding.

"Oh my God. I love this song." She turns up the volume,

bopping her head side to side, and belts the lyrics at the top of her lungs.

"Somethin' unexpected has come over me... I got my heart, my soul and mind... Hm-mm..." She points her finger at me. *"You're the kind of guy I've been waiting for... I've got a crush on you... I think I'm in love..."* Chloe raises her hands, wiggling her fingers. *"Every time you're near, baby... I get kinda crazy... I don't know what to do."*

Chloe hums, shimmies her shoulders to the beat of the song.

The lack of connection for the last three days overwhelms me. It took every ounce of strength to hold myself back.

I miss the feel of her warm lips, her delicate body in my arms and the silky curls of her hair between my fingers. There are no words that could fathom my growing feelings and the gravitational pull she has over me.

A smile spreads over my lips and Chloe is the one who put it there. A smile I hadn't had in a long while. I love seeing her this way, happy and so relaxed.

I absolutely adore her. I've never had to struggle this much to resist a woman.

Not just any woman. Chloe Channing.

THE SURF-SHACK WAITER PICKS UP the menus after taking our order. We were lucky to get a table tucked in the corner of the large dining area and it allowed me to lean back against the wall and view the open space.

The crash of waves and the roar of tourists below carries to the upper deck. A humid tropical breeze coming from the shore, cools the beads of sweat trickling down the back of my neck.

Keeping my instincts in check, I assess every employee, the patrons at each table, points of entry and all emergency exits. With the latest information I received from Tyco, the ticking time bomb is out there, hidden in the shadows and Chloe's safety is my priority.

The waiter returns, tray balancing on one hand with a beer and Chloe's tropical drink embellished with a pineapple and umbrella floating atop. He places complimentary taro chips and special sauce for dipping on the table.

My cell buzzes with a text. And I can't help the anxiety that washes over me.

Lincoln: Call me. New intel.

"You look so tense. You okay?"

"Yeah, I'm fine," I answer, glaring at my phone. "It's just a text from a buddy."

Me: Busy. With the contract. Can it wait?

Lincoln: Ninety minutes. Then I'm calling your stupid ass.

Me: Ninety minutes.

"Is it important?" she asks.

"He's gonna call me later." I tuck my phone back in my pocket. "I hope this place is alright." I take a chip from the basket and pop it in my mouth.

"It's perfect." Chloe sips the pink liquid, then licks her lips. "So, tell me about your friend."

"Lincoln?" I tip my beer back. "He's like a brother. We met in basic training. Both of us, so young and wet behind the ears. We went through six weeks of hell."

When I graduated high school and joined the Navy, I found a brotherhood and camaraderie no one else would ever understand. And although the training was brutal, it was worth it.

"We nearly shit bricks when we first saw our commanding officer. My C.O. was scary as hell and fucking intimidating." I chuckle. "I swear, with one look, I knew that man could destroy me. I was either going to win or lose. I chose to win. My C.O. always said two things to us: 'The only easy day was yesterday,' and my favorite, 'If you feel pain, that means you're still alive'."

"Do you miss being a soldier?"

"First of all, we are not called *soldiers*… Sailor is the correct term."

"I stand corrected…so do you miss being a *sailor?*"

I play with the label of my beer bottle. "Sometimes. There was purpose for me. But now, I have a new purpose."

"Which is?"

I take in a breath, needing the stint of silence, careful of how I answer.

Was it the right time to tell her my job is to protect her? Feeling conflicted, I answer the best I know how.

"My new purpose is to make sure you don't think this is our official first date."

"Date? Did I agree to go on a date with you?" She curls a lock of hair behind her ear.

"Actually, Channing, I told you I would show you what a real date is like. You said you would check with your vacation planner. And all things considered, I think your vacation planner would be very accommodating and squeeze in one night out with me?"

"If this is not a date, what would you call this?" She twirls the umbrella floating in her glass.

"Friends having a casual lunch and a couple of drinks." I raise my beer and clink it against Chloe's tall glass.

"Is that what I am to you? A friend?"

And there it is, out on the table to be picked apart. I still for a second, my beer halfway to my mouth.

"Chloe, you are more than a friend to me." I lick my lips and tip the bottle back. "And you know it."

This assignment is eating me up and the conflict is fucking with my head. Having one of the guys replace me has crossed my mind. But, as much as I can easily get a replacement and get the hell off the island, I can't do it.

I can't bear the thought of letting her go, again. Chloe's more than just a call of duty.

Chloe levels her gaze on me. "You can't say that to me and act the way you have been the last couple of days."

I stare deep into her eyes. The glare she returns scares the hell out of me, as if she can see the truth.

Shit would hit the fan if I just blurt out how I was hired as her protector from some unknown threat that could be roaming the island.

"I guess we'll just get to the heavy stuff before the main course is served."

"I just need to know…why would you kiss me and then switch like it meant nothing to you?" Chloe says, her eyes pleading.

A hurricane of emotions swirls in my chest. I need to figure out how I can have her heart without breaking it.

"Like I said, I have a new purpose… Everything I do has a purpose."

"So that's it? That's your cryptic answer?" Chloe asks, narrowing her eyes.

I take a swig of my beer, stalling.

What can I say? That I've been having nightmares of Amber and her? Making love to both, then the next image, Chloe dead in my arms? And that my past and present are colliding, screwing with my head.

"What do you want me to say? I had shit I needed to figure out," I clip.

"Well, did you figure it out, Julian?" Her blue-green eyes wait for an answer I don't submit. "Can I ask another question?"

"Better than anyone I know." I take another swig of my beer and realize I may need another if our conversation keeps going at this pace.

Her lips twist and she leans forward. "Does it have anything to do with your wife?"

I freeze, nearly choking on my beer. "Where did… I mean, how do you know?"

"I don't mean to pry…actually, yes I do mean to pry. I have a right to know. You said all those things to me…wanted us to work out…making me believe we have a future. You kissed me and you're married? And that makes you a cheater. And I refuse to be the other woman."

A freight train hits me full force, guts all my emotions, as I need a moment to gather my thoughts.

"For Christ's sake, Channing." I peer over her shoulder, my eyes on the waiter coming toward our table. I'm rattled by Chloe's knowledge of Amber. And I'm not able to get a word in edgewise. "Please. Give me a minute…this isn't as easy for me to answer."

Silence hangs between us as the waiter places our burgers in front of us. From his stained apron, the man retrieves a bottle of ketchup, mustard, extra napkins and sets them on the table, then scurries away to check on a family at the next table.

Will Chloe up and leave once she knows the truth?

The very thought of answering her question makes me sick and the thick burger doesn't look appealing. This is the one thing I never wanted to talk about with Chloe and should remain buried in the abyss of the deepest parts of me.

It's the reason I feel conflicted. A painful stab, the proverbial knife gutting my insides for betraying my dead wife the moment Chloe made a crack in my armor that surrounds my heart.

"Amber." I struggle to say her name, but I owe her an answer.

"I see…so there is a wife," she says softly, disappointment in her voice.

"It's a touchy subject for me. But you deserve to know the truth." I pinch the bridge of my nose. "Amber is…*was* my wife."

"Do you still love her?"

"With all my heart." I observe Chloe's eyes and I can see the hurt in them. They soften when I confess, "Amber died five years ago."

Silence ceases all her reaction. A hitch of her breath as she takes hold of my hand.

"Julian…I-I'm so sorry. I should've never…we don't have to talk about it."

Her comforting touch pulls out the demons I've tried so hard to exorcise. With that one angelic look, one healing touch, Chloe seems to rip them out and shred them into a million pieces.

"It is hard to talk about it. Like you said the other day, talking about it keeps her alive." I watch a passing waitress.

Chloe nods. "We don't have to."

"This thing I needed to figure out…it wasn't just about Amber. It was you."

"Me?"

"I haven't been able to open my heart since she died…till I met you."

"I don't understand. What are you saying?"

I bring her hand to my lips. "You had me from the first moment we met. You are all I think about. You're like my personal medicine, Doc."

"Julian," Chloe whispers. "I don't know what to say."

I stand and round the table. I pull her up and off her chair, cup her face and gently kiss her lips I missed so much.

Is it wrong to kiss her, all the while keeping yet more secrets from her?

"I've missed you," I whisper.

AFTER LUNCH, WE WALK AROUND town. Our conversation is lighter and upbeat. She tells me about her childhood, and I share funny stories and the pranks I played on my teammates when I was a SEAL. It's like a heavy boulder has been removed from my shoulders, which I had carried for so long.

Chloe looks so beautiful walking next to me, where she belongs. After Chloe purchased souvenirs for Celina, her coworkers, and her dad, we enter a jewelry store.

Chloe gazes at the trinkets and fine jewelry inside the glass cases.

I lean in close. "See something you like?"

"What a lovely piece," she says, her finger pressing on the glass.

I call for the clerk behind the counter, "Can she try it on?"

"Of course," the sales lady says.

"Oh no. I'm just browsing."

"Nonsense," the lady says, unlocking the case. The dark woman smiles tenderly, pushing back her long, braided hair as she holds up a key and points to the glass.

"I believe when our jewelry grabs your attention, it's for a reason…and must be tried on. It's like a calling. Now, which piece did you like?"

"The green and blue turtle shell," Chloe tells her.

"Ahh, yes…the turtle has so much symbolic meaning." The woman holds it up for Chloe.

"Oh?" Chloe turns to allow the woman to lock the clasp behind her neck.

"Yes. For one, the turtle reminds us to take life slowly. Just look." The woman gestures to the small mirror on the counter.

I snicker at that. "Ma'am, we can relate to *pace*," I joke, catching Chloe's half-smile in her reflection.

"It also symbolizes longevity, endurance, emotional strength, and protection," the woman continues.

"That's beautiful," Chloe says, peering closer in the mirror.

I stand behind Chloe as she admires the sparkling jewelry. *"You're beautiful,"* I whisper.

A blush of pink tints her cheeks. "Pace, huh?"

"Like I said, your pace, sweetheart."

"If my memory serves me correctly, Mr. Cruz…you changed the pace on us. Remember?"

"Well, the pace changed when you took a hold of my heart and healed it, Doc." I kiss her cheek.

The clerk coughs to steal our attention. "Should I wrap it for you to take home today?"

Chloe shakes her head, removes the necklace and hands it back. "Oh, no. But thank you for letting me try it on."

"You don't want it?" I ask.

"I think it's a beautiful piece, that's all."

"But you like it."

"Just because I like it doesn't mean I'm going to buy it." Chloe moves to the exit.

"Then I'll buy it for you," I tell her as my phone rings, and I take it out of my pocket. *Shit. Lincoln.* "I have to take this. It's Lincoln."

"You're not buying it," Chloe insists. "Understood?"

"You're being a brat," I tell her, as my phone rings again.

"Yes, I know... Now take your call." Chloe kisses my cheek. "I'll be next door. I saw a sundress in the window I want to try on. Maybe I'll buy that one."

I nod with a smirk on my face. "I'll meet you there."

I force myself away from Chloe and watch her enter the other store. I swipe the green icon. "Your timing is impeccable, stupid ass."

"Well, hello to you too, sweet cheeks," Lincoln teases. "For the record, I'd rather watch paint dry than shadow this douche-canoe. Anyway, he booked a charter. He's on his way to you."

"When?"

"His flight leaves in a couple of hours and he got a room at The Atlantis. Tyco is tracking his cell phone and credit cards. We'll know his every move." Lincoln's irritated voice sounds through the line. "Why am I watching this fucker again?"

"He's Chloe's ex-boyfriend. A possible threat and I don't like him."

"You don't like him?" Lincoln asks. "You fell for her, didn't you, asshole?"

"Fuck you, Linc."

"You're not my type, pretty boy... So?" Lincoln will continue to nag, like a damn gnat, till I give in. "I'm waiting."

What could I say? She's my heartbeat, the lifeline I've been searching for. But I'm not about to let Lincoln know that.

"Is Jensen coming alone?" I ask.

"Nice way to avoid my question. He's got a woman with him. Tyco is running her name."

"Keep me posted. I want to know every move he makes. This prick is not to come near Chloe. If I see him, so help me God, I will beat the living shit out of him, cut him up into pieces and hide his body parts all over this goddamn island."

"Slow down, Hercules. I really think you need to explain yourself."

"Linc, she's my responsibility. I will protect her at all costs. And that's all the explanation you need."

"Fine. You want to play it that way—I'll be seeing you soon. I'll text you once I've landed. Lincoln out."

CHAPTER

Nineteen

CHLOE

"HELLO. EXCUSE ME," I SIGNAL, trying to get the attention of the salesclerk engrossed in her cell phone rather than the customers roaming the boutique. I walk up to the young lady leaning over the counter. I peek at the employee's name badge pinned to her blouse.

I clear my throat. "Jenny…do you have this in a size four?" I ask, holding a purple sundress with pink and yellow tropical flowers.

Jenny looks up at me, then at the sundress. With a nervous smile, the young lady tucks her phone in her back pocket. "Um…sorry. I think so. I will have to check in the back. Give me a sec." Jenny disappears to the back of the store.

I circle a rack, riffling through more dresses.

Not my color. Too short. This one's nice.

By the time Jenny returns with the size-four dress, I have another dress and a couple of blouses over my arm.

"Did you want me to start a dressing room for you, ma'am?"

"Yes, that would be wonderful…also, do you have this in black? I only see an orange and pink one out here."

"We just might. We got a shipment this morning. It will take me some time to go through the boxes. I can doublecheck," Jenny says.

"Thank you."

"Be right back." Jenny smiles and scoops up the dresses from my arm and retreats again to the back of the store.

A ding sounds from my cell.

Ryland: How are you feeling?

Me: Better. Went to lunch with Julian.

Ryland: Will you be able to meet us for drinks later?

Me: I think so. So much to tell you.

Ryland: Like?

Me: He was married.

Ryland: What? Holy hell. What else?

Me: Long story. She died years ago.

Ryland: Damn. Now what's up with you two?

Me: I'm letting my hair down.

Ryland: It's about time. We are next to board the plane. Tell me more tonight.

Me: Don't splat on the ground.

Ryland: Not funny.

Me: LOL. See you later.

Ryland: Laters.

I tuck my phone back in my purse.

Phoebe has planned dinner and dancing for my birthday in a few days and this is the perfect time to shop for an outfit now that my spirits are lifted. The silver lining finally peeked over the horizon with Julian opening up about his past.

As comfortable as I am, a dozen thoughts still roam my mind.

Knowing more about his naval career, his friend, Lincoln, and what makes Julian who he is, warms my heart. Julian opening up about his wife is also a step forward and it explains why he's been so distant the past couple of days.

Definitely two steps forward…

But there's one piece still missing.

I can't place his face and where I've seen him before. It's within my reach yet so far away. For now, I'm going to accept this break-through and hope the more time I spend with Julian, something will click.

It has to, everything else is.

I hum to the lyrical melody I sang in the Jeep on the way to town. Seeing Julian's smile, dimples and all, made my heart skip. Singing softly, I sweep through another rack of blouses while I wait for Jenny to return. *Somethin' unexpected has come over me… I got my heart, my soul and mind… Hm-mm…*

I look out the window and he's still on the phone. Butterflies swarm in my belly and an emotional tingle curls down my spine just thinking about him.

Am I in love?

I suck in my bottom lip, thinking how foolish that sounds. It's asinine when it took me months to figure out if I loved Luke and even at the end of that relationship, I still wasn't sure I truly loved him.

Fumbling through the clearance bins, a sudden chill seeps into my bones and the hairs on my arms stiffen. The stench of cigarettes fills the air. A familiar smell; it suffocates my nostrils.

My instincts whisper to leave the store. My steps falter when I bump into a wall of a man.

"Excuse me," I apologize, trying to skirt around him.

I jolt as a rough hand yanks at my arm, holding tight. "Don't turn around and don't make a fucking sound." His voice is low and evil. "Feel this?" *A gun.*

Tears threaten as I swallow, then nod, not able to get any words out.

"You're going to be a good little girl and we're going to walk out of this store nice and quiet. Don't try anything stupid," he murmurs dryly. "My boss has been waiting for you."

Oh my god. Oh my god. It feels like I'm reliving a moment, the morning I was attacked. Only it's broad daylight and I'm in a women's clothing store. I want to scream, but nothing comes out.

"Drop. Everything," he says, the gun digging deeper in my back.

I do as I'm told, dropping my purse and shopping bag.

I take a deep breath and then comes a flash: my attacker's gaunt face, brought to life. The knife, the stench of his breath, those harrowing eyes.

Is this that man?

I want to see his face—maybe something would trigger my memory from that morning's attack. Piece it all together as one.

Inching our way to the door, I try to glance at the full-length mirrors scattered throughout the store. But with the tight hold the asshole has, I only get a quick glimpse of his ball cap and sunglasses covering his face.

I want to scream, a plea for help. The other shoppers have no clue of what's happening.

My heart shutters and my insides tighten. I choke back a sob and the bile that is creeping up my throat.

"Shh…it'll be over soon." The man's grip holds firm under the crook of my arm.

I search anxiously for the meaning behind his words. "Wh-who are you?"

Tears assault my eyes, blurring my vision as I try to rationalize with the asshole jabbing the hard metal against the backside of my ribs.

I wince, biting back the pain. My hands shake and my feet feel like boulders with every step forward.

"What do you want from me?"

"Shut up, bitch...no more talking." His chuckle is low and threatening.

My stomach heaves at his awful breath as his body is pressed against mine.

His nose touches my earlobe as he whispers in my ear, "You've been a bad girl and my boss is very disappointed." His fingers dig deeper into my bicep. "Open the door nice and slow. Once outside, move to the right. There will be a black delivery van where my partner is waiting for us."

I reach for the handle and ease the door open. This is a time to step up and get a grip. Because once I step outside those doors, into the crowd and in the black van, I know I'm a dead woman, for sure.

I have to be brave, shove my fear aside. I know I'm not the strongest, by any means, but I can try the MMA moves Julian showed me. But this asshole has a gun and he's much more powerful than I am.

Julian didn't show me any moves against an armed captor. If I kick or punch him, he could easily pull the trigger. But would the asshole risk it in public? This is a chance I'm willing to take. I have to.

Fight or flight.

Humidity hits my face the moment we step out of the store, then my stomach churns with panic. Every step the gunman takes, I'm forced to do the same.

I look around for Julian but he's nowhere to be seen.

The roar of tourists floods the small town and my anxiety rises when I see the van. It's parked in the alley about fifty yards ahead. Fear surges through my body, my heart racing to keep up.

Think, Chlo, think.

Just ahead, a group of Asian tourists wearing bright green shirts with the same logo on it is approaching us. The perfect diversion. I suck in a breath and count backward from ten.

Ten, nine, eight, seven, six, five, four, three, two, one…
Now!

I throw myself into the Asian man who's waving his yellow flag. My captor's grip slackens as I tumble over, holding on to the Asian man. The tourists gather around as I force him to roll on top of me, a protective barrier between myself and the man holding the gun. I hold the unsuspecting man for dear life, as tight as I can. My human shield.

"You *bitch*," my would-be captor hisses. "You'll pay for this."

Sweat forms over my temples, the world spinning around me. A ceaseless ring strikes my ears. The rumble of people mutes, voices fade in and out.

Then, only darkness.

"You're next… There's a black van…"

"There's no such thing as a hunky, secret-undercover agent who will come to my rescue."

"My boss has been waiting for you… It'll be over soon…"

"Do you need to be rescued?"

"You've been a bad girl and my boss is very disappointed. You'll pay for that, bitch."

"Hi. I'm Chloe Channing."

"I like your babbling."

"Sounds like you may need someone to give you a foot massage."

"Booker… it's just Booker… Booker… it's just Booker…"

. . .

I LURCH AWAKE AND BOLT UPRIGHT TO AN UNFAMILIAR ROOM. I'M disoriented. I rub my eyes to clear my vision.

Where am I?

The last thing I remember is my captor lodging a gun in my back. My heart races as I scan the bedroom. I must have passed out and my attempt to get away was a fail.

I gotta get outta here.

I turn on the lamp next to the bed. At the corner of the room lay my Converse and my duffle bag that was once in my bedroom closet. Now I'm really confused.

I shuffle out of bed, quickly slip on my shoes and open the duffle, taking inventory.

Shirts, shorts, jeans, panties, bra, toothbrush.

Someone obviously packed for me. But who? And where am I going? Whoever wants me must want me alive if I'm going on a trip.

Voices come from the other side of the door. I press my ear against the wood.

Two men. Talking. And fear strikes me as footsteps ricochet closing the distance, coming closer to the room.

My mind is spinning. Desperate and anxious, this time I'm ready. I have to be.

The door opens and I throw an uppercut to the man's jaw and kick him in his groin. The man tumbles to the floor, hands between his legs.

"Fuck," he grumbles.

I seize the opportunity to escape since he's down for a minute, or ten. I run down the hall and collide into a hard chest and muscular arms that wrap around my body.

"Let me go, asshole!" I yell, wiggling out of his grasp. "Get off me."

"Doc, calm down." A familiar voice that immediately calms my panic.

I look up. His hand curves at the base of my neck, the other at the small of my back.

Our eyes meet.

"It's me." Julian rubs my back, pushing back the hair from my face.

I just stare at him as my lips fall lax.

Now I'm more confused than anything else.

What is Julian doing here? Is he the other man that was waiting in the van?

All these questions and I can't fathom a single thought racing in my head.

"What are you doing here? Where am I? The guy in there..." I point to the bedroom as I ramble anything that spits out of my mouth. "Who is that?" My breathing evens as I try to calm my panic.

"Lincoln," he answers.

Julian's friend? Was he the one with the gun? None of this is making sense.

"You're safe here. I promise." Julian's voice comforts me. "I'll explain everything—"

"Holy fuck, woman," Lincoln yelps, wobbling down the hall. "Did Booker teach you how to hit like that?"

"Booker?" Whiplash. I spin my head to Lincoln then to Julian as he closes his eyes and presses his lips together.

The Hoover Dam has cracked wide open and the memories flood my thoughts.

"Do you need to be rescued? It's just Booker... Booker... just Booker..."

Julian is Booker.

Booker is Julian.

The flashing images and dreams that had pestered my mind have finally collided.

Anger and confusion ball up as all the missing pieces finally fall into place.

I push out of his arms and lean against the wall, hand pressed over my stomach, feeling nauseated.

I squeeze my eyes shut. It's as if I'm sent back in time, two years ago at the gala fundraiser. The scene replaying in my head.

Holiday music in the background.

Beautiful gowns and bowties all around.

Waiters carrying champagne flutes.

Laughter and chatter filled the air.

The vision of Mom as she gracefully rubbed elbows with the elite, pecked cheek to cheek and flattered all the guests. I followed suit as Mom introduced me to every eligible bachelor in attendance.

Dad stood closely, displeased with Mom's matchmaking scheme. I am his princess, after all.

"No one will ever be good enough for you, Pumpkin," Dad whispered, but loud enough for Mom to hear.

"Frank, that's why you're here. One cough for yes, two coughs for no." Mom winked. "Remember?"

"My sweet Sarah, everyone will think I have a cold. It will be two coughs every time."

"Okay, you two." I scoop my arm in the crook of Mom's elbow. "I know how to find my own man."

"Well, dear. Can you please hurry?" Mom chided. "Your future husband is here... I feel it. You need to get me some grandchildren soon."

My eyes veered to the ceiling as I rolled them. "If it's meant to be, Mom...it'll happen."

The evening's event wasn't about finding my Mr. Right, it was about the children and the women. But, to humor Mom and satisfy her matchmaking, I played along.

Some of the men were too consumed with their careers, their money, looking for someone to wrinkle their sheets, needed a trophy wife, too young, too old, too boring. But after the umpteenth suitor Mom pawned off to dance with me, not only were my feet throbbing, none of the men had sparked my interest.

I snaked a flute from a passing waiter's tray and downed all the bubbly champagne to take the edge off. Needing the respite from Mom's endless introductions, I snuck away and exited the ballroom.

It took me but a second to notice the attractive specimen standing at the check-in desk. I surveyed his broad shoulders and tight ass in his tailored black slacks.

Sophisticated. Drool-worthy.

I got a glimpse of his profile, chiseled jaw, dark chocolate hair with the adorable messy-spiked look and his megawatt smile that flaunted sexy-as-hell dimples. I could barely manage to pull away from his gorgeous face.

Hello, sexy suitor.

It was impossible to resist his gravitational pull. The man exuded a raw power, owning his surroundings. There was darkness and mystery I wanted to uncover.

My heels clicked forward, straight to where he stood. I surveyed his hands.

No wedding ring: check.

I leaned against the table, played with the heel of my shoe and mumbled to myself, desperate to steal the man's attention.

He let out a cough.

Got his attention: check.

I glanced at him through my lashes, gave my best flirty smile.

The air was electric, making every hair stand on my hypersensitive skin. Our eyes locked and his penetrating gaze commanded my attention. My breath hitched seeing him up close and personal.

My perfect Adonis was all I could think of.

The man looked like a model fit for the cover of *GQ magazine.* The scent of his clean, crisp cologne carried to me.

Handsome and smells good, too? Check and check.

Butterflies swarmed in my tummy. There was an instantaneous chemistry that couldn't be ignored.

Was he the type of man I could fall for?

I held out my hand. "I'm Chloe."

The corners of his mouth curled up, showing off his to-die-for dimples. "Booker." His low, gravelly voice sent warm waves spiraling through me, seducing me in one look, one word. His large hand engulfed mine.

Booker?

The vision of the past faded, while my name echoes and rings in the background.

"Chloe, you okay?" Julian asks, rubbing my arm.

I slowly open my eyes.

At first, words fail me as I come to standing in Julian's arms...or should I call him Booker?

My stomach turns upside down, a tension knotting in my abdomen. My head spins, temples pounding.

Confusion tightly woven together with my anger.

The clouds of emotions, overanalyzing the past several days, has come into fruition.

"The gala." I begin to pace the wood floor, pushing back my errant hair. "Julian, you were there. I mean Booker…it was you. Oh my god…it was *you* this whole time. You knew, and you didn't say a word. You lied." My hard stare pins him motionless. "You're not just the handyman or the chauffeur."

"Dude, what the hell is wrong with her?" Lincoln asks, adjusting his crotch.

"She rambles when she's nervous."

Blood boils in my veins.

I step closer, raise an eyebrow in disbelief.

My hand balls into a tight fist as it sails over his jaw. "*You asshole.*"

CHAPTER

Twenty

Julian

"**D**AMMIT, CHLOE." I RUB THE sting in my chin.

"Ouch." Chloe winces and shakes her fist out. "I hope that hurt you more than it hurt me."

I give a half-cocked smile she doesn't deserve. Mom always told me my jaw was made like a tank. "You're gonna need to ice your hand, Doc."

Chloe's bottomless eyes lock with mine in a high-voltage stare. *I deserve it.*

Silence hangs in the room for a moment.

The only sound is Lincoln's footsteps that echo toward the kitchen. Lincoln grabs a hand towel from the counter and ice from the freezer and bundles up a makeshift icepack.

Lincoln coughs with wide eyes, breaking the awkward stillness.

"Come on, Miss Fists of Fury, let's sit," Lincoln says as he extends his hand, gesturing Chloe to the couch. "This icepack is really for me, but it looks like you need it more." Chloe flinches when Lincoln rests the icepack on her knuckles. "Glad those lessons paid off. You're lucky Tweedledee and Tweedledum didn't get a hold of you."

"Who?"

"The kidnappers," I quickly answer as I turn and face the window. "I still fucked up and those clowns got away."

I stare at the setting sun over the horizon leaving iridescent clouds of pink and orange in the sky. A small road leads up to the secluded safe house hidden in the hills and surrounded by palm trees. Just like the estate, the safe house is secured, and a few cameras keep watch around the perimeter.

My new orders are to keep her here and out of sight for the next few days.

"I need my phone," Chloe says. "I need to call Ry—"

"Your phone is gone," I tell her, casting a veiled stare when I turn to look at her.

"What do you mean, my phone is gone?"

"I needed to disable your phone. With all the different apps to find you, we can't take any chances. We've got people looking at who tried to take you."

"Why would someone want to take me?" Chloe's forehead creases.

Lincoln speaks up, "Sweetheart, that's what we're trying to figure out...can you tell us what they said to you?"

"Not much. Just that their boss has been waiting for me."

My stomach twists, fury boiling in my veins as I look at the scratches on her arms and the ice pack on her hand. All reminders of how I found her on the ground outside the shop. One slip is all the kidnappers needed and I fed it to them on a silver platter.

Now, Tyco's been working diligently tracking down Tweedledee and Tweedledum, hoping to get a lead to the unsub. He hacked into the street cameras only to discover the black van had no plates and a bearded Tweedledum wearing sunglasses and a cap waiting in the driver's seat for Chloe.

Tyco had also retrieved the boutique's CCTV cameras. Tweedledee, who had Chloe at gunpoint, overshadowed and overpowered her. He was over six feet tall, about three hundred twenty pounds and most likely redheaded from his goatee and sprigs of hair that peeked from his hat. It was clever for the unsub to have hired the two bozos to masquerade the unsub's involvement.

Lincoln juts his chin at me. "He's got new orders now."

"Orders?" Chloe asks, confusion written all over her face. And it fucking kills me that she has to find out this way.

"Linc, that's enough," I grumble. "You're saying too much." *She needs to hear it from me.*

Chloe's vacant eyes switch from Lincoln to me then back to Linc. "Can one of you please tell me what the hell is going on?" She purses her lips. "How can I be sure you guys aren't the ones who tried to kidnap me today?"

I sit in the chair opposite of Chloe and Lincoln.

Elbows on my knees, my head falls between my shoulders. Rage vibrates through me seeing the images of the large man running from the huddle of people and the screech of the van's tires burning rubber after the bastard hopped in the passenger seat.

Sheer black fright swept over me when I found Chloe's body lying still on the concrete. I had checked her pulse, looked for any wounds. I was relieved to see her breathing and unharmed with only a few scratches.

I lift my head, eyes locking on Chloe. "We are not the bad guys. You were knocked out on the ground when I found you. Then I brought you here."

"How long have I been sleeping?" she asks.

"A couple of hours, give or take," I answer softly.

"Tell me what's going on," Chloe huffs, then darts to Lincoln. "Why are *you* here?"

"First, let me formally introduce myself. My name is Dylan Marshall. But that idiot calls me Lincoln." He points his thumb to Julian.

"So, you're Lincoln." Chloe raises a brow.

He winks at her. "The one and only."

"Sorry about kicking you in the balls, Dylan."

"Yeah... I'm still feeling it." He shifts in his shorts. "But, you're forgiven, sweetheart."

"Why *Lincoln?*"

"Because I tell it like it is. No bullshit, no lies," he answers then glances my way.

"Then tell me like it is, *Lincoln*. Since your friend is full of bullshit and lies." Her eyes volley to mine then back to my friend.

"Chloe, I had no choice," I answer hoping she'll understand and forgive me.

"Everyone has a choice." Chloe rises from her chair still holding the icepack over her hand. "You lied to me, Julian…Booker…whatever the hell your name is." She walks into the kitchen, tosses the icepack in the sink making a loud thud. "Everything we talked about… You told me things…you made me believe you had feelings…" Chloe takes a breath. "Was that all part of your *orders*, too?" Her voice cracks.

I can hear the hurt lacing her tone and it kills me that I've been lying to her, except about my feelings.

"Nothing's changed. I'm the same person." I roughly rub my face. "I know you're shocked—"

"Shocked? That's an understatement. Words cannot begin to describe half the shit I'm feeling right now."

Lincoln stands, looking at his watch. "Oh wow, look at the time…it's getting late." He smiles at Chloe. "Fists of Fury, it was a pleasure…until next time. And I suggest you keep putting ice on your pretty little hand."

Lincoln walks to the front door, opens it and looks back at Chloe. "One more thing… Don't bust his balls. It's important to hear the whole truth. Booker, I mean Julian, really does care about you." Lincoln's eyes shift to me. "Hey man…go easy on her. She's had a rough day. I'll call you in the morning with an update." Lincoln gives me a chin lift and closes the door.

A veil of stillness sucks the air out of the room. I try to formulate words to say to her. But I can't. There is no getting out of this mess.

She needs to know the truth.

I rise from the chair and walk to the bedroom, leaving Chloe in the kitchen. I squat down, open the small door that reveals the safe. I punch in the code and turn the lever to open the heavy door.

It's time for her to know the whole truth.

I take the folder out and return to the kitchen, where Chloe still stands. Her arms cross over her chest. She narrows her eyes, looking at my hand and what I'm holding out to her.

"What's that?"

"The truth." I place the folder on the kitchen island. "I'm so sorry… I can explain—"

"The last time a man said that to me, I walked out on him." Chloe wipes a fallen tear. She slowly opens the folder and flips through the documents, police reports and photographs. "What the hell is all this?"

"Your father hired us to protect you. We've been shadowing you since your attack."

"Oh. My. God. Are you saying the man who tried to kidnap me is the same person who stabbed me?"

"We aren't sure. An associate of ours, Tyco, is looking into that as we speak."

"Tyco…Lincoln…and you. Who are you guys?"

I begin to tell Chloe about KSIG and my assignment. As expected, Chloe doesn't take it well. I anticipated it would be a clusterfuck once she found out the truth of who I *really* am. This mission is like walking on a road of shattered glass. No matter how careful my words are, I would still be cut with every step.

"You weren't supposed to find out this way. Or at all."

"Not find out? Are you kidding me? A freakin' maniac killed my mom and is now after me? And you're telling me I wasn't supposed to find out." Her cold voice raises.

"Your father wanted it this way."

"And did my father tell you to whisper sweet bullshit in my ear so I would fall for you?"

I want to look away, but I can't. She just told me she's fallen for me. I stare deep into her blue-green eyes, hoping she can see that I'll do anything for her.

"No," I mutter. "I meant what I said. From the moment I met you at the fundraiser, I couldn't stop thinking about you. The timing was all wrong—"

"And the timing is just so fucking perfect now, isn't it?" she clips.

I cup the back of my neck in frustration. "What do you want me to say, Chloe? I never lied to you."

"Last I checked, omission is a form of lying. And you've been lying to me since the moment I landed… Is your name really Julian or is that fake like our relationship?"

"Yes, that's my name. My *real* name. Is that what you think of us…fake?"

"I don't know what to think. I feel so numb." Chloe presses her fingers to her temples. "I need some time alone. This is just too much."

I nod in acceptance, but Chloe doesn't move. I cautiously step closer, hoping she won't shove me away again. I need to be close to her, need to touch her.

She's my weakness and my strength. She's alive and safe.

"Chloe, please." I take her hand, the one she punched me with, and kiss her knuckles. "Don't push me away. Please understand…"

"I need to take a shower. I can still smell that asshole's stench on me." Chloe pulls her hand back.

"I got a few of your things from the house."

"Why did you do that? Are we going on a trip?"

"We need to stay put for a couple of days."

"This is so surreal." She shakes her head. "I can't…"

"I am not going to put your life in danger again. I fucked up. I should've never taken my eyes off you." I swipe a fallen curl behind her ear. "Please, I need for you to trust me. There was a time you did, remember?"

"Right now, there are things I wish I didn't remember." Chloe presses her lips together, slowly turns on her heel and retreats down the hall, leaving me alone in the kitchen.

After a couple of hours, Chloe hasn't come out of the room. I softly knock on the door. No answer. I slowly turn the handle, open it a few inches. I whisper her name then scan the room. The lamp beside the bed dimly lights her body lying peacefully on the bed.

"Can I come in?" I ask, but she doesn't answer.

I round the mattress, seeing her eyes closed and the twisted towel still wrapped around her head.

Snuggled with the pillows, I pull the blanket and cover her.

Although I want to lie down and wrap her in my arms, I sit on the chair opposite of the bed. It kills me giving her the distance she demands.

I just stare at her and my lids become heavy.

I can use the sleep since it's well into the night, but I would rather take the pleasure of watching every breath she takes.

My heart aches knowing how I hurt her. Will she forgive me?

Emotions whirl inside me, cursing to myself more times than I can count. The day started out good and got even better until I let my guard down and the perfect storm ravaged the rest of the day.

The only reason I let Chloe out of my sight was to go back into the jewelry store. I asked the clerk to hold the necklace for me so I could buy it later.

Anger possesses me and all I can think about is getting my hands on the kidnappers. It guts me and my stomach knots knowing their intent to kidnap Chloe is to kill her. But why?

What is it about Chloe that makes me forget why I'm here? Never once had I failed a mission. I'm skilled in protecting my clients.

But Chloe isn't just a client, she's my reason to love again. All the more to keep my guard up. But I screwed up royally...for the last time.

My biggest fear is Chloe walking out of my life. I've been so lost, walking blindly until I found her. I rise from the chair and lower my head to kiss her softly on the cheek.

I love you, Chloe Channing.

I quietly close the door behind me, and I collapse onto the couch in the living room, prop up a pillow and tuck my arm under my head. My legs stretch over the length of the couch and my sluggish body sinks into the cushions as the weight of the world presses against my chest.

My sweet Chloe. I need to keep you safe. I can't let anything happen to you. This is a damn clusterfuck...fucking complicated like a Rubik's cube. What did I expect? That you would just jump in my arms and think the shit that I've been hiding would just be swept under the rug?

I fucked up... I should've told you. But I couldn't. I was under orders... damn case. I need you to trust me again. And what the hell is wrong with me? I haven't even made love to you and I just told you I love you.

But that's all it took. Her delicious kisses, her touches, and her scent.

I'm not going to lose you...not like I did with Amber.

Amber... Fuck, can I love two women, the woman of my past and the woman I hope will be in my future?

It is true.

Chloe is the first woman I've loved since Amber. My feelings for her go deeper than I ever imagined possible. The thought of almost losing her today validated just that.

Even though this woman has healed the wounds of my past, grabbing my heart and bound it to hers, my past is still here. I have to find a way, deep down, to say goodbye to her and move on.

CHAPTER

Twenty-One

Judge

"Judge." Red's nervous voice cracks through the phone line. "She um…got away and ran into the crowd. I couldn't risk it. There were too many witnesses."

"Did I hear you right? You lost her?" I hiss, drumming my red fingernails on the wooden countertop. "You idiots keep fucking things up for me. It's not like this is a hard job…all you had to do was grab the bitch and throw her ass in the van." I signal to the handsome bartender, lifting my empty short glass once filled with Scotch. "Bartender, another scotch on the rocks."

The bartender grabs a clean glass, drops a few ice cubes in it and fills it with the amber liquid. He places the scotch on a white napkin in front of me. I wait for the bartender to step away.

"Where is she now?" I ask.

"That's just it—we don't know. We've been camped out in front of the estate for hours and she hasn't arrived."

"Find her. You have two days. You don't get paid until this job is done."

"What if we can't find her?" Red asks.

"Consider our contract terminated and I go straight to the cops."

"Our chances of getting to her now are slim to none, boss. That boyfriend of hers—"

"I don't give a flying *fuck* about her boyfriend or her airheaded friends. Chloe's a problem and a loose end." My voice is slow and threatening. "Need I remind you? I have enough information on you two asswipes that I can have you put away for a very long time? I have the knife with your fingerprints that you stabbed Chloe with. And the proof your pathetic brother dropped off those pictures at her apartment."

"Yes, Judge...but—"

"No buts. *Find her,*" I order, hitting the red 'end' button on the disposable phone and dropping it into my clutch.

I square my shoulders, smooth my long hair. I'm a confident woman and I am not about to lose my shit over Red and Larry's sloppy mistake.

I stifle a laugh, love how those two idiots call me the *Judge.* I take pride in being just that...judge, jury, and executioner.

Everything was going according to plan until Red lost her. Nevertheless, I have my bases covered. I always have a backup plan and there's nothing that will trace back to me. I was pleased with Larry's driving skills when he rammed the truck into Sarah Channing's Mercedes. I was equally satisfied with Red stabbing Chloe even though he almost got caught by a Good Samaritan.

This time, Red and Larry's job was to snatch Chloe and take her to the docks.

I gave those idiots enough chloroform to render her unconscious once they got a hold of her. Once Chloe was captured, I wanted to make sure Chloe knew everything wrong about her not-so-perfect parents.

Sweet revenge is my reward, wanting to see Chloe break after revealing all the family secrets before killing her.

This kill, is what I am looking forward to and it would most definitely paralyze Frank for the rest of his life. *That bastard.*

I take pleasure in how easily I can have any man at my beck and call. Russell Kollsson was an easy target. He met me at the St. Regis Hotel for lunch on the notion I was a client to discuss business. But my flirtatious skills paid off with our many rendezvous at the very same hotel during his lunch and after work before going home to his wife and kids.

Cheating bastard. All men are cheaters.

Blackmailing Russell to gain access to Sarah Channing's bank accounts was too easy. But to later find out Chloe is the new account holder.

My plans took a different route. She's another loose end I need to kill off.

The evidence is in the banking information and it's just a matter of time before Chloe will figure out where the money was going…to me. And I'm a greedy bitch.

I want more.

Frank Channing. He ruined our lives. Mom, this drink is for you. Frank will feel the pain he deserves.

I take in a deep breath and hold up the glass, swirl the ice before imbibing another sip. It's not a drink to toss back in one gulp even though the temptation is there.

Scotch is a drink to appreciate, slow sips to savor the smooth flavor. Just like the perfect revengeful plan. All three, in a casket, six feet under, covered by dirt as they are meant to be.

"Another scotch, ma'am?" The bartender smiles with his warm hazel eyes. "And are you staying at The Atlantis so I can charge it to your room?"

"Yes. The Presidential Suite. Room 8920."

CHAPTER

Twenty-Two

CHLOE

FRESHLY BREWED COFFEE AND THE aroma of bacon welcomes my senses. The break of waves that can be heard through the open window slowly rouse me from my sleep. It takes me a moment to gather my bearings as I rub my eyes with the heel of my hands.

I blink a few times, adjusting to the sunlight sneaking into the room between the slats of the blinds and gray curtains.

I suddenly remember I'm not in my bed.

Drunk on last night's betrayal and revealed truths, I'm completely drained. I cried myself to sleep after the hot shower last night. I only wanted to lie down and rest my eyes for a little while, but the kidnappers played a helluva day on me.

I don't know how to feel anymore, so I sit here feeling alone as I take in the solace the room gives me.

The comfort of the bed, soft sheets and plush pillows tempt me to ball up and stay in bed all day. Although the grueling emotions wore me down, I have to find my strength to pull myself out of bed.

Without panic or anxiety, my patient eyes roam the plain room.

One large framed artwork of the beach decorates the stale tan walls. No other pictures, no décor.

Then it dawns on me, this isn't Julian's home.

A book on the nightstand catches my eye. I pick it up to read the title, then turn to the page where the bookmark peeks. A set of one-inch black-and-white pictures from a photobooth.

They are of Julian and a beautiful woman with gentle eyes and curls of ash-brown hair tumbling down her shoulders.

The first image, her enduring smile looking up at Julian.

The next, him looking at the woman.

The third, both of them making funny faces.

And the last, kissing each other.

I flip over the photo strip and read the inscription on the back. It warms my heart as tears sting the back of my throat.

'Jules, you're the reason I smile... I love you. ~Ambs'

This was his late wife. I gaze at each image and my fingers trace Julian's face. He looks the same, yet different.

His smile reveals his straight white teeth and those dimples that I adore so much.

Questions fill my mind. What was Amber like? How was their life together before she died? Could I ever be enough for him?

I slip the photo back within the pages and return the book back to the nightstand.

Is there any truth to what is stirring between Julian and I? Or is it all an act and part of his assignment? Just the thought of it breaks my heart because Julian is truly a great guy and I've fallen for him.

I take in a deep breath and look at the door. Julian is on the other side and sooner or later I have to face him.

Tension knots in my belly. I can't stay mad at him forever. He's only doing his job and I need to come to terms with it.

There's one other person who knew about me being in danger and I need to get in touch with him.

Dad.

How much did he know?

What else is my father hiding?

I'm sick and tired of being forced to look through rose-tinted glasses. His fatherly duties of protecting his only child are under-standably, his right. But to completely hide the fact that my life is at risk for the last several months is completely unacceptable. Dad still wanted to slay the monsters in my closet as if I'm the little girl I once was.

But this monster, Dad can't slay alone.

All this time, I've had an eerie feeling of someone watching me. There were warning signs. But it wasn't my paranoia taking a hold of me.

The postcards and the picture of me and Mom. My God, I feel so stupid —I should've paid more attention. Trusted my gut.

How could I have been so naïve not to realize a threat lurking beyond the shadows? Now, the truth lay right in front of me, vali-dating all of it.

I push off the covers and swing my legs over the edge of the bed. My bare feet touch the wood floor. I walk into the bathroom, look at my reflection in the mirror and gasp at the puffiness under my eyes from crying myself to sleep.

I turn on the faucet and splash water over my face. The coldness soothes my aching eyes. I brush my teeth, pile my hair in a messy bun atop my head, shrug and take a deep breath in.

It's now or never. Can't stay cooped up in this room forever.

I move quietly through the hall. The rise of Julian's voice piques my interest, curious who he's talking to. I stop at the end and peek around the corner to the open living room which leads to the kitchen.

He's talking on his cell phone. I draw back and lean against the wall to listen in.

"I'm not playing, Linc...yeah, I know, I know... I fucked up, man... Yes, I do, I really do care for her. But you know my rule... After I showed her the file. She knows everything... Any word from Tyco... Mm-hm... He needs to work on those magic fingers of his and pull a damn rabbit out of his hat and find this fucker...I'm going to keep her here for a couple of days until I hear from Tyco. And what's the news on your douche-canoe you're shadowing? Lying by the pool? Any word on the female companion?

Hmmm…alright, keep me posted…yeah, I'll let you know… Later, man."

It's strange how the floodgates opened, and all became clear to me of when we first met. All it took was Lincoln to blurt his name, *Booker,* and it rushed back to me with force. Our conversation outside the ballroom. How he made me feel with just a handshake and simple flirting.

I laugh to myself, thinking he was a *super-secret agent* coming to my rescue after all.

I peer around the corner again now that he's done talking on the phone. Standing in front of the stove, spatula in hand, Julian is flipping a pancake on the skillet.

There's something so sexy about him cooking.

The dominating package of the man moving around the kitchen is hot as hell. It's like watching a cooking show. A very sexy cooking show and I can't wait to try out the recipe. I press my lips together as I watch him take a sip from a coffee mug.

When I get a glimpse of his front, I'm pinned motionless, as I gaze at the cords of his abs and the oh-so-sexy 'V' that disappears beneath loosely fitted jeans.

He hijacks every thought to a place I've only fantasized about. How is he able to make me feel like this just by looking at him? The only answer is he's absolutely perfect.

I suck in my bottom lip, stand here in silence, watching him. My libido awakens; an aching throb between my legs. A bottomless craving overwhelms me.

Is it lust? Desire? Curiosity?

Or am I falling deeper and deeper in love with him?

I take a deep breath and analyze everything Julian had said to me since I landed.

"I would never hurt you… I want you, Chloe Channing… You're all I think about… We will go at your pace…"

Cupid's timing is less than impeccable and makes this situation so much more complicated. But my smile grows as butterflies take flight in my belly. I've fallen for him and the emotions wash over me like the tide outside the windows.

I clear my throat to get his attention. "Good morning," I say.

"Hey, how'd you sleep?" he asks, putting down the spatula. He pulls out a chair. "Come sit... I hope you're hungry. I made scrambled eggs, bacon and more pancakes than I should've."

"I'm starving." I sit in the chair and Julian scoots me in. "Thanks."

"Coffee?" he asks.

"Yes, please."

Julian pours hot coffee and creamer in the mug.

"How's your hand?" he asks as he hands me the mug.

I open and close my hand, gingerly fanning my fingers. "No broken bones. How's your jaw?"

"All good...see?" Julian smiles, wiggling his chin.

A giggle escapes. "Sorry I punched you."

"I deserved it. I should've been upfront with you. It's just that—"

"I get it. You had orders." I stare at the steam coming from the coffee. Am I too quick to forgive? Maybe I am. If I can only control my heart and let logic take control. But it's useless.

"You were right though...I did have a choice." Julian sips his coffee, leaning back against the counter. "I truly am sorry."

I can see he's sincere and there's hurt in his eyes, as if he's asking for forgiveness. And the brief smile that lifts the corners of his mouth, tells me he cares.

"I just hope you don't think differently of me now," he says.

Think different of you? Are you kidding? You're the man keeping me safe and trying to find out who's after me. You are my real-life secret agent, the one I've truly fallen for. This thing we have...only exists in the movies. Every time you look at me, it rattles a desire within me I didn't know I had. What's different is this chaotic pace has me running in circles, dizzying me. I thought of you so many times since I met you the night at the gala. Wondered if you would ever try to find me after, come look for me. I wanted to hate you for being a chicken-shit, for not seeking me out two years ago, now I want to love you for finding me again.

The words are stuck in my throat as tears well in my eyes.

"Doc?" Julian sets his mug on the counter, then kneels down so he's eye level with me. His thumb wipes my cheek to catch a fallen tear. "What's the matter?"

"I want to tell you something. So, please give me this time." I look down at my fidgeting fingers.

He pulls the other chair and brings it closer to me. "I'm listening," he says, his brown eyes making my thoughts falter.

All I can think of is how perfect this man is in every way.

I smile as I gaze over the food he cooked. And how he managed to get all my necessities from my bedroom to make me feel at home in this safe house. This man thought of everything, making my stay as comfortable as possible, knowing this situation is such a clusterfuck.

I've lost all train of thought, feeling winded at the sight of this beautiful man in front of me. And I know he will protect me no matter what. His ratted spiky hair is so adorable, and I want to comb my fingers through it. His clean-shaven jawline shows off the dimples on his cheeks, calling for me to kiss them.

I crave the feel of his lips to be on mine.

I lean in and my mouth meets his. It feels silly to be so forward, but this is the only way I can express how I feel without saying another word. I kiss him with a hunger that belies my outward desire.

He hooks his hand behind my neck and gently pulls me closer to him. My hands grasp his shoulders, my fingernails pressing into his skin. I part my lips and he takes the unspoken invitation. His tongue sends spirals of ecstasy, igniting a yearning desire within me.

The warmth of his breath makes me dizzy with emotion and the throbbing between my thighs grows stronger. The heady mixture of lust and love thunders in my heart, so loudly I swear I can hear it in my eardrums.

A moan escapes when I inhale the combination of soap and his crisp-clean cologne. He's intoxicatingly delicious. All my rationality flies out the window and an oddly primitive courage awakens all my senses.

Confidence seizes my legs as I rise from my chair and straddle over him, never disconnecting our lips. His erection is imminent as I rest my hips over his lap. I angle my head and our tongues dance in a passionate frenzy.

He groans as my fingers lace through his hair.

My breath hitches when Julian's warm hand sneaks under my t-shirt, touching the small of my back, sending sparks of heat up my spine. The feelings soaring through me are unfamiliar, yet my body welcomes it, calling for him.

I'm so turned on. I no longer have power over my body. The need to have him is unbearable as our kisses intensify and hands explore.

I need to feel him.

Skin on skin.

Disconnecting our lips for a mere second, I pull my shirt over my head, toss it on the floor. My lace bra meets his chest. A ball of emotion forms at the back of my throat, knowing I'm in uncharted territory.

It doesn't matter.

I want this, want him.

"Chloe." His silky voice holds a question I knew he would ask. "Are you sure?"

"Julian, I have never been so sure in my life," I reply, panting.

His assessing eyes take me hostage. Our ragged breaths are the unspoken words that make me feel more intimately connected to him.

What am I thinking? He still loves Amber. He carries her picture with him.

I shouldn't be doing this.

"I'm sorry," I say as I slowly edge myself off his lap. But his grip tightens at the small of my lower back.

"Uh-uh... You can't start something and try to get away... because I'm not sorry." He pushes a lock of hair behind my ear and his thumb caresses my cheek. "What happens after this, there's no turning back... You will be mine and I will never let you go."

"You promise?"

His lips crash onto mine, claiming me. The very thing I've been waiting for since we met at the gala.

CHAPTER

Twenty-Three

JULIAN

THE BEACH'S DISTANT-SOUNDING SURF echoes through the open window above the kitchen sink. Only our heavy breathing can be heard in the room. Being near Chloe tempts me to sink my concentration and self-control to the bottom of the ocean, breaking my last, and most primal, rule.

I need to stay focused on the mission, figure out who those bastards are and why they want to hurt Chloe. My orders are to keep her at the safe house for the next several days. But even I know this is the test of all wills.

The peachy scent of her hair invades my senses; those soft curls tickle my shoulders. I hold her close, pressing her softness against my chest. Damn, I can't get enough of her, needing and wanting to touch and taste her in every possible way.

I'm no longer *Booker*, the hired bodyguard, the protector.

I want to be what she wants me to be, *Julian Cruz*.

A hum escapes the back of my throat when I taste coffee and vanilla on her tongue.

Fucking delicious.

Chloe's innocent eyes and soft lips taunt me, and I am not about to deny her. We are secured in the safe house, away from reality for a while. The only thing that's no longer protected is the fortification that once surrounded my cold heart.

This woman decimated those walls and takes hostage of every thought, every fiber and every part of my soul.

Initially, I tried to resist her and should receive a medal for holding off this long. But there's no denying it any longer. The chemistry between us is undeniable and her gravity pulls me to her.

I've wanted this woman since day one and on so many levels. Then realization hits and invades my mind, a sting in my past pricks my thoughts. As much as I loved Amber, the guilt is finally dissipating.

Amber is no longer tugging at my heartstrings. Remorse and shame are no longer holding me back and choking my soul. The only logical reason I can think of why Amber is disappearing into the haze is that I love Chloe.

I want Chloe in my life.

Her legs circle my waist as I lift her and move towards the bedroom, one arm under her ass, the other bracing her neck. Our lips never disconnect, tongues licking and nipping one another as her fingers rake my hair, caressing the back of my neck, sending cataclysmic sparks right down to my groin.

I finally pass through the bedroom's threshold and my shins barely touch the bed. Gently lowering her to her feet, her taut nipples press through her lace bra against my chest.

The riot in my head and my pent-up sexual frustration is finally unraveling as her fingers fumble with the zipper of my jeans and she tugs them off.

My eyes flash to her cleavage.

I pull down the bra strap to hang loosely over her arm then lower the fabric over her breast. My mouth brands her perfect globes, nipping and licking one, then I work my way to the other.

"Julian," she purrs.

My name coming from her lips is the sexiest sound making my dick even harder, if that is even possible.

I trail my mouth to her sexy collarbone, then to the curve of her neck, back up to claim her lips. I reach behind to unsnap the clasps of her bra, the whisper of the fabric hitting the floor.

Her soft skin and perfect tits are now on display.

Fucking breathtaking.

My eyes never leave sight of her curves, savoring the vision of her body. I'm fighting every primal instinct. The temptation to rip off her cotton shorts and panties and fuck her every which way I can is worse than fighting a battle during my deployments.

I've waited too long. I need to go at her pace, nice and slow. I want to savor every taste of Chloe to satisfy not only her desires, but mine.

Chloe is the make-love-forever kind of woman, and not the fast-fuck-forget-my-past type.

My mind wanders to the condom in my wallet that took residence there for the last several months and I hope I won't explode before making her climax. Ever since her name appeared in the case file and I saw her picture, I haven't had another woman.

At first, Rocky assumed Chloe was one of my conquests. But Chloe is much more than that. Chloe Channing is my *last conquest*, my holy grail.

What the heart wants, the heart will get. And dammit, Chloe's here with me, the treasure of all priceless treasures.

A seductive gasp escapes her mouth, as my fingers trace the hem of her cotton shorts and I see the sprouting goosebumps on her creamy skin. I'm spellbound by her simple sighs and it's making me lose control. My balls tighten and my cock suffocates beneath cotton boxers.

My fingers slip under the pink elastic of her shorts and Chloe shimmies out of them, the girly fabric pooling at her feet. This woman in front of me is too good to be true, standing naked in all her beauty.

Sheer perfection.

I moan as her fingers draw lines down my sternum and over my abdomen, tracing the ridges of muscle to the front of my boxers.

"Here, let me help you with that," I whisper as I push down the cotton briefs and kick them aside, not caring where they land. My eyes roam over her body, my hands skimming her bare arm. "You're absolutely beautiful."

I cradle her face and pull her mouth to mine, reclaiming her lips again. My kiss is slow and measured. My mouth and tongue explore the soft fullness of hers. Luxuriating in each second of this moment.

"Julian?" her sexy kitten-voice purrs again.

"Hmm," I murmur between kisses.

"I've… I've never done this."

I pull away slightly, my eyes lock on her beautiful blue-green eyes, then I tuck a strand of hair behind her ear. "Done what, Doc?"

"I mean, I've never done *this*. You'll be my first."

The floor bottoms out.

She's never done this before?

"Are you sure?" I ask, dumbfounded by her confession.

"Am I sure you're my first?"

My mouth turns up and I softly chuckle. My fingers pull her chin, so she is looking up at me. "Are you sure you want—"

"I want you to be my first, Julian."

CHAPTER

Twenty-Four

CHLOE

MY DORMANT SEXUALITY AWAKENS AND the aching need for Julian is spiraling out of control as liquid heat warms my body like a blanket. Desperate desire to feel him, connect to and consume him is all I can think about.

There's a surging need, a rising want and intensified greed, pent up and crying to break free.

I trust Julian with every fiber of my being.

There's something intoxicating about him that makes me want to give every ounce of my vulnerability to him. And I know Julian will most definitely satisfy all my senses of pleasure.

Not only is my body ready and willing, but my heart is as well.

I'm hostage under Julian's impenetrable eyes as he gently eases me down on the bed. His lustful gaze locks on my face. His jaw clenches and with his hands on both sides of my shoulders, he props himself up between the 'V' of my legs.

Something in his stare, a soundless voice, has emotions begging.

The arousal of the initial weight of his rock-hard body puts my hypersensitive skin on high alert. I work to swallow in anticipation of what's to come as the wetness between my legs increases.

I have a full image of the statuesque vision of Julian hovering over me.

My eyes trace the lines of his broad shoulders and every tense muscle on his perfect torso. My fingernails skim over his pecs, to his ribcage, down his abs and finally to his shaft. Julian hisses when I grip his rock-hard length. I start to stroke him and pray I'm doing it right.

"Christ," Julian groans through gritted teeth, his Adam's apple prominent. "You're going to make me explode before I can make you feel good, Doc."

I bite my lip, loving his reaction, from the intake of his breath to the momentary closing of his eyes as he enjoys my assault. He reaches for my hand that's wrapped around his cock, then raises it above my head. Then he takes my other hand, lacing his fingers with mine.

"Keep your hands there…" He pins both my wrists above my head, leans down and places a teasing kiss on my lips. The tip of his tongue traces my bottom lip before he slips it in my mouth. Then he breaks away, and I immediately miss his lips.

Julian leans on his side, elbow bent, head in his hand and his erection pressing against my hip. "Don't move, understand?" he demands.

I nod. "*Yes*," is all I can muster.

"I want to pleasure your body, make you tremble and come so hard you won't know where you end and I begin…and you'll be begging for more of me and only me."

"You're all I want, Julian…my first and last."

"Yes, Chloe, your first and last." He places a chaste kiss on my lips. "Now, close your eyes. All I want you to do is feel." His velvety voice feathers in my ear sending a message of arousal between my thighs.

The cool brush of his fingers leave tingling sparks as he trails the valley of my breasts, toys with my diamond-jeweled bellybutton, then between my thighs.

His fingers gently slide between my damp flesh, manipulating my sensitive clit with the ever-so-perfect pressure. I arch my back as a cry of ecstasy fills the otherwise silent room.

"Fuck, baby…you're wet and ready," Julian growls.

I fist the sheets, as I try to gather my thoughts. The friction of his deft fingers sliding and stroking, teasing the small bud of sensitivity, send pleasant jolts throughout my body.

A momentary pause as he eases his way down between my legs, his warm lips graze one of my thighs and then his lips graze on the other. He scours my body, provoking the inferno already ablaze.

Then Julian's tongue spreads my wet flesh, tantalizing the vibration of my impending orgasm.

"Fuck, you taste so good." I barely hear Julian's silky whisper.

He fondles one of my breasts and my pink nipple marbles, as his soft and stiff tongue nuzzles within the walls of my pussy.

I scream and my panting is almost incoherent as I spread my legs farther apart, giving him free rein to seize my openness.

His name falls from my lips, over and over, as his tongue continues to massage me as a tidal wave of arousal explodes, reaching my climax and crashing all at the same time.

His touch is light and yet painfully teasing, satisfying every desire that's been bottled up inside.

"Julian…you are…oh God," I cry out.

"Not quite, baby…but this is as close you'll get to heaven."

Hungover from my euphoric state, I prop myself on my elbows and look down at him between my legs.

"You are hopeless. Always a comeback."

"Speaking of comeback. You ready for the next round, my sexy boxer?" Julian sits on his knees between my thighs.

"You mean there's more?" I can kick myself for how stupid that sounds.

"Oh, there's definitely more for you, Doc." Julian chuckles as he tears the packet open and rolls the condom over his erection.

The desire in his gaze meets mine after he protects and centers himself at my entrance.

He hisses as he slowly enters my center.

"Christ, you're so tight," he mumbles.

I tense at the initial burn. His body stiffens as his hard length eases into me, gently pushing farther and filling me.

I welcome the weight of his perspiring body as he slowly tucks his iron cock, thrusting in and out of my wet canal, base to tip.

Although I'm conscious of where his warm flesh touches me, my mind is spiraling out of control. It's tortuous yet rewarding.

A moan of bliss falls from my lips.

His hardness electrifies me as erotic pleasure jolts through my body.

Julian picks up the pace, grazing inside with circling movements of his hips, angling on the one spot that makes my moan increase. Julian is so deep inside the pressure starts to build.

His raw sensuousness carries me to greater heights.

The scent of sex fills the room. I breathe in the intoxicating scent of Julian's cologne, clean soap, and the sweet pancake batter, all arousing my senses.

He's my personal aphrodisiac.

Heat ripples under my perspiring skin, a burning sweetness. I tighten the muscles around his large shaft.

"Chloe." His ragged groan sends goosebumps down my neck. "You're gonna make me come, baby."

"Oh God, Julian, don't stop," I whimper, begging for more. "Kiss me. Please."

His mouth crashes onto mine, more demanding this time. I hook my hands around his neck, needing the closeness as electric shock scorches my body, sending me to the edge and stealing my breath away.

It's a take-no-prisoners, no-holds-barred, soul-reaching kind of kiss.

We both moan in unison. Our pleasure and desire mutually exchange.

My apex arouses with fire and ice, not knowing which way is up or down. My toes curl and my back arches, trembling with intense pleasure after he dominates every fiber of my body and the wave of ecstasy collides around us as my second climax rips through me.

My body is in overdrive, an amplifying heartbeat hammers in my ears. My wanton body sated, butterflies settle in my belly, resting in a dreamlike haze.

Julian lays his head at the curve of my neck, warm breaths giving me goosebumps as I brush his messy hair from his face. I calm my breathing from my ultimate high. My orgasm continues to vibrate as his semi-hard dick is still inside me.

Julian props himself on one side pushing wispy strands from my face. "You okay?" he asks.

Somehow, I nod as my gaze locks with brown eyes, where I can now see a golden glimmer in his stare.

He's so beautiful.

Julian leans in, caresses my mouth with tender kisses. Addicted to his drugging kisses, I savor every taste of him as I cup his face.

"I guess I needed to be rescued after all, my hunky, super-secret agent." I laugh, remembering our flirty banter the night of the gala.

"I think it's the other way around, Doc," he says, then he kisses me again.

It's late in the afternoon and the sun's orange rays peek through the open window; the breakfast Julian made that morning is now easily forgotten.

After I told Julian I was on the pill and wanted to truly be with him, skin on skin, no barriers, we spent the rest of the day making love, exploring one another.

The warmth of Julian's arm is around me, as I rest my head on his chest. It's comfortable and peaceful.

I've forgotten about the outside world. It's me and Julian in our own utopia.

I'd fallen for Julian before our intimacy and now in his arms, in my nakedness and vulnerability, I am truly in love with him.

My thoughts drift back to what my nana told me: *"The best kind of love is where two people find each other with just one look before even making love."*

Then my mind returns to the photo of Amber and Julian in the book, and I contemplate on bringing it up. Should I overstep the forbidden line of the past and ask about Amber?

This is all new to me. Julian said he still loves Amber. How can he move on if she is so much a part of his present?

"Julian?"

"Hmm," he lazily moans as I trace the crests and ripples of his abs.

"What was she like? Your wife?"

Julian's breath hitches for a beat; the circling of his thumb pauses on the ball of my shoulder. A sound of discomfort rumbles in the back of Julian's throat. "Why do you ask?"

"The book on your nightstand. I saw your bookmarker." I change positions, prop up on my elbows and point to the book on the nightstand. "You look so happy in those pictures."

He turns to see what I was pointing at. Julian pushes a lock of hair off my shoulder. "I'm sorry you had to see that."

"I'm not mad. She was your wife," I tell him.

"I don't want you to think that I would ever compare you to Amber…and I don't know if I can tell you what she was like. Every time I try to remember her, it breaks me. It's kind of hard for me to talk about her." Julian takes a deep breath. "The thing is, I was angry for a really long time. At her, at me. I was living two lives. One where I pretended everything was okay and the other where I walked around with an empty soul. Amber took my soul when she died. And although I think of her often and talk to her in my dreams, she's told me so many times to move on, to fall in love again. But I refused to listen to her…until I met you."

He pulls me on top of him, his knuckles tracing the line of my jaw.

"I still remember the feelings when I first met you. That night at the gala, when you *pretended* your feet were in pain and leaned against my check-in table, you jumpstarted something in me. You took me by surprise and that shit is rare."

My mouth turns up as tears of joy stream down my face. "Julian, did you just say you love me?"

"Mm-hm, I do… Now that I have you, I'm yours."

My heart swells and my chest tightens at his words. The hum of the ceiling fan and a seagull's squawk from the open window interrupts the momentary stillness.

"And those assholes out there"—his jaw clenches—"they're not going to get their hands on you. I'm going to protect you, whatever it takes. You're my life, Chloe Channing."

My hands cradle his handsome face, and I pull him to my lips. I give him a kiss so tender, full of emotion and harmony.

I break the connection, needing to tell him something else. "One more thing, *Booker*… I wasn't pretending. My feet really did hurt."

Julian chuckles. "Oh really?"

"Try wearing four-inch-high heels for several hours."

"No thanks." Julian's hands go up in surrender.

"So, what now? Where do we go from here?" I ask.

"Well, I'd still like to see those fat-pants you love to wear."

I still for a moment. My thoughts filter to when I told Julian about my fat-pants. When my mother was still alive, and life was good.

Although I'm safe in his arms, I wonder for how long.

"When will this be over?" I lay my head on his chest, listening to his heartbeat.

"Not sure, sweetheart." He takes a deep breath as he plays with my hair. "Maybe things would be different today if I'd asked you out back then. But things happen for a reason… My fucked-up past and your situation brought us back together so we could fit perfectly."

"Like a puzzle." My eyes look upon his gorgeous face.

"Yes. Like a puzzle." A lopsided grin turns the corner of his mouth, deepening his dimples.

I ruffle his messy hair, adoring every feature of his beautiful face.

After a moment, his mouth meets mine, our tongues dance and taste one another. He switches our positions, putting me on my back.

"I wish we could stay like this forever," I whisper.

"Me too, Doc." He kisses the tip of my nose. "But sooner or later, you'll want to eat."

My eyes widen. "Oh my God! I totally ruined breakfast. Scrambled eggs, the bacon… You cooked and your pancakes…"

"Shh, it's okay. Stop your rambling. We can have pancakes for dinner."

"I like that. Pancakes for dinner."

CHAPTER

Twenty-Five

JULIAN

M Y BREATH STILLS AS I watch Chloe through the closed sliding
window that leads to the open patio facing the ocean. The
sun's rays radiate her tanned skin. With a glass of lemonade in her
hand, she looks at peace sitting on the lounge chair as the island
breeze blows her chestnut hair around her face.

I wonder what she's thinking, hope she trusts me that I would
keep her safe from whoever is after her. It's been a few days and
Chloe misses her friends, being cooped up at the safe house.

So, I broke protocol.

It's risky, but I knew it would make her happy. I had Lincoln pick
up Phoebe and Ryland in the morning so they could spend the day
with Chloe.

The trio's laughter can be heard through the glass and it warms
my heart knowing how much she loves her friends and they love her
back.

Not wanting to chance more exposure with Chloe's safety, I

discussed with Phoebe the importance of it being just them two coming to visit.

When they arrived, Phoebe didn't waste any time giving me an earful. Phoebe berated me about scaring the shit out of her and Ryland, the secret of Chloe's whereabouts and being blindfolded on their way to the safe house. It did not sit well with either of the ladies.

But after a few calm moments, Chloe told her friends being in the safe house is the best thing while the kidnappers are being located.

"So those are Chloe's friends, huh?" Lincoln juts his chin toward the women on the porch.

"Yup. That's all Chloe talks about. I had to let her see them."

"They're hot…especially the brunette."

I stifle a laugh. "You interested in Phoebe?"

"Nah, she's got a mouth. Too feisty for me." Lincoln removes his cap and scratches the top of his head. "You know that chick did not keep her mouth shut, saying we were a bunch of Neanderthals, keeping them from Chloe?"

"Yeah, that's her. Phoebe's bark is bigger than her bite, at least that's what Chloe's told me."

"Damn, would love for her to bite me, with no teeth of course." Lincoln's shit-eating grin turns up.

I choke on my coffee. "Always thinking with the head below the belt…besides, you're probably not her type."

"Fuck you, dude. Why not? I've got charm that can melt any woman's panties off with just one look." Lincoln pulls a small bag of Skittles from the grocery bag of goodies the women brought with them.

"She was with Sam at one point and then later engaged to some high-class corporate guy. Had money behind his name."

"She a gold-digger?"

"Nah, she doesn't come across that way. Phoebe has a solid career. From what Chloe told me, she's been burned and not into settling."

"A challenge?"

"Don't even think about it."

"You're very protective of Chloe's friend." Lincoln raises a brow. "I take it you broke your rule."

"None of your business, Linc."

"She got under your skin...and your tighty-whities." Lincoln chuckles. "Seriously, I'm happy for you, man."

I stare at her as I take another sip. She gives me a quick smile and returns back to talking to her friends. And that slight curl of her lips tells me what I need to know. She trusts me.

"I've got to keep her safe and need to figure out who the hell wants her."

"And what's the deal with Ryland?" Lincoln pops a few Skittles in his mouth.

"She wasn't around much the last several years. Went to UCLA, got a job in Switzerland, now she's moving back to San Francisco. Sounds like she's going to be bunking with Chloe and Phoebe." I place my empty coffee mug in the sink.

"Did you tell her yet?"

I scrunch my eyebrows, my eyes glaring at Lincoln only because I know where this is going.

"Did you tell her how Ambs died?"

"She knows enough...doesn't need to know the details... and how I fucked up."

"How many times do I have to tell you, it wasn't your fault. You had no idea—"

"Look, I know that asshole followed us to get to Amber. I don't need to relive this shit again. Can you just drop it?" I snap at him.

Lincoln's arms raise in surrender. "Sorry, man. Just thought—"

"You thought wrong. No need to resurrect the past." I pinch the bridge of my nose. "Just thinking about what I've done to the Shelton family is enough shit to handle in this lifetime."

After Amber's death, I investigated the shooter's background. Turned out the shooter was the brother of Kent Shelton, a fellow SEAL and my teammate. On my last deployment prior to Amber's death, I was in charge of the team's mission and it was my responsibility to ensure my men's safety and that everything went according to plan. I studied the blueprints of the compound and the underground tunnels.

It was a simple rescue. At least, so we thought.

"Kent shouldn't have died. That was my fault," I mutter between gritted teeth.

"Again, taking the blame. Booker, I was there, you selfish prick. Smitty and I had his six. Shell wanted to be a hero…radio connection was bad in those tunnels, something we didn't anticipate. He wanted to go left when we were supposed to go right and meet up with you. If it's anyone's fault, it was mine. Blame me, I let him go the other way and who would've thought the little boy would fool us, making us think he was a prisoner too…until that little fucker put a bullet in Shelton's throat."

"I should have predicted there would be children soldiers."

"Look, we knew what we were doing. Smitty shot that kid…and instead of carrying three dead bodies, it was only one."

"We should've stayed together," I bite back. "I fucked up that call."

"Can you please just shut the fuck up and stop being a pussy? It could've happened to any one of us. Shell was our brother and didn't deserve to die." Lincoln rubs his face with his hand. "I've come to terms with it and you should too. Who knew Shelton's brother would've sought you out for revenge?"

"Revenge? It's like a fucking curse," I spit out. "Sounds like history is repeating itself with Chloe." My gaze locks on the woman I love just out the window. "I can't lose her."

"And you won't. I've got your six, man. We're going to find this bastard and put a bullet in *his* throat."

Silence stretches between us standing in the kitchen. Then my phone buzzes in my pocket. I pull it out to see it's Tyco.

We walk into the bedroom so the ladies can't hear.

"Hey Tyke, you're on speaker with me and Linc. What do you have?"

"Good news. Tweedledee and Tweedledum are Larry and Dwight Folsom. We got those dumbasses," Tyco's confident voice comes through the line.

"What do you mean?" I ask.

"They were picked up by the Royal Bahamas Police Force. They were stopped for a traffic violation and of course, the van was stolen and they were taken into custody."

"No shit... Are they talking?" Lincoln asks.

"Nope. Their mouths are tighter than a mosquito's pussy."

I choke on a laugh. "A what?"

"Ah, you know what I mean. They're being flown to Miami where they're wanted for violating their parole."

"I'm assuming that's the good news. What's the bad news?" I ask.

"So far, there is nothing that shows they're connected to Chloe. I spoke to Mr. Channing and he doesn't have a clue who the Folsom brothers are except they have a rap sheet longer than Prince Harry and Meghan Markle's wedding guest list."

"We need to find out who hired them. That's the connection. Someone doesn't just up and go through all this bullshit...killing Mrs. Channing, attacking Chloe and then to follow her all the way here to fuck up their kidnapping attempt on her," Lincoln says just before shoving the rest of the Skittles in his mouth.

"I agree. All we can assume is the unsub's got some vendetta against the Channings... or maybe me?" I say, wondering if there is a connection just like with Kent's brother.

Would someone be that obsessed with me to plot this whole thing?

"With you?" Tyco asks. "What makes you think this shit has something to do with you?"

Lincoln glares at me. "Tyke, don't listen to Booker...he's just trying to cover his bases." Lincoln mouthed to me so Tyco couldn't hear, *"What the fuck is wrong with you?"*

I perk up at the faint sound of the women's laughter. "Forget I said anything...what else?"

"Well, these bozos are from Miami so definitely a long shot for any connection between the Channings and *you*. Their flights were paid for in cash as well as the shitty hotel they were staying at."

"What about Jensen?"

"Nothing. The guy's taking a vacation and hasn't left the resort. Maybe it's just a coincidence."

"No such thing," I retort. "Who was the female he's with?"

"Some nurse, a Reyna Donovan..." Tyco tapers.

"Okay, keep us posted."

"Will do. Tyco out."

I shove my phone back in my pocket.

"Man, seriously? Do you think Chloe's attacker has anything to do with you?" Lincoln tosses the red candy wrapper in the small tin trash can.

"Hell, I don't know. What do you think? You got any other ideas?"

"If that were the case, don't you think this asshole would've gone after your mom and Fabi? I would have to give credit to the unsub... luring you in on this case and plotting it this good to get to you if it were a vendetta against you. But seriously, I don't think so."

"Yeah, I guess you're right. I know I'm stretching." *But was I?*

"Hell yeah, you are." Lincoln looks down at his watch. "I gotta take the ladies back home, it's getting late."

"Alright." I brush my hair back with my fingers and cup the back of my neck. "I'm taking Chloe out tonight."

"You think that's a good idea?"

"I'm not stupid, Linc. The plans I made are secluded and safe. Besides, you heard it yourself. Those bastards are in custody and half the danger is dissolved."

"You want me to have your six? You won't know I'm there."

"No need. I will be fine. Thanks anyway."

"WHERE ARE YOU TAKING ME?" Chloe asks, fidgeting in the passenger seat.

"If I told you then it wouldn't be a surprise, now would it?" I gaze over at Chloe as I breathe in the salted air and ocean breeze.

With the top off the Jeep, her hair whips around her beautiful face. The spaghetti-strapped dress shows off her supple skin. The twinkle in her eyes shimmers like the stars above as I hold her hand while the other hand steers to get to our destination.

We arrive at an impressive mansion where a gray-haired man greets us at the front door. We follow the old man to the back of the house and through French doors to the picturesque garden with a view of the ocean's cove.

"Julian, oh my goodness, it's beautiful here." Chloe's eyes light up, awe in her voice. She places her hands over her mouth as she walks a few steps down the stoned pathway ahead of me.

I take her hand before Chloe takes another step. I love how her soft hand feels in mine. So tiny and delicate. Linking her fingers with mine, I pull Chloe closer to me.

"I love that smile of yours." I'm lost in her eyes as I lean in and kiss her gently. I tighten my hold around her waist. "I can't lose you," I whisper in her ear.

"You won't," she answers. "I'm not going anywhere. I'll be more aware. Besides, I have you to protect me, right?"

Would God be that cruel to punish me again and again?

First, for losing my father, Amber dying in my arms, Shelton, letting Kent's wife and children down and after all that, take Chloe away too? Death is around me.

Or maybe it was Satan himself laughing it up, lurking and waiting to snatch everything good from my life as a fucked-up joke for his own jollies.

The reoccurring nightmares that keep me up at night and the image of Chloe dying in my arms scares the shit out of me.

"Julian?" Chloe touches my face, shaking me from my thoughts. "Did you hear what I said?"

"Yes, every word," I say coming out of my daze. "I was just remembering something, that's all." I kiss her nose. "I will always protect you, Doc."

We continue our stroll through the gardens, our fingers linked together.

"Thanks for letting my friends come over today. I know you broke a few rules."

"You missed them. And Phoebe was blowing up my phone demanding to see you."

"That's Feebs, so persistent. Ryland is heading back to San Francisco tomorrow morning, so the timing was perfect."

"Heading back? Why?"

"Ry got a call from her brother. Their mom is in the hospital. Linda wants all her children to be with her. I'm worried about them."

"Well, as soon as the coast is clear, I will take you to see Mrs. O'Hare."

As the sun descends, we take in the sculptures, the exquisite landscape and the architectural details the gardens offer and I don't believe him .

"I thought this was private property and tours were no longer allowed here," Chloe says.

"I called in a few favors. I knew you were getting restless being cooped up in the house. Thought you might want a change of scenery."

We come to a pillared gazebo that faces the sunset just over the alcove water view. Two chairs and a white linen-covered table with two silver domes on it await us.

"What's this?" Chloe asks in amazement, covering her mouth with both hands.

"Dinner for two." I pull a chair out for her. Chloe sits down as I scoot her in, then I sit across from her.

There's a free-standing silver bucket with a bottle on ice next to me. I pour the liquid into our glasses.

"Let's make a toast...to lasting firsts."

"To lasting firsts." Chloe sips the liquid. "Sparkling cider?"

"I need both of us sober until this is all over," I caution. "I can't afford to be off guard."

"But you had alcohol at the club, remember?"

"Yes. A sip and to blend in. I babied that drink and then your one disgusting shot." I raise my glass. "This is what we'll have to settle for from now on, okay?"

With everything unfolding, it was only a matter of time until the ticking time bomb, the one person who hired Larry and Dwight, would finally explode.

"So, what's for dinner?" Chloe asks, trying to peek.

I smile, my hand on the handle. "Before I lift this, it's nothing fancy…but I know it's your favorite." I lift the silver dome.

"Margherita pizza! I haven't eaten pizza since I left home."

After about an hour of eating and talking more about our childhood, I'm ready to take Chloe on to her next surprise.

"Speaking of childhood memories… You ready for dessert?" I stand with my hand extended. Chloe nods and places her hand in mine.

I drive for several miles and kill the engine in front of a small cottage with a wraparound porch. The yellow door is dimly lit by low-hanging flower-shaped lampshades. There's a swinging bench and sunflowers decorate the porch.

After a few knocks on the wooden door, a smiling, spunky woman wearing an apron stained with pastel colors greets us.

"Julian! Welcome, welcome, please come in," she says, patting her braided black hair wrapped in a bun at the top her head. A whiff of sweet sugary aroma escapes from inside the cottage. "You're just in time." The woman extends her arm, inviting us to enter.

Chloe's smiling eyes meet mine. "What is this place?"

I place my hand at the small of Chloe's back, leading her in. The wood floors creak as they walk across to a stainless-steel countertop. A glass case lights up various colors and flavors of ice cream just on the other side of it.

"Another favor I called in with an old family friend. Izzy meet Chloe. Chloe, Izzy."

The woman embraces Chloe.

"Oh child, this man must love you very much to call and ask me to stay open just for you and give you a private lesson on how to make ice cream…but not just any ice cream. This is my special recipe and I only do this for very special guests." Izzy walks to the other side of the counter, pulls out a menu showing the different flavors of ice cream.

"Izzy and my mom go way back," I say as I take the menu from her and give it to Chloe.

"Yes, Bella and I were childhood friends." Izzy wipes her hands on her apron. "Now, I want you to pick a flavor of your choice and you, my dear, will get to see how it is made. But, before I show you, you must promise that it will be our little secret."

I embrace Chloe from behind, resting my chin on her shoulder. "Izzy's ice cream is famous for a reason. She'll make it for us, but Izzy will still keep the one ingredient a secret which makes her ice cream the best in the world."

"A lady never reveals her secrets," Izzy says, winking at Chloe. "So, what will it be, dear?"

"Chocolate hazelnut, please." Chloe answers.

"Make that two, Izzy."

CHAPTER

Twenty-Six

CHLOE

I WATCH AND LISTEN WHILE Izzy narrates every action as she mixes the ingredients together. She whips up the milk, cream, eggs, and sugar at different stages until it becomes custard-like. Izzy pours the mixture into a silver rectangular aluminum tin.

Of course, it has to freeze for at least three hours.

But the woman was prepared and has a tub already made in the freezer for us, since apparently, Julian had gotten intel from Phoebe about my favorite ice cream. Izzy scoops a large round serving into a cone for me and Julian.

"This is very delicious, Izzy," I say, licking the sides of the cold concoction. "The best ice cream I've ever tasted."

Julian leans in, and presses his cold mouth on my lips, sending warm goosebumps up my spine. "Mm. Maybe you're the best ice cream I've ever tasted." His charm is irresistible as he turns up a boyish smile.

Butterflies flutter in my belly as our lips graze one another's. I melt into his kiss because the man can kiss. And he tastes delicious.

A slight cough from Izzy breaks our connection as I almost forgot she was there. "So, Chloe, Julian tells me you are a doctor?" Izzy says more like a statement rather than a question as she puts the aluminum container back in the freezer.

"Yes, a pediatrician."

"You don't say. Being a doctor takes a lot of your time."

"It does, but I love my job. Wouldn't trade it for anything in this world."

After we finish our ice cream, I tell them about my patients and the silly things they say, and I ask Izzy how Julian was as a kid. Izzy is able to conjure up a photo album.

She points to sepia-colored photographs of Julian as a little boy then a teenager. The dark-haired, brown-eyed boy, with a smile so enduring it deepens his adorable dimples, warms my heart and swallows me whole.

To get a glimpse of his past, I'm utterly head-over-heels in love with Julian Cruz.

"Julian had his moments, but he was a good boy. Helped Bella from cooking in the kitchen to sewing," Izzy says as she closes the album and tucks it back in a box.

"You can sew?" I raise a brow.

"Yep. Mom made me sit there with her. I was a quick study. She wanted me to be part of the business."

"That's why the ladies loved him. So many girlfriends to tell you—"

"Okay." Julian's hands hover over my ears. "It's time we get going and say our goodbyes to Izzy."

"Aww, I was excited to hear about the girlfriends," I chide, hopping off the barstool. And I love the sheepish look on Julian's face, redness on his cheeks as he seems embarrassed of the stories that may follow.

"My mom kicked my ass when she heard I was dating more than one girl. She made me imagine a man doing that to her or Fabi. Then I became a one-woman man."

"Oh yes… Julian's a gentleman. A one-woman man once he met Amber…" Izzy tapers off, pressing her lips together and sliding an apologetic look to Julian. "I'm sorry, I didn't mean to… I've said too much."

I catch a glimpse of Julian as he purses his lips. It's a slip of the tongue and I know Izzy didn't mean to cause any miff or bring up any bad memories. Julian puts his arm around Izzy as she whispers in his ear. He nods and kisses her on the cheek.

"I'm okay," he whispers back then looks my way. It's the same look he gave me earlier when he didn't want to talk about Amber. A look of contradiction and confusion, which makes me feel a bit self-conscious.

Izzy moves closer to me and wraps her arms around me. "Take care of our Julian. He's got scars and I know you can heal him." Izzy pulls back and frames my face with her hands.

"I will try my best," I return a sincere smile then wave goodbye.

Back in the Jeep, Julian drives in silence and I know Izzy struck a chord by bringing up Amber. I gaze at his profile while the moon illuminates his face and I need to tread lightly, knowing he must be thinking about her.

The 'Wall of Amber' is a strong fortress and something he doesn't want to talk about. Every time I've brought it up, he's deterred the conversation to the psychopath and made me go through my mental rolodex of potential suspects.

I picked up on the hints when I saw the pictures of Amber and Julian in Izzy's photo album. One picture resonates with me, a prom picture. They shared a lifetime together and I wonder, were those blissful memories coming back to Julian? Is it the reason for his silence?

"Are you okay?" I break the reticence over a Bob Marley steel-drum melody softly playing on the radio.

"I'm fine. Why do you ask?" His answer is short and voice low.

"The moment Izzy mentioned Amber…"

"Like I said, I'm okay and she's not someone I want to talk about."

"Why not, Julian? I'm okay with you talking to me about her. She was your high school sweetheart. You shared a life together and I think it's healthy to talk about it."

Julian puts the Jeep in park, and I look out the side window. I recognize the hilltop where we had our picnic and our boxing lessons.

"Stop psychoanalyzing me, Doc." His fingers rake his hair back. "She's dead, okay? And that's all you need to know. I don't want to talk about her to anyone and especially not to you."

Taken aback from his snap, I push his buttons, knowing I shouldn't. He needs to talk about it especially if there's a future for us. "Bullshit. There's more and I hate to pry—"

"Then don't." Julian cuts me off. "The more you pry, the more you'll see what a failure I was. I fucked up and I don't want you to see that side of me."

And there it is. Julian's confession.

"You think I would see you as a failure? Are you kidding me? I could never. Please, Julian… I want to know that side of you too. I want to see not just your strength but your vulnerabilities. I also need to know what makes you so riled up at the mention of her name so I can be sensitive to that too. Please, talk to me."

Julian takes in a breath, pinches the bridge of his nose, as if trying to clear his head. I saw the hurt in his eyes and it kills me to see him this way.

"Talking about Amber is tough for me. It hurts too much to remember." He looks up to the stars then back at me. "Every year I visit her in San Diego, where we grew up. This is the first year I missed it."

"Why didn't you go?"

"Two reasons. One, the pain gets worse every year I'm there. And the day I buried Amber, I also buried my child. Amber was three months pregnant. No parent should ever have to bury their child and I was the reason for that."

I reach out and touch Julian's arm. "Oh God, Julian. I'm so sorry." My lips tremble as a tear falls down my cheek. "But, what do you mean *you* were the reason?"

Eyes blur and there's a lump in the back of my throat as Julian tells me about the day Amber was shot, the shooter being the brother of his fallen teammate and how that man got his revenge against Julian by killing his wife and unborn child.

"So, you see how fucked-up this whole situation is. I should've seen it coming. I wish he had just killed me. Amber didn't deserve to be in that lunatic's crosshairs. I'm the one who deserved that bullet. I'm the one who let the Shelton family down."

"How can you say that? None of this is your fault. The only person to blame for Amber's death is the guy who pulled the trigger."

"You, Linc, and everyone else have told me that time and time again. But it doesn't register. I've talked to shrinks about it and nothing helps."

I look into Julian's eyes, torment still residing there. He still struggles with the loss. Every part of me wants to help him, to cope with his agony. The haunting pain sears so deep even I'm afraid these demons are only his to fight and face alone. I open my mouth, but Julian speaks first.

"And the second reason I didn't make it to see Amber is because I'm here with you..." he softly grazes the back of his hand over my cheek, "moving on."

"Julian, moving on is good, but as long as this pain is still there, you can never truly move on."

"I love you, Chloe. Please give me time to figure this out. The only other person who knows about this is Lincoln. He's been my six since the beginning."

"Your six?"

"Sorry, Doc... Navy term meaning he's had my back." Julian nods after a beat and a smile turns up the corners of his mouth. "Let's not talk about this anymore. This evening is about us, okay?"

"Okay," I say as I watch Julian climb out of the Jeep and collect a blanket from the back seat.

He rounds the car and opens my door, extending his hand.

"Last stop." With his free hand, Julian tugs my hand as I hop out of the passenger seat. He spreads the blanket on the grassy hillside under the stars.

He's thought of everything. The secluded walk in the garden, pizza and ice cream, and now our little paradise on the hill.

I see the smile on his face as he kisses my forehead, my nose, then my lips. His hands frame my face.

"Ready to stargaze?" he asks, extending his arm for me to take a seat on the blanket. Julian scoots himself behind me. We lay down and my head rests in the crook of his arm.

"Thanks for everything, Julian," I whisper, looking up at the stars.

"I wanted to give you tonight. I know it's gotta be hard being stuck in that house for the last several days." His fingers graze my arm, leaving goosebumps in its path.

"It's definitely a memory I will never forget and will cherish forever." I let out a slight giggle.

"What's so funny, Doc?"

I'm wrapped in his arms like a silken cocoon of euphoria, remembering the last several days. I take in a breath as memories flood back. Making love to Julian at the safe house, sharing and exploring our smoldering passion. Recalling our conversations when we met at the gala and now to this very moment, being in each other's arms.

It's as if we've shared a lifetime together, but it had only been a couple of weeks.

"It's ironic how life brought us here to this very moment," I say, playing with the button on his shirt.

"How so?"

"Well, bad things had to happen to both of us in order to find each other. I was trying to remember and all the while you're trying to forget."

Julian clears his throat. "The irony of it all is that we both needed to be rescued, don't you think, Doc?"

Our hands link together as a content silence blankets us for a few minutes.

Sounds of nature around us. Crickets chirp in the tall grass. The tranquil ocean's surf ebbs and crashes down below us, and the bristle of the palm leaves dance in the salty breeze.

"I have something for you," comes Julian's silky voice. He stands and reaches for something in his pocket. He pulls out a small black box and sits back down. His legs stretch across the blanket as he hands me the box.

I tuck my feet beneath me. "What's this?"

"An early birthday gift. Open it," he tells me with excitement in his voice.

I slide the top off, revealing the necklace I eyed at the jewelry store. "Julian. You shouldn't have."

"Here, let me put it on you."

I lift my hair and turn my body so Julian can clasp the necklace around my neck. Julian kisses the back of my neck. My breath hitches, lost in the feeling as the rough pads of his fingers trace my shoulders.

This is surreal and happening so fast.

His touch is a tangible reminder that he's real, this moment is real and it's better than what I've read in my romance novels.

I snuggle against him, closing my eyes as we lay in a quiet comfort. No need for words, our fingers linked together, our bodies connected with the warm feel of one another.

Julian's fingers dance up and down my arm as I hum *Just a Kiss* wishing I could stop time and remain in this fairytale bubble forever. But sooner or later, the glass slipper is going to fall off and with every fairytale, there in the shadows lurks the evil stepmother, but in this case an unknown villain.

"Julian," I whisper.

"Chloe," he says.

"What if I put myself out there? Like Cinderella?"

"Cinderella?" Julian's fingers stop caressing my skin. "I'm not following."

"Hear me out." I sit up and tuck my legs under my bottom. "Cinderella was locked up in her room by the evil stepmother until the fairy godmother and those cute mice helped get her to the ball to meet her Prince Charming."

"Okay… And?"

"Well, when midnight struck, the prince chased after Cinderella and hunted her down to match her tiny foot to the glass slipper."

"Doc, you're rambling." Julian props himself up on his elbow. "You're confusing me."

"I'm getting to the point… When the stepmother figured out it was Cinderella who attended the ball, the woman's evil ways were exposed. Cinderella was brave to go to the ball and come out of her locked room. So, I was thinking—"

"*No.* Absolutely not. Are you crazy?" Julian springs from the blanket, paces in the dark, and roughly tugs his hair back. "Are you saying to come out of hiding and be bait for a goddamn maniac?"

"Julian. It's the only option." I rise to meet him eye to eye and stop his frantic pace.

"There's no way I'm going to let you do that." Julian throws his hands in the air and takes a deep breath. He's angry with me for making this suggestion, but what choice do I have. I just want this to be over with. I want to move on with my life.

"Let me? I believe this is my decision, not yours," I hiss as a contradictory laugh escapes from my mouth.

"That's where you're wrong, Doc. I am responsible for your life. And the fuck if I'm going to let you be bait—"

"Are you Booker the bodyguard talking, or Julian who just told me he loved me?"

"Christ, Channing." Julian scrubs his face with his hand. "I'm both. This is what and who I am. Don't you see that? I love you so much it hurts. And I'd be stupid to agree with you."

"It's the only way we can move on." I cup his jaw, pull his face close to mine. "Julian, please. I think it's something to consider. At least discuss it with Dylan."

"You are persistent, you know that?"

"Yes, but you still love me?"

"More than you'll ever know."

Julian's mouth is on mine. The taste of his kiss calms the chaos that roars through my head. Being bait and exposing myself to whoever is out there is still a good idea, in my opinion, and somehow, I need to convince Julian and Dylan it's the only choice.

I'm so wrapped up in Julian's addicting lips, rendering me help-less and weak in the knees that we ignore the raindrops falling from the sky. The intimacy of our prolonged kiss is no match for the tropical downpour.

Julian's mouth brands and claims my lips.

One hand curls around Julian's neck as I play with the ends of his hair. The other hand fists Julian's black shirt as his hands glide down my hips. He slowly hikes up my skirt and his fingers brush the backs of my legs, causing chills to race up my spine.

We stumble back to the blanket on the ground.

I unbutton Julian's jeans, push them down along with his boxers, over his waist and down his legs, exposing his dick that is already rock hard. I slide out of my panties and straddle Julian's hips. My skirt gathered at my waist and his pants just at his shins.

I need him. I want him.

But most of all, he needs to know that I'm not a victim. That I'm stronger than he thinks I am. So, I take control as I ride him, he's not setting the pace this time, I am.

There's something erotic about making love in the rain on our paradise hilltop.

It's just us and the sky water that cleanses us with a new pace.

Julian pushes his pelvis up as I press down, his cock fitting perfectly in my crest. The pressure of his fingers on my hips guides my rhythmic motion.

My body melts as he penetrates my sensitive velvet walls, stroking every nerve, sending shockwaves throughout my body.

Liquid heat ignites my skin as the flush of desire paralyzes me. I'm under Julian's spell, always have been and I always will be. I can't get enough of him. And it feels like forever since I've had him, though it had only been earlier that day since our last passionate encounter.

The pleasure is pure and explosive. My head tilts back, and my broken cries drown out his moans as the rain continues to coat our skin and drench our clothes. Julian pulls down the straps of my dress and palms my breasts. His grip is possessive, sending a tingle down to my pussy, heightening my arousal for him.

In unison we reach our climax, shuddering in exquisite harmony.

"Chloe," he murmurs in a gravelly tone. The echo of my name in the dark turns me on and my God, I love this man.

"Julian," I whisper back, and savor the emotion as I frame his face with my hands and press my lips to his. The buzz of my orgasm still lingers, as I let out a deep soul-drenching sigh.

I slowly ease myself off of him and slide my panties back on. Julian zips his jeans and the tropical rain dissipates.

We laugh as we fold the drenched blanket. "Sex in the rain… That was kind of hot," I say, wringing out my wet hair.

"Talk about having soaking-wet sex on another level." Julian throws his head back laughing.

CHAPTER
Twenty-Seven

JULIAN

DARKNESS IS ALL I SEE. The buzz of white noise in my ears. My head throbs. Aware, yet unaware, unable to move.

The fogginess hums throughout my body, paralyzing all of my senses.

I narrow my eyes, now on the prowl. Instincts on full alert, but the constant banging of chaotic percussions echoing in the distance begin to annoy my last nerve, breaking my concentration.

What the hell is that banging noise?

I hear soft breathing. Goosebumps rise on my arms and I feel a presence.

With my Glock ready, I quickly turn and aim.

The fog clears. I measure my steps, then my heart accelerates at the sight that renders me speechless.

Confusion seizes all my thoughts.

"Amber?"

"Hey, Sailor." *Amber's outstretched hand reaches for mine. I holster my weapon and reach for her delicate hand, pulling Amber in my embrace.*

"God, I've missed you."

I lean back to look into golden-hazel eyes and take in her porcelain face as I finger a familiar wayward curl behind her ear. I circle my arms around my wife again, kiss the top of her head, and breathe in her jasmine scent.

"Am I dreaming again?"

"Possibly."

"Possibly?" I ask. *"Am I dead?"*

Amber giggles into my chest. *"You're not dead, Jules."* She looks up at me. *"Take a walk with me."* With hands linked, we walk through the haze.

More bangs echo and I look around. *"What the hell is that noise?"*

"Jules, forget the banging for a moment... I need to talk to you. What's the last thing you remember?"

"Ambs, I'm not sure. I-uh... I'm confused. My head hurts like a bitch... Last thing I remember I was with..."

Amber frames my face and meets my eyes. *"Yes. You were with Chloe."*

"I'm sorry." I squeeze my eyes shut, bow my head. I hook my hand around my neck, feeling wetness and wipe it from my skin.

Blood.

"What the hell?"

"Hey, look at me." Amber's fingers pull my chin up. *"You're okay. Do you remember what your commander told you during BUDs about pain?"*

"If you feel pain, that means you're still alive."

More loud bangs boom in the background. *"What the hell is that banging?"*

"I'm glad you can hear the banging." Amber smiles. *"But I need you to ignore the noise for a moment...and listen to me. I don't have much time. This will be my last visit."*

"What? Why?"

"I came to tell you that you need to move on."

"I'm moving on."

Amber raises a brow. *"Are you sure about that, Sailor?"*

"What do you mean?"

"Come on, Jules, a question for my question? Some things never change."

"You're asking or telling me to move on?"

"Stop avoiding the obvious. You're letting all this pent-up guilt eat you up."

I hold her soft face in my hands. *"You shouldn't have been there. Shelton's brother killed you and that bullet had my name on it, not yours."*

"Oh, Jules. Let it go. You always had a problem holding a grudge."

I throw my hands in the air and pace in the fog. "A grudge? Ambs, that sick bastard took you from me. From us. I'm angry, pissed off. We were going to have a baby, for Christ's sake! What kind of husband and father am I if I can't hold both of you? I let everyone down. I let you down."

Tears sting my throat as I kneel in front of Amber, grasping her shins.

"The grudge isn't against Kent's brother. You're holding a grudge against yourself." Amber places her hand on my head, her fingers playing with my hair. "Please, baby, stand up and look at me."

I stand and lock eyes with shimmering hazels.

For the last time?

"It's been five years. You need to forgive yourself."

"I'm trying. It's so hard."

Amber's hand moves to cover my heart. "Do you love her?"

"Amber...please don't make me answer that."

"You don't have to. I can see it in your eyes." She takes a breath. "That's all I ever wanted for you. A second chance. She's beautiful, Jules. And if you truly love Chloe, we can't keep meeting like this...here in your dreams, where you keep me alive. You now need to ask yourself what kind of man would you be to Chloe if you keep holding on to me? That's not fair to her, or to you."

"I'm afraid to lose her, like I lost you."

"Then you need to wake up. Chloe needs you right now."

"What do you mean she needs me?"

"She needs you...now. Wake up, Booker!"

Another series of bangs sounds to the right and I spin my head. When I whirl back to Amber, she's gone, leaving me in the misty fog.

"Dammit, Amber...please come back. What do you mean Chloe needs me?"

"Booker," comes a distant voice.

Lincoln? Is that you?

"Wake up."

Another loud bang rings out. "Wake up, you pansy-ass." Then a sting to my face. "Stop fucking around."

Lincoln, stop your yelling... And did you just slap me, asshole?

"Come on, jerk-face. I need you to wake up."

Then flickers of blurred pictures, like an 8mm movie caught on a broken reel plays over and over. I shut my eyes and force myself to breathe as shrapnel images flood my head, in slow motion, wrapping around my consciousness.

Blackness grows around me.

A tall, dark silhouette appears in the shadows.

Olive eyes shine through the murky darkness.

Tears stream down Chloe's face.

An evil grin triggers my hairs to stand on end.

Red manicured fingers hold a gun to Chloe's head.

A woman.

Anger sears and heat boils in my veins as the torturous visions of Chloe replay in my mind.

A draft of air forces into my lungs as I leap up, grasping my chest.

"Well, it's about fucking time," Lincoln bellows, banging on a pot with a wooden stick.

"Where is she? Where's Chloe?" I yelp, faltering as I try to stand, but still dizzy from the blow to my head.

"Whoa, buddy, take a seat." Lincoln takes a hold of my arm and pulls me back down on the couch. "She's not here. They got you good last night. What's the last thing you remember?"

I stare at the tangled rope and my shattered phone on the floor.

I scan the room.

The wooden coffee table destroyed, and furniture tossed around haphazardly.

I give Lincoln a play by play of what I recall when Chloe and I returned to the safe house just after midnight.

It'd been unusually dark, the porch light off, and my instincts went on high alert. I pulled my Glock from my holster and secured Chloe behind me, using myself as a human shield to protect her from danger.

Then chaos broke out.

Chloe screamed, hands grabbed her from behind and pulled her from me.

A scuffle, a blow to the back of my neck.

I stumbled to the ground.

Kicks to my ribs knocked the air from my lungs.

Fade to black.

"How long have I been out? What time is it? Have you called Tyco?" I ramble questions I need answers to.

"Slow down, buddy." Lincoln hands me an icepack. "We'll get those answered one question at a time."

I shake my head and push away the icepack.

"Take it, fucker. You need it to cool down your hot head." Lincoln looks at his watch. "And it's just after seven."

My chest tightens at the thought of how much time has passed.

"We need to find her." I wince when I press the ice to the back of my head. "It was a woman, Linc. That fucking bitch took Chloe."

"Did you recognize her?"

"Not that I can recall."

"Tyco's been scouring the street cameras for the last couple of hours trying to locate Chloe." Lincoln rises from the couch and sets the pot on the counter. "The question is, how did they find the safe house?"

"Hell if I know." I throw the icepack on the floor.

"Do you think it was her friends?"

"No way." I shake my head. "They would never, and besides, you had them blindfolded."

"No one followed me, I'm sure of that." Lincoln reassures me.

"It doesn't matter now. We just need to find Chloe. God, if she's—"

"Don't even say it. We're going to find her. *Alive.*" Lincoln pats me on the back. "If that bitch wanted her dead, I would be calling the coroner rather than banging pots and slapping your sleepy ass up. That woman has an ulterior motive."

A sheen of sweat coats my forehead and adrenaline courses through my veins. All I can think about is getting Chloe back.

"I can't lose her, Linc."

"You won't." Lincoln's phone rings and Tyco's name appears on the screen. "Ty, you're on speaker. Sleeping Beauty finally woke up."

"Welcome back to the living. So, here's what I got." He clears his throat and sounds of keys being clicked fill the line. "Two dark figures approach the safe house then the cameras were compromised.

Leaving me to work the street cams. Between the hours of midnight till the moment Linc showed up... Two vans. Both pulled out at the same time and split up. I tracked the one going southbound down a dirt road to a secluded part of the docks. There's an old abandoned fish house at the end of this road that went out of business several years ago. My guess, Chloe was in that one."

"Good work, Tyke," I say as I watch Lincoln place a black case on the table. He opens it, displaying several weapons and binoculars.

"Hey, one more thing... Frank Channing is missing too. He didn't appear in court yesterday morning. And when SFPD went to check on him, his home was ransacked. Since I'm a betting man, I'm all in for Frank and Chloe being together."

My chest tightens and a sliver of fear runs through my gut. I don't believe in coincidences. This woman's vendetta runs deep to have Chloe and her father kidnapped, then brought to the island.

But what's her motive?

"That's if Chloe is still alive." I shake my head, images spin out of control of Chloe hurt, or worse.

"What the hell did I just say, Book? She's alive. And we're going to find her," Lincoln snaps back.

"And guys," Tyco adds, "it's primetime news over here."

"Shit...that means Phoebe knows." I let out a breath of defeat knowing how worried Chloe's friend will be. I pull out a G17 from the case, holster it to my waist. "They took Chloe and my gun, Linc. The bitch had my gun pointed to Chloe's head."

"Fuckin' A," Lincoln pipes out.

"Send us the location," I instruct Tyco.

"Already on Linc's phone."

THE BREEZE FROM THE OCEAN is a relief as the sun berates my

damp skin. I wipe the sweat trickling down the side of my temple. I raise the binoculars and peer through them at the beat-up shack in the distance.

This part of the dock is empty and explains the reason why the unsub would use this location. A large burly figure crosses the windowpane and looks outside, most likely inspecting the surroundings.

Relief overwhelms me and there's no doubt in my mind, Chloe is in there.

My grip on the binoculars tightens and I clench my jaw when I finally see a glimpse of Frank through the lens.

He's not looking so good, head hung low and face bruised. A fist smacks Frank's face; blood sprays from his mouth. I only hope they didn't lay a finger on Chloe, or so help me God.

Time slows, minutes stretching to hours. I run several scenarios through my head, trying to figure out a plan. This is not a recovery mission, it's a rescue mission. She's alive, and I feel it deep down to the marrow of my bones.

Kill the targets and rescue Chloe and Frank.

My patience is running thin and I'm bloodthirsty, needing to put this charade to an end. I can't make any irrational decisions that will cost the lives of Frank and the woman I love. The problem is we don't know how many people are holding them captive. And as much as I want to rush in there and get Chloe back in my arms, I can't risk their lives.

"One man," I spit out, looking through the lens. "But no woman."

"Piece of cake," Lincoln says as he chews on his gum, looking in through his own binoculars.

"I'm guessing the fucker has a hold of Frank and Chloe."

Although I want to crumble at the thought of Chloe hurt, I have to push it all aside. It's tearing me apart. All I want is to have Chloe back in my arms more than my last breath.

She's my lifeline. I've finally come to terms with a revelation—although my love for Amber will always remain, what I have with Chloe is good, and that it's okay to move on.

The pounding in my chest and heat racing throughout my body is making me antsy. I shut my eyes for a brief second, hoping I can channel a message to her.

Hold on, sweetheart. I'm coming for you. Stay strong.

"You alright?" Lincoln asks, putting his gun in the holster wrapped around his shin.

"Yeah, I just want to get in there."

Lincoln pats his hand on my shoulder. "So, what's the plan, Booker?"

CHAPTER

Twenty-Eight

CHLOE

THE HUMIDITY CLIMBS AND A sheen of sweat coats my body as daylight filters through the dull shattered windows of the abandoned shack. I can hear the crashing waves and seagulls overhead through the holes of the wood-paneled walls.

I fight the urge to vomit from the stench of rotten fish and the staleness that permeates the walls of my shiplap prison. My dress is torn at the hem. My shoulder is dislocated, and I lay motionless on the grimy and dusty floor, as an occasional cockroach scurries across it.

The nylon ropes cut into my wrists with every feeble attempt to set myself free. My ankles are tied together, and it's no use trying to get out of them because they did a good job immobilizing me.

I fought through most of the fatigue and forced my eyes open. But I'm exhausted and in pain from the strikes to my face throughout the evening. I don't know why and how long I've been held captive since I was knocked out several times from the blows.

At some point, I'm tossed in the corner like a ragdoll and they moved on to torture their next victim. This time Dad is on the other side of the room in the splintered chair I once occupied.

Dad was brought in sometime in the middle of the darkness and beaten to a bloody pulp. I pleaded with my captors to stop hitting him as tears deluged from my eyes at the sight of Dad being used as a punching bag.

I need to stay awake, be strong for him, so he can draw any strength he needs from me.

The woman who didn't say a word sat on the table, legs crossed, laughing as if she was watching a comedy show. With each hit the tattooed man connects to Dad's unstable body, the woman's sneer cuts into my chest like shards of glass.

"Reyna, please stop," I plead. "Why are you doing this?"

Reyna raises her hand at the man to cease his beating and her malevolent eyes pitch to me. "Ace, give me a minute."

Ace moves away from Dad and leans against the wall, lighting a cigarette.

Reyna hops off the table and moves across the room with purpose. My body trembles and triggers my heart to race.

There's only rage in Reyna's eyes.

She crouches down to rest on her haunches. With her manicured fingers, she grips my aching chin forcing me to look at Dad.

"Why? I'll tell you why," she hisses, evil lacing her voice. "Your father fucked my mother and left her with nothing. He's a piece of shit, and every blow to his handsome face is for every day my mother cried for him."

I wince. "Your mother?"

"Get your hands off my daughter." Dad's voice is low, as he struggles to get his words out.

Releasing my chin, Reyna quickly moves to grab Dad's hair and pulls his head upright. "I'm your daughter too… Take a close look at me, Frank. Who do I resemble? You know damn well who I'm talking about. Say her name! Say it! What's my mother's name, you bastard?"

Reyna's face is inches from his, as Dad's swollen eyes meet hers. "Denise…" he chokes out.

Dad's head sags when Reyna's grip releases his hair and she claps her hands to applaud him. "Ding, ding, ding! Otherwise known as *DeeDee.*"

"DeeDee?" I still, remembering the familiar name. "My Nannie?"

"Oh, Chloe. Don't look surprised. Frank knew how to fuck-em and chuck-em. Isn't that right, *Dad?*"

"Chloe, don't listen to her." Dad's voice is a painful whisper.

"Is it true?" My eyes meet his. "Is Reyna my——"

"Half-sister?" With her red painted nail, Reyna taps her chin, sarcasm written all over her face. "Oh, Chloe...tsk, tsk, tsk. Take off the rose-tinted glasses, you silly girl. Daddy dearest wasn't so perfect after all."

"Reyna, please let Chloe go. This is between you and I."

"No can do, *Dad.*" Reyna pulls a journal out of her purse and waves it in Dad's face. "I found my mother's diary after she committed suicide." She tosses the journal on the table and pulls out a gun from her purse and parades around the room. "There was a picture of you and my mother in your perfect house"—Reyna points the gun at me—"with *her.*"

"Reyna, no, please!" Dad screams as he winces through the obvious pain in his chest.

Fear grips my throat seeing the gun aimed at me. Reyna squints as her eyes lock onto mine and her finger trembles upon the trigger.

There's a beat of silence before Reyna retracts the gun and speaks again. "In my mother's diary, it says you like stories, Chloe." Reyna spins to Frank. "Let's tell Chloe about the sappy story of you and Mom, shall we, *Daddy?*"

Reyna clears her throat. "Once upon a fucking time...there was a handsome king named Frank who married a pathetic duchess named Sarah. King Frank was a horny bastard and set his sights on the beautiful young maiden, Denise, as she was out in the garden. The king pursued Denise and whispered sweet bullshit and empty promises. One day, Denise told the king she was pregnant with his child. Not believing her, the king broke the maiden's heart and she ran away without looking back." Reyna stops parading around the room, her hand on her jutted hip. "That about sum it up, *Daddy?*"

"Dad?" I swallow as tears spring from my eyes.

"DeeDee told me she miscarried and left without a note or anything. If I had known she was still pregnant, I would've been there for her—"

"Lies! You lie." Reyna swings the weapon toward Dad, her hand still shaking.

"Reyna, no!" I beg. "Please don't. Please don't hurt him."

"My mother loved you, Frank. But you know what's even more sickening, she loved Sarah too, and that's why my mother hid her pregnancy and ran away."

"I didn't...please, Reyna... If I...if she had told me..." Dad mumbles, desperation in his voice as he shakes his head slightly. "I'm sorry. I'm so sorry."

"I've held onto that diary since I was seven years old and read it every day like it was my lifeline. Instead of locating the next of kin"—Reyna levels her eyes at Dad—"I was shuffled from foster home to foster home. Mom's blood is on your hands, and payback's a bitch. Just like you took my mother's life, I took Chloe's pathetic mother's life, too."

My breath hitches and the pain in my chest makes it hard to breathe. "You killed my mother?" I cry out, tears falling from my face. "Why? She didn't do anything to you."

I sympathize with the little girl Reyna once was, for going through life without a mother and father. But this evil woman in front of me is not to be pitied.

Reyna straightens, smooths her hair behind her shoulders. Reyna's scars run so deep it chisels the marrow of her bones and revenge is etched through and through, taking this moment as her victory.

"Sarah was just as guilty as dear ol' Dad... I searched and searched for him since all I had was a name in my mom's diary. Do you know how many Frank Channings there are in this goddamn U.S. of A? Then my search was over... I planned for the perfect time to meet him…introduced myself, hoping we could rekindle, make up for lost time. See, after I started working at the hospital, I was trying to get under Sarah's good graces and since my mother loved Sarah, I thought it was only fair she should know what happened between my mother and her husband. So, I confronted Sarah a couple of years ago and showed her my mother's diary. I should've known better, reputations needed to be upheld." Reyna turns to me. "With Frank's election, your mother wrote a check to keep my mouth shut and stay away…but I got greedy. I told Sarah I wanted more money and more and more…"

Ace lit another cigarette and let out a billow of smoke. "More is good," he chuckles. "Now that Red and Larry are locked up, it'll be split two ways."

"My mom would never be so cruel," I grit out. "She would never pay off low-life scum—"

"Who are you calling scum, bitch? The plan is brilliant." Ace's jaw pulses as he glares at me.

"Oh, but she was, Chloe," Reyna feigns. "She was cruel and a thief from the very women she sheltered."

Anger flows hot in my veins, refusing to believe Reyna's words. The woman is sick in the head, psychotic. Mom would never turn away Dad's lost child, let alone pay Reyna off to keep her out of Dad's life.

"Why tell us this when you're going to kill us anyway?" I ask, fear and anger knotting inside me.

"Because I want you to suffer as I have."

"So why kill her if you needed her to keep giving you money?" Dad utters, grit in his voice.

"Since she was the only one who knew about our little secret, I asked her where the funds were coming from. At first, she refused to tell me. But since I had the upper hand and would reveal our secret, she eventually told me it was coming from her precious charity funds."

Reyna pauses as a repulsive grin spreads over her face. "Once I figured out who your accountant was, it was so easy to get any banking information from Mr. Two-Time-Cheating Russell Kollsson.

A man puts his dick in a woman's pussy, he'll give her anything her heart desires. Isn't that right, Chloe?"

"Fuck off, Reyna," I clip through clenched teeth remembering the sight of Luke with her many months ago.

"Actually, don't mind if I do. Luke's waiting for me back at the hotel." Reyna licks her lips. "The poor guy thinks I'm out shopping...idiot."

"Reyna, please let Chloe go. She's done nothing to you. I'm the one who's guilty."

"Oh *Daddy*, you most definitely are guilty, and you are in *my* courtroom. I am judge, jury, and executioner. Your sentence is death. It's time for you to pay for your crime."

"You can't do this!" I scream. "He told you he didn't know about you!"

"Will you shut the fuck up, Chloe?" Reyna turns to the tattooed man and points to a piece of cloth on the floor. "Ace, put a muzzle on both of them. I'm tired of their whining."

Ace pushes himself off the wall, picks up a dirty rag from the floor, and tears it in two. He punches Dad, knocking him out, then ties the cloth around Dad's mouth. Ace moves toward me and wraps the other around my mouth.

Next, he pulls Reyna into his arms and their lips crash together.

"Rey, I need to fuck you before you go back to your loser boyfriend." His voice is low and brusque. "You're fucking hot when you're angry."

"I'm not in the mood, Ace." Reyna's hands frame his face. "But you can have my sister."

Panic surges in my stomach. Bile rises at the thought of having Ace's hands on me. I send up a silent prayer, hoping Julian will find me before Ace sets his eyes on me, then kills us.

"Come on, Rey... You know my dick can satisfy you better than that Jensen boy." Ace licks his lips. "By the way, when are you going to kill the poor bastard?"

"The date is set. Once I'm his wife and the life insurance policy's signed, we can be together."

"God, you're fucking brilliant." Ace pulls on Reyna's hair and his mouth is on her neck.

I gasp through the muzzled cloth. Reyna looks over Ace's shoulders and chuckles, her dark eyes narrowing at me. "Tsk, tsk, tsk… Oh Chloe, do you still love Luke? You were such a tease, leading him on. God, the look on your face when you found us together."

"Enough talking to her, Rey. I want to fuck you, right here, right now." Ace's mouth crashes on Reyna's.

I squeeze my eyes shut, trying to mute the sounds of their kissing and moans. I concentrate on the numbness in my dislocated shoulder.

I only see darkness behind my eyelids, as I'm biding my time with the terrifying realization. I'm afraid I will never see Julian again and those words pain me to think them.

The heartache is more excruciating than the earlier blows to my fragile body. The thought of never seeing his beautiful face, his dimples and his brown eyes that can see into my soul are tearing me apart.

Images skitter through my mind as I remember the time I've spent with him. These past couple of weeks, feel like I've spent a lifetime with him. The moment I landed at the airport; I knew immediately there was something special about him. Our flirty banter and his wisecrack comebacks. Our first kiss at the club and seeing his protective side that night. The hilltop picnic and surprises that never ceased to amaze me.

I manage to laugh to myself, remembering the punch to his jaw during our Ronda Rousey session. And the last several days, making love to him, feeling his arms around me. Just twenty-four hours ago, we were on our date that he promised me the first night I arrived on the island. And then, making love in the rain.

I cling to the memories as I would to a life preserver in a stormy sea.

The sound of Julian's voice fills my thoughts when he told me he loved me. And the thought of Julian going through this a second time, of losing someone, intensifies the pain in my heart.

I come back from my drifting thoughts and take a fortifying breath. I have to grip every ounce of strength I have left.

Julian's words ring through my ears, *'If you feel pain, that means you're still alive.'*

All Reyna and Ace have to do is make a mistake. And as revolting as it would be for them to have sex in front of me and Dad, it may be their weakness in letting their guard down.

Determination courses through my veins and I'm going to do whatever I can to stay strong and get out of this hellhole.

But how?

CHAPTER

Twenty-Nine

JULIAN

I NEED TO REIN MYSELF in.

All I want to do is barrel through the doors, mark my targets, and lodge a bullet in all of their heads. But I have to be smart, keep my cool, remain in control.

Chloe and her father's lives are at stake.

Lincoln is covering the back of the house while I'm covering the front entry. Lincoln, Tyco and I had done a radio check to confirm we can hear one another. Tyco's on standby, ready to contact the local authorities and medics when its time.

Tyco was able to confirm the woman's identity as Reyna Donovan, daughter to single mother, Denise Donovan, who committed suicide when Reyna was seven. Father unknown and no next of kin, therefore putting Reyna in the foster care system until she aged out. Studied nursing. Born and raised in Las Vegas until she moved to San Francisco and worked at SF General Hospital the last three years. Tyco also discovered this was the same woman Luke Jensen had hooked up with.

But it's still unclear to me why Reyna wants Chloe and Frank.

I take measured steps. The hallowed planks below my boots creak with every move. Beads of sweat coat my skin and I wipe the dew from my forehead with the back of my wrist.

All my senses are on hyper-alert and I'm relying on my natural abilities and years of training.

I mute out the sound of the surf, the whistling wind and the seagulls that gawk above. My shoulder barely touching the splintered shiplap exterior. My ear is close to the wood so I can hear something, anything, on the other side.

The muffled voices of a man and a woman.

Footsteps and shuffling.

I cautiously lift my head and peek through a dull window.

Reyna's hair is in disarray, her hip leans on the table slipping her panties on. She then grabs a gun next to her and points it at Frank. Frank's body, hands tied behind his back and feet bound together, lay on the floor. It isn't clear if Frank is still alive, I only pray he is.

The unknown man, belt buckle undone and his jeans hanging low, has a cigarette dangling from the corner of his mouth as he checks his gun.

"Charlie-one to Charlie-two," I whisper. "What's your status?"

"I'm at the back door now. Locked and loaded." Lincoln's whisper can be heard loud and clear in my earbud. "You got eyes on them?"

"Two targets. The *bitch* and her *bastard*. Both armed. Frank's on the floor, status unknown."

The man buckles his pants, hands his gun to Reyna then moves across the room. His hands swoop under Chloe's armpits and he drags her to the empty chair. I can see her mangled hair, ripped dress, scrapes, and bruises marking her bare skin. Her limp body shows there's no more fight in her and it's ripping me to shreds.

I grit my teeth. My grip tightens around my Glock when the bastard backhands Chloe across the face. Her head swings, and the blood from her nose and mouth is soaked up by the threads from the dirty rag gagging her mouth.

"That fucker just hit Chloe." Adrenaline infiltrates my body.

The man stretches out his hand and grabs the gun from Reyna, then raises it to Chloe's head.

"Fuck! He's going to shoot her. Go, go, go! Execute now!"

I kick in the front door, in one fluid motion, my gun aiming at my target.

The man aims his gun at me... fires and misses.

From my peripheral, Lincoln rushes in with his weapon poised and ready upon the man. In unison, both of us riddle our intended target with bullets.

The bastard falls to his knees, then topples down like a redwood tree, his finger still pressing on the trigger as random shots ring out around us.

Reyna evades the bullets, her own gun still in hand. She lunges for Chloe who is still sitting in the chair.

Both women stumble to the floor.

Reyna quickly shuffles to her feet, holding Chloe in her arms, using her as a human shield. With the barrel of the gun lodged in Chloe's neck, Reyna takes faltering steps toward the door behind her.

The gunfire, the smell of burning metal, the trails of smoke seep from the barrels of our guns. In an instant, there's an eerie silence, a ringing in my ears. But my eyes lock and follow Reyna's every move as she nears the front door.

My jaw clenches as I see tears stream down Chloe's bruised and bloody face. The fear in her eyes just about shreds me to a million pieces. I need to stay focused and as much as it hurts me, I can't continue to look at her. My eyes meet Reyna's glare. I need just one clean shot, but with the tip of her barrel pressed into Chloe's neck and the woman's finger on the trigger, it's too risky.

Lincoln moves about the room, closer to my side, our guns aiming at Reyna.

"It's over," I threaten.

"Stay back," Reyna hisses, panic in her eyes.

"You've got nowhere to go, Reyna." I take a small obscure step closer.

"Are you blind, dickhead? I have a gun pointing at your girlfriend." Reyna presses the gun deeper into Chloe's neck. "I will shoot her."

"Let her go," I grit out, my voice more aggressive, determined.

Chloe whimpers under the muzzled cloth when Reyna tightens her grip.

I've just about had enough of this shit. The embers of rage are now a full-on inferno as sweat trickles down my back. I meet Reyna's evil olive eyes staring back at me.

I steady my aim and pull the trigger.

It's all in slow motion.

I can see the bullet slicing through the air before catching the center of Reyna's forehead. Chloe flinches as blood spurts on her face from the hole the slug made.

The bitch falls to her knees, bringing Chloe down with her.

Another shot rings out—from Reyna's gun. The last shot from the dead woman's gun struck Chloe's fragile body as her head hit the wooden floor.

"Chloe! Fuck. No, no, no, no." I shout.

I run to Chloe, afraid to touch or move her, so as not to disturb the bullet's penetration. "Tyco, call the paramedics," I yell into the two-way satellite radio. "Chloe's been shot."

"*Fuck*," Tyco yelps through the line. "They're on their way."

I remove the rag from Chloe's mouth and gently press it to her abdomen where the bullet punctured her frail body.

She's unresponsive and doesn't flinch.

Flashes cut through my thoughts, an excruciating déjà vu. An image of Amber, then a vision of Chloe, Amber and back to Chloe. Sirens come from the distance, but it feels like an eternity before they arrive.

"Come on, Doc. Open your eyes. Come on, baby. Let me see your pretty blue-greens." I caress her face, attempting to wake her. Chloe warbles in and out of consciousness, opening and closing her eyes, yet still unresponsive.

Time stands still as the ache in my heart grows, making it difficult to breathe.

Chloe, my lifeline and she lies here, motionless.

"Sir, please step back…sir, please let her go…" the medics' voices echo.

I don't want to leave her side. I don't want to break the connection, I want to continue holding Chloe's hand, somehow letting her know I'm still here.

"Booker, you gotta let her go. Let them do their job," Lincoln's voice calls to me.

Tears burn my throat as I give the medics room to do what is necessary. To keep her alive and bring her back to me.

I look down at my bloodstained palms.

So much blood.

Her blood.

Chloe's body lay on the gurney as the medics wheel her into the back of the ambulance. I'm not going to leave her side. I clutch her hand and watch as the medics move in such a high-paced rhythm in the small space, their medical battlefield.

Undisturbed by my presence and the bumpy ride, the medics cut Chloe's blouse open, her torso bloody, as they apply pressure to the bullet wound. They give the necessary IV fluids and secure an oxygen mask to her blood-splattered face.

All I can do is pray and hope they can keep her from bleeding out before we arrive at the hospital.

CHAPTER

Chloe

A HAZE OF DARKNESS IS all around.

Where am I? Oh God…the pain. It hurts so much.

"Come on, Doc. Open your eyes. Come on, baby. Let me see your pretty blue-greens."

Julian, is that you? Where are you? I can't see you. The fog is too thick. I raise my voice, but Julian is nowhere to be found.

A bright light, a flash of his beautiful face.

I see you, Julian.

My eyelids feel heavy. Then darkness again.

"Booker, you gotta let her go. Let them do their job," comes Lincoln's voice.

"I'm not leaving her," Julian shouts.

Julian…don't let me go. Stay with me. I'm scared.

I try to move my arms, but they won't budge. Feeling trapped, a heaviness bears down on my chest and pain knots in my stomach, making it hard to breathe.

I remember. I was shot.

Unfamiliar voices muffle around me and I hear beeping sounds in the background.

I'm so cold.

"Blood pressure is dropping below one hundred."

My blood pressure is dropping! Shit, I'm losing blood.

"Hang in there. Three more minutes to base."

Three minutes. I can do three minutes.

Warm hands grip mine. They belong to Julian. "Come on, Doc. Stay with me. I need you."

I need you too. Please don't let go of me, Julian.

I hear doors open and a rush of my body in motion.

"What do you have?" another voice calls out.

"Female. Late twenties. Single gunshot to the abdomen. Administered IV and fluids. Going in and out of consciousness. She's stable…"

"Okay…on my count. One, two, three." My body lifts from where I lay to another firm surface. And I know what's next to come for me.

Holy hell. This bullet hurts.

"Meds are in," a female voice says. "Heart rate 128. BP dropping below 100…"

Don't die… Hang in there, Channing. Think of Julian, your lifeline.

"Prep her for surgery. Now." A male's voice calls out in the cold room. My body hurts so much. I want the pain to go away.

I could just let go and let it all slip away.

More voices call out various numbers. A cold fluid seeps into my body, chasing the pain away and covering me in blackness again.

CHAPTER

Thirty-One

JULIAN

ALL I WANT TO DO is rewind the clock.
Go back to the hilltop where we last made love in the rain. Or go back even further, to the day we first met. Maybe things would be much different now. The one woman who healed my broken heart and the deep scars of my soul, now needs to be fixed.

Agony.

The only thing I feel is pure hopelessness and I want to jump off the ledge. The lead of guilt weighs heavily in my stomach and fire rages within me all at the same time.

My blood-soaked cargo pants and dried blood on my hands are reminders of the fucked-up rescue that had gone completely wrong.

Waiting.

That's all I can do.

Time has no place within the sterile white walls of the hospital. Minutes feel like hours and hours feel like an eternity. I pace the laminate floors of the long corridor as the blur of nurses that pass by me starts to make me dizzy.

My boots move me into the waiting room. I lean against the doorjamb and scan the room. Sam's face in his hands as Sage's arm comforts him. Ezra and Olinda, their foreheads touching, embracing one another for support and comfort.

Remorse stirs in my chest when my eyes meet Phoebe's. I swallow the lump in my throat and slightly shake my head, sending her unspoken apologies.

Phoebe rises from her chair and puts her arms around me. She pulls back slightly and frames my face, wiping a fallen tear from my eye.

"This isn't your fault," Phoebe says, her red-rimmed eyes filled with tears.

I shut my eyes because it is my fault. "I fucked up, Phoebe."

"Hey, look at me. Chloe is the strongest person I know." Phoebe chokes back a sob. We stare at each other for a beat until a soft smile pulls at Phoebe's lips. "I need you to be strong for her."

"I can't lose her… I just found her."

A squeak of rubber shoes behind me. Then a woman clears her throat breaking the tension in the room. "Family of Chloe and Frank Channing?" the nurse announces, clipboard in hand.

Sam steps toward the nurse. "I'm Chloe's cousin. Frank's my uncle."

"Yes, sir. Mr. Channing is in recovery. He's got a couple of broken ribs, lacerations, and contusions." She flips through the papers. "Other than that, he will be just fine."

"Can I see him?" Sam asks, fingering his hair back.

"Yes, but don't push him. He's had a rough ride and may be out of it from the meds."

"Thank you," Sam replies, letting out a breath of relief.

"And Chloe?" I quickly ask.

"They did identify some hemorrhaging and right now the doctor is doing an exploratory laparotomy to locate where the bleeding is coming from. I'm sure the doctor will come out and let you all know once he's done." The nurse warmly nods, and her outstretched hand motions for Sam to follow.

"I'm going to see my uncle…let him know what's going on with

Chloe." Sam takes a hold of Sage's hand. "Let me know if you get an update." Then he follows the nurse down the hall.

A momentary silence joins the small waiting room. I anticipate the doctor's forthcoming final words. Even now, they tear at me like bear claws shredding my skin.

I reach in my pocket, pull out the turtle charm necklace I picked up from the shed before getting in the ambulance. I stare at the trinket for a moment, hating the lump forming in my throat and the tears blurring my vision.

I so badly want to see her smiling face.

Parallel images collide of Amber and Chloe, knocking my breath loose. The doctor's words that came out… *'I'm so sorry for your loss'* hammered my heart when they couldn't save Amber.

I pray I don't hear those same words again. I send up a silent prayer hoping for some kind of sign that Chloe is going to come out of this.

I need to remind myself to breathe, to stay strong for her. But it's almost impossible when the woman I love more than my own life is fighting for her very own.

My head pounds as images of her brittle body, the bang of Reyna's gun firing one last time, then Chloe falling to the floor—all play in a loop, over and over.

I tuck the necklace back in my front pocket. "Don't you dare die on me, Chloe," I whisper to myself, letting out a deep breath I didn't realize I held in my lungs.

A heavy hand rests on my shoulder. "She's gonna pull through, Book," Lincoln says as he hands me a cup of coffee in a paper cup.

"Linc." I shake my head not wanting the coffee. I can't eat, drink or sleep until I know she's okay. "This is all my fault. I keep replaying what we…what *I* could've done."

"Don't fuckin' do this. You'll make yourself crazy."

"It's like the gods are punishing me, again."

"*Bullshit.* What you need to focus on is what you're going to say to her when she wakes up."

I roughly scrub my face. "I can't breathe without her."

"I can't either." Phoebe's voice wavers as she clings to my arm. "We have to stay strong."

"Go back to the house," Lincoln instructs. "Take a shower, clean yourself up, pretty boy. There's nothing you can do right now. Chloe will be in surgery for a while. I'll stay here with Phoebe and call you as soon as I hear anything."

"I'm not going to leave—"

"For once, will you listen to me, asshole," Lincoln snaps. "When she gets out of surgery, you wouldn't want her to see your ugly mug, would you?"

"I'm not leaving, Linc. I need to be here."

"Please. I'm telling you not only as a friend, but your bro. It'll do you some good. And you're scaring the shit out of the people here with all that damn blood on your clothes."

"You think I give a flying fuck what people think of my fashion statement?" I survey the dried blood on my clothes.

"Well, I do. Not only do you look like shit, you smell like it too."

Only Lincoln can lighten up any stressful situation. A feeble grin perks my mouth as I stifle a weak laugh. "You've smelled worse, asshole," I tell him.

I look over to Phoebe as she fiddles with her necklace.

"I'm scared, Julian," she says as a tear trails down her cheek.

I wrap my arms around her. "Me too, Phoebe. Me, too."

CHAPTER

Thirty-Two

JULIAN

ALL I WANT IS TO hold her in my arms again. My heart thumps so hard it bruises my chest. Guilt consumes my thoughts and sadness weighs me down.

I miss her so much. There are days I can't breathe without her.

I need to finally say goodbye.

I need the peace to put it all behind me.

Although the scars are there, time would at least ease the pain.

I miss the sweet scent of her perfume, her soft hands wrapped around mine and the gentle peck on my cheek.

I swear I can still hear her tender voice in my ear.

Bent knees on the grass, I wipe the leaves from the cold embossed surface. My finger grazes the edge of the small headstone. A tear escapes as I rest her favorite flowers on the grass between the granite markers.

For a moment, I stare at my palms, remembering the blood that once covered them. Phantom pains crush my heart as the image of the casket being lowered into the ground return, and the sounds of sobered cries whimpering around me.

A cool breeze rustles the grass. Chills race over my skin as I slowly open my mouth to speak.

"Hey there…sorry it's been several months. Just got back from an assignment. Work's been busy."

I look up into the brisk December blue skies of California, a bittersweet feeling knots in my belly. I'm happy to be home from an overseas assignment, able to sleep in my own bed, but hate being in the spot I currently occupy, staring down at the memorial.

"I don't even know where to begin. It's so hard being here. I actually hate coming to this place." I ramble, pulling out several blades of grass and tossing them aside. "This fuckin' sucks… I'm not good at this, ya know?"

Another tear falls as I remember what could have been.

"On my way here, I saw a kid holding his dad's hand. It breaks my heart that I couldn't have that with you. He would've been a mini version of me, of course." I stifle a chuckle. "He'd be devilishly handsome and would definitely have my wits. But he'd have your caring heart, be playful like you, with that cute-as-hell giggle when I tickled you."

The knot tenses in my belly.

"I miss you… Holding your hand, playing with your crazy hair… your cheesy jokes and just…everything." I let out an exasperating breath. "You should be proud. I'm moving forward…can't live in purgatory anymore."

I rub the overgrown stubble on my jaw and drag my hair back with my hand, then laugh to myself. "Yeah, yeah…I know what you're going to say, I need to shave, and a haircut. I'm headed to the barber after this. Satisfied? That's what I came here to tell you. Tonight's the fundraiser gala and they're honoring your name with a plaque. It will be a permanent fixture at the Los Angeles shelter. It's so beautiful…just like you."

Before I stand, I kiss the two pads of my fingers and press them to her cold headstone and proffered another to the other smaller one.

"I gotta go. I'm going to be late to your party. I will love you always. You know you can check on me, once in a while... it would be nice to hear your voice from time to time."

Hours later, I arrive at The Ritz, where it all began. The melancholy feelings all come back like a tsunami.

I take in a deep breath. Tonight is a special night.

I pace the hall, my stressed nerves rattling within me. I can't seem to calm the swarm of bees in my stomach, fluttering and stinging me, as familiar faces approach to shake hands and console me during this sentimental, nostalgic event.

Mom and Knox, my dad and boss greet me at the check-in table being manned by Jonathon 'Hawk' Hawkins, a fellow teammate at KSIG.

"Hey there, son." Knox gives me a stiff handshake. "You doin' okay?"

"Hey, Dad. I'm good." I smile then turn to Mom and kiss her cheek. "Mom, you look stunning." Her dark wavy hair tumbles past her shoulders. The diamond necklace that glitters around her neck is the perfect accent to her elegant black gown.

Mom embraces me and returns a kiss. "Thank you, Mijo. You cleaned up good," she says, wiping her lipstick off my cheek.

"How was your mission? Any issues?" Knox asks, seriousness written all over his face.

"Easy in, easy out... Gathered intel and Tyke is examining it now."

"Good." Knox nods, pleased. "I want to talk to you about another matter—"

"Darling, not tonight." Mom elbows Knox. "There will be no talking business tonight."

Knox laughs. "Yes, dear." He rests his hand on Mom's lower back. "She's right. Let's talk Monday at the office."

I nod at my boss and father who taught me about being a man. I only hope someday I can be as happy as my parents are. A warm fuzzy feeling takes over my heart seeing Mom get that second chance she deserves.

"Mijo, I've got a surprise for you." Mom shifts and motions for me to look over her shoulder.

My eyes widen and my smile grows as Fabiola wearing a royal-blue gown walks toward me, her hand hooked in a man's arm. He's tall, caramel-blond hair and wearing a dark suit.

I laugh to myself, wondering if this is boyfriend number five and it isn't even Christmas yet.

"Hey, big brother." Fabiola releases her hold from the man and stretches out her arms. "Miss me much?"

"Fabs...what the hell?" I embrace my kid sister, lift her off her feet and swing her around. "Damn girl, I've missed your ugly face. You told me you couldn't make it."

I set Fabiola back on her feet, steadying her.

"I wouldn't miss you making a fool of yourself on stage. My alpha big bro scared to speak in front of a room full of people... You ready for your fifteen minutes of fame?"

"Yep. Ready as I'll ever be," I say all the while calming the nerves rattling my bones.

"Doesn't your sister look amazing?" Mom's question is more like a statement.

"Like mother, like daughter," Fabiola's date says, with a hint of a British accent.

"Okay, turd-face, let me introduce you to Remi McCoy. He's in security just like you and Dad."

We shake hands.

"It's a pleasure to meet you, Remi." I pause for a second. "McCoy, huh? By chance related to Liam McCoy?" I ask looking at his familiar face and recalling the name.

"Yes, actually. He's my brother," Remi replies.

"LR McCoy International Ops?" I confirm.

Remi nods. "Hm...small world?"

"Liam helped with an op a while back—"

Mom coughs with obvious irritation and my cue to shut my mouth. "Julian, no business. Tonight is special, remember?"

"Yes, Mom. No business." I wink at her, then turn to Remi. "We can talk later."

Remi nods. "I look forward to it."

Knox kisses Mom's cheek. "Shall we go inside and find our table?"

Mom hooks her hand in the crook of my stepdad's elbow, Fabiola and Remi follow suit and together the foursome walk through the ballroom doors.

I still and can't move. "I'll see you guys inside. I need a minute."

"Okay, see you in there," Fabiola says as she softly smiles. "Break a leg."

I pace the grand hallway. I steady my breathing with every step.

The nervousness and anxiety overwhelm me. I cup the back of my neck and there's a thin sheen of sweat.

I look over to where Hawk stoically stands as he checks in the remaining guests. I can't help reliving the moment when I saw Chloe for the first time in that very same spot.

Lock it down, Cruz. You got this.

Hawk juts his chin. "You okay, man?"

"I'm good." I hold up an index card. "I have to give this speech."

"Public speaking is the number-one fear. You'd think it'd be death, but believe it or not, death is fifth..." Hawk rambles the facts, his mouth turning up in a proud grin.

"Thanks, Einstein. Isn't it ironic we can fight on the battlefield, kick ass, come face to face with things we wish we could erase from our minds...and I'm fucking hyperventilating over some words I have written down on this three-by-five."

"I know how you can overcome your fear while you're on stage. Just focus on..."

I tune out Hawk's statistical chatter when my eyes veer to a mirage. A vision—of *her.*

I have to blink a few times to make sure I'm not dreaming.

Damn...I missed her so much.

She gracefully approaches, hypnotizing every one of my senses. I hold my breath as desire overwhelms my logic, not caring about Hawk's trivial rants.

She fingers a lock of hair behind her ear that falls like a thick curtain down her back.

Several guests stop her as she smiles and shakes their hands. That damn smile of hers still gets to me every time, knocking me breathless.

She nods politely at the woman she's speaking to, then motions for the guests to enter the grand ballroom.

Her magnificent ever-changing blue-green eyes lock on mine and her sexy gait moves across the hall toward me. It's difficult for me to look away and why would I? She's stunning, enchanting, and breath-takingly beautiful.

Just over five months ago, it's hard to imagine the state she was in. It broke my heart and ripped me to shreds seeing Chloe on the gurney, fighting for her life and then the road to recovery in ICU. A ghostly shiver creeps up my spine, recalling the nightmare we both lived through.

But, just like Phoebe told me, Chloe is strong, and she had the fight in her that willed her to live.

"Hey there, hotcakes." Chloe's sexy kitten voice breaks through my haze.

I take Chloe's hand and pull her into an alcove at the end of the hall. I cup her face and press my lips to hers. I hunger for the taste of her sensual lips, had been longing for them since I landed in San Francisco.

I press my body against her softness from shoulder to knee as her back bumps the wall behind her. Her soft sigh follows a sweet moan I love so much it sends a tingle down to my groin.

This woman owns me. And I love it. Love her.

My thumb grazes the side of her breast as my hands caress down her hourglass figure. I want to ditch the party and take her to my bed. Feel her bare skin against my own. Bury myself deep inside her.

"Damn, Doc, I've missed you so much." I struggle to break away.

Chloe licks her lips. "Wow. Maybe you should go away more often if those are the kisses I will get every time you come back."

"This trip killed me. Two weeks, too long." I stroke the frame of her face with my fingers.

"Everything go well overseas?"

"Yup…and I'm glad to be back home." I kiss the tip of her nose.

"I'm so sorry I didn't know you were here already. This event has been keeping me busy. There was so much to do to prepare and—"

"Shh…I just want to look at you for a sec." I stare at her, suddenly feeling like a little boy who believes in magic. My palms frame her delicate jawline.

Chloe angles her head into my hand, smiling contently, as her eyes lock on mine.

Fucking enchanting.

She is the woman who owns me inside and out. She's the air I breathe and the other half of my heart. It's a bit sappy, but all true, nonetheless.

"You okay, Julian? You're scaring me."

"I'm perfect now that I have you in my arms." I kiss her forehead. "I, uh…I'm a bit nervous giving this speech today."

"Oh, come on, hotcakes…" Chloe's nickname for me when I made pancakes for her, sounds so cute coming from her lips. "My hunky, super-secret agent…*nervous?*"

I laugh, tossing my head back. "I'll show you hunky."

"Promise?"

"I promise you an all-nighter, Doc."

I SIP MY RUM AND Coke to ease the anxiety that stirs in the pit of my stomach. My eyes roam the round table. A grin perks the corners of my mouth.

The people who have meant the world to Chloe and I are here.

I raise a brow, laughing to myself.

Phoebe swirls her wine chatting with Ryland, something about a hot date and a Code Red. *Women.*

I study Sam as he fingers a strand of hair behind Sage's ear and kisses her cheek. Sage giggles at something Sam whispers in her ear. The two have been joined at the hip and I predict Sam is going to propose soon. The signs were there.

There's my long-time friend, Dylan 'Lincoln' Marshall, who got his callsign because he's so damn honest.

Lincoln interrupts my thoughts when he opens his mouth. "Man, Phoebe is hella fine." His voice is low so only I can hear.

"Linc, cool your jets. Besides, you finally got your date with Roc." I point my chin to Rocky sitting on the other side of Lincoln.

"This isn't a date, Booker," Rocky snaps.

"Call it whatever you want, Princess. We arrived together," Lincoln teases.

Rocky raises her hand in Lincoln's face. "And I'm banking I will be leaving without you if you keep eyeing Miss Powell."

"Jealous much?" he retorts before he lifts the amber liquid to his mouth.

"Don't flatter yourself. You're not my type. Besides, I'm here for Booker, not for you. Tonight's a big deal."

"Yeah, it is a big deal," I confirm, imbibing another sip of my rum.

"Linc, why don't you ask her out?" Rocky says, motioning toward Phoebe.

Lincoln shakes his head. "Eh, she's too feisty for me."

"Translation. You can't handle her?" Rocky raises a brow in amusement.

"I can handle any woman who comes my way. The question is, could she handle the Linc-Man?"

"Okay, you two…settle down. I swear you bicker like Fred and Ethel." I chuckle.

A deep cough interrupts from over my shoulder. "Announcements will start soon. You ready?" Judge Channing asks.

"Yes, sir." I stand, shake his hand and nod. "I just want to say thank you. This means the world to me."

I need to shake his hand again, let him know I remember our conversation from a couple of months ago. Not only had I never killed a woman point-blank, but it was Frank's daughter and Chloe's sister. The intense discussion between the two of us was uncomfortable, to say the least. If the information was known to me prior to the rescue, I would've had a different plan. And Reyna could've gotten the help she needed.

After Judge Channing fully recovered, he'd asked for the details of the rescue since he'd been unconscious the entire time. I gave him the rundown, feeling more guilt and anger than ever before.

Judge Channing told me the fuel that was behind Reyna's vengeance and why she wanted him and Chloe dead. There was evil in Reyna and that woman was not Frank's daughter, as far as he was concerned, and Frank assured me he didn't hold any ill-will against me for doing what was necessary.

"No need for thanks." Judge Channing warmly smiles. "I owe you my life, son. What's more, you saved my daughter."

"I would do it again," I promise.

"I know."

A tap on the microphone vibrates through the speakers and echoes in the enormous room. The guests' voices hush as a red-haired woman in an emerald gown takes the stage. Judge Channing sits back at the table with Knox and Mom, and I sit down in my chair.

"Good evening, ladies and gentlemen. My name is Stacey Hampton, Campaign Manager of Concrete Angels Foundation. It is truly an honor to stand before you all and humbly thank you for being with us this evening, and for your generous donations. I would like to give a brief history of this special foundation and tell you about the late Doctor Sarah Channing. A woman whose heart was bigger than California. A woman with a vision…"

I look to where Chloe stands on the right side of the stage. Her eyes meet mine, and then her smile just about knocks the wind out of me.

Beautiful.

There isn't a doubt in my mind I want to spend the rest of my life with her.

Chloe is my future, my present, my everything.

Tonight I will embrace that very future.

I will say goodbye to my past.

Move on but will never forget.

CHAPTER
Thirty-Three

CHLOE

M
Y HEART SWELLS AS MY eyes lock on the man I love. His eyes tell a story of a tortured past and I hope the scars the demons left behind are healed. The man helped me remember my past, and I cannot see my future without him.

There was a new hunger in his kiss in the alcove after I saw him in the hallway. I welcome it but it also unnerves me.

Is he hiding something, or did something terrible happen on his overseas mission?

It's going to take some getting used to, him going away on assignments. The last one he was gone overseas for two weeks and it nearly broke me since he was unable to make any contact with me except through Tyco.

Julian doesn't talk about his missions with me, as confidentiality is ever critical in his line of work. He told me the less I know, the safer I am. *No news is good news*, he assured me before he left. I find it hard to believe. All he would do was kiss my nose, tell me he'd be back, and make love to me before he left.

Little did I know my world would flip upside down and my life would turn out to be the very romantic-suspense novel Phoebe gives me a hard time about.

I laugh as her words ring through: *Get your head out of the clouds and come back to earth because there's no such thing as a hunky, secret-undercover agent who will come to your rescue.*

I look out to the crowd and get a glimpse of Phoebe, gesturing to the heels with the red bottoms. I twist my lips. A reminder of the bet I lost. Damn Louboutins nearly cost me a thousand dollars...but worth every penny.

An applause fills the room and Lincoln has two fingers in his mouth, letting out a loud whistle. "You the man," Dylan bellows. "You got this."

Julian takes the stage, stands behind the podium and pulls an index card from his jacket pocket. He smiles at me for reassurance and I smile right back. I'm lost in him.

I bite my lip, tilt my head at the man who looks so damn sexy in his tuxedo. Licks of desire flutter my belly as I gaze upon my six-plus alpha man, with broad shoulders, strong jawline, and those sparkling brown eyes.

How does he do that?

I shake my head slightly, needing to stay focused for my cue to step up on the stage and remove the cloth over the easel that's hiding the plaque.

"Thank you, Stacey, for the wonderful introduction," Julian starts. "Tonight is a very special evening and I stand before you, honored and humbled. Five years ago, Ambrosia Cruz, my late wife, was gunned down at a convenience store during an attempted robbery..."

As I stand stage right, listening to Julian and waiting for my cue, I can't help that my thoughts wander to the day I told Julian my idea of the dedication to the Los Angeles chapter. Images flash to the morning when Julian had again made his famous pancakes I love so much.

"Julian, you're being ridiculous," I huffed. "I am capable of eating at the kitchen table." I sucked in my bottom lip as I gawked at the shirtless man, showing off his rippled abs and the sexy 'V' line trailing in his sweatpants that hung low around his hips. "But then again the view of you serving me breakfast in bed wins any day."

Julian had come from the kitchen and was carrying a tray with a plate of pancakes, a cup of coffee, and a glass of orange juice.

"Don't give me any grief, Channing. Doctor's orders. You need to stay off your feet, rest, and eat lots of food."

"Did you forget I'm a doctor too? And I don't recall the doctor telling me to eat lots of food. If you keep feeding me like this, I'm going to turn into an elephant."

"Will you just let me take care of you?" he chided.

"It's been over a month. I was lucky there were no complications during the surgery. I'm perfectly fine. I go back to work in a week."

"You are so fuckin' stubborn, you know that?" Julian placed the tray on the nightstand next to the bed. "Look, I know Phoebe's been taking care of you too and frankly, I'm sure she's getting sick of me hanging around here. I just want to spend as much time with you as I can since I have to return to work in a few days."

"And I love that you're taking care of me, and the time we've spent together. But I'm not going to break."

"Baby, you're the strongest woman I know. Been to hell and back…"

"And I appreciate it and you." I scooted on the bed and patted on the mattress. "Sit."

Julian sat at the edge of the bed and brushed my hair behind my ear. "I just want to take care of you. Is that too much to ask?"

"No, it's not… But I want to talk to you about something very important."

"What's up, Doc?" Julian chortled, lightening the mood with his impersonation of the cartoon character.

"Cute…but seriously. I've been thinking about what happened to me and Amber."

Julian shook his head. "What happened to you and to Amber are not the same thing."

"I beg to differ. Both people wanted revenge. The only difference is, I survived, and Amber didn't." I let out a breath. "So, I've been thinking… Hear me out…"

Julian quirked a brow at my infamous last words, the ones I spoke when an idea sparked. "Yeah, last time you said that, it was absolutely ludicrous. And it still got you this damn hole..." Julian lifted the hem of my tank-top and his thumb grazed the stitched scar on my stomach.

"At least I'm here," I reassured him.

"And so am I." Julian cupped my jaw and closed the distance, our faces just a feather apart. "I'm not going anywhere." He pressed his mouth to mine. The kiss intensified to a hungry soul-devouring kind of kiss that melted my heart as our tongues tangled in an intimate dance. He pulled back and looked in my eyes. "God, I can't get enough of you, Channing. I hate that I have to leave you in a few days. I'm going to worry about you, there's no denying it."

Our foreheads touched and the comfortable silence was welcomed.

"Listen, it's over. Reyna is dead and Dad is back at work. Business as usual," I tried to comfort him.

"It's not business as usual. I know you're still troubled about Reyna. Shit, she was your half-sister for crying out loud." Julian pulled back and studied my face. "How have your sessions been with Doctor Zhang?"

"Good, I guess. Talking about it helps. It hurts to know Reyna as a little girl going through the abuse." I picked at a piece of lint from my top. "I wish Mom had known her as the little girl, maybe she could've done something."

"Reyna lost her way, Doc. You can't save everyone."

"And you can't either."

"What's that supposed to mean?" Julian cocked his head.

"You taking care of me, hand and foot."

Julian chuckled. "You know the guys are giving me shit for playing Nurse Nightingale all the while the workload isn't lightening up. I already have my assignment. I'll be gone for a few days and although the team is happy your recovery is going well, they know I'm milking this time off."

"I'm going to have to get used to you being gone days or maybe weeks at a time."

"It's what I do… I'm going to miss you like crazy. But the best part of returning home is coming back to you." Julian gently kissed my nose.

"Speaking of returning home… The fundraiser event is around the corner."

"And?"

"And we usually have one of the ladies give their testimony, how the foundation has helped them. But I want to do something different this Christmas. I want to gift the Los Angeles chapter with an official name. A dedication." I pulled out a paper from the drawer next to the bed and handed it to Julian. "I want to name it Ambrosia's Angels."

Julian surveyed the paper for a moment. "I don't know what to say…"

"Amber's the reason we're together. I know it's foolish for me to say, but I feel like she was watching over both of us."

"I like that. Ambrosia's Angels." Julian grinned. "Yeah, our guardian angel."

"The dedication is fitting, don't you think?"

"It's perfect." He placed the paper on the nightstand and kissed me again.

"So, the event… I want you to get a hold of Amber's parents, your sister, Mom, Knox, and anyone else you want to be there for this event."

"You're amazing, you know that?" He smiled with his eyes and it comforted me knowing he was pleased.

"So I've been told by a hunky, super-secret agent."

"Oh really? Should I be jealous of this hunky, super-secret agent?" he teased as he raised a brow.

"Well, I don't remember much about him except he goes by the name of Booker."

"Booker, huh? Should I be jealous of this Booker character?"

"Maybe. He does look sexy in a tux."

"Does this Booker come with a last name?"

"Nope, just Booker. I think he got that nickname because he has a little black book with hundreds of women's names in it. He's a player."

"Oh, really?" He leaned in a bit closer making my tummy flutter with his cocky grin.

"Something like that. I was hoping he'd ask me out on a date."

"And did he?"

"No, he disappeared. Vanished. Poof. Gone." I wave my hand in the air.

"Well, that was a jerk move on his part."

"I know, especially when he said he was going to give me a foot massage for wearing four-inch-high heels that I wasn't able to break in."

"I can remedy that..." Julian took my foot and began to massage the ball of my heel. "How's this?"

"Mm," I moaned. "Feels nice. But maybe you can go a little higher... I have this knot that needs to be massaged."

Julian's hands moved to my calves. "Here?"

"Mm-hm, yes...that feels good too. A little higher." I sucked in my lip, the throbbing at the apex of my legs called for his touch.

"How's this?" Julian slipped through my panties. "Hm...feels like someone is wet and ready." His thumb massaged back and forth along the slits of my flesh.

Julian slid my panties down my legs and tossed them aside. He grabbed my ankles and gently pulled me, so my back was flat on the bed. He pushed down his sweats and centered himself between her legs.

"Is this what you had in mind, Doc?" Julian's husky voice sent shivers up my spine.

My gaze locked on his brown eyes as I traced the ridges of his biceps. My libido called for every part of him. He was absolutely gorgeous...*and all mine.*

"I guess I got two for the price of one."

"I'm double-trouble, baby," he mused. "And right now, I want to be your player."

"God, you are *so* cheesy. Don't tell me that line worked on other women?"

"Nope, just you."

Julian's intense stare held me captive, as if he were looking deep in my soul like an open door. Briefly, I wondered what Julian saw when he looked at me. His smile radiated warmth, but it was his eyes I was drawn to.

"I love you, Agent Booker."

"And I love you, Doctor Channing…"

A roar of applause pulls me back into the ballroom. I'm in such deep thought, I hope I didn't miss my cue.

"…Finally, I would like to bring Doctor Chloe Channing up here. The woman responsible for this evening's event," Julian concludes, and his outstretched hand gestures for me to come up on stage.

That's my cue.

I lift my gown as I cautiously step onto the stage. I take the microphone from the stand, hold it close to my mouth, bracing myself to speak as I calm my nerves. As much as I prepared for the event, public speaking is never as easy as it looks.

"Thank you, Julian, for sharing your story," I begin. "And thank you all for being here this evening and for the contributions that will benefit the women and children who are on the road to recovery from their battered pasts. I would also like to thank the many volunteers who spent countless hours getting this event together and I'd like to thank the women who participated in the dating auction. The final numbers have been calculated and I am pleased to announce we have exceeded our goal this evening."

The roaring claps and whistles fill the ballroom. I peer out into the crowd, taking it all in.

My heart swells to see the standing ovation and the many people in attendance. I look down at my best friends who mouth *'you owe me'* for bribing them to participate in the dating auction. I laugh internally knowing exactly who their suitors are.

I raise my hand to silence the crowd as they all sit back down in their chairs. "Thank you again. I know you are all ready to start dancing and get your groove on. I promise we will get to that in just a few more minutes."

The audience laughs and a whistle or two sounds.

"This evening I wanted to do something different. Normally, we would have one of the women give you their testimony, but we decided to change it up a bit. Not only is it a privilege for me to stand here in front of all you, but also a blessing. This man" —I extend a hand toward Julian—"for those who may not know, saved my life several months ago. So, I wanted to return the favor to honor him and his late wife. From what Julian told me, Ambrosia had so many wonderful virtues. She had so much love not just for her husband, but all the people around her." I glance at Amber's parents. I smile at her mother as she wipes a tear from her cheek.

"She loved to make people laugh, had a boundless energy, and she loved children. She was a woman who was compassionate, caring and had a heart of gold. I thought it fitting to recognize her and her amazing qualities, which is exactly what this foundation is all about. So, with that said, from the bottom of my heart, I would like to reveal the beautiful plaque that will be dedicated to the Los Angeles chapter in honor of Ambrosia Cruz."

Together, Julian and I remove the heavy cloth and reveal the plaque with the embossed inscription.

Ambrosia's Angels - May her wings protect you and guide you to safety.

Claps erupt as the guests stand to their feet. I place the microphone back on the stand and begin to clap with the crowd. The applause lasts for a moment and slowly descends as the guests sit back down.

Julian lifts the microphone and begins to speak again. "Thank you. This means the world to me… But I have something else to add to this evening's event."

I furrow my brows in confusion since this is not part of the ceremony as Julian and I rehearsed.

"After Amber's passing, I was going through life blindly. I didn't want to love again because I feared it. Love does that to you. I realized I needed to face my fear and love again." Julian takes my hand and meets my eyes. "When I met this beautiful woman, I knew she was the one…and the fear of losing her scared me. She says I saved her life, but it was the other way around."

Julian kneels on one knee and pulls out a small black box from inside his jacket.

My breath hitches and a trembling hand covers my mouth as tears pool in my wide eyes.

"Doc, the first time we met we had an immediate connection. Our first conversation happened right here. Not one of my finer moments, but you were cute as hell. Do you remember? You were babbling about high heels and fat-pants." Julian laughs as I nod, tears tumbling down my face.

"What you did to me the night we met—you ignited something in me I didn't think could come back to life. We've been through hell and back and now I just want to stop time and spend every moment with you. I want to wake up every morning with you in my arms. To look at your hypnotizing pretty blue-greens, kiss your beautiful face, and although I may not agree with your crazy ideas, I will always listen to them. You not only healed my soul and made my heart beat again, but you are my lifeline. You told me life is about pacing yourself. Well, I want to go on that brisk walk with you, hand in hand, create our own journey and grow old with you."

Julian opens the black box, reveals a platinum ring with two glistening halos that surround the monstrosity of a sparkling diamond. "You have my heart, Chloe Channing. I hope you trust me to have yours too. Will you marry me?"

My gaze locks on Julian's brown eyes. "Yes, yes, and a trillion more yeses!"

"Thank God!" Julian lets out a long breath.

Tears now stream down both our faces. Julian slips the ring on my finger, rises from his knee and we both stare into each other's eyes, savoring the moment. So much intense love and adoration.

"I love you, soon-to-be Doctor Cruz," he says, then kisses the ring on my finger.

"I love you, Mr. Cruz."

He looks out into the crowd and yells. "She said yes!"

The standing ovation is so loud it would've blown off the needle on the decibel meter.

I giggle and peer out to the sea of people that are standing on their feet. Hoots, hollers, and clapping burst throughout the room.

My best friends, Phoebe and Ryland, cell phones in their hands, snap pictures and wipe tears from their faces.

Sam winks and smiles at me, his arm around Sage.

Lincoln stands with a shit-eating grin, his fist swirling in the air. Next to him, Rocky with two thumbs up.

At the next table over, Julian's parents and sister smile, wiping their cheeks. Amber's parents also applaud.

Then there's the first man who first captured my heart—Dad. His hand moves over his chest and he mouths *I love you.*

Julian turns to face me, his hand at the small of my back. His mouth comes close to my ear. "I had this speech planned out and was nervous as hell. But one look at you, and I just spoke from my heart. Didn't need to look at the paper anymore."

I frame his clean-shaven chiseled jaw. "This is what you were nervous about? Did everyone know you were going to do this tonight?"

"Yeah, they all knew. The speech about Amber and the proposal, it scared the shit out of me." Julian's knuckles caress my cheek, as another tear escapes his eye. "And I'm a big sap…it's been an emotional evening."

"My hero sappy and scared?" she asked, dashing a tear from her own cheek.

"Yes, scared…to not spend the rest of my life with you as your husband. I wish I could explain how you make me feel. You take my breath away, Doc. Your eyes, your voice, and that beautiful smile that lights up my day. I didn't just fall in love with you the first night we met, or on the island when I saw you again. I fell in love with you in between and every day after that. I can't wait to make you officially mine. Earlier I told you I promised you an all-nighter, but I promise you more than that. I promise to make every day better than yesterday and I promise I will find the next rain so I can make love to you as it soaks us."

I inhale every word Julian says as his eyes swim with emotion. He came looking for me and found me. He's brought back the memories I thought I lost for good. Julian changed my life completely.

Tears blur my vision as I gaze at my hunky, super-secret agent.

"I'm yours forever, Booker."

Julian
Seven years later

I HAVE TO BE LIGHT on my feet as I turn the corner of the long hallway. The intel I received from my informant indicated where the microchip was hidden. It's secured by one guard, heavily armed.

My steps are stealthy, pistol upright, ready to aim at my target and protect myself. I had gone over the plan of attack multiple times. There is no room for mistakes.

Easy in, easy out.

I need to put the operation to bed. I am not going to let my guard down because if I fail there will be ridicule from the boss.

Vigilantly, I poke my head around the corner again before I make my next move. I need to keep my cool and stay in control since my patience is growing thin. I wipe the sheen of sweat off my forehead before I dart from my barrier to the next one, concealing myself from the target.

Work the problem. Aim for the target.

I cautiously peek over the pony wall and see my enemy's reflection from the glass window behind him. With narrowing eyes, I focus to look more closely.

There are two guards now.

Shit. My intel source is a double agent. Traitor! She's going down.

I need a diversion. I duck back down, lean against the small barricade and take out my cell from my pocket. I pull up the electronic blueprints of the location and with a press of the 'lightbulb' icon, the room goes dark.

I make my swift move and I am only able to nab one of the scoundrels and pin him down under my legs. A scream breaks out, then I tickle the rascal wiggling himself to escape from my grasp.

The lights come on as quickly as they were turned off.

I lock eyes with the little boy's deep blue-greens that mirror his mother's and chocolate hair like my own. Then I look up at Chloe, fingers on the light switch, with a smirk on her face.

"Dad! No fair," my son squeals, still trapped under my legs. "That's cheating."

"Yes, Agent Booker...totally cheating," Chloe scolds, hand on her jutted hip while the other points her fake gun at me.

"Says the beautiful double agent." I cock my head and raise a brow at my wife. "Who's the cheater again?"

"We're both double agents, Dad. I'm Oliver Dwew Cwuz, the bestest agent in the whole wide world. And I'm going to *save* everyone and *punish* the bad guys. That's what double agents do." Ah, innocence at its finest. "And I'm going to punish *you*, Agent Bwooker." Oliver fires his last rounds of Styrofoam bullets at my chest.

"Ah, you're killing me, Ollie!" I drop my fake gun, putting one hand up in surrender and the other over my chest.

"My name is Cwuz, Agent Ollie Cwuz." Oliver continues to shoot as he wiggles from under my legs, letting him escape from my hold.

Chloe laughs, arms across her chest as she lazily leans against the wall to witness the shootout. "Get him, Ollie," she calls out.

Oliver finally runs out of bullets, then it's my turn and I scowl at my son. "Hmm. Seems you ran out of bullets, Agent Ollie."

"Dad, I shot you good and you're dead...you can't talk."

"Aha! That's where you're wrong." I lift my t-shirt, pat my chest a few times, showing off my makeshift bulletproof shield made of construction paper. "I came prepared. Microfiber Kevlar, steel-plated bulletproof and nothing can penetrate this sucker."

I quickly lift the toy gun I dropped next to me. Oliver's eyes widen and he sprints around the living room as I shoot my last rounds. I take in the view of my son running in his Avenger pajamas that cling to his small frame as he dodges the soft bullets.

Oliver slides around the sofa and ducks behind it. His breathing could be heard in the silence.

"I got you now. Nowhere to go, Agent Ollie!"

I quietly tiptoe around the couch seeing my son crouching on all fours. His back to me, his head poking around the other side. I sneak up behind him, swoop my arms around Oliver's waist and swing him over my shoulders.

I roll him on the couch and it's a tickle fest for several seconds. Then I lift Oliver's shirt, press my mouth to his tiny belly and blow raspberries on his skin.

"Dad, stop… I can't bweathe!" he yelp-laughs, catching his breath. "You're too stwong, I can't move you," he giggles, trying to tickle me back. "Stop, please, Daddyyy…no more!"

Our eyes lock and my heart stops and swells all at the same time. Damn, I love my son's smile, showing off the dimples on his cheeks.

"Tell me who's the bestest agent in the room." I hold my fingers above Oliver's sides, threatening to bear down with more tickles.

"Me," he giggles and wiggles, trying to escape. A mischievous grin blankets my son's face. "Agent Ollie's the bestest!"

"Wrong answer, son!" I love Ollie's laughter. My fingers send another onslaught of tickles.

"Okay, Daddy! You are! You are!" Oliver's breathing is heavy.

I chuckle, tousling my son's hair out of his face. "An agent's job is to do whatever it takes to get the job done." I then look up at the clock on the wall. *Eight forty-five.* "And right now, Agent Booker needs to put Agent Oliver to bed or the boss"—I slide a look to Chloe —"will have my head."

"Time for bed, munchie." Chloe puts her toy gun on the coffee table then picks up a few of the orange bullets scattered across the living room floor.

"Aww…can't I stay up a little longer, pwetty please?" Oliver's hands fold together, pleading with pouted lips. "Please, Mom. Please, Dad."

I sigh, look over to Chloe then back to Oliver. How could I say no to those blue-green eyes when tomorrow is his fifth birthday?

"Okay, another thirty minutes. You better brush your teeth, be in bed so I can read you the next chapters." I raise my pinky finger. "Got it?"

Oliver hooks his little finger with mine. "Got it, Daddy."

"Now kiss your mom goodnight."

Chloe kneels to eye level with our son, frames his small face and kisses his tiny nose. Her arms wrap around his petite body.

"I love you so much," she whispers, as Oliver kisses her rosy cheek. Chloe stands and fingers his brown hair back out of his face.

"Love you more, Mommy. Goodnight." He runs down the hall as fast as his little legs can take him. The pitter-patter of each step he takes as he disappears up the staircase warms my heart.

"You think he knows?" I ask, my arms circling Chloe's waist, as I rest my chin on her shoulder.

"I don't think so. We hid all the decorations and the big-ass box in the garage."

Chloe turns to face me and presses her lips to mine. "Now, you need to hurry and put that kid to sleep. You have some work to do."

"Work?"

"Yes. You need to build his safe house and I need to clean up this mess…"

"What? You're kidding. Linc, Tyco and Sam are going to help me put it together tomorrow. How the hell am I supposed to build the safe house in the backyard without making any noise? Ollie will hear me. And have you seen how big that thing is?"

"Come on, Hotcakes. You can do it…use your head."

"I'll use my head alright." I wiggle my eyebrows, licking my lips as I gaze over her sexy as hell body.

"At this very moment, I need you to use the head above the belt, mister." Chloe smacks me on the ass. "Besides, I don't think it requires any tools. It's like one jigsaw puzzle, insert A into B, right?

"I'll insert my A into your B."

"Julian, I'm serious. You need to fix it tonight and you're a smart guy, you'll figure it out."

My fingers pull at Chloe's chin, and she looks up at me. "Just like I figured you out," I say.

"I beg to differ, Agent Booker." Chloe grins. "I figured *you* out."

My mouth meets her soft lips once again. Chloe did figure me out, unlocked the cage that held my heart and soul captive. I would've never imagined my life as perfect as it is in this very moment.

Chloe had a difficult pregnancy with the scar tissue damage from the stab wound and Reyna's bullet to her abdomen. She'd needed constant care and monitoring by her doctor. But Chloe was the strongest woman I've ever known. Nothing ceases to amaze me of my wife's willpower.

"Agent Booker, build his spy house tonight, and I will have a surprise for you later." Chloe's fingernails tease the side of my neck, sending a spark down to my shorts. Every part of my sensitive body stands at attention, anticipating her next touch.

"Oh, yeah? Why don't we make a deal…give me the surprise now." I lick my lips. It's such a turn-on when my wife teases me.

"No deal." Her hand snakes between our bodies; fingers skimming over my gym shorts where the fabric clings to my nuts.

"Holy hell, woman. You know how to bribe a man," I groan.

"Safe house first. Then you can play handyman on me later."

"Handyman, huh?" I raise a brow and stifle a laugh remembering my undercover assignment when I had to be her protective detail, which felt like a lifetime ago.

"Yes. My sexy hunky handyman."

"What happened to the hunky, secret-undercover agent?"

"Well, right now the handyman needs to build that very expensive toy house right now before it gets too late."

"That damn plastic house cost just as much as a real house. I swear that kid not only is eating us out of house and home. He's put a hole in my wallet too."

"Oh, stop your complaining. You love it!" Chloe pinches my cheek.

And I do love it.

Every day, I thank my lucky stars and the heavens above.

My heart swells looking into my wife's intriguing eyes that still hypnotize me. My fingers weave through her chestnut waves and the same feeling returns, just as the day when I first laid eyes on her.

"And I love you." I lean in to kiss Chloe. My tongue glides between her lips. The instant our tongues touch, it never fails, passion erupts. A jolt of electricity zips down to my groin.

Our tongues dance harmoniously, tasting one another. My fingers knot in her hair and all I want to do is take her to bed and strip her down.

There's about thirty minutes to make out with my wife before I have a bedtime date with my son. Letting go of her hair, I grab Chloe's ass with both hands, lift her and lay her down on the couch.

My hips settle between her legs, my hardened dick against the inside of her thighs. My hand slides under her tank-top, pulling down her lace bra as my thumb plays with her taut nipple, to add to her arousal.

Chloe releases a throaty sound that drives me wild, as her legs grip around my waist. Her hands roam up my shirt, nails skimming my back, sprouting goosebumps on my skin.

"Dad! I'm readyyyy!" Oliver screams from his room. "Daaad!"

"Fuck," I grumble against Chloe's mouth, lift my head and yell back, "Okay, son. Give me ten minutes." I press a chaste kiss to Chloe's lips. "I gotta go to him."

"I'll make a deal with you. I will read to him while you build Ollie's safe house, and you can work your DIY hands on me later. Anyway, you certainly can't go into our son's room sporting a woody."

My forehead rests on hers. "Since my woody is ready, how about I skip the DIY session on Ollie's house, use them on you instead and wait for the guys to help me tomorrow?"

"No deal," she retorts, determination in her stare. "No spy house, no nooky."

"You play unfair, sweetheart."

"I played double agent tonight, remember?"

"Fine. I will build that damn house in record time." I press a kiss to her mouth. "Then I will use my handyman skills to insert my A into your B, and when you come, you'll say my name over and over. And baby, there is no sweeter sound I'd rather hear than my name from your lips, feeling you naked trembling against my skin."

"Promise?"

"An all-nighter, Doctor Cruz."

"Daaaad!"

"Hold your horses, Agent Ollie... Mommy will read to you instead!" I bellow back.

"Okay." A moment of silence. "Mommyyy! I'm readyyy!"

"That kid is killing me." I shake my head, raise my eyes to the ceiling. I push myself off the couch, my hand extending as I pull Chloe up. I adjust my crotch, swat my wife on her ass before I walk down the hall to the garage. "See you later, Doc."

Two hours later, after reading the foreign instructions, I quietly built the two-story house fit for the Seven Dwarfs. I give myself a proverbial pat on the back, proud of how it turned out.

It's equipped with all the fixings. Water guns, battery-operated two-way radios, endless Styrofoam bullets, just to name a few. Oliver's pseudo-uncles, Tyco and Lincoln, bought more high-tech equipment to supply Oliver's fantasy of being a secret agent and were going to bring them for his surprise birthday party.

I crawl out of the small door and shake it a bit to make sure the damn thing wouldn't fall down like a house of cards. I walk around the little house that has taken a good chunk of real estate in our backyard and gleam.

Ollie's going to love it!

I make my way back into the house. When I clear the doorway through the sliding-glass window and lock up, silence stretches throughout the house. After entering the code to alarm our home, I shake my head and chuckle softly, seeing dozens of orange pellets that litter the hallway.

Agent Ollie versus Agent Booker is my favorite mission of all.

I climb the stairs, down the hall to Oliver's room. I lean on the doorjamb, taking it all in. A freight train comes full force and nails me in my chest, making it hard to breathe. The sight of the woman I love more than my own life holding our miracle son.

My God, they're beautiful.

My soul and heart aches so much with love. Every fiber of my being fills with adoration. Watching them, thinking how lucky I am. I can't imagine my life without them.

Both of my lifelines, their eyes closed, sleeping peacefully.

I look up to the ceiling, sending up a silent prayer. I kiss the two pads of my fingers and press them over my heart, remembering Amber and our unborn child.

I know you two were watching over me...put Chloe in my path. All I wanted to do was forget my past. But I've come to realize, I'm not supposed to. And now I have Oliver Drew... Oh, Ambs... I remember the name we decided for our unborn son. Drew was a piece of me and you...that's why I named Oliver after him. I promise I will never forget you and I will love you both. Always.

I move across the room, sit at the edge of the bed as Chloe slowly opens her eyes.

"Hey, babe. You dozed off," I whisper, taking the *Secret Agent Jack Stalwart* book from her hand and placing it on Oliver's nightstand. "Go to bed, I'll finish tucking him in."

Chloe gently shimmies her arm from under Oliver, kisses him on his forehead then slides out of his bed.

"I'll be waiting for you in bed, my handyman." Chloe leans down and kisses me then retreats to our bedroom.

I finger back Oliver's outgrown hair, ponder over his angelic face and the freckles sprinkling across his little nose and cheeks. I begin to reminisce about the day my son was born, one of the happiest days of my life when the doctor laid him on Chloe's chest to hold Oliver for the first time.

Half me, half Chloe.

Our miracle.

A son that would carry on my name.

Oliver Drew is perfect.

I turn on the nightlight, dimly illuminating dancing stars on the ceiling, then pull up the blanket to cover him. Ollie's mouth slightly opens, and he moans as he turns to his side.

"Do you know how much I love you, son?"

"Love you more, Daddy," Oliver mumbles sleepily.

I press a kiss to his forehead. "Goodnight, my super-secret agent."

The End

SNEAK Peek

TILL I KISSED YOU

PHOEBE

"Do you know how much I despise you right now, Channing?" I hiss through gritted teeth, as I glare at my childhood friend adorned in a strapless trumpet chiffon white gown.

We've known each other since we were eight years old, disagreed and argued frequently, then with a glint in our eyes and our typical smirk to one another, wonder how in the world we remained best friends throughout the years.

As Maid of Honor, I fulfilled all my obligations.

I'd gone with Chloe to pick out the perfect wedding gown and shoes, invitations went out on time, and I hosted a weekend bridal shower. The morning of Chloe's big day, I gifted a massage to destress the bride, then on to hair and makeup.

Everything went according to plan with no hiccups. I accomplished my duties except for one more thing the bride deemed mandatory…

"It's not Channing anymore," Chloe scolds, giving her mauve and lavender calla lily bouquet a shake in my face. "It's your last requirement and a tradition."

"Tradition my ass." I shove the flowers down.

"And that traditional ass of yours has been so uptight that if I stick a piece of coal up there, it will be another engagement ring…so

I need that ass of yours for one more duty to fulfill for the new Mrs. Chloe Channing Cruz." She raises a brow, and proffers a shit-eating grin.

"I don't care if your new name is Chloe-freaking-Kardashian." I park my hand on my hip. "I refuse to be part of this shenanigan."

I look over Chloe's shoulder as the DJ brings the microphone close to his mouth. "Come on, single ladies… Don't be shy. I need you out here on the dancefloor if you want the bride's prize."

The bride's prize? Yeah, right! More like a curse. I huff and fold my arms.

Ladies from around the reception hall sprout from their chairs. Some move slowly and some quickly, ready to claim their spot on the wooden surface, shimmying to Beyoncé's "Single Ladies" playing through the speakers.

I scan the large room.

Many familiar faces sit around the white and silver linen-covered tables embellished with a variety of purple flowers and crystal glass-ware. Every guest is dressed to the nines. Long gowns, classy cocktail dresses, three-piece suits, and bow ties.

I mentally roll my eyes.

This is a 'Chloe kind of wedding,' not just because she's the only child of Judge Frank Channing. But it's a fairytale where my best friend married her knight in shining armor, Julian Cruz.

"This is your fault, you know?" Ryland's slender hip bumps mine.

I twist my lips as I glare at Ryland, the third best friend to our trio, the other Maid of Honor and my roommate.

Ryland Marie O'Hare resembles a Barbie doll, with crystal-blue eyes, peach lip gloss, rosy cheeks and her wavy blonde hair that tumbles down her shoulders, looking ever so elegant in a violet gown.

Ryland moved into Chloe's old bedroom when she returned from Switzerland after working there for a few years and I'm happy to have her back. But at the moment, Ryland's comment has put her on my shit list, driving the proverbial bus over my back.

"How is this my fault?" I ask.

"Feebs, you were the one who pushed Chloe to let her hair down and unlock her chastity belt. And look what she did…married the hottest guy on the island. I hope the next time I go on vacation, I find a hot guy like Julian." Ryland's eyes veer to the groom and his friends at the bar.

"You can get out of the driver's seat, Ry. The skid marks are burned onto my back," I retort. "You're supposed to be neutral, like Switzerland, and remember... I know where you sleep!"

But Ryland is right.

I told Chloe to take a chance on the hot chauffeur-handyman. Little did any of us know, Julian had been Chloe's undercover body-guard assigned to protect her from a psychopath.

A chill slithers up my spine remembering when Chloe was in the hospital after she'd been shot. Their love story is made for the movies and of course, they got their fairytale ending.

"My husband *is* hot, isn't he?" Chloe gloats, her gleaming eyes on Julian at the bar.

Ryland nods, turning with Chloe to watch Julian raising a shot glass to cheer. "Of course, he is. And girl, he knows how to work a tux! I need to find a man like him."

"Then it's settled. You go out there for the both of us." I press my hands to Ryland's shoulders pushing her toward the dance floor. "Besides, I gotta go make."

"Make? Now?" Chloe asks.

"Yeah, I gotta pee. I've been holding it since the ceremony."

"I call cock-a-doodle-bullshit!" Chloe rebukes with her infamous made-up words as her French-manicure finger points at me. "If you don't get your tight ass out there, I may use my blackmail card and slip about the diarrhea Pampers episode," Chloe sing-songs the last three words.

"You wouldn't dare," I grumble, giving the death stare.

"Try me."

The dreaded story of a nine-year-old little girl's mistake. I ate a piece of my dad's chocolate Ex-Lax and being a lover of chocolate, I ate more. How was I to know what the damn chocolate bar did? Needless to say, I wore diapers for almost a week and wished I'd never told my two best friends. Anytime Chloe or Ryland got a chance to blackmail me, this was their ammo.

Ryland laughs. "Ten points for Doctor Cruz."

"I swear you've become a changed woman now that you married a former SEAL." I wiggle my mauve fingernail at Chloe. "You seriously need to get laid again, Bridezilla."

"Oh, I plan on it. On our honeymoon in Fiji, baby." Chloe bit her bottom lip, winks and walks toward the DJ.

I glare at my best friend's backside and watch her short train of fabric sweep the floor. "God, she's infuriating."

Ryland hooks her arm in the crook of my elbow. "Let's go, Feebs."

"Did I mention this totally sucks?" I pout as Ryland pulls me to the dancefloor.

"Hey, what gives?" Ryland asks, concern in her eyes. "I thought you'd be the first one out there. Always trying to win the prize."

"That prize is not one I care to win. Anyways, I've got work on the brain. Been under a lot of stress lately, not to mention my mom is here."

"Everything okay at work?"

"It's my creepy boss, the promotion…and I've been getting these weird texts and notes."

"I don't know why you won't report your boss. It's sexual harassment, you know?"

"He hasn't really done anything that I can make a serious complaint about. It's his word against mine."

"Phoebe, seriously? It's obvious he's making you feel uncomfortable by his suggestive jokes or sexual innuendos or asking you out on a date."

"Thanks for your concern, *Mom*. When it goes too far, I'll report him… Besides, I've got it handled."

"And what weird texts and notes are you referring to? Are those from Mr. Bauer?"

"I don't think so because he's been so forward. I think it's someone else that's sending me flowers, secret-admirer notes, and text messages."

"You think you should tell the guys? I mean, they are a security company with all the high-tech gadgets. They can find out who's behind all the text messages." Ryland's head juts toward the three men at the bar, Julian, Dylan, and Tyson who work for KSIG, Knox's Security and Intelligence Group.

"There's no need to get them involved. It's probably harmless—a crazed fan, maybe. Besides, I've got it handled."

"Just promise me if it gets too scary, you'll tell the guys. Because if you don't, I will."

"I promise."

My harassing slimy boss isn't anything I can't handle, tolerating his undertone innuendos of sex after hours or the many times Mr. Bauer has asked me out on a date.

The creepy love notes and texts from a secret admirer have made me feel unsettled, but though disturbing, none had been life-threatening. The last note I received on my desk a couple of days ago concerns me the most.

Enjoy your friend's wedding. Purple looks good on you.

I thought about going to the guys at the firm where Julian is now Head of Security since Charles 'Knox' Fremont retired, but didn't want to scare my friends, especially Chloe. She'd been through enough.

I decided to ask one of my contacts at SFPD, Detective Lopezleon, to look into it. There had been flower deliveries, love notes, and even pictures of me at my random onsite locations during my segments sent to my phone.

Anytime I received them I forwarded them to the detective. So far, no leads, and although the messages had progressed, they were harmless.

I have a brown belt in Krav Maga and I'm ready to test for the next and final level. I'm a woman ready to defend myself and kick some ass if necessary. Skilled with the training I received, I also invested in pepper spray and a TASER gun as my backup.

"And what's the deal with your mom?" Ryland brings me back from my wandering mind.

"I'm going to do my best to show her I'm still the picture-perfect daughter of Penelope Hawthorne." I stand firm on the wooden floor, avoiding eye contact with my mother, knowing Penny's eyes are leveled at me.

"You never told her, did you?" Ryland's question is more like a statement.

"Are you kidding? If I told Penny that Bryan left me for his career and another woman, I'd never hear the end of it. Failure is not an option for her. I had to tell her *I left him*, that I wanted to focus on *my* career. I need to save face every time with my mother and if I don't, my ears would bleed from her damn nagging. I only tell her what she needs to hear. Heaven forbid I ruin her reputation in her celebrity world. The gossip pages and headlines would say, *Daughter of Penelope Johansen Hawthorne left in the dust by cheating fiancé.*"

"Feebs, I'm sure Penny cares for you."

"When someone like her was once top model turned most influential fashion magazine editor, it's all gotten to her head and image is more important to her than her daughter. Hence the façade I need to show right now—*Picture-perfect Phoebe.* Being part of this mythical toss is so stupid, but she'll be watching."

"So you believe in the superstition?"

"Not in the least."

"Well suck it up, Miss Poopy-Pants," Ryland teases. "I think catching the bouquet is kinda romantic."

"This thing is for a pathetic woman who's desperate for love, so why should I take part in this?" *I'm definitely not desperate.*

Ryland laughs. "Oh, come on. You don't have to catch the damn thing. Just act the part." Ryland nudges my shoulders with hers.

"Pretend? I can do that. I've been doing that practically my whole life with *Mom*."

I study my mother sitting next to husband number six. She's definitely on her way to Elizabeth Taylor status. Penny's massive six-carat ring glitters brightly, red nails skimming the glass's stem, short bob black hair barely touching her shoulders, and her makeup is perfection as if she just stepped out from a photoshoot.

I square my shoulders and take a deep breath, remembering how my mother told me to stand…with confidence.

It was all about image and this saddens me knowing I would never have the kind of relationship with my mom that Ryland and Chloe had with their mothers. I miss the mom Penny once was. The mother that had wrapped her arms around me when I had a nightmare in the middle of the night. The mother that had kissed my scrapes and nursed them with Sesame Street Band-Aids. I especially wished Penny could've been the mother that was there to give me advice on boy crushes and heartaches.

"You think that'll be the last one?" Ryland asks, referring to Penny's wealthy husband, William Hawthorne, CEO and owner of Glass House Creations jewelry company.

"I don't know. And frankly, I really don't care at this point." I shrug, disappointed at my mother's gold-digging ways. "She's all about status quo and being with the rich and the famous...*Picture Perfect*, remember?"

"I don't see how being married six times is considered picture perfect, Feebs."

"Neither do I."

"Well, she looks happy." Ryland angles her head as she looks at Penny.

"She's happy as long as Willy buys her whatever she wants, takes her to the Canaan Islands, Montenegro, France, or maybe just hanging out on his yacht for shits and giggles."

"It could be worse."

"How?"

"Penny could still be married to your dad." Ryland wraps her arm around me, resting her chin on my shoulder.

"True. I remember those fights like it was yesterday." I look over to my dad sitting with Gage, my younger brother, on the other side of the room. The screaming, throwing glassware, and the door slamming when Penny finally walked out the door and never came back. "Dad was so patient with her."

The dredge of memories surfaces as I remember my dad and husbands number two, three, four, and five. Penny left all of them for all the same reasons—they didn't make her happy and she wanted more. Grant Powell, my selfless Dad, a software technician, couldn't satisfy Mom's red-carpet lifestyle.

"Why didn't he remarry?" Ryland's chin juts toward Dad.

"I think because deep down Dad still loves her. He won't admit it, but I see it in his eyes. He still has a picture of her hiding in his top drawer next to his bed. It's sad." I shrug letting out a sigh. "He's the other reason I don't ever want to get married."

"Why not?"

"It's not guaranteed the other will love you back. Why open your heart to disappointment?" My gaze meets Dad's green eyes and I softly smile at him. Unspoken words are shared as we look at each other, knowing how much love I have for him. The only man I will always love.

I giggle to myself, remembering the night Dad drove me to the junior high dance and made a show when he dropped me off in front of the gym. My date had been waiting on the steps. Dad got out of the car, shook the nervous Danny Knight's hand, as the boy stuttered a greeting to Dad and told me how pretty I looked, holding a corsage nestled in a clear plastic box. Dad shook Danny's hand so hard; it could've come off. Maybe that was the reason Danny didn't kiss me goodnight after the dance. Poor guy was scared.

"Oh, Feebs. After seeing Chloe and Julian, you still feel that way?" Ryland asks.

"I'm happy for those two lovebirds. I really am. But love and especially marriage is not for me. Sure, I *love* men, dating, and the sex. But I'm not in love with the thought of being loved by them. And I'm incapable of loving them back. Been there, done that. What can I say? I'm a cold-hearted bitch who will end up growing old with a dozen cats." I purse my lips together, admitting to myself what I fear the most.

Being alone.

"I have hope for you, Phoebe Powell. I *double-bet* Cupid will bite you in that firm ass of yours and love will sneak up on you."

"You want to *bet* me that I'll fall in love?"

Ryland squares her shoulders with confidence. "Why not? Let's put a wager on it."

"That's absurd, you know?" I raise a brow. "A bet to fall in love?"

"Are you saying you're too chicken-shit?" she challenges.

"To love or to bet?" I ask.

"Both."

"Ry, it's a dumb bet. Plus, you know if you gamble against me, I always win."

"Maybe this will be your first loss." Ryland raises her pinky finger. "Seal the deal?"

"What's the winning pot?"

"Hmm…how about the loser pays for a weekend trip to Napa?" Ryland's mischievous smile perks up.

"Okay. You're on." I hook my friend's pinky with mine, then stifle a laugh. "Napa here I come."

"Don't celebrate too soon. I have a good feeling I'm going to win."

The DJ's voice roars through the speakers again while music fills the air. "Two more minutes, ladies. Get your booties out here."

Superstition or not, I still want out of this traditional game. I think about what Ryland said about love sneaking up on me. Would that really happen for me? To fall in love?

I shake my head, then laugh again. *No way!*

I survey the herd of women in front of me. It's actually silly, giving false hope, to think the bride's bouquet is some magical cherub and would lead them to their future husband if they catch it.

Unease flows through my veins as I stand on the dancefloor. I need an escape plan.

Slowly and stealthily, I ease a step backward then another, leaving Ryland's side. She's too busy chatting it up with one of Chloe's colleagues to realize I've stepped away.

With every step back I take, success reigns, celebrating a proverbial pat on the shoulder. Until my back bumps into a wall of a man.

"My apologies. Am I in your way?" A low gravelly whisper warms the edge of my earlobe. Goosebumps sprout, my breath hitches, sending tingles down my spine. "It's nice to know how responsive you are to my touch. Very sexy."

I wobble in my heels, heart thumping into high gear at the

warmth of his hand grazes up my arm, rendering me speechless. Damn, he smells nice, like clean soap layered with a crisp woodsy cologne, making the apex of my thighs suddenly throb.

I mentally cross my fingers, hoping he isn't with a date or worse, married. Curiosity piques my interest of who the man may be since I know all the guests.

I quickly fix the drape of my one-shoulder-strapped dress, smooth the satin lavender material over my torso, and square my shoulders. I wet my lips with my tongue, ready to bat my long lashes, and face the man behind me.

I slowly turn to him.

"Dylan?" I gasp, surprised and flustered I let my body react to him.

"As far as I can remember, that's the name my mama gave me." A cocky grin turns up the corners of his mouth.

Dylan Marshall, Best Man. Not only is he Julian's best friend, but he also works with him at the security firm, KSIG.

I think of Dylan as Julian's longtime friend, nothing more. He's a bit obnoxious and arrogant. But when he has his moments, Dylan can be charming and it's absolutely sexy. Much like this very moment.

The worst combination.

His sandy-blond hair is in a messy spike, and his broad shoulders fit perfectly in the white dress shirt, like it's made for him. The top two buttons are undone, bowtie loose around his neck, and shirt cuffs folded up his forearms.

His mesmerizing blue eyes lure me in, then my stare moves to his mouth, wondering what his tongue tastes like and the things he could do with it.

I slightly shake my head, recovering from my fantasies. "I thought you were—"

"Your Romeo?" he whispers as he leans closer.

"Don't be an ass." I push against his hard pecs. "Now, if you'll excuse me."

"You didn't answer my question."

My momentary gaze meets Dylan's. My hand presses to my belly, calming the flutter of bees, not sure if they were stinging or stirring in my insides, feeling like a prepubescent teenager.

"I, uh…need to get out of here."

"And leave the infamous game of catch? Never known you to be a quitter, Powell." He smirks, holding his short glass of amber liquid close to his mouth.

I clear my throat. "If you must know, *Romeo*, I'm giving all the other ladies a fighting chance."

"Says the woman who makes bets and doesn't believe in losing." He sips the liquor and licks his bottom lip.

"I don't lose. But I figured—"

"Save it for the choir, Phoebe," Dylan chides, cocking a brow.

My lips are agape as I watch Dylan open his mouth to take another sip. "Want some?" he asks, before the glass touches his lips.

"Huh?" I let out a nervous cough. *Damn, why is my mouth suddenly dry?*

"Wanna sip?"

Without a second thought, I snag his glass and toss back the remaining liquid, hoping to take off the edge.

Why am I suddenly seeing Dylan differently?

He wasn't the kind of guy who would give me flutters in my insides. Sure, we've bantered in the past, but only to get under each other's skin.

He's been the thorn in my side and shouldn't be the warm throb between my thighs.

He's Julian's best friend and not to mention a large man-child I have no interest in getting involved with, but tonight, he's so damn intoxicatingly sexy.

"Thanks." I wipe my lips with my finger and hand the empty glass back to him.

"Thirsty?" Dylan looks inside the glass, then meets my eyes. "So, are you going to answer my question?"

"What question?"

"Was I in your way?" He leans in again, his breath feathering my cheeks. Something about his gaze makes me feel naked and vulnerable.

Get it together, Powell. Stand tall. Don't let him get under your skin. It's only Dylan, for Christ's sake.

I lean back, and scoff. "In my way? Dylan, you're always in my way. Now if you'll excuse me, I need to get out of here."

His hand presses over his chest in mock surrender. "That hurts, Phoebe. When are you gonna give me a chance and go out with me?"

"Dylan, the answer is *still* no." I roll my eyes. "Besides, we would never work out."

"And why not?"

"I don't date within my circle. Too awkward if we didn't work out. Second, you're...*you*."

"Yes, I'm *me*. Handsome, sexy"—he huffs over his knuckles, then rubs them over his chest—"lady-killer...should I go on?"

"How many times have you used that bullshit pick-up line?"

"It works every time. Women fall for my charm and this irresistible smile." Dylan points to his cocky grin as it widens.

"Are you serious? Those poor souls."

"Jealous, sweetheart?" he goads, reaching out to push a lock of hair behind my neck.

I gently shove his hand away then step back to distance myself. "Jealous? Hardly. I hate to bruise your ego, *Romeo*. I've got my own game and you are definitely not allowed to play."

"We'll see about that." Music plays as Dylan's chin ticks up. "Hey, Feebs..."

"What now?"

"Heads up!" Dylan's eyebrows lift and his gaze flicks toward something overhead.

I look up and my eyes go wide. In slow motion the lavender petals descend from midair, the mob of women screaming, their wiggling fingers reaching out as they barrel toward me.

I lift my arms to dodge the bouquet, a second too late, and it lands in the last place I wanted it to.

My own hands.

I gasp, "Oh. Holy. Hell!"

Acknowledgments

I have so many people to thank, where do I begin?

FIRST AND FOREMOST,
TO MY READERS, REVIEWERS AND BLOGGERS:

Thank you, thank you and many more thanks!
Without you, there is no reason to write! This is my debut novel and
I have more to come! There are heroes, heroines and a circus of
people in my head that are dying to get out and be part of your
world! You are the reason why I want you to meet them! Love you all
so much! XOXO

TO MY SPECIAL READERS:

You are absolutely amazing!
Nikki, Leta, Rosario, Liz, Anne, Lace, and Lainey: Your support,
your attention to detail, questions about my timelines of who, what,
where, when and how only makes me a better writer! Thank you for
your friendship, loving me and all my quirkiness. Thank you for your
ideas even though you had no clue you were giving them to me.
Remember… anything you say to me may be used in my book! To
my proofers for V2: Michele Ficht, Janice Owen and Fiona Wilson…
thank you! This project was a do-over and the second time is a
charm!

TO MY "G-SQUAD":

Liz the Lizard: My sissy for life... I freakin-turtley-love you forever! Thanks for having my hard shell back that I crawl into from time to time. Then pulling me out of it so I can be goofy and dancing with me like no one is watching when I needed to let out the stress! A toast to the Three Wisemen! And don't forget Jimmy Dean!

Anne: Thank you for letting me use Olie's name! He will always be in my heart and now in this book! That boy is probably playing secret spy games or maybe basketball... what do you think?!?!

Leta: My sister... we share the same blood and vision. Thanks for your relentless support and love throughout my journey!

Rosario: I've known you almost half my life, seen me prego with my munchies, been in my wedding and watch me marry the man of my dreams... thanks for being such a loyal friend!

Lainey: My friend from across the ocean but can chat with you like you're the next city over. Thanks for being an awesome PA and watching my back. Words cannot express how blessed I am to have you in my life and on this journey! Your relentless social media posts and promotions are amazing. And thank you for encouraging me to rewrite version 2. You are my Rockstar!

Michelle M aka Dallas: Thank you for being an amazing coach, editor, and friend. Thank you for seeing the potential and the grit within me to be an author! After I finished *Till I Found You*, I reread the first draft I sent you what feels like a lifetime ago and *Oh-Holy-Hell* (Chloe's words)! Just reading it made me want to crawl under a rock or bang my head with it... what was I thinking?!? The first draft was horrible! But aren't first drafts usually bad? Your 'red pen' constructive feedback, suggested edits, 'starred' compliments and accolades are the reason why I have become a better writer. What you did for me has no words of expression, I'm speechless with a lump in my throat and tears pooling in my eyes (Can you pass me a tissue please... Ok where was I? Oh, yes...) Thank you for believing in me and loving Julian & Chloe just as much as I do.

To my Parental Units:

Mom and Dad: As a daughter, I am an imitator of great parents and I only hope I am as awesome as you were with me, as I am with my children and grandchildren! Love you to the moon and back and forth and back and forth... (you get the picture)

Nancy, Jerry, Tony, Saida, and Jimmy: I love you so much and I married your son because he is a piece of you... So, does that mean I married you too? LOL! Wow—we are so goofy, aren't we? Your love is a huge part of my assurance and believing in me!

To my Husband, Paul:

Your unconditional love and amazing support pushed me to do this (this is your fault, you know?) ... You bared the worst part from this project, and I know your ears have bled from my *Julian-Chloe-loquaciousness.* Regardless, you never once rolled your eyes and covered your ears... You have been so patient, believed in me even when I didn't, pushed me when I thought I couldn't go on and pulled me away from my MacBook to a date night with you when I desperately needed it! You read me like a book, know me so well and saw the end game. *How'd you know?* You're the butterflies that flitter in my tummy, my BFF I joke around with, my tickle buddy, my forever sleepovers, my everything and the air I breathe! I love you to infinity and beyond!

Lastly, and to the most important people To the Party of Five:

My Munchies: *Nathan, Nikki, Celina, Danny, and Nicholas...* I did it! There are no words in the dictionary, or any other book ever written to express how much I love you more every day! I've pushed Sunday dinners to the side and my bad… I even forgot to go grocery shopping because I've been so consumed with this project (At least there were Hot Pockets or Domino's to survive on)! Thanks for being wonderful kids and understanding my new author life and having a full-time job too! Thanks for your advice on social media input/output, hashtags tips, how to take selfies and spreading the word for me! I love you more than you know!

OTHER BOOKS BY

Michelle Fernandez

TILL I KISSED YOU

COMING SOON:

TILL I PROMISED YOU

IF YOU ENJOYED READING TILL I FOUND YOU (v2), PLEASE TAKE A MOMENT TO GIVE IT A RATING AS THESE RATINGS ARE SO IMPORTANT TO INDEPENDENT AUTHORS, SUCH AS MYSELF.

ABOUT THE *Author*

MICHELLE FERNANDEZ LIVES IN SOUTHERN California with her husband and children. When she's not writing, she loves spending time with her family, laughing it up with her 'squad' or simply relaxing with her two pups.

She's always been passionate about reading and impressed by the influence it has on people. Which is why she started writing in the first place. It started as a hobby. One chapter turned into ten, then a novel was born.

Till I Found You is her first book. She writes Adult Romance with a dash of suspense. The sassy heroine and the gentleman hero are who she loves to write about. Making up worlds and characters for readers to utterly fall in love with, is the most rewarding for her. It's all about the swoony, seductive and suspense when it comes to her novels.

Michelle is currently working on Book 2, the story of Phoebe and Dylan: *Till I Kissed You* which is set to be released in Spring 2020 and Book 3, *Till I Promise You*, is set to be released Fall 2020. Stay tuned for more of *Till I*....

Made in the USA
Columbia, SC
05 June 2021